FATE FORGED

BOOK 2 OF THE GIFTING

Fate Forged

The Gifting Series #2

Jacqueline (Jack) Dunois struggles to find a man not intimidated by her career as a law enforcement instructor, especially in the small town she calls home. She would sacrifice a kidney to find someone who would make her ovaries clap and didn't live with his mother. Then she meets a supreme commander from another world who thinks the stars in the galaxies shine in her eyes... What's not to love about that?

Supreme Commander Ulriq doesn't believe in love, an archaic term for a volatile and untrustworthy emotion Etterians were no longer subjected to. Until he meets Jack who triggers the Ethera, the soulmate force that irrevocably changes a male when he finds his ideal female. In that moment, his world, his focus, his very loyalty shifts. But when she is taken from him, it is too much to bear. Under the influence of the Ethera, he launches a rescue. He'll start a war and kill anyone who dares stop him, just to have her back in his arms.

Also by Sevannah Storm

The Blood of Legends Series

The Huntress

The Healer

The Gifting Series

Soul Forged

Fate Forged

Sun Forged

War Forged

Star Forged

Shadow Forged

Earth Forged

Lust Forged

Standalones

Xiaxan Fox

Ire of Silver

The Shikari

Sol Survivor

Plump Playwright Series

Plump Jane

Seducing Amelia

Loving Finley

Keeping Tessa

Kissing Navy

FATE FORGED

COMING SOON
Inkoded
Fire Forged
The Crucible of the Eternal

Contents

Chapter One

Etterian battleship, Kushin
Orbiting mid-grade planet, Earth
12252 years, 4th Month

AT THE MALE'S GROAN, Ulriq tightened his arm around his throat, halting his ability to breathe. From behind, he had both legs wrapped around the warrior's torso, his thigh muscles as taut as his arm cutting off oxygen. Four seconds, three seconds...kill him, the darkness whispered. Ulriq's vision tinted with red; his focus intensified. A need to fight, to kill, roared at him. The seductive allure bombarded his control, and he released the warrior, rolling away from him, from the temptation.

"That's the fourth warrior this morning, Ulriq." Nerx—his sub-commander—strode toward him. Ulriq snarled, bounding to his feet in a smooth motion.

"I needed the exertion." He accepted the cloth Nerx handed him, wiping the sweat dripping off his chin and drenching his chest.

"What we need is a distraction," Nerx frowned. "What I truly want is the heat of Etteria's suns on my face, to crunch the gray sand beneath my heels, and the sweet nectar of our hahyt blossoms to fill my lungs."

Ulriq grunted, the urge to see his homeworld was as strong. Too many distant memories flashed in his mind. The setting of the magnus sun on their scarlet oceans. The bright white of hahyt blossoms nestled in blue leaves, and the taste of fresh kreso in the king's hall. He glanced at Nerx, remembering their shared experiences, the number of times they had saved each other's lives, and the long journeys endured with shared determination. Staring at his glowering battle-bond, a little warmth flooded him, reminding him relationships mattered.

The moment he had received command of the battleship *Kushin*, an energized Nerx had bounced around him with rarely observed enthusiasm. Then they had notified him Nerx would second Ulriq's command. It was one of his fondest memories, seeing Nerx step off the docked scimitar. In that moment, peace consumed him; all was right with the universe. This decision solidified his respect for his king.

"Any sunlight would appease you. Yet we are surrounded by uninhabitable planets, or low and mid-grades, at best." Ulriq released a slow exhale, hoping to ease the pressure squeezing his chest.

"This I know. I propose we change course and discover a planet with wildlife worthy of a hunt." Nerx shifted his bulk, an indication of his restlessness.

"Fair enough." Ulriq forced a smile. The unused curl cracked his lips. He hid his wince by tossing the cloth into the waste disposal.

With a last nod at Nerx, he strode to his quarters. His footwear made no noise on the grated-metal flooring. As an Etterian, each movement must be in silence no matter the terrain. Disrobing en route to his cleansing room, he stepped into the cubicle. It sensed his core temperature and judging by the scalding water pouring over him, he was hotter than usual. Yet further evidence his emotional stability affected him. Adjusting the temperature, he hoped the icy water would cool his inner turmoil. Tugging the Maloidian clip off his braid, he flicked it to the floor. His hair unraveled, then swirled and danced in agitation.

With a deep sigh, he raised his arms and splayed his hands against the white bulkhead, lifting his face to allow the water to cascade over him. He gargled a mouthful before spitting it out. Slumping his shoulders, he lowered his hand and took care of his morning chore. For the briefest of moments, the torment eased. Yet his fulfillment remained lackluster, the fleeting joy overshadowed by irritation.

He stepped out, and the water switched off. After activating the air-dryer with a press of the blue button, he waited for it to complete its task. His body once more trembled with pent-up energy. The moment it shut off, he scooped up his clip and strode naked to the replicator to punch in an order for another set of armor.

"Malia pa," he mumbled.

His hair tugged and pulled as it braided itself. He caught up the end and slipped on the clip. Something in the metal placated his hair. They hadn't found another restraint that kept it calm.

Dropping his braid to brush his heels, he hovered his hand above the reflective surface of the replicator. He would order his usual armor, except the thought of its confines made him feel trapped, within his body, within his circumstances. A tension rose, pressing on his senses. At the sight of his trembling hand, he growled and punched his requirements into the replicator. Yanking the standard armor off the counter, he pulled them on and reached for his footwear. The auto-servos would take care of this morning's armor he had discarded. If in good order, it would stack them within the airing closet for later use.

He stilled, staring at his old armor. The dark pieces splattered his floor like lifeless shadows scarring his soul. He grumbled at his fanciful thoughts, wondering if he descended into the void at a faster rate.

Requesting a container of water from the rehydrator, he stomped to the communications room. He nodded at Pilot Ksal, dropped into a chair, and slid his data tablet closer. With each tap and swipe of a finger, his irritation increased. Over two hundred requisitions later, he realized he had reread the same one for the third time. His head jerked as his gaze focused on his data tab, to verify he had indeed read the same words.

Disgust followed next, and as his lips curled downward, no reaction reflected within him. He almost grunted, not liking that smiling had become a rare mannerism for him. There were moments spent with Nerx and his other battle-bonds when they would share giyua juice, laugh and share past events and gika kills. But it had been a while since Ulriq had enjoyed such a time.

After another hour, he gave up on his data tab and took note of his communications room. On one side, large display vids revealed the surrounding stars and a tiny blue planet with its single orbiting moon. Ksal frantically typed on his multi-lit console, his concentration intense as expected of an Etterian warrior. His long black braid pooled on the floor behind his metal chair. Ulriq was proud of his males, of their dedication, their honor as indicated by their braids at heel length. Each dishonorable action cost them a foot of hair. It served as a visible symbol of a warrior's obedience, of his willingness to serve Etteria.

On the other side of the room, three males—led by Data Officer Prex—surrounded this galaxy's holographic model. They cataloged all data received from the scans, though how much of it they analyzed, Ulriq didn't know.

"Supreme Commander?" Pilot Ksal's voice reached through Ulriq's distraction.

When he gave the male his attention, Ksal tapped a button on his console. A strange male voice reverberated through the comm room. His words synchronized, joining in a melodic flow. It was a strange way of speaking indeed. The cessation of movement around him drew Ulriq's notice. His males had stilled to listen; they faced the large display vids despite there being no image alterations. He understood, accepting their curiosity as it echoed within him.

"What language is he speaking? Is that his homeworld?" Ulriq peered at the planet that from this distance showed promise and mineral wealth.

He couldn't assess whether the planet was rich in resources when everything looked appealing from afar. Data analysis of the planet's population, communication, history was never his forte. He lacked the patience for it. Focusing on the console, he frowned. Tension rippled through his body, tightening his muscles, increasing his heartbeat a fraction. It wasn't the unusual situation that had Ulriq tensing. He stilled the urge to clench his fists. For the past few days, his emotions had been unstable, fluctuating from irritation to impatience which he couldn't reveal to his warriors.

As their commander, he had to remain impassive, and in control, as expected of an Etterian male. He blamed the confines of the battleship. During peace, they navigated and charted their expansive universe. Their mandate was to extend Etteria's knowledge and star charts. It was a repetitive task no warrior enjoyed. The long journeys tended to scramble their brains. They were simply not capable of handling extended periods of inactivity with no testing of their battle-honed skills. More to the point, Ulriq struggled to endure this.

"Yes, Supreme Commander. That is Earth, a mid-grade planet. It is home to a volatile species. They have managed to travel within their system but no farther." Ksal didn't look at him, but he hadn't expected him to. "Their air is breathable, if a landing is required."

"And we have their informational databases?" Ulriq asked.

"Yes, according to protocol. I am uploading their language now." Concern etched across Ksal's features a few minutes later, and Ulriq waited for the pilot to clarify his annoyance. "They do not have a planetary language, Supreme Commander. I have sent three of their most-spoken languages to you." The unit activated the three for themselves as well as an analysis tool to assist with language recognition. Expectantly, Ulriq activated his Optical Data Implant, or O.D.I., embedded in his wrist. A sensation rippled up his arm and the Earthian's words—still echoing through the communications room—were, in an instant, translated. Not a medic, he couldn't go into detail as to how the O.D.I worked, just that it was powered by his neural system, and utilized those pathways to connect with his mind.

Of the looped message, the birdsong was the first understood. Its meaning increased Ulriq's pulse, and his core temperature rose. The words were evocative as the Earthian addressed a sister he had failed. He had a deep affection for his blood-bond, evident by the level of emotional intensity in his voice. The pain, sadness, despair tainting the Earthian's voice, was strong enough to reverberate through Ulriq. He barely contained the shiver raking his body.

"That is love?" Ksal asked.

Love? Ulriq frowned at Ksal's words, at his reverent tone. It was an archaic term in Etterian culture. Acceptable emotions didn't include 'love', unless under certain circumstances which were rare. Affection was tolerated, but love was too volatile an emotion. It was uncontrollable and distrusted.

"Yes. He loves his... sister." Ulriq took a moment to wonder what 'love' might be like. Unfortunately, he couldn't begin to imagine. His range of emotions was limited as expected. Yet an ache pressed on his chest, heavy, dark, and noticeable. The strangeness of it tugged his lips downward.

"May I share this Earthian's words with our males, Supreme Commander?" Ksal asked.

The hope on his pilot's face would pass onto his males. They could use the distraction, he noted as he tossed his data tab onto the table. To encounter love without suffering under its influence; it was a gift from the Maker.

"Yes, you may share it, Ksal." He listened to the words again. "He believes he is dying."

"Jack, I hope this gets to you, my sister. I love and miss you, and I'm sorry I couldn't return to you as I promised." The male followed the words with the melodic birdsong which echoed his message, that of loving his sister for an eternity and beyond.

"He is breaking a vow?" Ulriq asked the communication room, in general. That this troubled the male implied he was honorable. "Scan the vicinity, Ksal. He might still live." Ulriq jumped up to stand closer.

Ksal's fingers flittered across the console with practiced speed. The display vids altered to focus on the source of the Earthian's voice. Suspended in mid-animation—a creature in a white-constrictive suit—drifted against a backdrop of stars.

"Can he not return to his space station?" Ulriq pointed at the alien's structure on the horizon.

"Scans show there are twenty-one life signs on the station; their pulses slow and steady. I suspect they are resting, Supreme Commander, and are unaware of his predicament."

"Has he requested assistance?"

"No, but there is a sadness to his voice as if he believes no assistance could be forthcoming." Ksal shook his head, the frown on his face mimicked Ulriq's own.

This species intrigued Ulriq, with their emotions and their *damu*-like vulnerability. He hadn't experienced such vulnerability, not since he was six years old. To evoke intense emotions for an Etterian meant an impactful event had occurred like the loss of a blood-bond. His warriors knew the creed. To feel is to fail. Their joy and hope might hasten the void. He scowled, concern deepening as Ksal's dark-blue eyes briefly paled.

"To feel is to fail." Ulriq's voice conveyed the fiery burn of anger he struggled to contain.

Ksal stilled, then squeezed his eyes shut for a second before nodding his thanks.

Ulriq sighed, strolled to his chair, and dropped his bulk into it. He had overestimated his warriors' ability to resist the tug on their souls. He didn't like that this Earthian could affect his ever-vigilant males with his strange emotions. As if this Earthian's love was contagious.

Charge after charge buzzed up his arm, startled him, and stoked the angry burn coursing through his veins. Tapping on his O.D.I., he deactivated the notifications temporarily then flicked through forty-two messages from his crew.

"Our males request we rescue him. Alodon's balls." Ulriq roared his frustration and bounded up. He punched the ship-wide comm system on the console with more force than intended. It didn't matter that he was revealing his restlessness; this needed to end. "This male cannot be rescued. Cease comming me."

Ksal's fingers flew over the console with more urgency than needed. His posture stiffened as if anticipating a battle, yet his lips had curled in distaste.

"What alarms you?"

"I am tracking a Yithian slave ship. It travels past the first planet from the sun. Expected path is not near our current position. I will continue to monitor their trajectory."

"Why would you need to concern yourself? We are in stealth-mode, are we not?" Excitement skittered through Ulriq; the need for battle bombarding him.

"A slave ship, Supreme Commander. If we do not rescue this Earthian now, the Yithians might. His message is still broadcasting."

Ulriq scowled. He wouldn't doom anyone to the Yithian arena, not if he could help it. Yet, to rescue this Earthian would require they reveal their presence. This he couldn't allow. It was against protocol.

"Comm King Xeus." He didn't need to wait long. As expected, Adviser Cales answered the communications request promptly.

"Supreme Commander Ulriq," he said.

Ulriq gave a slight nod, in acknowledgement of the older male before him. He first noted the two physical attributes that mattered to an Etterian.

Cales's black braid was thick and long, a visual display of his unquestionable honor. As adviser, it was his responsibility to mete out the Foot of Honor. This was the removal of a length of hair from a disobedient male: a chore all knew he detested.

His eyes were dark blue. The color denoted control of one's emotions and since he was old enough to be a lima kuu, a great teacher, his control was formidable.

"Greetings, Adviser. We have a situation requiring the king's guidance."

"Cryptic but intriguing, Ulriq. Is this a matter of urgency?" Cales asked.

"Yes. We have encountered an Earthian stranded from his planet and station. An approaching Yithian slave ship is forcing my hand. I request permission to violate G.C. laws to retrieve him."

Violating the Global Council laws entailed a heavy monetary penalty, not that Etteria would feel the cost. The violation was more a matter of honor since King Xeus had been the forerunner in the creation of these laws. Having said that, the rumors or buzz indicated a rift had formed among the council with corruption running rife. It was an unstable time to bring the Etterian honor into disrepute.

"Has he requested assistance?" Cales arched a brow in query.

"He has not; however, his message is one I admire." Ulriq gestured to Ksal to share the Language Protocol and message with the Adviser.

Cales took a moment to listen. The adviser's expressions mimicked Ulriq's current volatile emotions, though, he knew, feeling them would cost Cales. The more an Etterian aged, the more the void claimed his soul, and the less emotion they dared to experience. It was for this reason they cultivated a tighter control. Any intense emotions siphoned the remaining light, bringing the darkness closer. When the void consumed a male's soul, it led him to sacrifice his life on the training battlefield at Calustrum. It was why only the youngins still revealed emotions; they had the luxury of time to do so.

"Is this love?" Cales asked, then shook his head.

"I believe so, Adviser." Ulriq frowned.

Ksal tapped the display vid, drawing his attention. He focused on the active scanning of the solar system from Earth itself.

"Earth scans their solar system. The longer the *Kushin* remains in orbit the greater the chance of discovery. We will need to leave stealth to rescue the Earthian."

"This is a matter of honor, Ulriq, permission granted. I will inform Xeus should the buzz reach the council's ears. Keep me informed." The comm ended from Cales's side, as expected. It was frowned upon should Ulriq have ended a comm on a higher-ranking warrior.

"Ksal, task Der, Kanzo and Sena." Ulriq leveled his gaze on Prex who had returned to his duties. "Prex, record the interaction. It might appease the G.C."

Data Officer Prex straightened to his six-foot-four height, typed on his O.D.I. before rushing out of the communications room. Ksal grinned and attended to his task. Ulriq reached across and tapped the comm button with less vehemence than earlier.

"Permission granted for the Earthian's rescue," he said to his crew.

With a deep sigh, he lowered his heavy frame into his chair and waited. Sitting didn't calm him. His black armored breeches were as confining as he had predicted and the urge to rip off his vest pushed against his control. Too energized, he jumped up and waited, spreading his legs wide and planting his feet firmly. His fists clenched as he fought the need to fidget. As an Etterian warrior, he commanded his body.

Minutes later, Prex had activated various security vids for the interaction. The display vids filled with the dark-gray interior compartment of the kuta shuttle. The four males suited up under the eager attention of the *Kushin* crew. Their air-suits were made of a Maloidian-nano polymer, similar to their armor but with additional sensitivity to the demands spacewalking, or spacing, placed on their bodies. The nanos in the suit monitored their oxygen usage and would recycle it for the short spacing required, otherwise they'd attached additional equipment to the suits.

Ksal punched his console and shared the rescue vids with the crew. Ulriq wondered what the consequences of that would be. More harassment?

En route to the Earthian's location, his males on the kuta, chatted among themselves, their words discernible with the advanced hearing of their species. It wasn't acceptable protocol to listen in on conversations, but in this case, it was unavoidable. Ulriq didn't appreciate their eagerness. An Etterian warrior was to remain vigilant, to stave off the void for as long as possible and to never bring shame upon their people.

Their conversations ceased, and they hovered around the door. The pilot must have aligned the shuttle with the Earthian. They flipped their visors over their faces when the compartment's lights flashed to green indicating a loss of pressure, life support and gravity. The shuttle's door opened, and Prex shifted into position with an additional vid to reveal the white immobile figure. Ulriq's battle-bond Kanzo launched himself at the Earthian, activating his boot boosters by tapping the heels together. He reached the drifting male with ease then deactivated his boosters to spin them using the Earthian as an anchor. Kanzo redirected them to the waiting shuttle with the aid of his boosters once more. A perfectly executed retrieval; Ulriq approved.

Inside the shuttle, the door sealed, and the green lighting altered to white with his males flipping up their visors. Ulriq ground his teeth as he tightened his jaw. Kanzo's eyes had swirled to ice-blue. Ulriq would need to talk to his males regarding their recklessness. He refused to lose a single warrior to the void, not under his command.

Prex scanned the Earthian to assess his breathing compatibility as was protocol when encountering an unknown species. At his nod, Kanzo pried off the Earthian's helmet; the latches unable to withstand the strength of an Etterian male. They stared at the Earthian, with his pale skin and white hair. Though his features were similar to an Etterian's, his coloring was startling. Not that it was unpleasant, just unusual. All Etterians, male and female, had black hair and dark-blue eyes.

"He is alive. His body needs oxygen." Der stepped forward, knelt in front of the sprawled male, and roared.

The Earthian's eyes opened, and he bolted into a seated position. Ulriq stared in amazement at the pale-blue eyes. The color was unexpected. Etterians were born with such eyes, but as they trained to control their emotions, the color transformed to dark blue.

"What... what happened?" The Earthian rubbed his face with his gloved hand. "Where am I?" He scanned the shuttle before blinking at the looming warriors. "You're not a known alien species."

"He is well," Der called out, a victorious expression on his face. The bright smile was incongruent with the older warrior's stoic demeanor.

Heat swelled Ulriq's chest with an unexpected joy, yet he wasn't willing to acknowledge it.

"Greetings, tiny Earthian. We are Etterian warriors and have rescued you," Kanzo offered his hand to assist the male up. Instead of using it, the Earthian did a strange thing and shook it—three times—before releasing it.

"What was that?" Ksal asked the console.

"Thank you. I believed I'd die..." The Earthian staggered to his feet. His white suit was of a poor design; it restricted instead of enhanced his movements.

"Yes, we intercepted your message. It is why you were rescued," Kanzo said. "Tell me, why did you pump my hand? It was meant to assist you to your feet."

"Oh." Pink splashed the Earthian's pale cheeks, the color of their Etterian sky as the magnus sun set.

What was the significance of such a reaction? Ulriq had never known a species where their skin changed color. The yellow of a Maloidian, the gray of a Yithian, the green of an Algri, and the bronze of an Etterian only darkened.

"I greeted you; we shake hands." He held out his hand again, and Kanzo accepted it to 'shake' three times. "Yes, like that." The Earthian studied the males staring at him and gave a nod of thanks. "I'm Michel Dunois, an Earth Space Agency astronaut, and you are...?"

"I am Warrior Kanzo, of the Etterian Elite forces. This is Data Officer Prex, Warrior Sena, and Medic Der. Did you require assistance when you sent out your birdsong?" Kanzo asked which Ulriq appreciated. The Earthian's response might appease the council. Although, in truth, he hoped they never learned of this incident.

"Birdsong?" Michel Dunois frowned then shrugged. Ulriq arched a brow at Ksal. Perhaps their data scan of the Earthian's language was defective. "I needed help, but I didn't expect it. Thank you again."

Ulriq strode out of the communications room, his destination was Docking Bay J where he would await the shuttle's return. He entered the bay as Michel Dunois stumbled down the lowered ramp, his gaze scanning the interior of the bay. One of many on the battleship. Ulriq glanced around as well, attempting to see his ship with fresh eyes.

The dark gray of the Maloidian steel bulkheads gleamed in the white lighting. Metal-grated flooring lined the large bay which housed two kuta shuttles and one scimitar as per protocol. Maloidian crates lined the walls, magnetically attached for safety. His males darted across the bay, attending to their tasks with utmost efficiency despite their obvious interest in the Earthian traveler. Warmth flooded his chest, recognizable as pride, at what his males had accomplished.

"Michel Dunois, this is Supreme Commander Ulriq, and this is the battleship *Kushin*," Kanzo said.

Ulriq accepted Michel Dunois's offered hand and shook it three times. Why the repetition?

"A pleasure to meet you, Supreme Commander." At the male's use of 'pleasure', disapproval swept through Ulriq, snatching a little more of his control. But the words were in a formal tone, therefore the use of the word 'pleasure' wasn't meant to offend. "Will I be returning to my planet?"

"This is impossible. In rescuing you, we have violated our Global Council laws regarding our dealings with mid-grade planets. Earth needs to believe you have expired."

"Then why did you rescue me?" The Earthian flushed pink.

Ulriq didn't appreciate the potent, yet controlled emotion directed at him. It was a mark of disrespect, of ingratitude.

"A Yithian slave ship was en route. Would you have preferred we allow them to capture you? To force you to fight in their arena?" He growled, his voice lowering. Adrenaline flooded his body, and even though there was no battle to fight, the burn of anger still resonated through him.

"Arena?" Michel Dunois gasped, his cheeks trembled, then he pinched his lips and raised his determined gaze to Ulriq. "I must go home...to my sister. She's all I have."

Impressed by the male's ability to contain his emotions, Ulriq opted to ignore the disrespectful outburst and acknowledge the strangeness of the situation.

He pasted on a stiff smile before gesturing to his observing males. "Your message was *felt* by all. But we cannot allow you to return you to your homeworld."

His fists clenched. "So if I remain on this battleship, what becomes of me?"

The Earthian wasn't aware of the significance of the word 'felt.' Etterians didn't use it often.

Ulriq sighed, his patience ebbing. "You will be an Etterian male, subject to our law. We will train and treat you as a warrior."

"I can't say goodbye?" Michel Dunois asked in a strangled voice. He paled making Ulriq realize these skin-color fluctuations were not controllable.

"What would you tell her, Michel Dunois?" Ulriq hated that he was in this situation. His booted feet were on a path he couldn't escape.

"I would tell her I'm on a long-term mission, and not to expect to see me for years. At least she'll know I haven't died, that I didn't break my promise to her."

"And you cannot do so via a comm?" Ulriq folded his arms across his chest, more to still his restlessness than for any other reason. "I will give your words further thought. More than this I cannot promise you. Kanzo, see him settled."

"Yes, Supreme Commander." Kanzo gestured to the male to follow him.

Ulriq scowled as Kanzo led the Earthian away. This new development didn't please him. He ignored his males's gazes trailing his pacing form. He wanted to grant the male his request, to bid farewell to his blood-bond, a sister. And he suspected the gender of his blood-bond tipped Ulriq's leniency. Females were rare, to be cherished.

But to visit her endangered his males and their mission. A hovering battleship would start an intergalactic incident. And setting foot planetside would increase the risk. In addition, he knew not the character of this species. Could Michel Dunois be trusted to keep his word and not attempt an escape? It wasn't that he considered him a prisoner. No. What Ulriq needed was to remain honorable in all things. He had to decide and soon.

He growled in frustration. An hour ago, the monotony of exploration had been his only concern. Now the requisitions were side-lined due to the number of reports he now needed to submit. With a grunt, he acknowledged he had already decided. Michel Dunois's plea hadn't changed his mind. Ulriq strode over to the Earthian's quarters, where Kanzo waited outside his door.

He greeted him with a nod, grateful Kanzo had the forethought to communicate the location of Michel Dunois's quarters to him. Ulriq didn't waste further time and opened the door. The Earthian had dressed in blue breeches and a soft-looking tunic. At least it allowed for better ease of movement. He gestured for Ulriq to enter while he rose to a standing position.

"You may comm your sister, Michel Dunois, but a visit is unacceptable."

"It's Michel, or Mich, Supreme Commander." He paced; energy vibrated off his body. "I understand the risks and your distrust. I'd feel the same in your shoes."

Ulriq bristled at the word 'feel' even as his gaze traveled to the Earthian's tiny feet. He would never fit in Ulriq's shoes.

"Please, hear me out," Michel pleaded.

Ulriq clenched his teeth, not liking that this male thought his decision was negotiable. "Usually, I notify Jack..."

"Jack?" Ulriq echoed, recalling the prior use of it.

"Jacqueline, but I call her Jack."

"Continue." Ulriq spread his legs and rested his arms behind him, waiting to hear Michel's plea.

"I'd let her know I was home, and we'd meet for dinner. I'd sometimes surprise her at her house, but if you allow this, I'd suggest we meet at my house under the pretense of a barbecue. It's far out of town and away from nosey neighbors."

"How long do you expect to waste our time further?" At Ulriq's words and unrelenting gaze, Michel grimaced.

"An afternoon, approximately four hours. I won't try to escape. I understand rescuing me violated some council law, and I'm sorry for my part in it."

Ulriq turned to Kanzo. "Allow him to communicate with his sister, and nothing more." He strode off, too irritated to endure the disappointment clear on Michel and Kanzo's features. Pausing in the passage where no male hovered, he struggled for control, hoping to silence his instincts screaming he had erred in judgment.

CHAPTER TWO

Earth
The outskirts of West Haven
Jack's workplace
Year Of 2252, April

HOLY SHIT, HER RIBS burned. As an instructor, she didn't dare react to any form of pain. It would create fear in her students. And fear of unarmed combat wasn't something she wanted to teach them. It was, for this reason, she'd endure this in silence. As fire scorched along her ribs, she couldn't decide what was worse, the pain or holding in the deep moan scratching her throat, demanding release. Her mind blurred for a few minutes under the shards lancing through her, almost as if she'd consumed too much cognac.

"Damnit. What do you think you're doing?" Steve, a fellow instructor, boomed as he rushed to where she sprawled across the blue training mats.

Her world settled, and she blinked at Steve, almost giggling at his girl-curls. She swallowed that too, instinctively knowing it would trigger hysterical laughter and call forth more pain. Flashing a forced smile at her recruits, she held up her hand, trying to calm Steve who looked close to losing his shit. Dragging in a slow, shallow breath made her wince, pulsing daggers at the outer edges of her consciousness. Her ribs were hopefully cracked with nothing broken. She didn't have the courage to test.

"It's okay, Steve. I'm just winded," she gasped, sitting up and wishing she hadn't as the icy-hot shards intensified calling forth a wave of nausea—she swallowed with care.

Nancy nibbled on her bottom lip with her brow furrowed. She rocked on her toes, as if readying to bolt.

Jack sighed and forced out what she hoped was a reassuring smile. "Well done. I didn't see that coming." She scanned Nancy and pinched her lips to quit gawking. Who would have thought five-foot-three Nancy could flip Jack over so effortlessly? Pride warmed her chest or was that the side effects of her cracked ribs?

Steve scowled as he helped her to stand, and she bit down hard on her inner cheek fighting the urge not to curse him for his jerky movements.

"You're laughing about this?" Anger skewered his features.

She stared at him, wishing she didn't have to deal with his melodrama. Not now, when her tolerance was understandably low. "Yes, why not? Look at how little she is, and she flipped me." Patting Nancy on the shoulder, Jack forced a faint chuckle past her aching ribs, hoping it appeared relaxed. "Proud of you, girl."

"You could have been seriously hurt." Steve pouted, irritating Jack to no end. One day she would catch his bottom lip between her fingers and yank it.

He had to have practiced it in the mirror, believing it made him irresistible. Averting her gaze, her focus fell on the recruits. They showed no emotion around Steve; experience had taught them he would rip them a new one if they reacted in any way. Their faces were pale, and their bodies tense.

"That's the point." Jack strode closer to the line of recruits, forcing her hand to release her ribs and fall 'casually' to her side. "Did you catch that, or should Nancy demonstrate on a few of you? Cranston, up for the challenge?"

Tentative smiles formed while their gazes darted between her and Steve.

"All right, split into teams of two and try not to hurt your partners too much."

Jack paused, raised her gaze to the beamed ceiling, and prayed for patience. Steve watched her with an intensity that was alarming. How did she know this? Thousands of bats swirled in her stomach then promptly plummeted to their deaths. The nausea curdling her insides was their tiny bodies decaying. She frowned at her morbid thoughts.

"I'm fine, Steve. I promise." She flicked him the tiniest of smiles, despite not wanting to. Any overt friendliness on her part encouraged him, as if her countless rejections meant nothing. Like she would miraculously change her mind, wowed by his impressive pout and his lack of height. "Thanks for coming right over."

His shoulders remained scrunched, narrowing his frame. "It's Friday, Jack. You got time for a drink after work?" He ran a hand through his brown curls. On him, the girl-curls looked good, if a bit effeminate. On Jack, if she styled her hair into curls, she'd turn her into a six-foot-two cherub—a creepy one.

"Sure. Just to show you I'm fine. But not as a date," she added and raised her forefinger at him in a threatening manner. "I don't want a repeat of last time."

"I told you, Jack, it was Dave's idea of a prank. He brought her in from up north so no one would recognize her. *I* didn't even know the woman."

"But you apparently cheated on her," she teased and tried to control her shiver. All the restaurant's patrons had looked at Jack with pity. A woman had even snuck a silk handkerchief into her hand. Worst date ever. "Did you prank him back?"

"Of course. I paid the same woman to hit on him at a bar in front of his fiancé." Steve's wicked grin was an unpleasant sight to behold, like a gleeful hobgoblin delighted with his mischief.

"Filmed it, didn't you?" Jack didn't need the answer; his expression said it all. He might as well have rubbed his palms together to complete the wicked joy twisting his face.

"Yup, showed it to all his friends, and come Christmas, the family will view it too." His anticipation was palpable.

"You know it's conflict escalation, right? He'll retaliate, and I won't be a part of it. You so much as consider including me in any of that, and I'll shave your head while you're sleeping."

"My brother is a dick," he muttered, tugging on his precious curls.

"Doesn't mean you have to be a dick too." For Jack, this was one of the reasons why she couldn't date him, his immaturity.

"He ruined my chances with you. I'll never forgive him for that."

"Chances with me?" She sighed. Her ribs throbbed as her patience drained from her body. Maybe she should have been honest, told everyone his constant lecherous gazes, touches, comments, and incessant whining about her dating him made her skin crawl. Lying about his height bothering her had seemed the simpler approach. She gritted her teeth. "You do know you're shorter than me, Steve?"

"I know you're sensitive about your height, Jack, but I'm shorter by one inch. I didn't think it would matter."

"It does, and yet you blatantly ignore my preferences. I'll be at Fred's after class," she said as Nancy flipped over the class bully—Jimmy Cranston—with more effort than she needed to. The man hit the padded floor with an oomph.

Despite Jack's ribs pinging in protest, she smothered a chuckle. *Damn right, girl.*

"Can't we ride together?" Did Steve just whine?

"Of course, we can; I have my spare helmet. You can be my bitch." She tried not to laugh at his disgruntled expression. He wouldn't find it funny if she explained it, with pictures, and it would just squeeze her ribs. Might be worth it, though.

"Damn. Forgot you bought a solarcycle. You know how dangerous those things are, right?" When he wagged his finger at her, she was tempted to bite it off.

"Yes, Mom. I promise to do less than the required speed limit." Gliding away ended the conversation, thank the Lord.

Jimmy lay on the mat wheezing, having had the wind knocked out of him. She strode toward him to assist. Despite wanting to congratulate Nancy on her epic throw, she was unable to show favoritism. She didn't crouch, but kept herself upright, gesturing to him with controlled movements how to avoid Nancy's techniques. And when he thwarted her next flip, Jack strolled across to the other sparring pairs. When an unexpected bolt of pain squeezed her lungs, she nodded at Steve before leaving the training room. Their full-time nurse, Melissa, was her destination.

JACK PEELED OFF HER faux-leather tavlex jacket, wincing as her ribs complained louder than their usual grumblings. Genuine leather made her sweat, not that she could afford it. But tavlex was better, lighter with steel fibers making it heat-resistant and durable. If only her academy jumpsuit was of the same stuff. They were testing out a new synthetic fabric that might as well have been leather.

She placed her helmet on the barstool beside her.

Melissa had strapped her ribs and given her pain meds. There was no known treatment for bruised ribs except immobility. A tumbler of cognac slid onto the counter, stopping inches from her hand. The brandy was expensive, but she needed it. She hadn't taken the meds yet since she wasn't sure how her body would react. It was unwise to ride a solarcycle or drink alcohol while on medication.

Sliding onto the stool in trepidation, she leaned her elbows on the counter with a grateful sigh. They were the only part of her body not in pain. Her head throbbed which meant she hadn't broken her fall fast enough. The back of her head must have bounced off the mat. Rest and pain medication would certainly help with that.

"Thanks, Fred." She forced a smile in greeting. The mirror lining the back of the bar reflected her grimace, so she gave up on a friendliness she was far from feeling.

"Bad day, Jack?" he asked as he polished a glass with a clean cloth.

His methodical actions seeped contentment into her. He didn't need to do that, but he said it put people at ease, and he hated to have idle hands. Fred Munroe had known her parents long before they died. Hell, he even knew her older brother Mich, the astronaut in the family.

"You should have seen it, Fred; little Nancy flipped me." With a wince, she shifted on her stool.

"Nope, don't believe it, Jack. I mean, what are you, six-foot-*four*?" He grinned. His humor was unappreciated yet warmed her heart regardless. He teased her by purposely forgetting her height since she was sensitive about it. Last week, she'd been six-foot-seven, the week before that six-foot-three. He'd randomly 'guessed' her height since she first broke six feet.

"Six-foot-*two*, Fred, I don't need you making me taller." She sipped from her glass and savored the explosion of flavor across her tongue. Intense, smoky, and dark made her taste buds hum with pleasure.

"I see pretty boy wore you down." Fred gestured to Steve who'd entered the bar.

Jack glanced at the door and groaned at Steve's persistence. Agreeing to this meeting had been easy when she'd had plans to come here, especially after the day she'd had. He bounced as he strode toward her, his enthusiasm worsening her day. Muttering, she buried her nose in her glass before raising it for a sip.

"Nope, not gonna happen." She winked at Fred before grunting a greeting at Steve who slid onto the stool next to her.

"Heard from Mich?" Fred asked as he slid a glass of beer over to Steve before he'd even ordered. Being in a small town, memorizing every customer's beverage of choice was a given.

"Nothing, not for a while now. It's worrying, you know?" She shrugged then winced when the slight use of her back and chest muscles rippled fire through her. "I mean, anything can happen out there. Space pirates are becoming a nuisance. The government is thinking of setting patrols." She shook her head in disbelief, keeping the sway to a minimum. "Our firepower is pathetic in comparison to the aliens out there."

"Ever thought of finding your own way among the stars?" Steve asked before he took a long draw from his glass.

"I did, once, but then Mich beat me to it."

"What? Where would you go?" He wiped his thumb down the glass, clearing the condensation.

"I'd work security, probably. Any of the space stations would do." She took another sip, and swallowed, relishing the sweet heat in her stomach. "I still might. I like the idea of me against the universe."

Steve scowled, unhappy with her for even thinking of going. Not that his opinion mattered. "You're insane. It's bad enough worrying where the shooter will be without factoring in the possibility of the air filtration system exploding, or losing gravity, or being hit by an asteroid."

"Pessimistic much?" she teased and pushed her empty cognac glass aside. Splaying her hand on the bar, she slid off the stool. She swiped her wrist over the paypad embedded in the fake-wood counter. "See you Monday."

"You're leaving?"

Scooping her helmet off the stool next to her, she waved at Fred before she tugged it on, not bothering to answer Steve. He'd witnessed the hell of a day she'd had.

"If you even knew her, you'd realize she only drinks cognac when she misses Mich." Fred frowned at Steve. At least he understood her.

Gratitude welled within her, strong and comforting. Every year, on the anniversary of her parents' deaths, she would be there drinking herself into oblivion. Fred made sure she got home safely. He'd also been there for her when it seemed as if Mich would never come home. Best of all, he was there on days like today where everything threatened to overwhelm her.

Strolling out of the bar, she swiped her thumb over the keypad, before throwing her leg over the 'leather' seat of her new purchase. Tugging her gloves from her jacket pocket, she slid them on, stroked the throttle, and flipped the stand back. She checked the traffic and pulled out, thrilling in the power beneath her and the wind sneaking into her protective gear. Purchasing the hybrid bike had been an impulse she hadn't regretted yet. Zipping through the small-town traffic gleefully, she was home in less than ten minutes.

After parking her cycle on her solar-paneled driveway, she flipped the stand and paused for a moment, leaning her weight back as she slid off her gloves a finger at a time. Unclipping the helmet, she lifted it off, tossed her gloves inside it, and cast a glance over her double-story old-style farmhouse. Painted in dark green, it matched Mich's house on the outskirts of West Haven. They had bought the paint in bulk. It had once been a wooden house, many years ago, but across its various owners, brick and steel had replaced the wood.

She paused on her stone porch doing a three-sixty, gazing at the domed mega-cities on the horizon. The powered domes contained their pollution, and to live under a clear blue sky was a precious gift. It was why most schools and academies were relocated to farming communities with their free, clean air.

With a sigh, she entered through the stained-glass aluminum door; it rattled when she allowed it to thud closed behind her. Dumping her helmet and gloves on the antique foyer table made of wood—a rare find and had cost her a month's salary—she stripped off her jacket and hung it on the hook drilled into the brick. Flashing a glance at the framed photographs of her parents who'd died when she and Mich were little. When she settled on the photograph of Mich, she stilled. Sniffing, she raised a trembling hand to slide a finger over her brother's face.

With slumped shoulders, she undid her braid and scraped her nails over her scalp, massaging as she did so. Her boots were next. She dropped them carelessly before climbing the stone stairs to her bedroom. The railing was wrought iron. The earlier owners had sold the original wood to collectors. Her footsteps were silent as she crossed the paisley carpet runner, past her empty spare bedrooms—indicative of her life—before entering the room at the end of the hall.

Along the way, she stripped off and tossed her clothing on the floor—as discarded and disrupted as her thoughts and hopes. In her T-shirt and panties, she crawled onto the bed and gingerly lowered herself, choosing to lie on her back. Only then did she let the tears fall.

Chapter Three

Etterian battleship, Kushin
Orbiting mid-grade planet, Earth

DECEPTION DIDN'T COME NATURALLY to Etterians which was why Ulriq knew his males were planning something. They stopped conversations when he neared. They peeked at him in passing with their gazes lowering. Alodon's balls. Ksal had stammered when he had informed Ulriq the Yithian slave ship had altered course, traveling in the opposite direction from Earth. By the time Nerx approached him, Ulriq was more curious than angry. It had to do with Michel since he was the newest addition to their mundane existence.

"They are planning on escorting Michel planetside?" he asked.

Nerx grumbled in response. The male had only one disposition and that was 'miserable', yet he was the finest warrior Ulriq knew.

"And what do you suggest I do, Nerx? I have not heard of a warrior disobeying orders."

"It happens, otherwise, Adviser Cales would have one less task to attend to."

"True." Ulriq sighed. He had permitted Michel to receive an O.D.I. At least they could trace him if need be. And judging by the Earthian's slumped shoulders, he wasn't participating in this disobedience. Even though he could control his emotions, he couldn't hide them.

"Your involvement is not necessary. Each male is prepared to lose a foot of honor for this, Ulriq. Perhaps leniency is required." Nerx words drew a scowl from Ulriq. Be lenient when he had denied Michel his request? "I suggest we commandeer the kuta before they do."

Ulriq's brow furrowed before an unexpected smile tugged his lips. "I assume you have a plan, my battle-bond?" The spark of excitement unfurled in his belly. Nerx nodded, though no expression of eagerness crossed his features. "And which warriors require my leniency?"

"Danic, Kanzo, Aaro…" Nerx ignored Ulriq's arched brow. "And myself." At Nerx's admission, Ulriq stilled, gaping at his sub-commander before he gritted his teeth. "I understand why you have taken the stance you have, Ulriq, which is why you cannot be involved in the planning. The records need to indicate this."

"And convincing me to 'commandeer the kuta' is part of your plan?" Ulriq's voice hoarsened. Fury vibrated through him, forcing him to focus on his calming techniques rather than the situation at hand. Yet underlying it all, was a sense of betrayal. "You would sacrifice your honor for an Earthian? We do not know his character. You risk punishment for an unknown." When tension stiffened his body, he forced his muscles to relax, limb by limb.

Nerx pinched the bridge of his nose. "Here we differ on what is honorable, Ulriq."

Sharp, stinging heat flushed Ulriq's face, and the released tension returned, hardening his muscles. He clenched his fists with the urge to hit something.

"Now you question my honor?" Ulriq boomed.

"You have not been yourself of late." Nerx's observation caught Ulriq by surprise, jerking his fingers open. "Under normal circumstances, you would risk your hair, our warriors' lives, and Xeus's wrath to do what is right."

"And you believe allowing this Earthian to say farewell is justification for your defiance?"

Nerx straightened his shoulders, assuming his full height of six-foot-seven which was one inch taller than Ulriq. "You can participate or remain here, either way, it is scheduled. Michel is notifying Lady Jack now."

"So that is it? Ignore—"

Nerx thrust his face close to Ulriq's. "If your closest battle-bonds are involved, what does that tell you?"

Ulriq glared at Nerx, not willing to acknowledge the truth. But his battle-bond's words beat at him, at his mind, at his heart. He hated that Nerx was correct. Historically, Ulriq would have thrown caution to the wind and done what was right, what was honorable. And bidding farewell to a blood-bond in person *was* honorable. But he hated that his irritation hadn't gone unnoticed. Shame clouded his vision, and his shoulders dropped a fraction.

"I would appreciate the feel of solid ground beneath my feet." Nerx wrapped his fingers around Ulriq's forearm and pressed a hand to his shoulder in a warrior greeting. "The visit is two days hence. Please...join us."

Chapter Four

Earth

West Haven

Jack's house

A FAINT VOICE INTRUDED on her sleep. Jack tried to crack one eye open, but they were swollen shut from the crying she'd indulged in last night. Everything was groggy as exhaustion pounded at her. Both symptoms were probably due to her pain meds. She had a vague memory of moaning herself awake, traipsing downstairs to find her medication in her jacket pocket then collapsing into bed.

"Jack Dunois."

Mumbling something again, she waved her hand dismissively to whomever the intruder was. If they were burglars, they could help themselves as long as they left her alone.

"I suppose I could eat the chocolate croissant by myself. It wouldn't be a hardship. You could say I'm doing you a favor with your ass as big as it is."

Jack lifted her head off the pillow. Sometime during the night, after the meds had kicked in, she'd rolled onto her stomach, and was now feeling the error of her ways. A vise clamped around her midriff, and her mind couldn't grasp the concept of moving.

"Are those your grandmother's panties?" the sweet voice teased.

"Taylor Montgomery, I swear," Jack threatened into her pillow which wasn't as menacing as she'd intended. Her friend's too-delighted laughter showed how ineffectual her threat had been.

"Come on, Jack. It's like ten already."

Jack released a deep groan, rubbing her hand over her smashed-into-the-pillow cheek. With the greatest care, she knelt before facing her best friend and adopted sister.

"I heard about the incident," Taylor said, drawing Jack's gaze to hers.

"Blue hair?" Jack groaned in agony as she shifted toward the edge of the bed. Taking a moment for the pain to subside, she gathered her strength to haul herself to her feet.

"Don't you like it?" Taylor bounced her platinum-blonde curls now with blue highlights. She'd also shaved it on one side exposing a pretty skull. Jack's skull would have too many scars to count, so shaving her head was O.U.T.

"I'm just jealous." Jack didn't have the guts to do that to her own hair. It fell down her back in a state of constant neglect. She had it trimmed when Taylor promised to nag her to death. Then she'd drag her ass to visit their adopted sister, Ava—their resident hairstylist.

"The girls will be here soon. They said something about a food hangover." Taylor pursed her lips as she picked at an oil stain on her T-shirt.

Jack frowned as dismay gripped her. She wasn't in the mood to watch illegal romance-comedies and eat until abdominal explosion. What she wanted was a run but—with her bruised ribs—that would have to wait a few weeks. The inactivity alone would drive her crazy.

"So, where's this croissant you mentioned?" Standing up, she bit her lip to stifle a full-blown moan. Only a whimper escaped.

Remaining immobile, she drew in a few gasps before shuffling into her en-suite to run her shower. Taylor leaned against the doorway while Jack used the toilet. Taylor, Ava, and Victoria, known to them as Vicky, were the only family Jack and Mich had. They'd met in the orphanage, and due to their advanced ages, had remained there until the age of eighteen. Mich had left first, and with a scholarship, had worked toward becoming an astronaut. He'd also inherited their grandparents' place which was on the outskirts of their farming town. Jack checked on it, ensuring all was in working order and neatened in case Mich came home for a visit. But that was a faraway dream with her heart as empty as his house.

Taylor was in love with him. Had been for as long as Jack could remember. She hadn't mentioned a thing to Mich. He'd deal with it when he was ready. Knowing her brother, he wouldn't claim Taylor no matter how he felt. He was never planetside, and to do that to her was heartless. Even worse, if he saddled her with kids once the Parenting Board gave permission. He probably hoped another man would come by and sweep Taylor off her feet. Jack almost snorted, in their town? The chances of that happening were slim to none.

She stripped and stepped into the shower while Taylor assumed the toilet seat, wanting to talk. The bandage was waterproof so Jack could wear it without fear of a rash developing. As she soaped her body, she tried not to make any jerky movements—just slow and steady.

"Fred said Steve managed to get you to the bar last night." Taylor chuckled; the sound merged with the running water. "He's going to wear you down, y'know."

"Small towns," Jack said as she washed her hair. "He's too short for me, and you know it."

"Nonsense. True love isn't fazed by height."

"True love?" Jack spluttered, not sure whether Steve was true-love material for any woman.

That was mean. He'd find his true love or more than one, of that she had no doubt. She used her facewash before rinsing her hair one more time. Stepping out of the shower, she accepted the towel Taylor held out.

"There are no decent guys in this town, Jack. The pickings are slim," Taylor said, unknowingly voicing Jack's thoughts.

"Not that you're looking," she teased and as expected, Taylor blushed a pretty pink. "I can't see myself with Steve. I have known him since he was twelve when he picked his nose like a gifted miner."

Squeamish Taylor shuddered, twisting her face in disgust. "Ew, Jack. I wish you hadn't shared that."

Jack grinned and dried off before she wrapped the towel around her head. Traipsing into her room, she carefully slid on a pair of leggings and a baggy shirt that had once belonged to Mich. It made her feel like he was nearby, that at any moment, he would storm in and demand the return of his T-shirts. Right then, the weight of her loneliness wrenched her gut, as if he didn't care about his shirts, his life planetside, or his sister.

Buying herself some time, Jack glided to the bathroom to brush her teeth then flashed Taylor a fake-cheeky grin. "My point exactly."

With Taylor trailing her, she climbed each step down to the kitchen to find a pretty blue box of chocolate croissants on the steel and stone counter.

"Did you sell another painting?" Jack turned to her in query.

"Yes, two to one collector."

Taylor—a famous artist—shipped her paintings internationally. Jack loved that her friend's art was well-known and respected. Her fingernails always had oil paint embedded in them, and the scent of linseed oil mingled with her jasmine perfume.

"Ava mentioned a mystery-spy marathon, but I dunno…"

"Oh. That sounds better than I-love-you's," Jack said as enthusiasm blessed her with a little energy. She didn't need to feel more emotionally unstable than she did now. Hours of you-complete-me would be torture. She'd rather have Nancy break another rib.

"You would say that, Jack."

"I sat through your favorites, so cut me some slack." Jack pointed a finger.

Taylor laughed showing her unrepentance. Knowing the kitchen as well as Jack did, she retrieved four small plates and scooped a croissant onto each one.

"Where Ava gets these vids, I don't want to know." Jack raised her hands in a show of innocence.

The governments had outlawed music, movies, and video games in 2021 due to a music vid that had caused over a hundred thousand deaths in young adults under the age of twenty. Jack didn't know much about the circumstances around this vid, just that the world had united to ban all three industries.

Therefore, any vids or music Ava got her hands on were contraband and ancient. At least, she disposed of them after they'd watched them, though Jack did know she kept a secret stash of songs she loved. Jack shook her head. As awesome and entertaining as some of these vids were, she would prefer not to risk it. Illegal viewing or ownership resulted in severe prosecution by the media police and a lifetime sentence on Mars's penal colony.

"Vicky might not make it, said something about having to bake a wedding cake." Taylor shrugged. "Or maybe she's bringing leftovers, I can't remember."

"These are Antoine's?" Jack gestured to the croissants.

Vicky was their baker. The thought of her chocolate salted caramel cake had Jack's mouth watering in longing. Antoine was an elderly French gentleman Vicky had lured to their backward town. He did some of the confectionaries when Vicky was too busy. Jack glided to her coffee machine and programmed in her requirements.

"Yes, and I was lucky to get them. Widow Miles had him pinned to the display case. I swiped the paypad and ran for my life." Taylor wiggled her eyebrows suggestively. "Come to think of it, maybe we shouldn't buy from there anymore. I mean, how hygienic are those counters?"

"Antoine knows better than that," Vicky said from the door, her red-gold hair spilling down her back. It brushed her elbows as she strolled into the room carrying way too many unhealthy confectionery boxes.

"What do you think of Taylor's hair?" Ava asked from behind Vicky.

Jack gently hugged her friends—her sisters—in greeting. Ava was average in height, so her head reached Jack's shoulder. Her skin was a lovely mocha color and with her striking green eyes, she was the beauty in their group. She'd pinned her black hair up with two chopsticks, and these poked Jack in the jaw. It was preferable to Taylor's hugs whose face landed somewhere in Jack's cleavage.

"Love it, of course." Jack sighed 'forlornly.' "Maybe you could put purple streaks in mine?" She asked every week, and each time she changed the color.

"No can do. You signed that code of conduct, remember," Ava said as always. "Quit that job, then I could do it. Besides, you're wincing again, so what happened this time?"

Jack explained the miracle that was Nancy. Her sisters commiserated even though they'd known five minutes after it had happened. Damn small towns, but Jack appreciated that they pretended not to know.

With croissants and coffee, they settled down for the movie marathon. And of course, Ava had stolen the ones with her favorite actors. Jack liked most of them, more so the ones who brought grittiness to overly suave roles. By the time the sun had set, they'd consumed too much confectionary. Jack waved goodbye to her sisters and groaned as she lay on the couch, variations of cake gurgling in her stomach, refusing to digest. In addition, her ribs throbbed; the pain steadily climbing to the point she had to pop two pain capsules just to numb herself.

She spent Sunday cleaning the house as best she could, doing laundry, resting in between chores, and planning lessons for the following week. But Monday hung like a dark cloud. Firearms training loomed. The recruits had learned the mechanics behind antique handguns as well as the cleaning protocol, the best way to holster them, safety first, and the importance of ballistics. On Monday, they'd learn to load and fire. She dreaded those days since she'd had quite a few close shaves. But she couldn't take sick leave. Not when her current set of students were so close to graduating. They'd covered the use of air and sonar weaponry, but they needed to know the antique weapons some street factions still utilized.

That evening, she received a mail from Mich. At the sight of it in her inbox, indescribable elation burst through her. The joy couldn't be contained, it bubbled out, vibrating her cracked ribs, calling forth a hiss of pain even as she indulged in a bark of laughter.

He was able to visit on Tuesday, asked her to get off work and to meet him at his house. The extensive shopping list he had for her screamed a craving for a barbecue and judging by the quantity, he planned to eat for ten men. She sent the mail to the girls, and they responded with due eagerness. Yes, Tuesday would be fine, Jack informed Mich. She'd stared at the mail in a daze of happiness. If it wasn't for the pain meds, sleep would have been elusive.

THE UNIVERSE HATED HER. That thought circled Jack's mind the moment the bullet penetrated her shoulder. Since she had been standing in front of the wall, it threw her back the final few inches with shards of brick spraying at her cheeks and throat. 'It burns' pierced her mind as the gasping pain ripped through her. Her vision faded, speckled with black spots, and her semi-digested lunch burrito threatened to present itself. Students gathered around suffocating her as she fought to control her reactions, the pain fighting for supremacy over her emotions, her motor control, and her vocal cords.

Her ribs throbbed, threatening to crush her pounding heart. The hot stickiness of her blood soaked her shirt. She threw out a hand and splayed her fingers over the coarse brick as she fought to stand. Many hands waved as if to aid her, but she grunted them away, words having failed her. Her booted feet wouldn't slide under her with her knees refusing to lock. Her actions served to drop her backside to the floor, jarred her, stabbing fresh shards of pain through her shoulder. Melissa burst in, parting the students faster than Steve ever could.

"Holy shit, Jack. What the hell? You couldn't go a week without an injury?"

"It's not funny," Jack mumbled before clamping on her bottom lip.

Melissa lifted the collar of her shirt to ascertain the severity, and the fabric tugged at the wound. A groan rumbled up Jack's throat, escaping as a hum from between her pinched lips.

"It will be." Melissa smiled as she pulled out her mobile device and made a call.

In her dream world, Jack would have preferred to calmly assure her students she was fine, pick herself up, and stride off the shooting range. Instead, she was on her way to the hospital with a gunshot wound on a freaking gurney. As far as it concerned her, a shoulder wound was better than the alternative. The bullet had been a through and through and had embedded in the wall behind her judging by the dust coating her jumpsuit.

She was proud of herself for not bellowing like an offended walrus. Her mind had racked over the last half-an-hour, trying to analyze how this could have happened. Perhaps Jimmy had preloaded his .22 and had accidentally waved it around? She would need to see the security feeds to be sure. And she'd known this would happen, at some point. She could only have so many close calls before her luck ran out. Of course, Melissa had organized a replacement instructor. And despite having not wanted her to call an ambulance, by the time it had arrived, Jack hadn't minded.

Her shoulder burned as if on fire with pain radiating down her body and across her chest. She gritted her teeth as the paramedics loaded her into the ambulance under the watchful gaze of her students. It hurt like hell, and Melissa was overreacting, according to Jack's expert medical opinion which she vocalized to the uncaring paramedics. Both she'd known for years, and both ignored her with blatant eye-rolls.

Steve's glowering countenance had her imagining what sort of berating Jimmy would soon endure. Melissa road with her, taking the time to contact Taylor who Jack had recorded as her next-of-kin. Melissa now stood at the edge of the hospital bed wringing her hands with her clenched lips revealing the depth of her concern.

"X-rays are clear, no bone or lung damage. Some muscle tears will limit your movement for a while. But knowing you, Jack, you'll pop the pain meds and do what you want anyway." Dr. Cooper snorted.

Jack grunted since he had the right of it. But he'd been her doctor for as long as she could remember, and would understand her urgency to be mobile. With Mich on his way, she couldn't stay in bed, no matter how much pain any movement cost her.

"So, I'm good to go?" She shifted her backside closer to the edge of the bed, even as the nurse wrapped the final bandage on. "Mich's coming tomorrow, and you know how he hates hospitals."

"Yes, you can go, but if you start bleeding again, you come right back, Jack. I need your word on this." Doc waited with a pointed look, his finger hovering above the med-pad.

"Of course," she promised.

He studied her face for a minute before throwing up a hand. After signing a form on the med-pad, he strode out, shaking his head.

"Are you sure about this, Jack? It looks bad." Taylor chewed on her lip. She hovered around her, in case of what, Jack wasn't sure. If she decided to faint, petite Taylor wouldn't be able to do a damn thing to catch her.

Jack groaned as she stood, feeling like a sumo wrestler had pounded her into the ground. Everything within her ached as if her body tried to carry the pain by spreading it to her extremities.

"It *feels* bad. I'll stay at your place tonight, Taylor, then you can make sure I don't do anything stupid. Of all the timing." Jack huffed, as heat warmed her cheeks. Frustration vibrated through her. She tamped it down, not wishing to exacerbate her injuries. "Why couldn't this have happened on Wednesday?"

"Or not at all?"

Jack nodded at Taylor's logic and acknowledged she had gotten off lightly. It could have been far worse. Climbing into the wheelchair, she slumped, exhaustion weighing heavy after the day's events. Mich coming was all that mattered. And there were things she needed to do in anticipation of his arrival.

"My cycle is still at work. I'll need you to drop me off in the morning. I'll pick it up and meet you at Mich's. You get the food?" Lists and logistics bombarded her pain-saturated mind.

"Riding your cycle? Is that possible?" Taylor asked. "We haven't left hospital yet, and you're planning something stupid. Didn't you just promise otherwise to Dr. Cooper?"

Jack grunted and offered a small smile. "I'm not leaving my baby there, and I can't see any of you girls riding her. Maybe Vicky?"

Taylor grinned at that imagery. "Her hair would look like trailing fire."

"Trust your artist's mind to go in that direction." Jack eased into the front seat when Taylor opened the door to her car. "I think I'll pop some capsules and crash."

"That's the best thing you've said today."

Chapter Five

Planet, Earth

Michel's housing structure

SILENT TENSION DESCENDED THE moment Ulriq strode up the ramp and into the kuta's compartment. He paused to glance at his anxious males before resting his gaze on a bouncing Michel.

"You thought I would let you travel to the surface...without me?" He forced a smile and almost nodded as Kanzo relaxed. His pseudo-joviality was well-performed, though deceiving his males bothered Ulriq. As it should have bothered them to betray him. He clenched his jaw and focused on calming his erratic heartbeat.

"You're coming with?" The happiness on Michel's features was too unbearable to observe. "You're going to love Jack, Supreme Commander."

Ulriq grumbled at the use of love, as if an Etterian warrior had the emotional capacity or Maker's blessing for such a gift. Nerx strode in, pressing the panel to seal the shuttle door behind him. He signaled Danic who slid into the pilot's seat to initiate the departure protocols.

"I am pleased you decided to join us, Supreme Commander," Nerx said, though no expression crossed his features, so there was no 'pleased' about it. "At least I do not have to look at Michel's sour expression for a while."

Ulriq's lips twitched. Michel's sour expression? Unexpected and unappreciated laughter rumbled up his chest, vibrating his throat before he smothered it. Nerx's usual expression made Michel's sour one look joyful. Ulriq turned his attention to Michel, who was recounting a memory from his *damu* days. Watching the Earthian, he found his mannerisms intriguing if not a little flamboyant.

"We spent the entire summer building that fort. Our neighbor was kind enough to supply the materials and tools." Michel gestured wildly with his arms. "We'd built it on branches extending over the river thinking it was a good strategy. It secured our fort, limiting access to the one branch which wouldn't hold an adult's weight. Little did we realize that meant it might not hold our fort's weight." Michel chuckled; his smile wide with his bright eyes sparkling. "But it didn't collapse, no. The real reason Jack fell was due to a squirrel. It startled her, and squealing, she plummeted into the cool depths of the river." His shoulders shook as he laughed. "To have her tell it, a *snake* as thick as my arm startled her, and she lost her footing. My Jack's hard on the outside, but all sweet softness on the inside."

"We are all hard on the outside and soft on the inside," Aaro said, confusion furrowing his brow.

"Oh, no…it's a saying. It means you give the appearance of being impenetrable like nothing can hurt you. But on the inside, you are kind, understanding, compassionate," Michel said.

"And your Jack is this?" Ulriq asked, doubting such a paragon existed.

"Yes, you'll see." Michel grinned, energy vibrating off the smaller male's body.

From space, skirting the atmosphere of Earth, the planet was beautiful. Pristine white, swirling against a backdrop of blue on one half of the globe. Having discovered numerous worlds, Ulriq assumed the illuminated circles seen from their approach were the Earthian cities. The blissful admiration was short-lived. Danic proved his mettle as a pilot when he dodged the extensive debris field orbiting the planet. A few pings indicated he hadn't been able to miss them all, but as expected, the shuttle's shields withstood the impact and the searing heat of re-entry.

They burst through the atmosphere without further resistance, into a vision of bright sapphire oceans, glistening under their one weak sun. It was spectacular, even with the scars of pollution mottling the water's surface. Navigation on reflex was the protocol for most excursions, but Danic preferred to pilot without assistance. He did so now with the aid of markers and was soon skirting along fields of gold, an oasis amid domed mega-cities.

He hovered the shuttle for a moment above an isolated housing structure before landing the shuttle toward the rear of it. They exited as per protocol, blasters drawn, eyes vigilant. As Ulriq lead his unit toward the door, he took a deep breath, filling his lungs with unrecycled air. By the time Michel had unlocked the structure with a swipe of his thumb and ushered them in, they had stowed their blasters and relaxed their stances.

They entered what appeared to be the food preparation room with a large enough capacity for three males. It overlooked a table with four metal chairs that would collapse if an Etterian rested his full weight on it. Ulriq's upper arms scraped along the thin walls of a narrow passage and into a casual seating area. Michel led them to the front of the structure and out into the open sunlight. Ulriq paused, as did they all, to scan the area before once more relaxing.

Within minutes, each had an ice-cold beverage shoved in their hands. Ulriq sniffed then sipped it, rumbling his approval the instant the bitter liquid pooled in his mouth. A beer, Michel had called it. He settled to watch the Earthian bounce around with impatience as he started a fire. Ulriq swept his gaze over his males, enjoying their jovial demeanors. Such moments were rare when danger might be on the horizon, and for now, contentment reigned. As warriors, they were ever vigilant, and despite being at peace with all species in the galaxy, they still prepared for war. This quiet time afforded them a respite from their vigilance. He was grateful to Nerx for showing him the error of his ways. He would have missed this pleasant relief from the monotony of space exploration.

Leaning against the bark of a tree, he was unusually warm in his regulation armor. The suit normalized his body temperature, and since this was failing, it must be defective. The shade of the large tree—an oak Michel had called it—offered relief from their one sun's heat. He found its colors to be pleasing, a variegated-brown bark and green leaves. The trees on the planet Lysara were as beautiful with their gray bark and red canopies. Still, both felt wrong when he was used to Etteria's dark green trees and purple foliage.

As Michel disappeared inside for more beers, something rumbled in the distance. It was as far as Ulriq's advanced hearing could reach. His males stilled with remaining laughter curling their lips and their heads tilted. The rhythmic drone was mechanical. Something black on two wheels raced along the dirt road toward them with a dust cloud streaming behind it. The approaching ground vehicle was against the backdrop of large, domed cities. The male riding it drew Ulriq's focus as if it was a pressing danger. While he fought to steady his heartbeat, his fingers twitched above his blaster, eager for action. Tension tightened his muscles, and fire fueled him, readying him for battle.

The rider wore black camouflage and a similar helmet to Michel's when they had rescued him. The vehicle roared to a halt amid dust, burned sol, and other odors that twitched Ulriq's nose.

Yet there was something sweet, spicy, and elusive in the air. He scented the metallic tang of blood as well, as if this male had a fresh wound. No weapons bulged his strange armor, but Ulriq's males were as alert as he was. The rider swung a thin leg over the back of the device and pulled his gloves off, revealing pale hands—long-fingered with short nails—delicate in size. As the male unclipped the helmet and removed it to reveal flowing waves of sun-white locks, everything within Ulriq quietened, as if time slowed.

This was no male but an Earthian female.

She buried her gloves inside her helmet before hooking it over the front of the device. Impatience beat at him, twitching his limbs; this need to see this female bombarded his control. He pushed off the tree for a closer look since his males had crowded around her vehicle, blocking his view. Michel ran out, tossed the beers at Danic to grab the female, and yank her into his arms.

"Jack." He held her against him in a show of affection Ulriq found intriguing.

"Holy shit, damnit. Put. Me Down." At her pain-laced command, Michel dropped her and held her at arm's length. "Damn time you came home," she said with what Ulriq assumed was a smile on her face. Not that he could see her, but her tone had carried a warmth to it. He tamped down a shiver; her voice had a captivating cadence to it, soft, husky, and hypnotic.

"What happened this time?" Michel ran a frowning gaze over her.

"I'll fill you in later. Tell me, why is there a stripper convention happening here?" Her curls bounced when she glanced at Ulriq's males. "And in bronze glitter?"

Glitter? His eyelids fluttered as his O.D.I. informed him what 'glitter' meant. He scowled at its description. He wasn't a sparkling male.

"Shit, I almost forgot. Come meet the commander," Michel said.

His males parted to allow them through. Ulriq snapped to attention and drew in a long, calming breath, squaring his shoulders. At last. His first Earthian female. Her sensual voice demanded his focus. Her white-gold hair cascaded around her in wild abandonment itching his fingers with the need to test its silkiness. Excitement skittered along his nerves, speeding his heart as if victory was his.

"Ulriq, this is my sister, Jack."

She smiled in greeting and raised her blue gaze to meet his. Her eyes were beautiful—the same color as Earth's sky and Michel's. He admired her upturned face, her skin exquisite and dusted with a fine sprinkle of spots. The urge to press his lips to each one took hold of his mind. Parting his mouth to greet her, all he managed was a grunt.

Pure white heat—a scintillating pleasure so forceful it bordered on pain—seared through him. It ignited and exploded, engulfing him in joy so sweet, so intense, it threatened to bring him to his knees. His muscles tensed then shuddered under the onslaught. He threw out a hand to steady himself, catching hold of the wall of the housing unit as a vision struck him.

Her pale skin, bare, glowing, enticing, undulated beneath his mesmerized eyes, and as he raised his gaze, still in the vision, two soft mounds—with taut pink nipples—trembled with her moans. She was writhing beneath him as he devoured her feminine essence, wisps of her hair curling around a breast. The tart taste of her saturated his tongue, and her aroused scent drenched his nostrils. He was in agony and in heaven, both states exquisite in comparison to his previous indifference.

Only the Ethera, the Etterian mating bond, could weaken his body, assault his senses, and brush aside his warrior control. Icy shivers feathered across his overly sensitive skin. He clenched his eyes closed, gasping for air. Alodon's balls. He recognized the intense joy and gratitude coursing through him, but none of the other emotions. They remained nameless.

Jack was his Dar Eth, his life force, the one female in all the galaxies who would conquer his encroaching void. Without her, he would have died a lonely death. If the Maker showed him favor, he would have fathered a female *damu* with an Etterian female he would never care for. *Damu* were rare but not as rare as Etterian Dar Eths. A true blessing from the Maker was to receive his own Dar Eth. And he had from the unlikeliest of planets.

"Ulriq?" Michel's voice reflected his concern. Such an emotive race, these Earthians.

"I...I am well, Michel." With all the control Ulriq could muster, he forced himself to stand, staggering a little. While cursing his weak knees, he tried to smile, to put Michel at ease, despite not having returned to his former self. But the irritation—that had plagued him for the past few days—had disappeared.

"Too many beers?" the young male teased.

Ulriq chuckled even though unknown and volatile emotions roiled within him. No one had dared to tease him, and he found he liked it.

"Perhaps." He studied her, his life force, finding he was unable to look elsewhere.

The supple black fabric clung to her long legs which were muscled, defined, and yet looked pliable. She wore thick heavy footwear; he suspected they served as protection while on her two-wheeled vehicle. A black jacket hid what he had seen in his vision. Her face was exquisite, a feminine version of Michel's. Her chin was small, her jawline squarish made entrancing by her soft, supple lips—the color of pink hahyt petals—with a nose long and tipped at the end. Her blue eyes met his after her gaze traveled over his form; they were wide and admiring.

He couldn't smother an answering smile—an outward sign of his inner joy. The Maker *had* blessed him with a Dar Eth. That she wasn't Etterian didn't bother him, despite what this venture had cost him. Then again if his Dar Eth turned out to be a tentacled, six-eyed Algri, he would be as grateful. Thankfully, she wasn't. She was an Earthian and as beautiful as any Etterian female. Such a gift needed cherishing, and he would never contest it.

"Greetings, Jack," he said, his hoarse voice and no longer his to control.

Her luscious mouth fell open for a moment before she clamped it shut. The dark interior tempted him more than he could admit.

"Hello," she said, a little breathless. She held out her hand in their Earth greeting. "It's a pleasure to meet you, Ulriq."

He accepted her hand intending to shake it three times. When his large one engulfed hers, a bolt of energy pulsed between them tightening his hold. Her skin was heated Kulaian silk. He stroked his thumb across her knuckles, unable to resist the temptation. Her expressive mouth fell open on a gasp, and he found himself stepping closer, almost succumbing to the urge to claim a taste.

"So, you bought that monstrosity? You know how dangerous solarcycles are." Michel gestured to her vehicle, stomping back and forth.

The unexpected flash of blue fire in her eyes stilled the air in Ulriq's lungs, and an eagerness to bathe in her emotions swept shivers over him.

"Yes, Mom, and yet I got one anyway. And it's the best thing I have had between my legs ever," she snapped. Spinning on Michel, she released Ulriq's hand as if she had forgotten she held it.

He missed her warmth the moment they separated.

"Ew. So didn't need to know that," Michel teased before wrapping his arms around her again, gentler this time. "Missed you too, sis." She paled, her mouth pinched into a thin white line, but she wrapped her hands around him anyway. "Come inside, and tell me what happened to you? How're the girls?"

Girls? Ulriq's O.D.I. flashed data and images in his mind, leaving him to wonder who the 'girls' or *damu* females were. The O.D.I. had to be in error, though, not that he could recall such a possibility having ever occurred. How could one planet bear such treasures and with this variety? Shaking his head, he tried to clear the images of red hair and brown eyes. Some had brown hair and green eyes.

Still reeling from the Maker's blessing and unable to help himself, he followed out of desperation, something deep within drove him to bask in her presence. He grabbed three beers from a gaping Danic who peered into Ulriq's eyes in disbelief. Danic's reaction served as a confirmation, and Ulriq thanked him with a brief nod and the broadest of smiles. He had a right to be joyful.

"The girls are on their way once they have everything on your list." Jack undid her jacket, her hand sliding from her throat to her belly, revealing inch by inch a thin sleeveless white tunic. It conformed to the gentle swell of her breasts. The very sight of them snatched Ulriq's focus. "I was going to ask why the shit-ton of meat and beers,...but then I saw these massive men, probably starving by the looks of it. I guess you lost a bet with a rugby team or something?" She shrugged and pinched her lips hard enough to pale them.

Seeing his Dar Eth suffering didn't sit well with Ulriq. His fingers twitched, the only outward sign of his inward battle. His instincts pushed against his control, bellowing that he port her to Der now. But sanity demanded he wait, listen, and learn. The impatience, the need, the frustration all culminated in said finger-twitch.

"Okay, out with it. What's got you jumping like a long-tailed cat in a room full of rocking chairs?" Michel accepted the beer from Ulriq who offered the other one to her.

She thanked him with a nod but was careful not to touch his fingers. Her caution teased a smile onto his lips. He liked that he affected her as she did him. What the Ethera would do to an Earthian he didn't know, but he was eager to find out.

"Which one?" she asked as she sipped the chilled beer.

He stared, wishing he could swipe the bitter flavor dewing on her bottom lip...with the tip of his tongue. A rumble formed in his belly, and he hurried to tamp it down. She sliced a glance at him, but her focus lingered on his legs, his hips, sliding side-to-side as she scanned his chest before resting on his lips. A flick of her gaze to his, she paused, then dipped her chin, her mouth parting on a silent gasp.

"Which...?" Michel grunted. "I don't know why you work—"

She laughed; a sound so full of joy and wonder it made Ulriq shiver. She cut it off with a groan. "All right, relax." Removing the jacket with care revealed sculpted arms. A large, bloodstained patch on her back mimicked the placement of a smaller bloodstained one in the front. "Got shot yesterday with a .22. It was a through and through, thankfully. Stupid clumsy rookie." She peeled her tunic up, exposing her sculpted abdomen with multi-colored bruising. "Cracked a few ribs on Friday. Overeager student flipped me over like a piñata."

Ulriq moved before he could rein in his instincts. Before she lowered her tunic, he stopped her with a touch. He withdrew a med-gun from a pocket in his armor and ran it over her stomach. Gripping her hip, he crouched, bringing his nose inches away from her. Her stomach quivered, and he wished he had the freedom to close the distance and press his lips to the pale flesh. He forced himself to swallow past the lump in his throat. As he scanned her, he widened his thighs, granting his Fuyra-hard malehood a little room.

The relief was fleeting. The scent of her hit him, and he stilled. He raised his gaze over her stomach, between the valley of her breasts to her eyes. Alodon's hell. His arousal throbbed and had they been alone, who knew where she would be now. He bit the inside of his cheek, relishing the pain and the return of his sanity.

Dropping his focus on the med-gun, he ran it up and down. It took a few seconds for the bruising to fade. The speed at which she healed showed the receptiveness of Earthian physiology. Her shiver raised the tiniest hairs on her skin. He touched before he could stop himself. When he ran his thumb, tiny bumps formed on her skin. She was as soft as in his vision. Etterian females were hard, muscled like the males, and firm to the touch. Earth females had muscle but still managed to be yielding. He withdrew an Etterian med-patch and placed it where the bruises had been as an added precaution, running his finger along the edges to ensure they adhere. Her breasts jiggled as she sucked in a sharp breath.

"That should heal your bones quickly." He shifted his focus to her more serious wound.

This close to her, the scent of her filled his lungs, like heated sand with the sweetness of exotic blossoms. He clenched his jaw, determined to see to her care. With a trembling forefinger and thumb, he pinched her tunic to slide off her shoulder, gaining the needed access. While removing her pointless patches, he grumbled at the sight of her wounds. Crimson and angry, they looked painful. Anger exploded like a chokaar's missile striking true. He hated that someone or thing had harmed her in the first place, that she suffered.

With the med-gun in hand, he brushed her lifeless hair aside, but his fingers tangled in the silken masses. He closed his eyes, wanting nothing more but to bury his face in her soft strands. Unlike Etterian hair, hers didn't undulate, but it did wrap around his fingers, clinging with a gentleness that was disarming.

He gritted his teeth, and activated the med-gun, watching and waiting as she healed. Her gaze rested on his face, her mouth parted for her teeth to dimple her bottom lip. Maker. He was stronger than this. Finishing the scan, he applied two med-patches, wishing he could port her instead. Der would care for her properly, and Ulriq *needed* her well-cared for.

"Better?" Sliding her tunic in place, he allowed his fingers to trail down her bare upper arm, marveling at the texture of her skin. The tiny hairs from her belly covered all of her, and they rose, eager for his touch. Etterians only had hair on their heads and around their malehood.

"Yes." Her voice cracked before she cleared her throat. "It's soothing; I don't feel the throbbing anymore."

"Thank you, Supreme Commander." Michel grinned.

Ulriq jerked back, having forgotten Michel watched him unravel. Ulriq sighed. His interest hadn't gone unnoticed, but it would have become apparent soon enough. He needed to speak with Michel, to assure him his intentions were honorable.

She fixed Ulriq with a stare, demanding and unflinching. "Um, I hate to sound ungrateful, but who are you exactly? How do you know my brother?"

Chapter Six

ULRIQ ADMIRED HER FEARLESSNESS. Standing so close tempted him to touch her again. Forcing himself to pocket the med-gun, he stepped back, despite his instincts demanding he claim her.

"They're astronauts like me," Michel intervened, but she didn't look away from Ulriq. Not that he minded. He took the opportunity to meet her gaze and to lose himself in her sky-blue eyes.

She frowned, furrowing the delicate skin of her brow. "But their accents—"

"Sound European, right? I thought so too," Michel kept his vow not to reveal the truth to her, but Ulriq didn't need to deceive her anymore.

She faced her blood-bond...brother, pinning him with the same stare.

"Mich Dunois, you know who you're talking to, right?" She pointed at Ulriq. "European? Are you shitting me? They're battle-honed. He could bench-press my solarcycle. So, quit being an ass, and tell me the truth." She flashed Ulriq a quick smile, letting him know she wasn't angry with him. He appreciated that but not as much as he enjoyed her heaving breasts and her fiery responses. "They talk like they have swallowed a dicto-tab. I bet you, old Queen E didn't talk like this. And judging by their gear, they're militarized rugby players. Yeah, like that would work. So, quit being an ass, and spill."

She folded her arms across her chest, thrusting her breasts up, hitching Ulriq's breath yet again. Maker. His grip tightened around the glass container. The cold condensation seeped into his fingertips, keeping him focused on the moment.

"We are here without authorization. If he tells you, you must leave with us." Ulriq raised the beer to his lips, but his gaze remained on her.

"And go where?" Her hair flew around her as she faced him.

The light reflecting off the white-gold strands tangled his tongue, snatching the words from him. His fingers itched from when it had touched him.

He studied the glass container to break her hold on him. "You will have to sacrifice your way of life…" Shaking his head, he struggled to focus on the conversation and not on the gift before him.

"I'm never seeing you again, am I?" She gaped at her brother, the realization draining her and slumping her shoulders. Ulriq didn't like seeing her so, for the same darkness in her eyes settled on him, like a ravenous void rising to engulf him. "How far away are you going this time? Ganymede?"

After a long moment of silence, Michel closed his eyes and squared his shoulders. "This is goodbye, Jack." His voice cracked, and pain skewered his face.

Ulriq shifted a foot and spread his legs to better bear the burden of his decision. He hadn't realized how it would harm the Earthian.

"Damn hell it is." She leaped to her feet. "You tell me right now why we have five aliens in this house?"

At her demand, Ulriq twitched, but he hid it well. She was intelligent, his Dar Eth.

"And don't think you can lie to me, either. They're drinking beer like it's their first time. They gathered around my solarcycle like it was a stripper parade, and they have bronzed skin. And don't get me started on his eyes. Where, on God's green earth, does a man's eyes change from dark-blue to ice-blue?"

"I…" Michel glanced at Ulriq in desperation.

"We are Etterians." He fought a smile as hot and sweet joy burst through him. She would have to travel with him, the probability was more and more in his favor. "We rescued your brother. He was disconnected from his space station."

Her skin paled. "You almost died?"

She lunged and wrapped her arms around Michel, crushing him to her despite her injuries. The Earthian male winced, but he managed to circle her with his arms, holding her for as long as she needed. She pulled away, then raised her gaze to Ulriq. When she tugged on his arms folded across his chest, he lowered them, not expecting her to slip hers around him.

The instant she pressed her body to his, he straightened, no longer leaning against the wall. Her gesture was unexpected, but the experience was indescribable. The level of peace that descended upon him was something he thought he would never attain. Her exotic scent surrounded him with her soft mounds crushed between them. He grew to his full length and harder than the rock in their Fuyra caves.

"What is this you are doing?" he asked, his voice hoarse with emotions he couldn't name. Not wanting her to stop, he mimicked Michel's example and wrapped his arms around her. The bottle in his hand hindered him, but he wouldn't take the time to put it down. And he was careful not to hurt her. Her silken curls tickled his forearms.

"It's called a hug," she said into his chest. "Thank you for saving my brother."

"You will have to come with me," Ulriq said. Either she joined him or he would remain on her world. There was no living apart from each other, not for him. How Earthian Dar Eths reacted to separation was unknown, but it crippled a warrior, as debilitating as the final stages of the void.

She sighed, resignation conveyed by an almost imperceptible nod. "Where Mich goes, I go. It's not as if humans haven't traveled into space before." She pushed away from him, forcing him to release her. His hand trembled. He wanted to yank her into his arms for another *hug*.

Human? Not Earthian? His eyelids fluttered, preventing him from reaching for her.

"She can come with?" The joy on Michel's face was too painful to look upon.

Another mechanical rumble preceded a squeal on the solar panel driveway. Not hearing it approach, didn't alarm Ulriq since his senses remained focused on Jack.

"Oh, shit, what do we tell Taylor?" She darted out of the house, forcing Michel and Ulriq to follow. Three human females disembarked from their ground vehicle halted alongside Jack's... solarcycle.

"What the hell, Jack? Are these men edible?" a black-haired, dark-skinned female asked as she hugged Jack.

Ulriq's body tensed as he anticipated his Dar Eth's pain. The urge to protect ripped through him, and he found himself gripping the front door frame, his strength denting the soft metal.

"They can hear you, Ava," Jack teased her.

The flash of her smile brought needed air to his lungs. The other female hadn't hurt her? Perhaps the med-patches had healed Jack faster than he had anticipated? Still, at the first opportunity, he would have Der assess her.

"What? Men who listen? Have we died?" A shorter female scoffed, her red-gold hair vibrant against her pale skin.

"Damn, and I thought Mich was tall." A female, almost *damu* in size, circled the ground vehicle. She wore a strange garment that brushed the floor. It swayed hypnotically as she walked. Her white-blue hair fell around her in waves, gathered to a shoulder.

"Is that my girls I hear?" Michel hugged each one, dropping kisses on their cheeks. "In case you can't remember, let me explain quantum mechanics." He chuckled at their longsuffering groans. "Okay, don't kill me. Come, I'll introduce you." He guided them over to where Ulriq stood. Jack followed. Ulriq admired the play of sunlight on her hair, the curve of her lips, but it was the warmth in her eyes that snagged his thoughts. "Supr...Ulriq, this is Ava, Vicky, and Taylor. We grew up together at the orphanage."

The three females smiled at Ulriq in greeting, not bothered by his height, muscles, or the strength he exuded. His lips twitched. They didn't touch him other than by the shaking of his hand. They behaved better than Etterian females who tended to believe all males were theirs to command. A generalization, but he hadn't dealt with many females to confirm or deny it. "This is Danic, Aaro, Kanzo, and Sub-Commander Nerx."

Ulriq shifted aside, choosing to remain beside Jack, wishing their shoulders could touch, wishing he could draw her into the arch of his body.

"It's a pleasure to meet you." Blue-haired Taylor offered her hand to Danic. "Such unusual names, whereabouts are you from?"

"Europe." Jack's skin flushed the color of Etteria's sky—a beautiful pink. "They're from northern Europe."

He liked that she was uncomfortable telling untruths.

With a soft cry, the black-haired Ava dipped as one of his males dropped to a knee. Kanzo shuddered at her touch. Ulriq winced, grateful Jack hadn't touched him at such a crucial stage in the Ethera. Studying his males and the human females, he waited for another to kneel. When they remained upright, he rubbed his chest, acknowledging the pure joy he would need to convey to the king when they returned to the *Kushin*. Two Dar Eths in one day?

"What is an orphanage?" he whispered into Jack's ear, pleased with himself when she shivered. "I disbelieve the understanding I have of this word."

"It's a place for abandoned children." She met his gaze, but her slight gasp and erratic heartbeat blessed his hearing.

He frowned at her explanation. It was in line with his O.D.I. He focused on her upturned face, traveling down her nose to her lips, and faltered there. "Your planet throws away *damu*? You have no blood-bonds?"

Her brow furrowed, but before he could run his thumb along the creases, her skin smoothed. "Throws-away is a little harsh, but this is my family...blood-bonds now." She gestured to Michel and the girls.

"I would like to hear more, please, Jack, if it is not too painful for you."

Her eyebrows arched at his request, her gaze meeting his before she gave him a curt nod.

"So, where's my stuff?" Michel headed for the back of the ground vehicle. Taylor trailed him to assist. Ulriq's males did, as well, but Michel chased them away, carrying the crates into the house.

"Jack." Ulriq snatched at any question, needing her gaze on him. "What do you do that injures you so?"

She offered him a tentative smile, as if what she did might offend him. "I'm a law enforcement instructor. I specialize in unarmed combat and hand-held weapons."

He rumbled his approval, leaning back to allow his eyes the luxury of admiring her toned form, lingering for too long on the swell of her backside. Alodon's hell, she was made for him. "Do these skills assist with determining the truth?" He inched closer to her, imagining her warmth reached across the narrow gap between them.

Her magnificent gaze rose to meet his. "Yes."

"Am I speaking the truth when I say I would like to take you to my quarters, spread those beautiful thighs, and claim you?" His voice tore through his throat like coarse stone. He dared not look away. He kept his unblinking focus on her face, analyzing every emotion, known and unknown as it flitted across her expressive features.

Her breasts heaved, but her gaze didn't waver from his, despite the splash of color on her cheeks. Although he couldn't say whether her flushed face was from embarrassment or excitement. As he drew in a deep sniff, he trembled. Excitement, the musky scent of her arousal attested to this. He rumbled, struggling to contain the need to touch her.

"Truth." Her voice rasped.

He closed his eyes for a moment. The quality of her voice evoked an intense reaction within him as sharp, almost painful sensations traveled from his chest to his malehood.

"Would you be offended if I vow it will come to pass?" He leveled his gaze on her again, but clenched his fists, fighting the urge to lunge for her.

"No."

His heartbeat paused, and he stared into her eyes, seeking the truth, seeing her interest in him. Allowing himself a brief squeeze of her hip, he strode away, the temptation too much for his current level of control.

It wasn't long before Nerx joined him in the shade of the oak tree. The male was smirking which Ulriq acknowledged was his right. With Ulriq's attention remaining on Jack, he grumbled. His muttered words on Nerx's attitude would only be heard by the male himself.

"Alodon's balls. Allow me a moment to bask in your good fortune, Ulriq. Your eye color does not lie. Jack is your mate. I am pleased we have stumbled upon Etteria's salvation. Two, Ulriq. Two Dar Eths. It has been decades since the last pairing, this you know." Nerx's eyes swirled between dark and ice-blue, indicative of the intensity of his emotions, his usual impassivity absent. "And if you had not joined us, Ulriq..."

Silence met this statement, and Ulriq scowled at the thought of no Jack in his life. As he sat there, the Ethera bond formed between them, like tendrils of light curling around his cursed soul. His priorities shifted with his thoughts and intuitions aligning to her needs. The darkness and irritation that had consumed him of late were...gone. Replaced by the glowing joy-filled life force of his Dar Eth.

"I am grateful, Nerx. I cannot portray how much." With the crescendo of emotion bombarding him, he wouldn't know where to begin.

"As to be expected, my battle-bond." Nerx leaned against the tree and sipped from his bottle. "Kanzo is not handling this well. He is a strong male. The Ethera shouldn't have affected him so."

Ulriq glanced at a pale Kanzo who stood to the side, stiff as a sheet of Maloidian steel. "There are no historical recordings on the effects of the Ethera, Nerx. Perhaps what I experienced was minor?" Ulriq grimaced as he spoke those words. If his Ethera had been mild, he couldn't imagine what his males might have to endure.

"I do not believe one male's Ethera can be compared to another's. I am curious. I will consult with Der as to whether there are any archives at all." Nerx ran his thumb along the bottle, catching the moisture glistening on its glass surface.

"And the other two human females?" Ulriq rested his gaze on the tiniest one, bouncing as she spoke with wide gestures and a ready smile.

"Human?" Nerx arched a black brow before his eyelids fluttered.

"They prefer human and not Earthian," Ulriq said with a dismissive flick of his hand.

"None have triggered the remaining males, proving that the Ethera is at work here and not interspecies chemistry." Nerx's gaze rested on the female with fire-kissed red hair.

"Good." Ulriq released a slow sigh. He preferred the work of the Ethera than fickle attraction, no matter how painful the occurrence.

"And if I understand Lady Taylor's expressions, her interest lies with Michel." Nerx sipped his beer. The cold bitter beverage didn't tempt Ulriq, not anymore. He longed to sip from Jack's lips, taste the nectar the Maker had blessed him with.

"It does?" His gaze snapped to the female in the strange garments. Her bright gaze followed Michel's form, her face changed color when he spoke to her, and her body angled toward him if he stood nearby.

Ulriq rested his senses on Jack, knowing her location as well as he knew his greatsword. He met her gaze, admiring her pink cheeks, and the rise and fall of her breasts as she drew in ragged breaths. He focused his hearing, picking up her staccato heartbeat, and when he inhaled deeply, her rich arousal's scent called to him. Maker. She tempted him, his Jack. He wanted to hold her in his arms, taste those parted lips, wallow in her intoxicating scent until it saturated his senses.

"They are an emotive species, Ulriq," Nerx said from alongside him. "I am concerned our males may not have the skills to handle such intensity."

"Regardless of their inability, that is minor to the lives these females will save." Ulriq accepted another beer Michel offered him, having heard him approach. "Tell me, Michel. How many human females are there?"

"How many women?" Michel echoed, his focus turning inward in deep thought.

"So emotive," Ulriq said to Nerx.

"Billions, Ulriq." Michel's head tilted when Taylor called him. He flashed a smile before rushing off. Air rushed out of Nerx's lungs. Not a word passed his lips as joy swirled his eye color again.

"Your Dar Eth is here, Nerx. You need only find her." Ulriq grasped his battle-bond's forearm. "You too will be blessed."

"King Xeus will be most pleased," Nerx said, his voice gruff.

Chapter Seven

Earth

The outskirts of West Haven

Mich's house

JACK GLANCED AT THE alien warrior again. She broke her daze for the umpteenth time, keeping her lips pinched against the need to gasp. So, she couldn't get enough oxygen into her lungs. So, her heartbeat stuttered. So, her hands were unstable, forcing her to grip her eating utensils with trembling fingers. All this could be forgiven in the wake of this man.

Oh, how arrogant she'd been, thinking all she needed was to meet a handsome man. Little had she known—in her naivete—that he would rock her to the core. His voice rumbled when he spoke to one of his soldiers, a man with a dour expression intermittent with bursts of joy.

To top it off, an alien man looked at her like she was the center of his universe. She'd probably stared at him the same way. Damn, he was a gorgeous man. Closing her eyes, she recalled his features with perfect clarity. When faced with his hooded and ice-blue eyes, she longed to stare, to absorb the sheer masculinity before her. Like raven's wings, his eyebrows peaked. His forehead was wider, emphasized by his black hair pulled away from his face. His cheeks narrowed into an angular jaw and led her to linger on his wide, uneven lips that promised to be feather soft. A fishtail braid as thick as her forearm fell to his boot heels, drawing her gaze to his tight ass every time his hair swayed. Overall, a delectable package. She sighed, the best damn man she'd ever seen.

She sliced her attention between Ulriq and the others. How did West Haven get so lucky? Her small town in the middle of nowhere now had five alien hunky visitors. And they weren't a species she'd heard of. Because, damn, had she known they existed, she might have traveled the stars sooner. They were taller than her and Mich; bronze-skinned and built like police barricades. All muscle in form-fitting armor. Black leather-like sleeveless vests exposing broad shoulders and muscled arms. Narrow waists into slim hips and long well-muscled legs. Large chunky boots adorned their feet. There were many gadgets on their armor, all with specific purposes she'd love to hear about.

But it was the way Ulriq spoke and looked at her that touched a part of her deep inside. She shivered in anticipation; excitement danced along her nerve endings like a spiced criminal dodging taser bolts.

"Are you cold?" he graveled from beside her.

Her gaze met his, and she wished she could stare at him without coming across a besotted idiot. "I'm fine, thank you." She lowered her chin but snagged on his untouched plate of food he grasped in his large hand. "Scared?" she teased, gesturing to his potato salad.

"Scared?" His eyes twinkled, showing he had a sense of humor. He had beautiful ice-blue eyes, made even more mesmerizing by his good mood.

"Of trying our food. I suppose cubes in white sauce wouldn't look appetizing to an alien." She leaned closer to him as if to share a secret. "That's the best dish on your plate. Vicky's potato salad is amazing."

"I am not hungry."

She nodded, unable to focus on food herself. Why he affected her so, she couldn't fathom. "Thirsty then? Another beer, a soda?"

Placing their plates on the table, she rose from the chair to fetch him his beverage of choice. But his fingers encircling her wrist froze her. They were so long they overlapped making her feel petite, a never-before-experienced emotion. But he wasn't hurting her. His touch affected her with her heartbeat rapidly increasing like stun grenades exploding in her chest.

"Stay," he whispered.

She studied every inch of his upturned face, unable to resist the allure.

"I am thirsty." The grumbling male beside him flashed a joyful smile, startling her out of her daze.

"Go ask another female, Nerx, this one's mine," Ulriq growled.

Heat burst across her cheeks.

Nerx laughed, said something in another language—lyrical and exotic—before bounding away. A tug on her wrist drew her attention to the man looking at her like she was a slice of heaven. It evoked a heady warmth in her chest, one she didn't recognize but wanted it to remain indefinitely. One moment she was gazing into his eyes, the next she pressed her hand to his jaw and cheek, her thumb a whisper away from his lips. His eyelids fluttered, and he captured her hand in his large one, trapping it against his heated, velvet skin.

"Jack." He met her gaze. The intensity of emotion he conveyed was overwhelming. Maybe it was different for aliens, but for humans, they weren't this intense on the first meeting. The heat in his eyes promised her something timeless, as if he'd love her for an eternity. She didn't know what to make of it, but by the way she felt, she wasn't about to run either. "I am pleased you are leaving with me."

"Planning on getting to know me better?" she teased.

"Yes." He chuckled.

A smiling Ulriq—his bright teeth against his bronze skin, a deep dimple denting his cheek—snatched her breath away. She struggled to align her thoughts, to gather her wits, because no man, alien or not, should affect her so.

Then Nerx bellowed something as a barrage of lights hit the ground around them, shooting up dirt.

Chapter Eight

Planet, Earth

Michel's housing structure

A SHUTTLED HOVERED ABOVE the housing structure. Yithians fired their blasters through the open compartment door. Before Ulriq could evaluate the situation, he took his Dar Eth to the ground, covering her with his body. He didn't crush her but prevented any harm with a hand on her head and one on her back. He held his weight off her by leaning on his elbows. With such an intimate position, her warmth and softness trapped beneath him, desire surged through him like the aftermath of a Gika kill. Her cheeks flushed pink, bringing forth a sense of victory.

"Ulriq?" Her hands fluttered along his shoulders.

He grinned, praying she would *feel* how much he wanted her. "Not now, Jack."

At the intensity in her eyes, he shifted, nestling his Fuyra-hard malehood into a more intimate position. Fire exploded across his shoulder and down his back. He grunted as he twitched. Pain lanced through him, burning from a blaster shot to his shoulder. The salty tang of his blood drenched his nose, as his armor attempted the healing process. He summoned his hardened control, calling forth his training, calming his erratic heartbeat that had more to do with Jack than his wound. She ran her hands over his upper arms in concern. He appreciated the gesture.

"Are you all right?"

He focused on her. They were inches apart; he wanted to taste her, to test the softness of her lips. Nerx lifted Ulriq off her and slipped under his arm to support him. Ulriq groaned, not only from the fresh wave of fire claiming his shoulder but at the lost opportunity. If he died today, he wanted to, at least, have kissed her. She scrambled to her feet; concern still etched on her face. Her gaze flew to the pocket in his armored pants where he had stowed the med-gun. His lips twitched into a smile despite the grimace that had taken up residence. His Jack was observant.

"You are bleeding," Nerx said in a casual manner. Jack gasped at Nerx, then circled Ulriq, searching for his wound, no doubt.

"I know, Nerx, but I am appreciative of the status update," Ulriq growled through clenched teeth. More ground spurted close to their position, proving their current location wasn't a safe one.

"Those bastards," she spat. "Get him to safety, Nerx, I'll follow."

"No, keep her safe." Agony strangled Ulriq's throat and strained his voice, but he persevered.

She switched her focus between him and the hovering craft. He wanted to take the time to admire the determination that burned in her eyes, but the need to protect her was too overwhelming.

"Shit. They're firing again." A loud boom-boom jerked his shoulders, and he bit his inner cheek as a fresh wave of agony pulsed outward.

She had pulled a handheld human weapon from where he didn't know. Two Yithians plummeted to the ground. He gaped, and his chest expanded with an inexplicable warmth. She fired once more at the front of the shuttle. If she hadn't demonstrated her accuracy by killing the Yithians, he would have assumed she'd missed. But her narrowed gaze, pursed lips, and curt nod said she tested the efficacy of her weapon against the shuttle's structure.

Nerx tugged, attempting to reach the housing unit.

The side of Ulriq's body blazed between fire and burning intensity. His patience evaporated. "Damnit, female. You cannot damage a K-Class shuttle; it is constructed of Maloidian steel." He gritted his teeth when Nerx pulled him forward, but Ulriq held firm.

"I can damage the aliens, though." She tossed him a smug smile while gripping her weapon in her hands.

His breath caught, despite the pain lancing through him. Maker, she was beautiful. A proud, confident warrior.

"She has you there." Nerx shuffled Ulriq through the narrow door. "Here." With his free hand, he offered Jack his blaster. "Hit the red button, it should be strong enough to worry them."

She snatched it from him, and within seconds, the unmistakable bolts of a blaster came from behind Ulriq.

"You gave her your blaster?" He sucked air through his gritted teeth with every step he took. "She is my—"

"I know," Nerx's calm tone irritated Ulriq further.

He gritted his teeth. Words lodged in his constricted throat, and his face flushed. He could do nothing about Nerx's attitude or Jack firing a blaster.

"But as you can see, my hands are busy," Nerx huffed.

In retaliation for his recklessness, Ulriq rested heavily on him, forcing him to carry more of his weight.

Nerx paused and glared at Ulriq. "You are a big bastard."

"It is a good thing you are my battle-bond," Ulriq managed through clenched teeth. The agony had spread upward, hindering his ability to speak clearly.

"If that is true, then help me get your big ass into the shuttle." Nerx carried him through the back door and out into the open area. He shuffled with determination toward the ground marking. This would have been the focus for the cloaked shuttle's location if the opened outer door hadn't revealed the internal compartment. His unit had relocated the human females with Mich having thrown Taylor over his shoulder, as well.

When Nerx boarded with Jack trailing them, the door sealed, and Danic initiated elevation. A quick scan confirmed all were onboard. Nerx eased Ulriq into a seat to strip off his chest armor. Tossing it to the floor, he prodded Ulriq's wound and hissed. His reaction confirmed Ulriq's original assessment. The blood loss was happening too rapidly.

While Nerx scanned Ulriq with the med-gun, its cooling touch lessened the vise around his chest. He settled his gaze upon Jack who clasped the back of Danic's chair. She leaned over the console assessing the display vids. Her pants clung to her muscular thighs and a firm backside, tugging tight or loosening as she moved to create shifting art. Ulriq was mesmerized by her, despite the black spots encroaching his vision. Everything about her mannerisms pleased him. She accepted the technology around her, unfazed by flying in a shuttle and among an unknown species. Yet another potential obstacle he need not deal with.

"Can you shoot it down?" she asked Danic. "Does this thing have any firepower?"

"Yes, of course, it has 'firepower.' And no, we will not be firing the weapons. We are here illegally, milady." Danic's tone brooked no further argument.

She smacked her fist in her palm, and her tense body brought a small smile to Ulriq's pinched lips. A huge explosion lit up the display vid, and she cried out before throwing her hands in the air.

"The house." A second explosion followed. "My cycle. Taylor's car. Do something, damnit. Shoot those bastards."

"To do something would endanger everyone on board." Danic steered the cloaked shuttle up and away from the carnage, filling the display vids with open blue skies.

"Kanzo," Ava screamed, her voice pitched high with fear.

Kanzo jumped up and roared like a wild creature.

Ulriq arched a brow at his battle-bond, unable to comprehend why there was pain and disbelief etched on his features.

"What now?" Nerx asked while he tended to Ulriq's wound.

"Ava," Kanzo bellowed and paced the short confines of the shuttle. He had drawn his blaster, but his wide-dazed eyes and agitated movements as he gripped and released the edge of the door brought Ulriq to his feet. Nerx yanked him down.

"Where is Ava?" Aaro gripped Kanzo's shoulder, trying to calm him.

They spoke in Etterian so Jack wouldn't understand. Her brow furrowed in an adorable manner, calling forth another lip twitch from Ulriq. He had no right to find anything humorous at this point, with pain pounding at his senses, and Ava taken from under their noses. Kanzo wasn't handling it well. Ulriq grunted. Had it been Jack, he would have lost his mind. Horror, disbelief, and pain flickered across Jack's face as realization dawned.

"She was ported from the shuttle. Why? How?" Kanzo's hands switched between clenching and rubbing his face. "We must go back."

"We cannot. Ulriq needs urgent assistance." Nerx's tone was calm and in control, as expected of a sub-commander.

Kanzo grabbed his head with his hands. "She is my—"

"I know exactly what she is, Warrior Kanzo." Nerx clipped his tone. "Who took her, where is she now?" He remained focused on Ulriq's back, even though he directed his questions to the berserk male.

"Comm Prex and Ksal, have them investigate immediately." Ulriq narrowed his gaze on his unstable battle-bond. He, of all his males onboard, understood Kanzo's reaction.

"Doing that now," Danic called from the pilot's seat.

"Ava needs you to remain calm. We are her only hope." Aaro attempted to reach through to Kanzo. He grabbed him by his upper arms, forcing Kanzo to meet his gaze.

"You did not see her fear, Aaro." Kanzo roared. "She was scared. I am supposed to protect her. And I—"

"Alodon's balls." Aaro punched Kanzo in the face, knocking him out. He caught Kanzo's slumping body, and with ease, lifted him to a seat before assuming one himself.

"Where's Ava? What's going on?" Jack challenged Ulriq with her hands on her hips. "Why's Kanzo yelling?"

Her scent dominated the stench of his blood. He inhaled, expanding his chest to snapping point, and ignored a muttering Nerx behind him.

"Ava has been teleported, sis," Michel said in Earth English.

Teleported? She mouthed the word. The slow splash of furious pink on her cheeks snagged Ulriq's gaze. She had worn the same color in his vision of her sprawled beneath him.

"She was kidnapped? Why would anyone want to take Ava?" she asked Michel. "And why the hell are you so calm about this?"

"Because to overreact when we don't know who or why isn't going to help." Her brother's sky-blue gaze flicked to Taylor crying in his arms, then at Vicky whose skin had paled. "You know better, sis."

Jack pinched her lips. She drew in a shuddering breath then faced Ulriq and Nerx. "I assume you have a plan?" Her gaze was unflinching. "Besides getting Ulriq medical attention?"

At Nerx's whispered cursing, she flashed him a cheeky grin. Ulriq smirked, happy to have caught that moment of brevity on her features before his eyelids fluttered closed again.

"We have males investigating. They should have more information by the time we dock," Ulriq mumbled, fighting the urge to admire her. He gripped the arm of the chair, forcing himself to calm his heart rate.

"Until then, we can do nothing but wait," Aaro said.

Silence descended upon the shuttle. She sighed but didn't look away from Ulriq. Through narrow slits, he watched her study his upturned faze for a while. She drew near, and the warmth of her thighs bathed his knuckles where he squeezed his knees. Her lips parted as she raised her hand and hovered an inch from his chest then his arm, to offer comfort. When she lowered her hand without touching him, a chilling sense of loss gripped him. At her unexpected stroking of his cheek, he fluttered his eyes open and drowned in her pale-blue eyes. Releasing him, she dropped to the grated floor before him, crossed her legs, and rested the blaster over her thighs.

"How are you feeling?"

"I am better with you near me," he said, confirming his interest.

Her eyes widened for a fraction of a second before narrowing. Her lips parted again, and the sweet, musky, addictive scent rose to tease him. He focused his hearing on her erratic heartbeat and couldn't halt his smile.

"How bad is it?" she asked Nerx but didn't look away from Ulriq while she touched him. The softness of her hand—cupping his cheek—tempted him to nuzzle.

"He is bleeding severely. Medic Der has been notified."

Nodding, she pulled her lips into a tight line. She grabbed Ulriq's hands, even though his dwarfed hers. Touching him with familiarity pleased him, and he flipped his hands to grasp hers. Her gaze darted everywhere before she sighed and gave up on avoiding his.

"You're going to be fine," she whispered, offering him a smile.

He chuckled through the pain, hissing as Nerx dug his fingers into his sides, conveying the need to remain immobile.

"Is this confidence in Medic Der's skill or in the power of the universe?" he teased her.

"In the power of God."

He closed his eyes briefly to acknowledge her faith.

"Just get better, okay." She squeezed his hands while rubbing her thumbs across his skin. Often, she would stroke his jaw, brush his hair along his temple before grabbing his hand again.

He was aware of every move she made, each tremble of her breasts as her chest rose and fell, of the way she studied the shuttle's occupants, of how her touch soothed yet excited him.

"If you do not calm your heart rate, you will bleed out before we reach Der," Nerx said in Etterian.

While Ulriq focused on calming his pounding heart and erratic breathing, he devoured her upturned face.

"Milady," Danic said from the pilot's seat.

"Danic is calling you." Nerx nudged his chin toward the console.

Her eyebrows arched, but she released Ulriq's hands, jumped to her feet with grace, and trotted to the front of the shuttle, still gripping Nerx's blaster. Sighing, Ulriq closed his eyes as he assessed the presence of another emotion. Irrational anger scorched along his nerves. He was furious at Danic for drawing his Dar Eth's attention away from him. Gratitude and this illogical anger warred within him, constricting his chest. He opened his eyes to watch Jack, unable to resist.

"We are approaching the battleship *Kushin*, should you like to view it." Danic smiled, the younger battle-bond able to enjoy more of life than Ulriq could...

He grinned. That was yesterday, this morning, hours ago. Finding Jack had changed him, his life, his future.

"Yes, please." She cast a glance behind her. "Vicky, Taylor? Wanna see?"

Three human females gathered around Danic to watch.

The sheer size of the battleship could be overwhelming. The bay Danic targeted was the size of Ulriq's fingernail against the battleship's image filling the shuttle's display vid. On Ulriq's first voyage, it had been a humbling sight.

With a skill honed over many years, Danic maneuvered the shuttle into the bay nearest to the front of the battleship. After he touched down with the barest of bumps, his males surrounded them, returning to their various tasks.

The shuttle door opened. Aaro hoisted Kanzo over his shoulder and marched out as Medic Der strode toward Ulriq. The medic's stiff posture and angry countenance revealed his displeasure. But when he met Ulriq's gaze, his eyes widened, and a slow smile formed.

"Congratulations, Supreme Commander." Without another comment, he had his males lift Ulriq onto a floating gurney. Der trailed him into the bay and through a door.

Jack was torn. Her body demanded she follow Ulriq, but her head told her she shouldn't, that she didn't know him well enough. Still, he had been a hero, protecting her with his body and receiving a wound for his efforts. She nibbled her lip and rocked back and forth on her toes. Perhaps her concern stemmed from gratitude. That wasn't all she felt, though. But neither did she want to analyze the maelstrom of emotions engulfing her. Michel's house was gone, her cycle destroyed, Ava kidnapped, and now they were on some sort of spaceship to who knew where. On top of it all, Vicky's and Taylor's lives were disrupted. Jack wasn't sure whether they could return to West Haven as if nothing had changed. And none of them would go home until Ava returned to them.

Vicky trembled, her skin a color Jack had never seen before. Taylor sniveled in Mich's arms. Her brother rubbed his hand up and down her back, keeping her close to him. His body language revealed what Taylor meant to him, even if he himself hadn't realized it. Jack smiled. It was about time.

"Come, Jack, let's go to my quarters. We need to talk," Mich said.

She frowned at him before returning her gaze to the door through which Ulriq had disappeared. The urge to follow was more powerful than her love of cognac, and that said it all.

"Go with Mich, milady. I will keep you informed."

"Thank you for tending to him," she said to the grumpy man called Nerx.

Mich grabbed her hand and tugged her behind him, with Taylor and Vicky trailing. She caught Nerx's arched brows as she threw another worried glance at the door.

Chapter Nine

Etterian battleship, Kushin
Mich's quarters

JACK KNELT IN FRONT of Vicky, cupping her bare toes peeking from under her pant legs. "How're you doing?"

Vicky pinched her lips and tightened her arms around her legs. "We almost died at the hands of aliens, Jack. How the fuck do you think I'm doing?" She shivered. "Then we were rescued by more aliens, traveled to a battleship with them, and Ava is gone, Jack. Poof." She raised a tumbler of brandy to her lips and took the tiniest of sips. Where Mich had gotten it from, Jack couldn't say.

The white chair Vicky sat on had adjusted to her shape, and in doing so, scared her half to death. Jack swept the tumbler out of Vicky's trembling hand and took a big gulp before giving it back to her. Less was more when it came to Vicky and alcohol. Jack strode the length of the room, relishing the burn of the smooth, smoky brandy. Heat flushed her cheeks, and she slammed her fist into her palm, desperate to do something worthwhile.

"Will you quit pacing, please, Jack?" Vicky snapped, folded her legs beneath her, and wrapped her arms around her calves. She rested her chin on her knees after she abandoned the tumbler on the circular table.

When they'd entered Mich's quarters, Jack toured it. Her limbs twitched, she flicked her hair out of her face then huffed when it blocked her vision again.

Mich's bedroom was huge, the bed large enough to fit two Etterian men. His bathroom held modified sanitaryware but nothing mind-blowing, and his kitchen had two glass surfaces. No sink, no appliances? If she stretched her imagination, it could be a kitchen, but she'd find out soon enough how things worked.

Mich tightened his hold around Taylor and buried his nose in the curve of her neck. Jack studied his body language and released a controlled breath. A sense of helplessness crushed her chest, and she struggled to keep herself focused. Ava was missing, and unconscious Kanzo was with Ulriq in medical. Sod's Law was in full effect.

"Sorry, babe." Jack assumed the closest chair which Mich had called a comfy. "I'm just worried. He took a shot meant for me, and it's killing me I can't be there."

Vicky patted Jack's hand, trying to offer comfort and failing.

Jack squeezed her hand and released it to grab the brandy. "With Ava stolen, I feel helpless. There's got to be something we can do."

"You better start talking, Mich, or so help me..." Vicky held her back ramrod straight.

He stilled, studied Vicky and Jack's faces then offered a curt nod. "Shit... Okay. About two or three nights ago, I was outside the station fixing a communications panel when I severed my safety cord. The force of the sever damaged my thrusters and launched me away from the station." He closed his eyes for a moment while Vicky and Taylor's eyes widened in horror. "It was the night shift, and yes, I shouldn't have gone out without back-up. Hindsight's a bitch.

"I recorded a message for you, Jack. To say how sorry I was for dying on you, and I sang our song, you know the one." His face paled in the bright lighting. He pressed a kiss to Taylor's forehead before continuing, "The Etterians rescued me and agreed to let me say goodbye to you. By saving me, they broke their Global Council laws, but if I went with them and Earth continued to think me dead..."

"You were leaving us?" Taylor squeaked, her cheeks trembling.

Vicky dipped her chin, trying to hide the shimmer of tears in her brown eyes. Jack pinched her lips at how close she had come to losing her brother. Like a bullet penetrating her flesh, her heart twanged. He had planned to abandon them with nothing but a goodbye kiss and cheerio.

"I was leaving you too," she said, acknowledging that she'd known about his departure.

"What?" Vicky met Jack's gaze then darted her focus between the two true siblings.

Taylor twisted in his arms to glare at him. He winced as guilt darkened his blue eyes, but he gave her and Vicky an imploring look.

"He's my brother, guys. If he goes, I have to go." Jack begged them to understand.

"And now? Can we come too?" Taylor's sweet voice was filled with hope despite the paleness of her skin, "I can paint anywhere."

"I... No, I can't leave," Vicky gave a determined shake of her head as tears slipped unheeded down her cheeks. "The most danger I'm in is burning myself with a hot cookie tray." She shuddered. "Those gray aliens were shooting to kill. Then they kidnapped Ava who knows how. One minute she was there, the next Kanzo's roaring like an injured lion."

A dark sinking heaviness settled in the pit of Jack's stomach, as if she'd swallowed a magazine of bullets. If Vicky stayed on Earth, it would mean the end of their time together. She was shit-scared but to let fear throw away such an extraordinary opportunity? The urge to shake Vicky, to make her see reason, had Jack death-gripping the comfy's arms.

"I think you should reconsider, Vicky, my girl. They don't know what baked goods taste like. They survive on replicated foods," Mich said, his blue gaze pleading.

Baking for a new planet should convince her to come with. Jack glanced at Taylor, wanting to implore her to speak, but Taylor's silent crying and her resigned expression said it was hopeless.

"Give me time, Mich. Maybe when I'm tired of being lonely and missing you guys like crazy..."

"You know we'll nag you to join us. Just warning you." Jack forced herself to smile, leaning across to squeeze her hand again. She was the fool. What had she expected? Her sisters would hear about her and Mich leaving and join them? One big happy family?

"Fair enough," Vicky's whispered.

"Regardless, what are we going to tell folks?" Taylor tugged Mich's arms tighter around her. "I mean, now that you're going home, they'll ask you all sorts of questions, maybe even accuse you of poisoning us with your croissants."

"It's possible; I die every time I bite into one." Mich grinned.

"We need to contact Fred to let him know we're all fine. Maybe our bosses too, and the sheriff." Jack ticked off on her fingers. "If we do a vid-con, they will see we're well and not dead by nefarious baked goods."

"Yeah, we just need to say where we are..." Taylor frowned. "So, where are we?" She pulled out of Mich's arms to drop into the comfy next to him.

At his disgruntled expression, Jack chuckled. Oh, how the tables had turned.

"Either way we're going to have to lie." He bounded up to grip the backrest of Taylor's comfy. His fingers twitched as if he wanted to do something else with them.

"We died in the explosion? Vicky hadn't arrived yet and missed the whole carnage." Jack slumped. Because damn, that had been a narrow escape.

"Or she was thrown by the blast and staggered back to civilization which might explain the delay in reaching town?" Mich threw in.

"Gas explosion?" Vicky asked with an arched eyebrow.

"If we're presumed dead, then you could be as moody as hell," Taylor said, her brown eyes large in her face.

"True, I wouldn't have to pretend to be sad."

"Vicky, please...just come with us." Taylor's eyes glistened with fresh tears. Mich squeezed her shoulder. She cupped his hand in recognition of his support.

Joy zinged through Jack at the sight of what looked like a beautiful couple.

Vicky shook her head. "I'm going home. If I must lie to keep you guys safe, then so be it."

"Fine, but can you get an O.D.I. fitted?" Mich touched his wrist to reveal holographic buttons. "If you get one, then we can communicate all the time. It's an Optical Data Implant. It's powered by your central nervous system."

Jack gasped, and excitement exploded through her. She bounced in her chair. "I want one." After Mich typed on the glowing letters, she bolted around the comfys to study his wrist the moment the buttons faded. "I can't see anything. Was it painful?"

"Painful? Ms. Walking-injury wants to know this?" He laughed.

"If it was painful, Jack, Mich would have cried like a girl." Taylor chuckled when he gaped at her.

"Whose side are you on?" His tone was accusatory.

"I have to pick sides now?" She glared at him. "Regardless of sides, I want one too. So, what do you say, Vicky?" The excitement in Taylor's broad smile didn't reach her eyes.

Vicky frowned in deep thought. "How does it work? I mean, powered by my internal energy is cool, but how do words, images travel into my mind?"

"The same way our body sends signals, I imagine." Mich shrugged. "It works, it's amazing, and that's good enough for me."

Vicky offered a tremulous smile. "I suppose technology this advanced would appear like magic to us. All right, but I'm not going first."

"Excellent. I have transferred all my savings into tokens, just in case." Mich rubbed his chest with his free hand.

"They don't use crypto?" Jack arched a brow when he shook his head. "If our currency isn't recognizable, how did you convert?"

"Aaro helped me." Mich shrugged. "I bought tons of salt online and sold it to the Algri—another race of aliens. Salt is like narcotics to them. I made a fortune. Though, what I'll spend it on, I don't know. Etteria covers all expenses for its people. Anything else they want, they purchase with their own tokens."

"All expenses?" Vicky gasped.

"Yes, medical, clothes, food, housing—"

"So, can you convert my savings for me?" Jack asked before she doubted herself. Converting her crypto would be a decisive step to leaving Earth. She couldn't return after that.

"Mine too." Taylor clapped, bouncing in her chair.

"Fine, but later. Nerx said he'd send Medic Der when he's done with Ulriq," Mich lifted Taylor out of her chair, stole her spot, then tugged her onto his lap.

Her face flushed, and she bit her lip against squealing in excitement. The sheer joy on her face prickled the backs of Jack's eyes. Taylor had been in love with Mich for as long as she'd known him. She was genuinely happy for them both.

Jack sighed and jumped up to stare at the door again. "Did Nerx say how Ulriq's doing?" She rolled her twitching fingers into fists then unfurled them one by one.

"Now don't start pacing again...," Vicky said as Jack strode to the door and back.

Jack couldn't help herself. The inactivity was killing her, and even though her shoulder and ribs didn't ache as they should have, it didn't mean she could be irresponsible and go for a run...or something. She did squats and a few press-ups, testing the movement of her wounds.

Vicky smothered a smile, and Taylor slumped against Mich's chest. At least, they'd been able to distract each other for a little while.

"He said he'd be around to talk to us." Mich's words were vague.

As she stretched her arms above her head, Jack frowned at her brother since 'be around' didn't sound promising.

"Don't glare at me, Jack. I'm just the messenger."

The door chimed, and she spun, facing it.

"Enter," Mich called out, and it swished open to reveal Nerx. "Thank goodness, Nerx. Jack's driving us crazy. Any news on Ava?"

Nerx stepped into the room, bringing with him a dark and solemn vibe. His navy-blue eyes showed no emotion, his face was as stoic. No polite smiles, just an impression he didn't appreciate this inconvenience. His lips curled downward in a perpetual frown.

"Nothing. A shuttle's shield is easy to bypass; we can only assume this is how they managed to port her. We have not ascertained her intended destination."

So no news. Jack scowled.

"Will they kill her, Nerx?" Vicky asked in a timid voice, her brown eyes pleading with him.

He grumbled something and addressed her, dropping into a military stance, legs spread wide, hands clasped behind him. To Jack, it showed how comfortable he was commanding.

"I do not believe they will harm her. They took her for a reason we have yet to determine. If we knew this, we would know her destination. As it is, we have altered the *Kushin*'s destination to the suspected planet as a precautionary measure. All captives are transported there. We may be able to intercept her en route if it is the offenders we suspect."

Jack blinked. Altered their destination? As in they were traveling through space toward another planet? She scanned the room, gritting her teeth at the lack of windows to show them moving.

"And Ulriq?" She exhaled a slow breath, then nibbled on her bottom lip, dreading news but desperate for it.

Nerx met her gaze before grumbling again. He activated the door, ushered her into the passage, and waited for the door to seal behind her, affording them some privacy. The ease with which he accomplished this amazed her. She swallowed a gasp. One moment she was in the quarters, the next she was facing the six-foot-seven man in the shadowy passage.

"He will recover," Nerx said.

Joy burst through her, along with relief and... hope? She squealed her happiness, throwing her arms around his neck, giving him a hug in gratitude. He growled something, grabbed her hips, and pushed her away. His glower was quick to rebuke her for overstepping an unknown boundary.

"Can I see him?" she asked, despite the heat staining her cheeks.

"He is still in hibernation. I am certain he will come for you after he surfaces."

She peered at the man, not willing to endure a single moment more of waiting. "I can't stand next to him and hold his hand?" Her question stunned the alien man.

He jerked back and arched a brow at her. "What purpose does that serve?"

"Medical studies have shown touch, especially during...hibernation, is appreciated by the patient." So much for scientific articles. Nerx continued to stare at her, his expression blank. "It's supposed to bring comfort." She changed tactics.

He sighed, his frustration coming through. A chill raced up her spine as her thoughts swirled and her one chance to do something slipped through her fingers.

"Would I be in anyone's way?"

He pinched his brow. "No," he said. "Come, I will take you to him."

She grinned which darkened his scowl. What a grumpy man. Turning to let everyone know where she was going, she stared at the panel next to the door. Not knowing what to do with it, she shrugged and gestured to Nerx to lead the way. She skipped while he led her along the passage with ill-concealed impatience. She'd gotten her way; she would see Ulriq soon, and that was all that mattered.

Chapter Ten

Etterian battleship, Kushin,
En route to Yithia
The common - medical

Ulriq awoke, blinking at the unfamiliar ceiling. If he didn't know better, he would say he was in the common. He lay still to assess his surroundings and his body. Location-wise, he was in medical. He remembered a wound on his back, but there was a dull ache there now.

Then he felt it. The most incredible softness wrapped around his hand. It slid over his fingers, wrist, along his forearm and down again. His senses narrowed in on the sensation. Accompanying this softness was a scent that rivaled the hahyt flowers in the Etterian royal gardens. It was rich, intoxicating, spicy, and one he would know anywhere.

He turned his head to gaze upon his Dar Eth seated next to him. She stroked him with her right hand while Medic Der inserted a chip into her left wrist. With her gaze on the wrist, Ulriq studied her expressions, taking the opportunity while she was distracted. She was fearless as Der sliced her skin, slipped the device in, then scanned the incision closed.

"That's a remarkable tool, Medic Der. Ulriq used one just like that on me."

"You are injured, milady?" Der's eyebrows rose.

"Yes, but please don't worry about me. Ulriq needs all your attention."

His heart fluttered at this unexpected revelation. An Etterian female would have demanded immediate attendance and wouldn't have sacrificed her health for a male. Sixteen males to one female meant they could choose whom to lay with. Jack had declined healing and requested all be done for him... Slowing his heartbeat, he drew in a shallow, calming breath trying to remain silent, despite the need to act. He wanted to pull her into his arms, the precious gift she was. Her not knowing her value was incredible.

"Please, let me scan you as a precautionary measure. It is the honorable thing to do."

At Der's request, she nodded.

He scanned her, paused on her ribs, and spent too much time on her shoulder. Ulriq didn't like that she had needed more care than he had given her, as if he had failed her.

"Is there a problem, Medic Der?" She twisted to glance at him over her shoulder.

"Supreme Commander Ulriq did well; unfortunately, you require synthetic skin to seal your wound. It is not available when out in the field."

Ulriq closed his eyes for a second and savored the swell of warmth at having done the best he could.

"Will it hurt?" Her voice had lowered as if she feared pain. This was an untruth. This day, she had shown remarkable courage and endurance, no matter in what circumstances she had found herself.

"You need to sit still for it to seal well. May I tear your garment to access your wound?"

"Please. And you have my thanks, Medic Der."

Der tore her stained tunic with a precise movement, ensuring he maintained her modesty while removing the med-patches Ulriq had applied. The wounds were scanned again, and the synthetic skin applied. It sealed well as it assumed her skin tone in the replication process. He had seen it done many times, yet with her appealing softness, he couldn't look away and refused to blink.

"It feels like a too-tight bandage." She gestured to the med-gun. "What exactly does that device do?"

He admired her inquisitive mind. She must have studied her surroundings, absorbed as much as she could, and would ask any questions should something confound her.

"It searches for anything unusual, broken bones, blood anomalies, torn muscle, then encourages the body's internal healing. We can set our O.D.I. to scan, but for serious injuries, we use the nano-meds which infuse all med-patches for on-field treatment." Der slid the med-gun into a pocket. "Each male carries it on his person." He withdrew the med-gun and rested it on the counter behind him.

"And you had to use these nano-meds on Ulriq?" Her voice thickened with concern, and she tightened her hand on his, revealing her distress.

Der faced her, spread his legs wide, and clasped his hands behind his back. "Yes, he will make a full recovery."

"But he shouldn't have been injured. It happened while he was protecting me." At her passionate cry, Der stepped back. His eyes widened at the unexpected emotional intensity in her voice.

He gave her hand an awkward pat. "Ulriq did as expected. All females must be cherished and protected."

"What?" she whispered. "*All* females?"

"Yes, the mothers of our offspring, the future of our people."

A smile warmed her cheeks and eyes. "Is that why Nerx is chasing after Ava?"

"Yes, partly." Der stacked items as he cleaned medical, relaxed enough around a female to do so.

Ulriq frowned, noting the disastrous state of medical. Objects littered the floor, some smashed, others leaking. The L-shaped counters were bare, as if someone had swung their arm and cleared everything off the surfaces. Thankfully, the Maloidian steel remained unblemished which meant no blaster fire, not greatswords, or daggers. Had Kanzo done this? Ulriq settled his gaze on Der who bore no wound.

"Is that also why we're addressed as milady?" Jack broke into a grin.

Immobile by choice, Ulriq listened to her. Lyrical yet firm, her voice held a hint of huskiness, spiking his temperature in reaction. He could listen to her speak indefinitely.

Der paused halfway through stacking empty nanotubes to flick a small smile. "Yes, as a sign of respect."

"You won't be calling me that, will you, Der? I mean, on my planet, milady means a woman...female of noble birth. We use ma'am or miss as a sign of respect, or missus if we're married."

"Married?" Der's eyelids fluttered as his O.D.I. updated him on the word's meaning.

Ulriq's did the same, flashing images of a human couple with *damu* between them. In Etterian terms, a pairing.

She gasped. "Why did your eyes do that?"

Ulriq wasn't certain he liked her concerned for anyone other than himself.

"Do not be alarmed, milady. When a word is spoken I do not know the meaning of, the O.D.I. instructs me with images and descriptions." Der kept his tone level. "I now understand this 'married.' Your language is charming, mil...Jack."

She stroked her thumb over her healed incision, taking her touch away from Ulriq's hand.

"We have learned your English but do not understand all the words, perhaps needing context." At her frown of confusion, Der continued, "The meaning is placed into our minds by the O.D.I. You speak, and it does the translation."

She grinned. "That's amazing." Bouncing on her chair tossed her hair, and the bright lights of medical caught it like the magnus sun.

Appreciating the emotion altering the tension in the air, a rumble built in Ulriq's chest. He tamped it down, not ready to reveal his alertness. Enjoying observing her, he wanted to do so for a while longer. She squeezed his hand without glancing at him.

"Some words sound the same but have different meanings. It is why your language is fascinating." Der laughed.

Ulriq had never seen the medic laugh or smile, for that matter. The softening of his features removed two decades from his age. Ulriq must have twitched because Der leveled his gaze on him.

"Ah, you are awake, Supreme Commander. Any pain, numbness?"

Ulriq focused on Jack, admiring the curve of her breasts in her tight tunic and the way her eyes widened, the pale blue entrancing.

"Shit, Der, I moved. Did I mess it up?"

"It is well, Jack."

She released a slow whoosh before smiling at Ulriq. "How're you feeling, Ulriq?" Her voice had grown huskier. He couldn't say why, but he did like the way it brushed across his senses like a caress.

"I feel well," he said—his voice guttural—and he was, *feeling* that is.

Hope, excitement, lust, need...bombarded his chest and mind, merging into one. He struggled to regulate his heartbeat and the heat coursing along his veins. But there was no pain. Flipping his hand, he laced his fingers through hers, trapping her. Sitting up but not letting go of her, he swung his legs over the side of the bed. Her other hand hovered over his bare chest, wanting to assist him, but she hesitated to touch him. He captured and pinned it to his chest, relishing the softness of her skin and the slight flutter of her fingers.

His gaze rose to travel her face, lingering on the color change to her cheeks. Focusing his hearing, he listened to her erratic heartbeat, her breathlessness. "What is wrong, *ensa*?" he asked, certain she wasn't ill.

"Um, Ulriq, shouldn't you put on a shirt?"

His laughter burst from him, filling him with intense and enjoyable warmth. Her heart danced as she stared at him, her mouth falling open; the dark pink tempting him again.

"Do you not like my chest, Jack?" he teased without mercy.

Her gaze darted across the muscled expanse of his chest. "I do, I mean, it's beautiful..." She bit her lip to halt her words; her tiny white teeth on that succulent petal hardened his malehood.

"How fairs Kanzo, Der?" Ulriq asked as he scanned the destroyed medical. He frowned, as concern rose within him for his battle-bond.

"He is calmer, Supreme Commander. I have tasked him to assist Data Officer Prex." Der glanced at Jack then at him. "I administered an ancient medication meant for Eths who have lost their Dar Eths. The one application will be sufficient. He was understandably distraught." He spoke in Etterian while flashing an apologetic smile at Jack. Without the Etterian language protocol activated on her O.D.I. she wouldn't be able to understand them.

Ulriq studied her hand in his, marveling at the smoothness of her skin as he ran his thumb across her knuckles. "Nerx has altered our course?"

Der nodded. "For Yithia."

Ulriq settled his gaze on his Dar Eth and switched to her language. "Come, let us go for a walk."

"A walk?" she echoed, confusion furrowing her brow.

He was tempted to run a forefinger over those creases. Instead, he shifted off the bed with her hands still ensnared.

"Yes, unless you wish to keep your hands where they are?" he teased and marveled that he could. Such an amazing feeling of gratitude swelled in him. This was all due to her, his Dar Eth. A new emotion surged through him, catching his breath. He couldn't yet name it, but it was potent and addictive.

"You have my hands trapped, Ulriq. Will you let go, please?"

He dropped the one at his chest, but he refused to release her fingers laced through his, needing the connection more than he could explain.

"Thank you, Medic Der," he acknowledged the observant male.

She blushed again, her embarrassment easy to discern. Ulriq smothered the chuckle tickling his throat. She had forgotten they weren't alone. It pleased him to think he captivated her as she did him.

"Thank you for the O.D.I. and for healing Ulriq...and me." She beamed at the male, flustering him.

Ulriq grinned at Der's reaction. "Did you and Michel talk?" he asked as he led her out of the common, up to the viewing deck, and away from curious gazes. "And your family?" He didn't spare the narrow platform more than a cursory glance. Nor did he focus on the expanse of space and Earth displayed on the floor-to-ceiling vids. What mattered was the female with him.

Her lips curled in delight. "Yes, my family and I talked. Everyone wants to stay except Vicky."

His stilled as shock rippled through him. She wanted to leave him? Did she not feel the Ethera's pull? A dark emotion coiled within him, recognizable... fear. He didn't like it.

"Stay?" he echoed; his voice lowered as his grip tightened. He wouldn't let her go; he couldn't face a life without her nor allow the void to claim him.

"Yes, with you. If we're allowed to, that is." Alarmed, her blue gaze flashed to meet his.

He calmed his erratic heartbeat, relief now flooding him. As wonderful as emotions were, it was also a battlefield. He had thought she wanted to leave him. The sharp pain and fear he had experienced weren't pleasant.

"You are allowed to," he whispered.

He tugged her closer to slide his hands up her arms. One he slipped into the pale curls at the nape of her neck, the other to cup her cheek, his thumb pressing against her jaw. With a little pressure, he tilted her head back. Staring at her upturned face, he attempted to memorize every glorious inch of her. He dipped his head to press his lips to her forehead while inhaling her scent.

"And we can return Vicky?" Her husky voice slid across his senses like a caress.

He smothered his smile against her skin.

"She...promises not to give our location away. Said she'd pretend we'd died, that the house exploded due to a gas leak." Jack rested her hand on his chest as he held her.

It was indescribable, holding her in his arms, having her body flush against his, her hand touching him, and the scent of her surrounding him. The way her heart skittered and the almost permanent splash of pink on her cheeks were the work of the Ethera. They had to be.

"You have thought this through." He trailed his mouth across her forehead to bury his face in her silky strands, inhaling an exotic fruity scent.

"We will have to ask Ava when you find her. But Vicky is a definite. I'll be sad to see her go. I think this attack has her running scared."

His chest swelled at her faith in him. She believed he would rescue Ava. Kanzo and Prex were tasked with investigating all information and possibilities. Nerx had altered the battleship course toward Yithia as a precaution. And they would locate Ava, he vowed. For Jack, he would conquer the known universe.

"And you? Are you scared?" He grinned when he remembered her firing on the Yithians. His fearless Jack.

"Nervous, yes, scared, no." She shifted to press her temple against his chest, forcing him to release her jaw.

Looping his arm around her, he gathered her closer. He fought the urge to rub his hand up and down her back, to drop it lower and have her soft backside fill his palm. His fingers twitched in anticipation, but he tightened his control. She wasn't Etterian. He couldn't afford to rush this, to push her away. His very existence depended on her.

"Why would you be nervous?"

"It's a normal reaction to starting a new life, to going off into the unknown." She sighed before continuing, "What will I do? I assume Etterian males don't need my kind of training."

"No, we are trained by our lima kuu, our teachers, and are battle-honed on Gikaet, a perpetual war zone."

"I was right?" She arched her body to meet his gaze, lifting her fingers to feather along his jaw. Her willing touch spread warmth through him. It was an encouraging sign. "You *are* battle-honed."

"You were correct. This is the life of a warrior, always searching for what he needs, many never find it." But Ulriq had found it...found her, his Dar Eth. He admired the thoughtful expression on her features. The joy cresting within him made him want to throw caution to the wind and kiss her, claim her.

"Our lives are the same, going through the motions until we find what's missing, what we need." Her voice was low when she mumbled the words, her gaze fixated on his lips.

She brushed her thumb across his bottom lip, and he shivered, unable to prevent it from rippling through his body.

"Here you are." Michel burst onto the viewing deck. "Ulriq, would you mind if I had a moment alone with my sister?"

Yes, Ulriq wanted to roar. His Dar Eth, his female. Instead, he gathered his disintegrating control and crushed her to him before releasing her, allowing his fingers to trail down her arm. Stepping away clawed at his instincts. He twitched, almost reaching for her.

"Yes, I would mind," he said to Michel as he caressed her waist. "I will see you at the evening meal, *ensa*." Unable to resist, he pressed a quick kiss to her temple before striding off.

"Wear a shirt, please," Jack teased.

Ulriq grumbled something in response but left them alone anyway.

"What's that about?" Mich sat on a molded seat built into the bulkhead. 'Windows' ran the length of the viewing deck. Earth sat at the bottom left of the panoramic vista.

"I don't know. Feels amazing though." She flashed her brother a grin. "You and Taylor?"

He shrugged as his cheeks flushed. "When I thought she might die, something in me snapped. I'm here to talk to you about everything that's happened and not..." He ran a frustrated hand through his locks.

"Shoot." Jack joined him on the bench.

"Are you sure about coming with us, Jack? You can stay on Earth, and it will be as before—"

She raised her hand. "With me missing you and spending my days getting wounded? No, thank you. I needed to change things anyway, Mich. I mean, I'm still a virgin." Heat exploded across her cheeks because discussing her sex life, even a non-existent one, with her brother was never comfortable.

"That's a good thing. I didn't fail Mom and Dad." He flashed a cocky grin, the same one that made her want to smack him or hug him.

She did neither. The scent of Ulriq clung to her skin, and she wanted it to remain for as long as it could.

"No thanks to you. You were gone most of the time. Besides, only Steve showed interest."

"Nose picker Steve?" Mich gaped.

She laughed at his shocked expression.

"The same Steve who used any excuse to touch you?" He shook his head. "I forbid you from dating him, sis."

That was one 'command' she wasn't willing to debate. "I'm happy to follow you into the wide unknown, brother. I just worry I'll be bored. What can I do to contribute to this great empire? Parasites we are not, you know that. What are you going to do? How will you fill your time?"

"Jack, Jack, Jack," he chuckled. "We have all this technology to learn. Look around you. Is there anything that appeals to you? I'd love to pilot...well, any craft. And Aaro was saying how they have been charting the stars. Imagine going beyond our galaxy, seeing other strange worlds and cultures? I mean, Earth isn't home to the aliens we know about, but there could be other places and races, Jack. There has to be."

She gasped, excitement exploding through her. The sensation was like a taser bolt minus the pain. The possibilities were endless. Security had been the only option open to her, but now, she could find something else to focus on. Exploration was one of them, but Mich was right, even learning how to pilot would be fun. "Oh, Mich, I was so worried. I'll speak to Ulriq about it and see what he says."

"Speak to Ulriq." Mich made kissy faces into his palm.

"And there is my immature brother. I was wondering where he went." She couldn't tamp down the mirth that bubbled up and giggled like a giddy teenager.

"Come, there's still time to shower and replicate an outfit before the evening meal. It's your first dinner with Ulriq, and you'll want to look good." Mich smiled.

"I always look good," she said but trailed after him. A shower would be nice.

"I disagree. What about that time your face was all splotchy?"

"I had a reaction to the river." She thumped him on the arm.

"Yes, I remember, where the *snake* scared you." He laughed. "Then a *snake* must have startled you again because when I walked in on you and Ulriq, your face was splotchy."

She froze, alarm raising her hands to her cheeks. A strong urge to smack him gripped her. She caught up with him to ruffle his hair, knowing it would irritate him even more than a punch to the gut.

He laughed and led her in another direction. "You have been assigned new quarters with Vicky, although I intend to keep Taylor with me." He gave her a pointed look as if to instruct her not to interfere. When he placed his hand on the panel beside a door, the color flashed white. It changed to green before the door opened.

Jack pursed her lips. So, that's how to use it. Simple enough, and Nerx could have taken the time to explain...if she had asked.

"I found her French kissing the commander. It's something I can never un-see," Mich called as he swaggered into her new quarters, a perfect replica of his.

"Liar." Taylor grabbed Jack by her hands to tug her farther into the room. "You can go now, Mich. Your job is done."

"Dismissed so easily?" he growled, before snatching Taylor's hands from Jack's and pulling her into the passage, letting the door close behind them.

"So, tell all," Vicky commanded from where she stood next to one of the glass surfaces in the kitchen.

"Nothing to tell." Her skin tingled when Jack remembered touching his chest, his kisses on her forehead, the way he held her hand, as if releasing it would kill him.

"You are all over yourself with that blush, Jack," Vicky teased but her gaze remained focused, intense, making Jack squirm.

"Okay." She huffed. "The man has a gorgeous chest and smells better than sun-dried sheets."

"And he's tall too." Vicky pressed a button. Within a blink of an eye, blue jeans appeared on the glass surface. Jack strolled across to stare at the materialized jeans, arching a brow at Vicky. "The Etterians call this a replicator. You enter in your dimensions, and after choosing from a range of garments, it creates the order. This one is the rehydrator; you can order any food item they have on the menu, and there are many. They keep all alien food types in their data banks. Mich says the rehydrator acts as a disposal unit as well.

Said something about converting everything into sludge from whence it creates a variety of flavors and textures."

Doubting such a device existed despite the proof of the jeans, Jack studied the nondescript surface. "Did you try a coffee yet?"

"Yes, why? Do you want one?" At her nod, Vicky ordered for her.

A mug of steaming Arabica formed on the glass. The aroma was as rich as expected. Jack snatched it from the counter and took a tentative sip. She moaned her pleasure as the dark and smoldering taste exploded over her tongue.

"The attraction started when we met," she said between sips, hoping Vicky thought her hot cheeks were from the steam. She dropped into a comfy and held her breath while it adjusted around her ass.

"No, you don't say." Vicky fake-gasped with her hand over her mouth. "Like we couldn't tell?"

"Any news about Ava?" Jack asked to which Vicky shook her head. "You should see what Kanzo did to medical."

"Kanzo? Isn't he the one who roared in pain when Ava vanished? And he fell to his knee in front of her?" Vicky squinted her eyes as she tried to remember the past events.

"That's strange. The same thing almost happened to Ulriq." Jack shrugged. "It could just be an adverse reaction to our air…"

The door opened to a stumbling, lips-swollen Taylor. Her glazed eyes had them all grinning.

"Damn, girl. Were the kisses that good?" Jack chuckled, then dipped for another sip of her coffee.

"Huh?" Taylor pressed her fingers to her lips in amazement.

"Mich's kisses? How were they?" Vicky pronounced each word in an exaggerated fashion. "Damn. It must be something in the air. I'm glad I am getting off this love boat."

"Have I died? Did those aliens kill me?" Taylor slipped into a comfy, her gaze unfocused.

"Let's get your clothes sorted and you showered before you melt into a puddle." Vicky sighed as she ushered Taylor out of her seat and toward the replicator. "Tell me, Jack, is an Etterian male worth the wait?"

Jack's gaze flew to her friend's eager eyes and smiled. "Yes."

"Let's see…he must be tall. Check. He mustn't live with mommy. Check. He must be able to take you in a fight. Check. And he is buff, so that's a bonus." Chuckling, Vicky ticked off on her fingers the items on Jack's official yet undocumented list. "He could be the one…but Jack, how can you tell them apart? They all look the same, ooze the same sexual allure. Why Ulriq? Why not one of the others we met today?"

"I don't know." Jack shrugged while a frown tugged on her lips. Her eyebrows dipped as she gave it more thought. "His presence? His command of his team, of his body, of this ship? His gentle yet firm touch? His raspy voice?"

"Fair enough." Vicky threw up her hands to concede. "Hell, I think I might like him too," she teased.

Jack laughed. No matter how gorgeous an alien, Vicky would still be leaving. When she made up her mind, nothing deviated her from it.

Chapter Eleven

Etterian battleship, Kushin
En route to Yithia
Their shared quarters

THE DOOR CHIMED, AND Vicky granted entrance on her way to the bathroom. An unknown Etterian male waited in the doorway. His gaze darted over Jack who stared at him in expectation. He kept his focus vague, and his stiff shoulders and sweeping glance sent a shiver of apprehension down her spine. Her instincts danced, and she rose from the comfy.

"Please, enter." She approached him, hoping to encourage the startled male. When she gestured to him, he stepped into their quarters. He stared at the door as it sealed behind him. Her eyes widened at meeting a timid Etterian male. She expected them to be bulky, sexy, and overpoweringly commanding—how she thought of Ulriq.

"Greetings, miladies," the male mumbled before squaring his shoulders. "I have been sent to collect the human female who killed two Yithian soldiers this day."

"Whoa, Jack, looks like you're in trouble again," Taylor teased.

"Well, you can take her," Vicky flicked her hand, her gaze focused on Jack's fake-horror expression.

"Gee, thanks, guys." Jack chuckled while closing the distance to the male. "I'm Jack. I believe you're looking for me." She arched an eyebrow.

The male studied her with a frown in his dark-blue eyes. Her appearance didn't please him. Well, she didn't expect every Etterian soldier to find human women attractive.

"I am Medic Teric, milady," he addressed her with a formal nod. "Please come with me."

She strolled along the narrow passage, trailing him. "Medic? You must know Der?"

"I do, milady. He is a valued male," Teric's voice held respect, and something else Jack hadn't expected, sadness.

"He is...valued." What could she say? She couldn't intrude on Teric's thoughts. That was beyond rude. Nor did she have the right to demand he shared what depressed him.

He veered down another passage, and she followed. Shadows, chilling silence, and the lack of foot traffic narrowed her focus.

"Where are we going, Teric?" None of the passages looked familiar, but she didn't know the battleship or its amenities well enough to be certain.

"We discovered a strange device and require your opinion. With your ability to kill two soldiers, you are now respected."

"What? I just shot them with my gun," she mumbled. Respected? Heat burned her cheeks. They implied the warriors hero-worshipped her. Her fingers twitched where she pressed them to her stomach. Nausea churned her gut. Deep respect often led to a too-high bar she needed to maintain.

"Your skill is revered." Teric continued onward without a backward glance.

Two warriors hugged the side of the passage to let her and Teric pass. Seeing faces other than the long, dark corridors in gray metal should have brought her some sort of relief. It didn't. Not when they stopped to stare. Low grumbles passed between them. They had behaved not with respect but with interest, as if she were an exhibition at a museum. It conflicted with what Teric had said. No hero worship here.

Shivering, she hurried her steps to catch up to Teric, needing him not to abandon her in the bowels of an alien battleship. He stopped outside a door, opened it, and gestured for her to enter first. She did so, the flickering red across the metallic walls intrigued her. A floating red pyramid pulsed and glowed. Circling it, she tried to make sense of the hovering device.

"I've never seen anything like this, Teric." She held out a hand, not to touch but to feel if residual heat emanated off it. "It doesn't look human-made." She raised her gaze to him. "What do your engineers think it is?"

Teric punched on his O.D.I., and she grinned. She had one too. When she touched where he did and holographic buttons popped up, a gasp slipped free. Now what? She hadn't learned what this implant could do. Ulriq could show her later, if she could keep her mind off his bare chest and blue eyes long enough.

A change in the light show of red triangles on the metal walls drew her attention as the pyramid spun faster and faster. Her hair blew back, and she dared not look away from it. Such momentum could only end in disaster.

"Um, Teric, should it be doing that?" she squeaked in her alarm, and her hackles rose, warning her of impending danger. Too damn late.

When he still didn't respond, she chanced a glance at him. He stared at the red swirling light with the saddest expression, his hands lying limply at his sides as if he were defenseless.

"I am sorry, milady," he whispered.

Strange tingling swept through her body.

Shivering, she lifted her hand in front of her. Parts of her fingers faded. She gaped and raised her gaze to Teric, cold slithering down her spine. But where he had stood alongside the pyramid, both were gone, and she was alone.

Chapter Twelve

Jack grimaced at her blurring vision. She stilled to allow it to clear, enough time for her to scan her new surroundings. Where the hell was she? What the hell had just happened? Where the hell was Teric? Gray metallic walls with a sickly yellow light near the ceiling told her she was in a whole lot of shit. The thick submarine-like door said 'impenetrable,' which meant there was no escaping this.

"Teric?" she yelled, her voice cracking as fear swarmed her like wild wasps.

Tamping down the seeds of panic that swirled in the pit of her stomach, she pressed her wrist and activated her O.D.I. She blinked at the holographic buttons before randomly typing on them, wincing at the wasp stings itching her throat when nothing she pressed helped her.

With a growl, she gave up and sat on the floor, leaning her back against the bulkhead. If she ever got her hands on Teric, she'd kill him. She welcomed the burn of anger flowing through her. It was better than the fear which skirted her anger, threatening to overwhelm her. Her heartbeat leaped as she panted. She wouldn't let hysterics claim her. It served no purpose.

"This isn't funny, Teric. I'm not laughing," she called out, but no response was forthcoming.

She didn't know how long she sat there when the yellow lights brightened to white. The door opened with a sucking sound and in slithered...a gray alien. It or he was large, bulky, his skin thick and silver, shining as if moist. But most noticeable was his head, like a great white shark with tiger teeth pressing down on his wide bottom lip. Black soulless eyes revealed no emotion. This close, he was scarier than the two she had shot.

Yithian.

He shifted aside and another two entered to surround her. Like she could take them on. The first alien lisped in what sounded like sentences. She blinked at him, showing her inability to understand him. She hoped her glazed look was a universal expression for "honestly, dude, I don't speak fish."

When nothing happened, she tamped down the itching hysteria scratching at her throat. The shark lisped something, lunged forward, and grabbed her arm. Cold and clammy fingers made her shiver. He activated her O.D.I. and punched something on the buttons. They must have watched her since he knew she had one. She hadn't seen any sec-cams, but then again, would she? Alien technology.

"Understand me now, human female?" he lisped as he stepped back.

"Yes. Why am I here? Where's Teric?" she asked, grateful to be able to communicate even if it was with a fish. "I tell you, if I get my hands on him, I'll kill him." She wrenched her fists in the universal throttling gesture, but when they frowned, she had to amend the thought to human-only gesture. Then again, their necks were too wide for her hands to reach around.

"You are onboard a Yithian slave ship. Teric will soon be of no concern," the slimy fish curled his wide lips into a smirk

She didn't like the look of it. "Why? If he's on this ship, I want him brought to me. Now." The fear gripping her was close to consuming her. Just in case, these fish knew what her trembling hands meant, she shoved them into her back pockets.

Although Teric had brought her here, there was something more sinister rolling off these aliens. Maybe she could swing Teric to her side; he was Etterian. There might be a minuscule amount of honor left in him. Not that she believed she was capable of swaying anyone to her side, but she sure as hell wanted to try. Besides, the longer she faced the cold shark, the more she understood her dire situation. He'd said a slave ship. That wasn't fish for 'vacation cruiser.'

"You make demands of me?" His lisps increased in intensity with what looked like venom forming dew drops on his fangs.

He flicked his three-fingers at the two aliens flanking her. They charged, triggering her training. She side-kicked one on the thigh and thrust her elbow into the stomach of the other. Ducking spared her from grasping fingers and granted her access to punch what she hoped was his groin. Her fist hit something soft, and the alien grunting was score one for her. But he didn't collapse to a knee. Instead, he lunged for her, grabbing her, pinning her arms in place. Her instinct was to use her head to strike his chin, but she hesitated. With their teeth, doing that might harm her more. So she shifted her hips to the left and threw a fist back, striking him in the groin again. He released her on an oomph. Before she could celebrate her small victory, fire exploded across her face. She hadn't seen the punch coming. Her head snapped to the side as blood pooled on her tongue. She clasped her jaw and winced at the tenderness. With her focus on the one who hit her, the fist to her eye took her by surprise. Crying out, she fell to the floor. So much for her pride in her ability to defend herself. Whimpering, she used the metallic wall to scramble to her feet. Her limbs twitched and exhaustion drained her strength, trembling her knees.

Sensing her weakening, they didn't hold their punches. Each strike at at her resolve. Pain lanced through her, the blows to her face and stomach debilitating. Staggering back, she swiped her wrist across her mouth, blinking for a second at the blood smear. Squaring her shoulders, she swung a wild punch with the last of her strength. The bastard caught her fist, grabbed her arm, and yanked. She screamed as they overextended her arms to the side and immobilized her. Unable to move, to fight, they twisted her arms, ripped a scream from her and forced her to her knees.

"Still wish to make demands?"

"May I *respectfully* request Teric be brought to me?" she spat in a sweet and polite voice, meeting the asshole's black gaze through her one un-swollen eye. She willed herself not to lick her burning lips. And her jaw ached as if the bottom row of teeth had been jarred loose. If her students could see her now...

"Why would you want him? He betrayed you."

Gritting her teeth summoned a wince. "You said he was of no concern. What would it matter if he died at my hands?" The more she knelt with her arms losing feeling, the more she realized Teric was as much a victim as she was. These assholes must have held something important over him, enough to force an honorable Etterian to betray his supreme commander.

"Very well since you asked with a respectful tone..." The alien left the cell, with his guards trailing him.

Jack groaned, as a thousand nerves feasted on her arms. Whimpering at the unbearable sensation, she rubbed, forcing circulation into them. Her swollen eye throbbed, and with her ring finger, she patted the swelling, groaning at the fresh throbbing her gentle touch summoned. When she lowered her hand, blood smeared her fingertip. Okay, that wasn't a good sign. She jolted, having not realized the door remained open. Struggling to her feet, she crept closer, the darkness of the passage tormenting her. Shifting shadows preceded an Etterian pre-teen shoved into the cell. Jack lunged to catch her, in case she stumbled. She shouldn't have bothered.

The girl caught herself before facing the door, watching it seal them in with the white light fading to yellow.

"Hello," Jack lisped a greeting. "My name's Jack, what's yours, little one?"

"Aala," she whispered and sat on the floor in the far corner of the cell.

"Hello, Aala. Have you been here long?" Jack mimicked her, choosing the opposite side of the cell, understanding that the girl needed distance from her, a stranger, and an alien. She almost chuckled at considering herself an alien. But to Aala, she was.

"Months," Aala whispered.

Months? In this fish-infested ship? Jack shuddered and relished the slow burn of anger uncoiling in her stomach. "And how did you get here? Why would these sharks want you?"

"Sharks?" Aala frowned. "That is not a word I know."

"They look like fish creatures from my planet, Earth." Jack stuck out her fingers and pressed her wrist to her mouth to show fangs, wincing as she brushed her split lip.

Aala shrugged. "They stole me off my mother's escort ship. Every year, she sends for me, and my father must let her have me for as long as she wants. Thank the Maker, it was only for one month this time."

Having any sort of maternal relationship was foreign to Jack. She had faded memories of her mother, but too many years had passed. The girls and Mich were her family, but they were siblings to each other, not parents. "I'm sorry your mother is horrible to you. Mine died when I was young."

"I sometimes wish mine died too." A tear slid down Aala's cheek. Her eyes were a startling ice-blue, like Ulriq's. "Does that make me evil?"

Jack's heart melted, and she hurried to shake her head. "Of course not, you have the right to your emotions."

Aala's laughter was cold, lacking joy. "Not on Etteria."

Jack frowned. "Why do you say that?"

Aala picked at the hem of her stained tunic. "Hundreds of years ago, uncontrolled emotions started a war that cost Etteria many lives, or so my lima kuu, my teacher, said. So the king at the time asked another culture to help us. The genetic modifications they made granted us control but impacted our fertility."

"Ah, why women are precious." Jack nodded. Hence the silly milady. "Well, when we escape, I'll take you to Earth where you can feel whatever you want to feel."

"If we get out." Her shoulders slumped, encouraging the despair Jack was barely keeping at bay.

"Of course we will. Ulriq and Mich will find me." She forced a large smile, despite not being particularly hopeful. "Do you need a hug?"

Aala frowned. "What is that?"

"May I cross over to you?" She gestured with her fingers to the distance between them.

Aala shrugged, but her gaze remained wary.

Jack shuffled across to sit next to her. "Don't be alarmed. If you don't like it, just tell me, okay?"

Aala nodded.

Jack picked her up, placed her onto her lap, and wrapped her arms around her thin shoulders. Reaching Jack's shoulders, Aala had to be no older than ten or twelve. She was heavy for a child, her bony backside digging into Jack's thigh muscles. Gritting her teeth, she adjusted the girl's position until the sharp poking eased.

She leaned against the bulkhead, shifted her backside to something more comfortable. "What do you think?"

Aala poked Jack in the stomach with her elbow. "I do not know yet. What is supposed to happen?"

Jack laughed. "Nothing, you just sit within the safety of my arms, maybe listen to my heartbeat."

"It is pleasant. You are soft, and you smell good too."

Jack rested her chin on the crown of the girl's head. "My brother would hug me like this. It told me I was loved."

"Love?" Aala grew heavier as she relaxed.

"Love is a strong feeling of affection," Jack moved her arms to a more relaxed position.

"I do not think my mother feels this for me."

"Then why does she send for you?" Jack stroked Aala's braided hair.

The girl shrugged. "To irritate my father, I suppose."

"Does your father love you?"

"In his way, but he does not know I am here."

Jack swallowed her gasp. Aala came across as too mature for a child her size. The thought saddened Jack, for a child should enjoy the freedom of growing up without the burden of adulthood.

"And if he did?" Jack pictured an Etterian father shooting his way into the cell. A ping of hope exploded in her chest like an emergency flare.

"He would come for me." The certainty in Aala's voice was precious, as if she still considered her father a knight, capable of untold feats.

Jack had looked at her father through hero-tinted glasses, thought of Fred like that too. "That is love, Aala."

"And does Ulriq and Mich love you?" Aala asked in a sleepy voice.

"Mich does; he's my brother." Jack couldn't say what Ulriq felt for her. They'd just met, and their relationship was too new.

"I will hug my father like this if I see him. To let him know I love him." Aala's voice was growing weaker and more incoherent as sleep called to her.

"I think he would like that," Jack whispered.

"Are you staying with me, Jack?" Her small voice rose as fear curled around its edges.

"As long as they let me, Aala. I will fight to stay with you." Jack tightened her arms and clenched her jaw. Just let the damn fish try.

"You would?"

"Of course, as girls, we must stick together."

"Girls? Another odd word."

Jack leaned back to focus on Aala's face, wondering why her eyelids didn't flutter as Ulriq and Der's had done. "On Earth, all females young and old can be called girls. It's an informal term."

Aala snuggled against Jack. "Girls," she whispered, testing out the new word.

Jack listened to Aala's soft snores as she slept. She held the child close, unraveling what had to have happened for an Etterian girl to be onboard a shark's slave ship. What kind of mother didn't report her child missing?

Jack wanted to find the Etterian woman to pummel sense into her. And why had they thrust Aala and not Teric into the cell as she'd 'respectfully' asked?

Mich had to have noticed her missing by now. But then again, what could he do? The red pyramid must have been a teleporting device, but how could anyone track teleportation? She wasn't an engineer or an inventor, nor could she wrap her human mind around alien tech. She wouldn't know where to start.

She tested the swelling again and winced. Her eye was swollen shut, and the throbbing rippled outward in waves. She didn't know why she couldn't stop touching it, checking on it as if it would miraculously heal without a med-gun. It was no longer a priority. Her survival focus had shifted to the girl in her arms. No matter what happened or where they headed, she had to keep her safe. God willing, or she would die trying. Children needed to be cared for. And Jack was damn well going to provide that for as long as she could.

She must have dozed off because the sucking sound of the door opening jolted her. Under a bright light, a shark strolled in and held out two packets of water and what resembled protein bars. She gestured that he could drop it on the floor, and he did so before leaving.

Well, at least starvation wasn't a concern.

Chapter Thirteen

Michel burst into the comm room with far more energy than was usual. "Ulriq, have you seen Jack?"

Not lifting his gaze from his tablet, he shook his head. "We are to meet at the evening meal."

"The girls haven't seen her. They said a male collected her."

Ulriq's whipped his head up to meet Michel's wide gaze. "A male? No name?"

Michel paced in the narrow confines of the comm room. "Eric or something. They said he asked for her specifically, for the female who took down two alien soldiers, but that was hours ago."

The fear in the human male's voice brought on a twinge of concern, but Ulriq brushed it aside. It was a large battleship, and Jack had an O.D.I. Rising, he placed his hand on Michel's shoulder.

"Calm, Michel. We will trace her." Frowning, Ulriq faced his pilot. "Ksal, locate Jacqueline Dunois."

Ksal's fingers flew across the multi-lit console as he punched the buttons. "She is not on this vessel, Supreme Commander."

"Look again," Ulriq growled; a sharp sensation pressed on his lungs. Emotions were new to him, but this one, this painful debilitating emotion he recognized as fear. He experienced it far too much since meeting Jack.

"I have, Ulriq," Ksal met his gaze.

"How is this possible?" Ulriq boomed. "We are on a battleship."

"I have verified no unauthorized ports have occurred. No shuttles have left any docking bays. No unusual spacecraft in our vicinity. There's nothing out of the ordinary across all stations."

"How can she just vanish?" Michel's voice rose in his agitation.

"Stealth porting can only occur with a temirian device. Those are rare and expensive. Such a device could penetrate the battleship's dampening shield," Ksal said with his fingers still flying across the console. "There was an unusual power reading close to the engine rooms. Because of its proximity to the fusion drives, the reading was ignored."

Ulriq stiffened. "Where?"

"Storeroom 516S."

"Ksal, send Prex to that location." Ulriq broke into a run, with Michel attempting to keep up.

His males dove out of his path, not that Ulriq paid them any attention. He prayed to the Maker as he ran, asking that he wouldn't find anything. As he burst into the storeroom, fear struck hard and fast. His chest constricted as he fell to his knees, his vision spinning. There in the middle of the room stood a lifeless pyramidal device.

His Jack was gone.

"What is it?" Michel panted and clung to the door frame.

Ulriq glanced at him and recognized the emotion on the human's face since it saturated his own heart.

"A temirian," he whispered, his voice cracking; emotions bubbled to the surface, and his control was at breaking point. He had to calm himself; he had to think. Jack depended on him to find her, save her.

"She's gone?" Michel demanded, fear and anger warring in his voice.

Ulriq understood what the male was going through. She was his sister…but she was more than that to Ulriq, she was his life force.

"Supreme Commander," Data Officer Prex greeted as he entered the storeroom and crossed to the device. He pressed a few buttons and extracted the pyramid section from its stand. "The last ported location should be stored on the device. However, I suspect it was next to this battleship at the time of port. That ship would not be there now."

"At least find who would dare—" Ulriq's voice broke.

"That is possible, Supreme Commander." Prex left the room with the temirian in hand.

"Why would someone take her? This makes no sense. Ava, now Jack?" Michel stormed. "Do you think the two are linked?"

"Let us talk to your girls. Perhaps they remember something more…" Ulriq strode to Jack's quarters. His heart stuttered, knowing she wouldn't be there to greet him with her mischievous smile, the one that melted his insides.

"Have you found her?" Vicky's face was pale, and her hands trembled.

"She was taken, ported off the ship by unknowns," Ulriq said. "I need you to tell me everything that happened. Please try and remember as much detail as possible."

"He said he was a medic." Taylor shoved a glass of brown liquid in Ulriq's hand. He accepted it but frowned at it, not knowing what to do with it.

"A medic?" Ulriq was grateful when Michel took the glass from his stiff fingers before downing it himself. With his hand free, Ulriq activated his O.D.I., sending instructions to Ksal and Der.

"He seemed scared, worried." Vicky tapped her chin. "Maybe even nervous, shuffling from side-to-side and not meeting our gazes."

"Yes, he wasn't at all confident like the other men we have met," Taylor offered, her expression was one of hope.

Ulriq's arm buzzed, and he activated his O.D.I. again. He read the message and scowled; his brow furrowed, exacerbating the headache forming.

"Medic Teric did not report for duty," he frowned. "This is illogical. Teric is an honorable male. Ksal," he spoke into his wrist. "Investigate Teric thoroughly. Has he received unusual comms? I want to know everything." He faced the waiting human females and sighed. They needed him to find their Ava and now their Jack, and he would, so he vowed, "I will locate your girls."

He left with Michel on his heels. When they stepped into the passage, Ulriq spun on the male. "Stay, offer them comfort. I will keep you informed with whatever information is brought to light."

Michel wavered then left Ulriq standing there in the empty passage. Finally, alone, he roared his anger, his fear, his pain and threw his fist into the bulkhead with enough force to dent it.

"TERIC DID SEEM AGITATED," Medic Der added as they watched Prex work on the temirian. The medic had found Ulriq in the Data Officer's narrow room. "I wish to remind you that Jack has an O.D.I. Could we not track her with that?"

Ulriq faced the medic as his eyes widened. "It is possible if she activated it. Ksal, place a tracker on Jack's O.D.I. as soon as she uses it," he spoke to his wrist.

"I have not shown her how to use it; did you or Mich?"

Ulriq's shoulders slumped, answering the medic without speaking.

Der pursed his lips. "Let us hope someone activates it."

Ulriq clenched his jaw, fighting the overpowering urge to punch something again. Hope, he was basing his life on hope.

"It was the Yithians," Prex said, indicating the letters on the large display vid.

"Yithians?" Der frowned. "Why?"

"She killed two soldiers..." Ulriq explained, not willing to go into further detail.

"She did?" Prex's eyes widened.

"Yes, with a human weapon."

"It is Yithian to seek revenge," Der commented.

They had been allies with Yithia for many centuries, though their data annals did mention a time when they had been at war. And the Yithians did lack honor.

"They would take her to Mascroba, to the royal seat," Ulriq said before raising his wrist to his lips. "Ksal, how many pulses to reach Mascroba?"

"One-week fusion pulse, Supreme Commander, it might have been longer had we not already set course for Yithia. I need you in the comm room." The pilot paused, "You need to see this, Ulriq," The seriousness of his pilot's voice spurred Ulriq.

"Good work, Prex," he called as he rushed out of the office, his long strides taking him to the comm room. "What is it, Ksal?" he demanded the moment he stormed in.

Instead of answering, Ksal loaded a male's face onto the display vid.

"I am Medic Teric, son of Base Commander Meric. Maker bless his soul. I have taken the human female as demanded by the Yithians for the safe return of my daughter, Aala. I apologize for the deception, but I saw no other recourse. I have released this scheduled message approximately half a day after departure. We will be en route to Mascroba, to the arena dungeons. I do not expect the Yithians to keep their word to liberate my daughter and myself. I... cannot lose my daughter." The male closed his eyes before opening them to stare into the vid, determination set in his shoulders. "I will accept whatever punishment you deem fit...if we survive."

The display vid went blank.

"Alodon's hell." Ulriq ran a trembling hand over his face.

"Her destination has been confirmed." Der sighed with relief. "We will still arrive a day or two behind them. This battleship is not as fast as a Yithian M class."

"Ksal, speak to engineering. Find out if they cannot increase the *Kushin*'s performance," Ulriq demanded. "I need to notify Michel and the girls."

"Girls?" Ksal repeated in confusion and paused as his eyelids fluttered with the O.D.I.'s explanation.

Ulriq, bouncing on the balls of his feet, was too irritated to wait those few seconds. "Michel's name for the group of human females."

"Thank you for the clarification. Before you depart, Supreme Commander, I have one more suggestion..." Ksal spun his chair, skilled enough not to catch his braid in the process. Ulriq faced Ksal expectantly. "Why not take the scimitar in Docking Bay G? It is fast and—"

"Thank you, Ksal." A massive grin warmed Ulriq's face. "Good work as always." He sighed, twice he'd given out praise, a rare thing for him to do. But under the circumstances, his males had risen to the challenge, and their exemplary performances would be documented. "I will gather a unit and leave at once. Have the vessel prepared. Der, I will need you. Ksal, summon Kanzo to the comm room. I shall await his presence. And wake Nerx, the male will need to take command."

When Kanzo staggered into the comm, he straightened at the sight of Ulriq. His exhaustion was palpable, and Ulriq could understand why. The male had been trawling through comm after comm, all in the Yithian language. He was searching for any mention of Ava.

"We were incorrect in our assessment, they were after Lady Jack," Prex told Kanzo as he stood beside him. "They have taken her, as well."

"A temirian?" Kanzo arched a brow.

"Good, now that you are informed, Kanzo, we leave within the hour," Ulriq growled, his impatience thrumming through him and twitching his limbs. He hated revealing it, showing his eagerness to be on the hunt. "The *Phoenix's* Data Officer Kemt—under Xan's command—has stumbled upon communications between a Yithian slave ship and their royal court."

"Lady Jack is destined for the arena," Prex told Kanzo. "A unit will port down to rescue her, while I escort you to the *Phoenix*. You will join Supreme Commander Xan and his unit, and rescue Lady Ava.

"It should take five days to reach Mascroba, even with the scimitar at full fusion pulse. By then, we will know her precise location, Kanzo," Prex said.

Five days? Ulriq swallowed a groan. Anything could happen to Jack in five days. But he couldn't reach her faster. The pressure on his tense muscles, vibrating through his chest and dropping into the pit of his stomach had red staining his vision. With slow, steady inhales and exhales, his focus sharpened. He had to remain calm, and somehow, appease the Ethera driving him.

The scimitar craft was small with sufficient capacity for eleven Etterians. It had an engine room and ten single quarters, similar in design as per their battleships. The officer's quarters remained unused if the craft was utilized for covert missions. It had a well-stocked recreational room and fully functioning replicators and rehydrators. The comm room, though smaller, held the controls and navigational diagnostics to pilot such a ship. It was fast, and the best they could do.

Ulriq strode out, heading for Jack's quarters.

When he requested entrance, the door opened, and Vicky shoved a cup of what looked like fruit juice. He accepted it automatically and took a grateful sip, humming at the strange yet tart flavor before strolling to the center of their gathering.

"We have learned the Yithians ported Jack and Ava." They stared at Ulriq blankly. He strode toward the display screen and navigated to the cultural studies section on Yithia. Images appeared of a male Yithian.

"Why would they want either of them?" Vicky's brow furrowed.

Taylor's confusion was mirrored in her heart-shaped face. She traced the Yithian's face with a finger.

Ulriq winced as he said, "They are taking Jack to their arena to fight."

"Like a gladiator, a contender?" Taylor snatched her finger away as she faced Ulriq. With fear twisting her features, she glanced at Michel who'd entered behind Ulriq.

"I am going after her in a smaller vessel we have on board. It is faster than the M class Yithian ship Jack is on and will bring us to within a day of her arrival on Yithia."

"I am coming with you," Michel announced.

Ulriq nodded, having anticipated this. Though, it appeared as if the human females hadn't. They gawked at Michel, their mouths falling open and their fear-darkened eyes widening. He could understand their concerns. Losing a single bond was hard, but to have two in jeopardy and now a third...

"How long will you be gone, Ulriq?" Taylor's voice was faint but as emotive. She rose to wrap an arm around Michel's waist.

"A week. The *Kushin* will be close on our heels. Once we have Jack, we will return to this battleship in stealth mode."

"And Ava?" Vicky asked.

"We have requested the assistance of the battleship *Phoenix* in orbit around Yithia. They are tracking Ava for us." He clasped his trembling hands at the base of his spine. "Warrior Kanzo will be escorted to the *Phoenix* and will launch a rescue with their warriors. We will unite with the *Phoenix* to retrieve Kanzo and Ava."

"Won't these Yithians try to stop you?" Vicky wrapped her arms around her knees. Her reasoning behind such a posture was lost on him.

"I look forward to any such attempts." Ulriq gritted his teeth with determination. To repay Yithia for their audacity was a task he'd appreciate. "We leave within the hour. Prepare yourself accordingly."

"I am prepared to leave now." Michel stepped out of Taylor's arms as if to follow Ulriq. He paused and shot a glance at Taylor, giving Michel a subtle instruction to see to her care first. "But I could do with a quick meal," he amended, acknowledging Ulriq's advice with a curt nod.

"Thank you, Ulriq," Vicky whispered, touching his forearm with her small hand. "For keeping your word. May God be with you." She closed her eyes to offer up a swift prayer.

Ulriq waited for her to meet his gaze. "I apologize, Lady Vicky. We have not yet delivered you to your home. We will do so the moment Jack and Ava have returned to us."

"I understand. I would prefer to remain on board anyway until they are found. Please don't worry about me."

He left, heading to Docking Bay G. Perhaps his presence would speed his males at their tasks, and the ship could leave sooner.

"I hear you are abandoning us," Nerx greeted as Ulriq entered the bay.

"You have the command, Nerx."

"So I have heard," the stern male said.

"Then why are you here?" Ulriq assumed a position next to Nerx. He was still worried about Jack, but knowing he was in pursuit eased some of the tension coursing through his body. The Yithians wouldn't harm her, not after going to all this trouble to capture her. His males had also risen to the challenge. He was grateful to them and would reflect said emotion in his reports.

"I am overseeing our males at their tasks, of course. I did assume you would prefer to leave sooner than scheduled." Nerx scowled.

At this, Ulriq laughed, the joy rising within him unexpected under the circumstances. "And we will with you glowering at them," he finished on a teasing note.

Nerx grunted. "A necessary skill this day."

Chapter Fourteen

"How did you sleep, Aala?" Jack stroked the little girl's hair.

"I slept wonderfully well, Jack." Her words warmed Jack's heart.

She hugged the girl, rubbing her chin across the crown of her head. "I'm glad. How many days has it been?"

Aala scrambled off Jack's lap to stretch. "Four since you arrived. The Yithian said we should reach our destination in two days."

"Where do you think our destination is?" Jack finger-combed her own hair before braiding it. She didn't have a hairband but doing this repetitive task kept her fingers busy.

Turning to Aala, she did the same thing, loving the way her hair danced as if she was underwater. The strands reached eagerly for Jack's fingers, and she stroked them, soothing them until they let her braid them. At least Aala had a metal bracelet-like hairband. It clipped at the end of her hair, and she had explained that the metal, infused with Ferusi crystals, had a calming effect on her hair.

She chewed on her bottom lip and picked at the hem of her shirt. "Um, Jack, they are taking you to their arena."

"Arena?" Jack scowled, not liking the sounds of that. If they tossed her in without Aala, then she would fight to survive. But if Aala went with her, the girl's life mattered more. "And you?"

"I do not know," she shrugged, but the slight stiffness of her shoulders told Jack she did know or at least suspected.

Before Jack could question her further, the yellow light brightened to white seconds before the door opened. They shoved an Etterian male into the cell, and the door sealed behind him. Leaping to her feet, she tugged Aala behind her as the beaten male crumpled to the floor.

"Father." Aala nudged Jack aside to rush to him, her hands hovering an inch from his skin as if she feared to harm him.

"Aala." Agony permeated his cracking voice. He tried to rise but slumped, curling into a ball with a hoarse groan.

"I prayed to the Maker you would come," Aalo said.

Jack pushed off the wall and circled the male, trying to ascertain what his injuries were. His fingers were purple and black, his breathing was shallow. He didn't gurgle, which might have meant a punctured lung. He had to be nursing a cracked or broken rib—she knew how that felt. His face was swollen, and he could barely open his eyes. Behind him, coiled on the metallic floor was his thick braid.

"How badly are you hurt?" She tried not to startle him.

"I will heal, Lady Jack." He squeezed the English words through his clenched jaw.

"You know my name?" Jack gasped, staggering back.

"I am the reason you are here, for which I am deeply sorry." His head dipped to his chin.

Jack frowned and bit her lip against the angry words she wanted to spew. This was Medic Teric? Had the pyramid ported him as well? She glanced at Aala who was watching her. Fear and concern marred her bronze face. Tensing her muscles against the fire burning her blood, Jack ground her teeth and pasted on a smile. She was livid, but she couldn't rant in front of the child. And having spent days in Aala's company, she understood why Teric had done it. He had no choice; the life of his daughter had been at stake. Regardless, her anger would have to wait. She'd strip him a new one when she had him alone.

"I understand now, Teric." Jack clenched her jaw before touching his bruised hand. "I might have done the same had I been in your shoes."

"Your tiny feet could never fit in my footwear," Teric mumbled as his brow furrowed.

Jack chuckled. "It means, had I been in the same situation."

He attempted to sit up, moaning in the process.

"If you need, I have water?" Jack lifted her shirt to chew on the hem, wanting to tear off a strip to bind Teric's fingers.

He raised his gaze to meet hers only to frown again. "You offer your water?"

"Of course." Jack fetched the packet carefully balanced against a bulkhead. She brought it to him and smiled in encouragement. "You may finish it. Aala and I have had more than enough today."

He accepted the packet, draining it with a trembling hand. "Thank you," he whispered as he tossed the empty packet to the side. It dissolved once the inside material was exposed to the air. "They mistreated you?" He pointed a finger at her swollen eye.

"Yes, but I managed to get Aala, so I'm not upset about it."

He flicked a glance at his daughter. "How did you get Aala?"

Jack worked a small tear in her T-shirt, sparing him a smile. "I demanded they bring you."

"Me?" His voice rose along with his thick, black eyebrows.

"Yes, I was planning on kicking your ass."

He chuckled before wincing, his arm clutching his ribs.

She ripped her T-shirt and shrugged. "Like *I* could take on an Etterian male."

"You have the heart, not the skill." Teric's compliment warmed her, soothed some of her anger.

Jack shrugged before smiling at him again. "I figured we could team up against the sharks."

"Sharks?" His eyelids fluttered before he nodded.

"Fish creatures from Earth," Aala giggled. "It is what Jack calls the Yithians."

"How are you, *minus susa*?" Teric examined his daughter, searching for any injuries, anything out of the ordinary.

"Better. I have you and Jack now." She frowned. "You still have not answered Jack, Father? How badly are you injured?"

"I will heal," he grunted. "Let us hope Ulriq finds us."

Jack stilled. Her thoughts flitted to Ulriq's intense blue eyes, to his decisiveness when dealing with her, his gentleness, and his looming masculinity. "He will."

"Agreed, your Eth will not give up until he has you back," Teric said.

Jack tore a strip off her T-shirt. "My Eth?" She tested the word on her tongue.

"He did he not tell you?" Teric's confusion had her taut nerves awakening to worse things than sharks. Whatever an Eth was, it had to be pretty bad.

"We only met a few days ago. Why don't you tell me now?"

"It is beautiful, Jack." With a beaming smile, Aala bounced on her toes. "For an Etterian male to find his Dar Eth, it is a precious thing."

"Dar Eth?" Jack glanced at Teric who sighed.

He shifted to lean against the bulkhead, needing the wall's support for his bruised body. "When an Etterian male finds his Dar Eth, his other half, he experiences the Ethera. It calls forth strong emotions long suppressed. A lifetime of smothered emotions will be released in one occurrence, hence the pain-pleasure Eths endure." He settled one eye on Jack, his arched brow conveying his hope she followed his explanation.

She snapped her gaping mouth shut and bandaged his worst hand.

"The male will fall to a knee. That is what my lima said. Something about it being so pleasurable it is painful, testing the male's control." Aala clapped with joy, bringing forth a small smile to Teric's bloodied face.

"They fall to a knee?" Jack whispered, her eyebrows arching in alarm as her cheeks burned. Like Kanzo knelt before Ava? Like Ulriq almost did before Jack?

"Yes, and their eyes change from dark-blue to almost white."

"What?" Jack squeaked, struggling to inhale as if a hand squeezed her chest. "Ulriq's my other half, my soulmate?"

"Soulmate?" Aala's frown mimicked Teric's.

Teric's eyelids fluttered, and Jack gave his O.D.I. the requisite time to update him.

"On Earth, it means the person with the other half of your soul," Jack mumbled, a little dazed. Her heart pounded with erratic excitement, making her chest feel too small to contain it.

"Yes, Ulriq is your soulmate," Teric said.

"Did he fall to a knee when you met him?" Aala jumped up and down, swinging her thick braid. "Did his eye color change to look like mine?" Aala pointed to her ice-blue eyes.

Jack nodded, unable to speak past the lump in her throat.

Aala grabbed Jack's hand to skip around her. "Then he *will* come for you."

"He cannot help but do so," Teric whispered with his eyes closed. He was in more pain than he had let on. "The Ethera will drive him to find you. His very being will be calling to yours." Teric's gruff voice vibrated his pain.

"Damn," Jack mumbled, torn between squealing like a little girl, or curling into a ball and muttering to herself. "Will the Ethera fade over time?"

"It is for life. An Eth will never look at another female, regardless of the Ethera fading or not." Teric tilted his head back, and in the sickening-yellow light, it highlighted the severity of his wounds.

"Never?" Holy shit. To find a man who would never cheat on a woman?

Teric clutched his hand to his chest, his breathing uneven. "They cannot, Jack. The Ethera is a powerful attraction with uncontrollable rushes of intense emotions which in turn creates an overwhelming compulsion between the Eth and Dar Eth. The bond is instant, and as you grow to know each other, the bond strengthens."

"This explains so much," she whispered.

Ulriq's instant attraction to her, the way sparks flew when they touched, the expression in his eyes when he looked upon her as if she held his heart, his world in her hands. It was a powerful feeling, that she was able to bring such a male to his knees. It was also humbling and a little frightening.

She stilled, trying not to think about what this entailed. Dating, sure, but to commit after one meeting? Look at her. Whining about the lack of gorgeous men available, and when one wanted her, she distrusted his interest, his sincerity. Crushing the dark whispers urging her to hide, to run, to reject this Ethera, she sat, leaned her back against the bulkhead, and braided her hair. She would cross the bridge when Ulriq saved her.

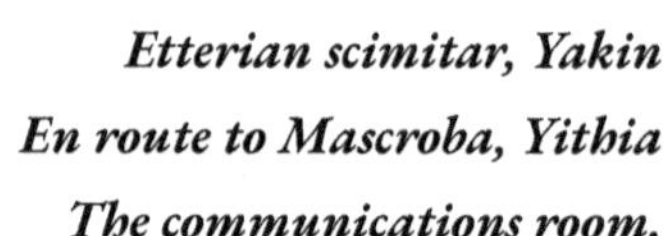

Etterian scimitar, Yakin
En route to Mascroba, Yithia
The communications room.

"Have you found anything yet?" Ulriq demanded.

Prex and Kanzo worked diligently in front of the console. "We are making good time, just two days out."

"I have translated enough Yithian to not need the O.D.I.," Kanzo mumbled, exhaustion clear in his sluggish mannerisms.

Ulriq dropped his hand on his battle-bond's shoulder. "How is the Ethera?"

"Bearable. Having her image helps." Kanzo activated his O.D.I. and showed Ulriq the sec-vid.

His heartbeat paused before it leaped ahead. "Is Jack on there?" he growled, desperate to see her.

"No, I commed only the minutes before Ava's phasing," Prex announced, then punched on the console keys, and the sec-vid from the shuttle appeared on the display vid.

The image of his Jack jumping into the shuttle hitched Ulriq's breath. Her stance was warrior-like as she hefted the blaster in her delicate hands. As the shuttle door closed, her hair swirled around her, hardening him...again.

"You two, go rest," and his tone brooked no argument.

Kanzo flashed Prex a grin as they left Ulriq in the communications room alone. The first thing Ulriq did was contact his king. Delaying the comm had been for Ulriq's benefit. He'd wanted to have accomplished something before this discussion. Asking Xeus for help should come from a position of competence. Under his command, Ulriq had lost two Dar Eths. If the king decided so, this might cost him many feet of honor.

"Ulriq? You too?" King Xeus barked as his eyebrows shot up.

"Yes, my king, Warrior Kanzo as well. It happened fast. And as much as I would wish to supply the details, it will have to wait. I am contacting you with an urgent request."

"Speak as needed," Xeus said, clasping his hands behind his back.

"The Yithians have kidnapped our Dar Eths. I request permission to retrieve both females."

"Permission granted," the king said without hesitation.

"And should it start a war?" Ulriq hoped for one. The fury had yet to leave him. Fear slithered between the fiery bolts of rage, disturbing his ability to sleep. Though that might be the work of the Ethera.

Xeus narrowed his eyes, meeting Ulriq's gaze. "Then a war they shall have."

"Tell me, Ulriq, is your Dar Eth human?" Prince Enyl drew Ulriq's anxious gaze to him. Ulriq twitched at the prince's ice-blue eyes. Why hadn't he heard of a royal pairing?

"Congratulations, my prince." Ulriq offered a curt nod. "Yes, Kanzo's is also human."

"As is mine, Supreme Commander."

Ulriq blinked at the prince, realizing the importance of Earth, now more than ever.

"Do you require assistance? The *Phoenix* is in Yithia's orbit," Adviser Cales said, his calming effect reached across the communication.

"We are two days from Mascroba. We pursued immediately, though, I am pleased to have your support. I have contacted Supreme Commander Xan and will be initiating a dual rescue." Ulriq ran a hand over his face before meeting Xeus's gaze. "Medic Teric betrayed us."

His voice was hoarse in reaction to this betrayal. Having seen the vid, he could understand Teric's motivation. But the male had chosen this option, chosen to steal Ulriq's Dar Eth, to hand over a helpless female to the Yithians. Teric could have sought assistance. Any Etterian male would have mounted a rescue for his daughter. He, himself, would have assisted.

Cales stilled and whipped his gaze up from his O.D.I. "Meric's Teric?"

"We will investigate from this side. All of Etteria be with you, Ulriq," Xeus ended the communication.

Ulriq stared at the blank display vid and shuddered. Two more days before Jack would be in his arms and safe. Then she would never leave his sight again, Maker help him.

When he activated the sec-vids from the shuttle, the vision of Jack consumed him. He couldn't state how many times he watched her, from the moment she climbed into the kuta, to Ava porting, to Jack touching his face, but he would run through the vid many times more. And even though it violated protocol, he sent the vid to his O.D.I.

In his quarters, he stripped off his armor, spread out on his bed, and activated his O.D.I. As the vid played, he analyzed every expression that crossed her features. There. He paused the vid and sighed. She raised her hand to stroke the hair at his temple, and the warmth in her gaze told him, she was his, forever.

He fell asleep to that image, the sight of her soothed the Ethera enough to grant him a little rest.

Chapter Fifteen

Yithia
City of Mascroba
Arena dungeons

JACK STARED AT THEIR new cell in the arena's dungeon. It had metal bars, thick and impenetrable, with dense black sand covering the floor. In the corner, a strange half-gnawed bone rose out of the sand. She shivered. By the size of it, the creature that had died or chewed on it had to be massive. The ceiling was a light gray rough-hewn rock. The cell had no windows to let in natural light, just hidden yellow lighting. The sharks had cast the three of them into one cell, for which she was grateful. The thought of being alone churned her gut.

"Father?" In a small voice, Aala hugged Teric, wrapping her thin arms around his waist.

He tentatively put an arm around her.

"Ulriq is coming, Aala, sweetheart. And they put us together, so that's good," Jack forced a happy note as she scanned the bars, searching for the lock. There wasn't one. No lock meant she couldn't pick it, as if alien lock tech was even remotely familiar. Her shoulders drooped.

"It *is* good." Teric tugged his daughter closer, wincing as he did so.

"Aala, come sit with me, and I'll tell you about Earth." Jack held out a hand, hoping to draw Aala away from her healing father.

Jack lowered herself onto the soft sand and waited. Aala crawled across the cell to climb onto her lap.

"Remember how I told you I was a law enforcement instructor?" At her nod, Jack smiled. "I was training recruits and a petite female named Nancy flipped me onto my back so fast and hard that I bruised my ribs. I had bruises all down one side of my stomach."

Aala's blue eyes grew wide, but her lips twisted as if she doubted Nancy existed. "How little was she, Jack?"

"The top of her head reached here." Jack tapped her shoulder.

"Truth?" Aala gasped, and a slow smile spread her chubby cheeks.

Jack laughed as she untied Aala's hair to stroke then braid it. "Now why would I lie?"

"But she was so small."

"Yes, she was...is. She used my weight and height against me. I don't expect one as tiny as you to take on an Etterian male, but remember, you're not helpless."

Aala splayed out her hands. "I am not Nancy, Jack, what could I do?"

Jack closed her eyes at the thought of Aala in danger. The cold fury seizing her stomach wanted to kill, to end anyone foolish enough to hurt a girl. "You can run and hide. If things get bad, that's what we need you to do. You do this for me, for your father, and when he's better, I will show you how Nancy did it."

"Promise?"

Jack changed the topic, hoping it would help keep her tears at bay. "Do you want to hear about elephants again?"

"Please." Aala bounced on Jack's lap with too much energy.

Jack spread her legs, hoping to settle Aala's boney ass anywhere but on her thighs. "Not sharks?"

"No, I know enough about sharks to never swim in your oceans." Aala shook her head, tossing her hair wild.

Jack gathered the masses and stroked them into obedience. "And your omeika aren't scary?" she teased, recalling Aala's description of carnivorous fish that were dangerous to catch, prepare, or eat since they had razor-sharp teeth and toxins tainted its flesh when it died. Similar to Earth's piranhas except humans didn't eat piranhas as far as she knew.

The sight of three Yithians striding along the wide passage stiffened Jack's shoulders. She rose to her feet, taking Aala with her. With a nudge, she tucked Aala behind her. The gate opened, and the three sharks charged Teric, who had struggled to his feet, his face pale and gleaming from perspiration. They punched him in the stomach, and he fell to his knees with a groan.

One of the bastards laughed and produced a wicked-looking knife. Jack screamed and lunged forward, to do what she knew not. She imagined the worst, Teric stabbed right in front of Aala. She wouldn't let that happen. When one shark swung his arm, Jack flew back, hitting the metal bars with a sickening thump before she slumped to the floor. She struggled to her knees, but the pain was excruciating, tearing through her, snatching her ability to breathe.

"No." Teric's voice held anger and desperation.

It pierced the ringing in Jack's ears. She rolled onto her knees again, willing her body to respond. With a pain-filled whimper, she snuck a glance. Teric's fishtail braid landed in the sand within her line of vision. The sharks then snatched a cowering Aala from the corner. Teric cried out, stumbling forward to stop them, but a shark kicked him in the face, dropping him to the floor. Hoping he was fine, Jack studied his prone body, silently begging him to rise. But when he remained down, she screamed and tried to claw her way to Aala. She could do nothing but watch as they latched a collar around her neck. It clicked closed with a finality that echoed through Jack's mind.

When a red light flashed on the collar, its purpose became clear. Pain cinched her chest, and spots circled her tear-filled eyes. She gasped and fought for air with her hand outstretched.

"What the hell do you think you're doing? She's but a child. You take that thing off her this instant." Gathering the last of her strength, and with every muscle in her body screaming in agony, she clambered to her feet. She lunge-staggered at the nearest shark. He swung his arm and struck her again. Flying back, she hit the bars a second time. She crumpled to the floor, and this time didn't have the strength to move. Lying in the cloying hot sand, she allowed the tears to fall as her energy drained from her.

"Jack?"

Jack stirred at a childlike voice in the far-off distance. Fire burned along her back. Her chest throbbed, but greater than these was the darkness welling in her soul. Something terrible had happened. Something to do with...Aala. Aala needed her. She shifted toward the small voice, determination casting fearful whisperings aside until she broke through the seductive warmth of sleep.

"What is it, Aala, sweetheart?" she mumbled.

"Are you in pain?"

Jack blinked awake to look at the girl leaning over her with concern darkening her eyes.

"I'm fine...." Jack gasped as the pain ripped through her. "Okay, maybe not so fine." She tried to sit up, embedding her fingers in the dark sand, using it as leverage since her trembling limbs couldn't manage on their own.

"They brought water. Would you like some?"

Jack pinched her lips against the moan threatening to escape her. "Yes, please." She accepted the offered packet, draining it before raising her gaze at Teric. "Teric, how are you—?"

"I am fine, Jack."

But he wasn't. He pinched his lips like she was doing which meant hers were as pale. "It is just hair..."

Judging by the way he reverently held his shorn braid in his hands, it wasn't. His hair fell below his shoulders and swirled around him in agitation. It too wasn't happy. Did it hurt when they were cut? She shuddered at the thought of squealing, squirming strands of hair. But his braid lay there lifeless.

"Will it grow back?" Jack asked, not knowing anything about Etterian physiology and whether losing one's hair was permanent.

"It is not the loss of the hair, but what it symbolizes. We earn the right to wear our hair long based on our performance in battle and in service. To lose one's honor will cost a foot of hair, for each offense. It is thus a visible indication of one's honor."

Jack gaped, now understanding his despondent shoulders, the misery rolling off him. "The sharks know this, right?" She received the expected nod from Teric. "I'm so sorry, Teric." Sorrow welled in her throat misting her eyes. All he had done was protect his daughter, knowing it would cost him his honor. But he had done it anyway. "I'll cut my hair too."

"I as well, father," Aala assured him, rubbing his shoulder with her tiny hand.

"Let anyone dare question our honor...," Jack said, even as determination curled her fingers into fists.

Teric chuckled, but it wasn't a joyful sound. "Thank you, but no, I must face this alone."

Jack clenched her jaw. So it was honorable to bear a burden alone? She sighed. "Come here, Aala-sweetheart."

Aala crossed to sit next to her, her concern for Jack's injuries admirable. She tugged the child onto her lap—despite her back protesting the additional weight—and wrapped her arms around her little body.

"What's this thing around Aala's neck, Teric?" Jack didn't touch it. Who knew what a caress could do, if it had sensors, a self-destruct. She tightened her arms and rested her chin on Aala's shoulder.

"It is a slaver's collar and used to locate, stun, or...kill," he said the last word in a hoarse voice, drawing Jack's startled gaze.

Kill? As in remotely? "Can it be removed?"

Teric ran a reverent caress over his braid before meeting Jack's gaze. "Yes, with a specific tool or sheer strength."

Relief was a drenched warm blanket draping her shoulders. She smiled, grateful for the first bit of good news. "You can break it with your bare hands?"

"Yes, but they will simply put another one on her." He leaned his head on the metal bars. "They will use it to force us to comply with their wishes."

"What?" Jack's eyes widened. The action wrenched her swollen eye, and she clenched her jaw to swallow the yelp.

"We fight tomorrow," Teric said with a finality that sent chills down her spine to churn her stomach.

Fight? Having her worst fears confirmed, she hugged Aala closer. Jack opened her mouth to ask him more questions but judging by his mulish expression, he would speak no more of it. He turned away from her, his braid still clasped within a tight fist.

Chapter Sixteen

"Come," the lisped words startled Jack awake. She groaned as she sat up to stare at the Yithian who waited at the opened gate to their cell. "The child stays," the bastard lisped, and Teric growled at him in warning. "If you wish for your contender to kill her then take her with you."

Teric jerked back at the suggestion, his shoulders slumped, and he knelt before Aala, despite the pain twisting his lips.

"No, Father, I want to come with you." She scrambled up to throw her arms around Teric, tears slipping free.

"Please, for me, *ensa*. Stay here where it is safe." He waited until she nodded. But she clung to his forearms to stop him from leaving. He untangled himself then stumbled back.

"Keep Jack safe." She wiped her cheeks and wrapped her arms around her thin body.

"We'll keep each other safe and be back before you can miss us." It wasn't a promise Jack had any control over, but she made it anyway.

The sharks led them along a broad passage with occupied cells on either side. She didn't pause to peer into the cells despite the curiosity to do so. Most were humanoid to some capacity, and if she survived this, she could gaze upon them to her heart's content.

They approached a gated entrance; the sunlight streaming in was blinding. Excited crowds cheered from beyond the gate that had to open onto the arena. She pinched herself in the hopes of waking from this nightmare.

"Choose your weapon." The shark indicated a shelf to the side, and Jack leaned closer, relieved to see human handguns of various sizes and shapes, all antiques. "If you kill a Yithian with any of these weapons, the child dies."

She lifted a Smith & Wesson and faced the shark. "Where's the ammunition? I can't use these without bullets."

"These are not suitable?" the shark lisped, his dark eyes widening.

She reviewed each weapon, checking the magazines for ammunition. Most had blanks, and only one had bullets, the Glock 26 Gen 3. The 9mm rounds would have to do, but she doubted their efficacy against alien creatures.

"What about these?" The shark gestured to the guns loaded with blanks.

She picked it up and fired at the wall, startling the unsuspecting Yithian. He withdrew his blaster and held it on her, a yellow light flickering.

"See? Blanks." She brushed her hand over the wall which showed no new indents.

"And the one in your other hand?" He lowered his blaster but didn't holster it.

"This one has real ammunition with only seven rounds. That might be enough for one match."

"Do I get a weapon?" Teric demanded.

The shark wheeze-coughed in his version of a laugh. "Weapons cost tokens, warrior."

Teric growled. "It is dishonorable to arm a female but—"

"We are arming her as validation for the cost of finding her." And with this, the shark abandoned them at the gate.

"Here, take this one." She shoved a Beretta Nano in Teric's large hand hoping his finger would fit in the trigger guard. "I'll give you some of my bullets; at least you won't be unarmed."

Teric stared at the weapon dwarfed by his hand. "No, I do not know how to use this. You do. I will use my hands." He placed the gun on the shelf.

A glance at the door stuttered her heartbeat. "I'm...scared." She rolled her top lip, keeping her gaze off Teric, lest she broke down and cried.

She systematically disassembled the Glock in her hands, trying to keep her mind focused on the moment, hoping to keep her tears at bay. She checked each piece before reassembling it.

Teric placed a hand over the gun, stalling her repetitive movements.

"We will survive this, Jack, I vow." His words were earnest, his voice filled with determination and a strength she gravitated toward.

"I just wish Ulriq would get here already," she said in a timid voice.

"The *Kushin* will be traveling at maximum speed, and even so, it will be approximately two days behind us."

"So, any day now is what you're saying." She flashed a tremulous smile, his lips twitched but an answering smile didn't fully form. "That's right; don't smile. I might die from the shock."

"You are being silly," he chuckled as his lips curled into a grin, revealing two adorable dimples.

"Be still my heart." Laughing warmed her chest, as if they weren't in a dire situation.

The gate swung open stripping the humor from her, replacing it the invincible flush of fear and adrenaline.

"Ready?" she whispered to Teric who nodded.

They marched to the center of the arena, amid praise and condemnation from the crowds. So many faces, alien races, colorful garments, and skin tones cheered. Their excitement reverberated off the walls and transparent domed ceiling. Rows upon rows of seating tiered outward and up three levels of black stone. Massive holographic screens hung from the top of the arena, beneath white perforated metal sheets in elongated triangles. The images flickered, alternating between her and Teric. Her bruised faced was the size of a house. She winced, then ducked her head when the image mimicked her. Gates lined the base of the arena, proving how far the dungeons went. How many were trapped in the bowels of this horrific place? How could the Etterians stand by and let this happen? Caged fighting was still underground for humans, but the authorities did try to stamp them out.

Two suns filled the sky. She raised her face to the sunlight and winced as it warmed her cheeks. No cool breeze blew. Nothing disturbed the sweltering heat shimmering off the black sand floor. She squared her shoulders and strode next to Teric. Whatever the sharks sent out to fight, they would face it together.

A wild roar ripped through her, sending fear skittering across her nerve endings. It sounded like an angry panther. If not pissed-off, then a hungry one. A terrifying rumble vibrated through the arena as whatever the creature was snarled.

"Alodon's hell," Teric groaned, drawing her attention. "It is a sogair."

A dirty burgundy six-legged creature sprinted into the arena, snarling and hissing. When it flashed its razor-sharp teeth, she swallowed a yelp. Fear spiked, threatening to choke her. Her limbs trembled with the compulsion to flee.

"How do we kill it, Teric?" She fixed her gaze on the creature while raising her Glock.

It looked like a panther, except it was the color of old blood and about the size of her solarcycle. Her hand gripping the Glock shook, forcing her to use both hands to steady her aim. A snarl behind her had her spinning to find another sogair prowling toward her.

"Two?" Teric bellowed, shaking his fist at the sky. He pressed his back against hers in a defensive stance. "I'll kill one, you kill the other. And do it quickly."

"What do I shoot at?" Desperation squeaked her voice.

The sogairs circled them, predatorial in their efficient movements, their gazes unflinching. Tension rippled along their muscles, fury in their snarls and rumbles. Nothing in her training had prepared her for this. Take down an armed man? Sure. Tackle a mugger? No problem. Kill a spitting cat? No way. She didn't know its weaknesses, and by the looks of its teeth and claws, it didn't have any.

"Teric?" She didn't dare dart her gaze away.

"Their eyes." He launched himself at the closest sogair. They went down in a snarling mess. For a nanosecond, she blinked at a man wrestling an alien tiger like it was something out of the ancient entertainment vids—Spartacus?

She sucked in a shuddering breath and raised her gun to shoot at the cat-like creature. But when she hit it in a shoulder, it shrugged it off. Her face flushed then chilled. She dived out of the way as it lunged at her. Claws scraped across her thigh, drawing a scream. Fire burned, like gun shots and cracked ribs combined. Rolling across the sand, she leaped to her feet and stamped her wounded leg, checking its usability. Not that she could check the severity, just pray its claws hadn't nicked an artery. She faced the creature charging toward her—its imminent attack more urgent.

Palming the Glock, she raised it.

Calm the eff down, Jack. Focus.

She took careful aim, using her good eye, and let the noise, the bright sunlight fade into the background, then drew in a deep breath before releasing it slowly. As the creature launched itself into the air, she fired. Time slowed. She stumbled back, her knee caving, sprawling her in the dirt.

The sogair landed on top of her, crushing her under its massive weight. Flicking her face to the side, she squeezed her eyes shut and waited for the burn of claws to dig into her flesh.

But it remained still. She peeked, then poked it with the gun's barrel. She'd killed it. Relief drenched her with heat melting her bones where she lay. Not that its death helped her in her current state. No wiggle, no shove, and no hip thrusts loosened the beast. She was pinned.

Winded, she gasped for air, her back screaming in agony. Regardless of what new injuries she had received or what her old ones had to say about the situation, foremost was her inability to breathe.

Teric's face appeared over the head of the dead sogair.

She opened and closed her mouth, unable to ask for help. Tears pressed against the backs of her eyes when he disappeared from view. Then the sogair was off her. She sucked in air, her chest burning from the lack of oxygen. The spots in her vision cleared, revealing the almost white skies of Yithia.

"Are you well, Jack?" Teric collapsed to his knees beside her, clasping his shoulder. Blood trickled from a wound to drip onto the black sand. This near to each other, they didn't need to yell.

"Me?" She groaned as she struggled to sit up. "I didn't take on a sogair with my bare hands."

She studied Teric's kill, its neck bloodied and torn where he'd ripped the creature's throat out. The crowd was going berserk, but neither paid attention to it.

"Now what? Does this buy us another day? Or will they release more creatures?"

He shrugged with his good shoulder, communicating with that slight gesture that no one knew what to expect from the Yithians. Unpredictability wasn't good.

"If they are done with us then we will have three days before the next arena."

"Let's hope they are done." She slumped. "I didn't enjoy killing these sogairs."

He patted her shoulder. "Is killing ever enjoyable?"

"If it's a Yithian, I just might like it," she whispered those words in case they were overheard. She didn't want to bring more retribution upon their heads or harm Aala.

"Agreed." Teric clambered to his feet, offering her a hand.

Grasping it, she let him hoist her to her feet, taking special care with her leg. It didn't matter. Jarring spurred on fresh agony. She bit her lip to smother a whimper.

"How bad is it?" Teric gestured to her shredded jeans and the crimson bloodstain.

"Can't say." While she limped to the exit, her throat tightening with each step, four armed Yithians ran into the arena. She tossed the Glock on the ground and followed them to their cell where Aala had better be waiting.

Chapter Seventeen

Planet, Yithia
Nearing the city of Mascroba

ULRIQ'S VISION FLOODED RED when the sogair landed on Jack. Everything within him stilled. His chest constricted, squeezing until pain filled his senses. His heart stopped beating, as it too waited, fearing the worst. The relief that flooded through him when Teric shoved the sogair off her was...indescribable. Every muscle in Ulriq's body relaxed, with heat rushing to his chilled extremities. He hated that he couldn't be there for her, that they hadn't arrived in time to prevent this.

Kanzo clasped his forearm, Eth to Eth. "Calm."

Ulriq drew in deep breaths, agreeing that he needed to control his emotions. He pressed his hand to Kanzo's shoulder. They were two hours from Mascroba, close enough to receive arena vids but not to port.

"She is wounded but alive," Der said into the quiet.

Ulriq didn't respond; his frown deepened when he glanced at Michel's pale face. They'd both seen how terrified Jack had been. Her expression was something Ulriq never wanted to see again. It tore through him, pierced his heart, his soul. The Yithians and sogair had hurt her. Her face was swollen with blue and purple bruises. Her thigh bore red scratches. He curled his fingers into fists, desperate to smash something—he was that enraged, frustrated...powerless. Etterian males didn't deal well with helplessness, especially him.

"Did you notice Teric's hair?" Der crowded Ulriq and lowered his voice.

"I did." Ulriq winced. "It changes nothing. I will have him bald for this."

"You have the right to demand justice, but as a supreme commander and an Eth…" Der offered a curt nod before crossing the comm room to scan Kanzo.

As a supreme commander? Ulriq scowled. Was he supposed to show Teric mercy when he'd endangered a Dar Eth to save an Etterian female? Was Jack's life less than Aala's?

"We will not be able to port into the dungeon. The dampening shields will prevent it," Prex said as he loaded a map onto the display vid. "I suggest we port near the outer wall of the dungeons." He indicated the landing point and the wall. "According to the structural layout, this is the weakest and most penetrable."

Ulriq analyzed the map, absorbed Prex's suggestions, then traced a finger along the path they would need to run. "This section will be without cover."

"So, we wait for the cover of darkness?" Michel arched a brow.

"No, Yithia has no darkness, not with three suns. The evenings are set by timers with most Yithians returning to the oceans," Ulriq said, though his focus wasn't on their conversation. His fingers had rested on the location of the arena dungeons, as if he could touch Jack through the map.

"What?" Michel gaped.

"The planet is three-quarters water. The majority of Yithians live underwater which is why Yithia cannot be targeted; our weaponry is unable to penetrate to those depths." Danic gestured to the map. "If we land here, we should make it to the wall without raising alarms. A large portion of this path is shadowed by structures."

"Yes, it is a sound plan. We are a small enough unit to slip in undetected. Have you managed to locate her yet, Prex?" Ulriq turned to his Data Officer who gave him a confident nod.

"Yes, hers and Teric's O.D.I. were activated and are in proximity to each other."

"How close a proximity?" Ulriq growled, the anger at the male's audacity still vibrated through him.

"They share a cell, northeast of the point of entry."

Ulriq's eyelids fluttered as his lips clenched. He would have to deal with Teric in front of his Jack, an action he hadn't wanted her to witness.

"This is good." Michel grinned, his spirits improved. "We can rescue them both."

"I do not need to rescue Teric. I care not if he lives or dies," Ulriq spat. Silence consumed the communications room. "Would you show leniency if Jack was your Dar

Eth?" He leveled his gaze on each of his males, challenging them to refute his right for retribution.

"His daughter may be with him."

Ulriq squeezed his eyes shut at Michel's reminder. A human male wouldn't understand the Ethera.

Only Michel would openly challenge Ulriq's authority. For that, he could do nothing since Michel wasn't a warrior and knew not the code nor the sacrifices Etterian males made.

"Switching to stealth mode," Prex said to the comm room in general.

"Time to prepare. Der, see to Michel's armor."

"Armor?" Michel squeaked with his eyebrow arching just as Jack's did.

Ulriq glanced away to ward off the memories. He needed her. His hands hadn't stopped shaking since they'd left the *Kushin*. The Ethera wouldn't rest, and worst of all, wouldn't let him rest. What energy pulsed along his veins was his last, the dregs he could dredge from his core. He was beyond exhausted.

"You will wear the armor or will remain on board," he commanded.

"I thought we would be disguised," Michel said.

"What do you mean?" Danic faced him with interest.

"A unit of armed Etterians moving through a foreign city will draw attention. But drunken ambassadors might not." He paused. "They do allow ambassadors planetside, right?"

Danic nodded, despite gawking at him.

Michel rubbed his hands together. "Good. Ulriq and I will be ambassadors, you three will be the security detail."

"The what?" Sena asked from where he leaned against a bulkhead, sharpening a ser- rated Maloidian dagger.

"He means guards. Ambassadors often have them; Prince Citus does not, but that is his preference. It is a good plan, and we have time to perfect these disguises." Ulriq tried to smile but gave up on it. "Intoxicated wealthy ambassadors."

Within an hour, they were garbed in their disguises. Michel was barely recognizable. Ulriq's disguise didn't please him as it hindered his ability to battle. However, he un- derstood the necessity. The leather breeches were too tight as was the tunic. He didn't appreciate the gold thread woven into the garments but had to admit he did look the part.

The need to hold Jack was overpowering him, taking control of his senses. He twitched, wanting to teleport and locate her now. As they gathered in final preparation, he went through his weapons; blaster strapped to his thigh, confirmed, daggers in his footwear, confirmed, explosives, two in his back pocket, confirmed.

Kanzo stood beside him, checking his personal artillery. "May the Maker bless your mission, Ulriq."

"Yours too. I do not know what Supreme Commander Xan has planned, but if I had to infiltrate the royal seat in Mascroba, I would use brute force." Ulriq shared a small smile. "It is best you are in Xan's hands."

Kanzo nodded. "I too prefer action rather than subterfuge. Let us pray the Maker blesses us both."

"Set to port?" Prex faced the unit.

Ulriq grasped Warrior Danic's and Michel's shoulders, Danic clasped Medic Der's and Warrior Sena's shoulders since they needed to be touching for successful teleportation.

"Five to port." Ulriq didn't bother to hide the excitement in his voice.

They phased out of the ship and onto Yithia, re-forming within the shadow of a black stone building. He assumed a fighting stance, prepared for an attack should their arrival have been detected. No alarms sounded with the narrow path abandoned.

"Good so far." He fought the urge to whisper. Punching his O.D.I., he activated the location marker Prex had issued to the unit.

"Let us retrieve your Dar Eth, Ulriq." Der adjusted his breeches as if they were too tight.

"Dar Eth?" Michel blinked.

"I will explain later." Ulriq led the team from shade to shade until he reached the last building before an open stretch of dark paved stone. The dungeon's wall was across the courtyard. They were close.

Two Yithian soldiers mumbled as they patrolled the area, but had yet to step into his line of sight. He activated the language protocol for Yithian and listened in as he paused beside Michel to activate his O.D.I. as well.

"Yeltz, you are an idiot to listen to your female. What does she know, after all?"

Ulriq almost laughed hearing this; even Yithians had female trouble.

Yeltz grunted in response. Two new Yithian soldiers came through a stone archway and greeted Yeltz and his partner.

"Anything to report?"

"No, Captain," Yeltz responded.

Judging by his tone, he didn't respect his superior officer. Ulriq would prefer to incapacitate them now rather than deal with the patrol *and* the prison guards inside the dungeons. He spun to instruct his unit to move forward, to draw the attention of the four soldiers, and to do it as swiftly as possible. However, running toward them would bring them within firing range and allow them sufficient time to sound the alarm.

Michel bumped Ulriq's arm and grinned. "Remember, I'm the ambassador." He laughed, too loud and boisterous. "Oh, Ambassador Jax, I like your sense of humor, indeed I do." The male then burped before stumbling over his own feet.

Ulriq gaped at him, then sliced glances between the patrol and Michel. He rested his fingers on his blaster, waiting for the cry of alarm to pierce the air. What in Alodon's hell was he doing?

"What was in that schtuff, anyway? I think you're tryin' to...." Michel oomphed as he hit the ground before giggling like a female. While sprawled on the dark paving, he glared at Ulriq before he 'laughingly' attempted to stagger to his feet.

Ulriq sighed and plastered on a fake smile. "Ambassador Mylor, it is you trying to deceive me." He slurred his words, mimicking Michel's speech patterns. Barking a laugh, he tripped as he assisted Michel off the ground. Ulriq 'fell' over his feet and landed on his back. He lay there 'laughing,' wondering how he managed to get himself into these situations and whether he was performing the mannerisms correctly. It had been years since he'd consumed a large enough quantity of alcohol to become intoxicated. And most symptoms lasted but a few minutes.

"What is this?" a Yithian soldier demanded.

Ulriq recognized the captain's voice.

"Oh ho. Jax, I think we have a new fwend." Michel made another strange sound before 'staggering' to his feet. "Humans share, an' I have jus' the schtuff." He whipped a bottle of golden-brown liquid out of his coat and took a deep drink from it. "Damn. This's issh good. Maybe I shouldn't share?"

Ulriq accepted the bottle Michel offered and drank deeply. He couldn't pretend with the Yithians so close to them. Then the scent of the liquid rose to greet him. It tasted incredible, dark, smooth, smoky, and sweet as it burned a fiery path to his belly.

"Explain yourself," the Yithian commanded.

"Be calm," Ulriq 'chuckled' from his position on the ground before he too 'stumbled' to his feet. While they kept the Yithians focused on them, Danic, Der, and Sena shifted into position, in silence.

"Goin' to a tavern, don'cha know?" Michel drew the captain's attention with an authoritative tone of voice. Then ruined it by 'hiccupping.'

"Tavern?" Ulriq asked before the captain could.

"A place to drink away your sorrows, and as Ambassador, I have many sorrows," Michel slurred and swayed on his feet, 'accidentally' nudging the Yithian away from him.

Said Yithian jerked back as three blasters fired on the soldiers, taking them by surprise. They were dead before their bodies hit the ground. Danic, Der, and Sena dragged the bodies into the shadows as Ulriq faced Michel.

"What is this?" He held the bottle to his nose to inhale before taking another deep pull.

"Cognac; it's Jack's favorite." Michel grinned as he gestured to the dead captain at his feet. "Want to help me move him?"

Ulriq grunted, capped the bottle before stuffing it into his coat pocket. Tugging the body into the shadows, he ignored Michel's attempts to assist. Tossing the corpse's legs down, Ulriq bolted to the target wall, eager to get inside and find his life force. He placed the explosives on opposite corners and set the timer. Not stepping back, he flashed Michel a confident smirk.

"Sonic explosives." He grinned, his gaze fixed on the devices. "It vibrates at a high frequency and disintegrates any construction material between the two devices." A rumble rippled along the wall. The collapse of stone and mortar obscured the breach with black dust.

He didn't wait for the cloud to dissipate. The stench hit him first. Strong overpowering odors of many species in various stages of cleanliness danced colors before his eyes. He adjusted his scent sensitivity to allow his vision to clear before he strode in, firing on any Yithians who dared to cross his path.

"How will we get through the bars?" Michel scampered after him.

"Blue button on the blaster; fire at the locks." Ulriq tapped the button he was referring to.

"It demagnetizes the metal." Danic glanced into each cell they passed.

Michel did the same and frowned at the trapped souls. He fiddled with his blaster, his intentions clear.

"Halt, find Jack first." Ulriq jog-strode to the northern side of the dungeons. His O.D.I. buzzed up his arm as he neared her location. The excitement that burned through his body had his heart fluttering; he was close.

"Ulriq?" Her lyrical voice caressed his hypersensitive nerves.

He groaned and veered in her direction, ignoring his O.D.I. vibrating up his arm in a steady rhythm.

He found her. She stood in the center of a cell, yellow light bathing her. Never had he seen a more beautiful sight. Firing on the gate locks, he pushed them open as she launched herself at him. He rumbled his approval, wrapping his arms around her, crushing her to his chest.

"What took you so long, my Eth?"

"You know?" he asked, his voice gruff, his eyes widening. He buried his nose in her neck and tightened his arms. The Ethera eased its hold making him sigh with relief. "Danic, arrest Teric." Ulriq didn't turn to see if his command would be obeyed, knowing it would be.

"No." Jack tugged on Ulriq to let her go, but he refused to loosen his hold on her.

"Wait," Teric pleaded as Danic neared him. "Aala..."

"Damnit, Ulriq." Jack pummeled his arms, and he grudgingly released her. She stumbled when her feet touched the sandy floor before righting herself. Spinning to look at Aala and Teric, she asked, "Can you rip it off?"

Panic squeaked her voice as Teric lunged past Danic to reach his daughter. He gripped the collar and tugged, careful not to hurt her. It snapped under the force he applied, and he tossed it away from her. An ominous sizzle emanated from the collar where it landed on the sand.

Ulriq stared at it, recognizing it and the implications thereof. A glance at Teric summoned a curse. The male's hair was unbound and brushing his shoulders as in the arena vid. Never had Ulriq seen a male's hair that short. Alodon's hell. He scanned the cell searching for the discarded braid, then winced at the sight of it.

"Father?" Aala whispered as she raised her arms to him.

The male gingerly picked her up, gathering the female *damu* close. "Ulriq came, Aala," Teric rubbed his cheek across his daughter's temple.

"Jack's Eth?"

He nodded at her words then faced Ulriq and Danic. "You may arrest me now, Danic, but my daughter stays with me."

Danic glanced between Ulriq and Teric, concern etched on his features.

"Thank you for coming. Jack said you would." Aala smiled at Ulriq.

"She did?" A flash of unidentified warmth spread through Ulriq's chest.

"Is Mich here too?" The *damu* met his gaze unwaveringly.

"Yes, he is freeing prisoners with Medic Der," Danic huffed.

Ulriq kneeled to run his med gun over Jack's thigh, not liking the additional musky scent of blood. "If he frees prisoners and expects us to house them, porting to the scimitar is impossible. It does not have the capacity." Rising, he pocketed his med gun, laced his fingers through Jack's, then using their clasped hands, pulled her toward him. "Danic, locate a suitable hide-out while we await the arrival of the *Kushin*."

"We need to move now, Ulriq. They might discover the bodies at any time."

Ulriq settled his gaze on Jack. "Can you run?"

She stomped her foot and tried to hide the pain pinching her lips.

He scooped her into his arms, then darted for the crumbled wall. Cries from deeper into the dungeons added energy to his legs. The freed prisoners crowded them, eager to leave as well. He shoved through them. "Danic, lead the prisoners out."

"Ulriq? Will Teric be punished?" Jack asked.

The fear in her eyes lanced his chest, squeezing his lungs. "We can discuss it later. Let me breathe freely now that I have found you."

Michel ran out of a cell to hug her as best he could with Ulriq still holding her against him.

"You stink." Michel stepped back, his nose crinkling.

"I missed you too, Mich," she chuckled. "And if they ever kidnap me again, I'll demand a cell with an en-suite bathroom."

As Ulriq stepped through the hole in the wall into the open sunlight, she lifted her face to the suns' rays. Her mouth curled into a beautiful smile, contentment in her hand stroking his shoulder.

"Freedom feels so good." She squinted to meet his gaze. "But it feels even better being here with you."

"I am pleased to have found you, Jack." He jogged to the nearest shade, needing them to be free of Mascroba and Jack secure without the threat of a Yithian retribution.

"What did you ask for that got you the black eye?" Michel gasped, bending over to grip his knees.

"Teric, so I could kick his ass. But they gave me Aala instead."

"I found an abandoned mine, but it is quite a distance. We need to move faster; I do not like the eerie silence." Danic jogged up to them before scanning their surroundings. The buildings looked empty, the narrow paths bare of Yithians and guards.

The prisoners trickled into the sunlight, some limping, others more mobile. Those able to help, did so. Behind them, Yithian arena guards appeared, firing indiscriminately into the crowd. Ulriq's team took them down. Der hurried to help the wounded. But the appearance of Yithians had spurred panic. The prisoners no longer strolled from the dungeon but sprinted toward Ulriq.

"How many prisoners are there?" He rubbed his chin across the crown of Jack's head.

"There was twenty-two." Michel frowned at the few bodies beyond Der's ability to heal.

Ulriq focused on the shimmering-white blips in the distance. He grimaced. Kill-drones. They were grazing kreso out in the open. "We need to move now. Split the prisoners into four controllable groups, a group for each of you to lead."

"Me as well?" Michel's eyes widened, reflecting his shock.

"You are the reason they are free, so yes." Ulriq looked at him pointedly.

"What will you do?"

Ulriq sighed, trying to remember that Michel wasn't Etterian. "I am taking Jack to the scimitar."

"What?" Michel squeaked.

Ulriq smiled, with Jack in his arms, his tolerance was restored. "I need to communicate with the *Kushin* on a secure comm."

"As long as you come back." Michel jogged ahead to confer with the other males in the unit.

"He can be trying." Jack squeezed Ulriq's shoulder. He nodded but didn't comment. "Would the scimitar have a cleansing room?"

"Yes, it does." He chuckled as he admired her upturned face.

"Then we'd better hurry."

Chapter Eighteen

Planet, Yithia
Abandoned mine
Mascroba outskirts

"I still cannot comm Prex, Ulriq." Danic snuck a glance at Jack. "We cannot port to the scimitar yet."

The prisoners settled within the dark enclosed spaces of an abandoned mine Danic had discovered. Maloidian males in pale yellow and black markings gathered to one side. Two Kulaian males glowed with their silver skin. One nursed his ribs. A few were unknown species sure to excite Prex. Among the prisoners were no other Etterians or humans. A few Yithians leaned against the rough-hewn walls, others sat where they'd stopped. Cringing as they gawked at Ulriq in gratitude, he glanced at Danic, relieved at the distraction.

"The rock must be blocking the signal. Der, extract a sample of it; we will have our males analyze it. Danic, take Sena and find a suitable porting site. Take care. I spotted kill-drones on our tails." With several gazes on him, Ulriq lowered his voice. "Should you reach Prex, give him the status, and await his response." Many souls were now reliant on Ulriq for salvation. He sighed. "We need to know how long before the *Kushin* arrives. If we remain on Yithia longer than a day, we will need a food source more than firepower."

"The dungeon guards should have sounded an alarm," Sena said. "I've set guards at the mine's entrances as instructed."

Ulriq searched for Michel, but his gaze switched to Jack. A familiar warmth flooded his chest when she laughed at something her brother said. Der scanned her with his med-gun while she chatted, often including Der in the conversation. Her pants clung to her legs, and the meager light caressed her taut backside. Her dirty hair hung limply down her back. Had they been able to port, her bright-yellow locks would once more tempt Ulriq to bury his fingers in the silken mass. But none of that mattered. Her laughter cut through the drone of whispered conversations and jolted his heart. Maker. He trembled with the urge to stride across, toss her over his shoulder, and take her somewhere private.

Ulriq gestured to the entrance, indicating they should commence with their mission. Danic hesitated, shifting from foot to foot. Eager to reach Jack, Ulriq struggled to still the energy burning through his veins. He leveled his gaze on the male, arching a brow to encourage him to speak.

"The mine flooded and jeopardized the structural integrity. I suspect the Yithians abandoned it for this reason. Sufficient drinking is available. I have asked Der to tend to the captives' thirst as well." The male squared his shoulders before continuing, "Sena spotted strikers. I suggest you arm Jack. I should return within two hours to report."

Ulriq stared after him. While Danic and Sena searched for a highpoint, Michel and Der would guard one entrance, and himself and Jack the other. Ulriq settled his gaze on Teric, sitting aside with Aala.

"Der, give Teric your blaster. Tend to the prisoners." Ulriq shoved the bottle of cognac into his hands. "Teric, guard the bigger entrance with Michel. Jack and I will take the rear."

Der frowned, lifting his gaze from the bottle. "The kill-drones?"

Ulriq nodded. "And strikers." He marched to Jack, needing to instruct Michel but took the time to admire her. "Michel, please guard the entrance with Teric." Ulriq clasped Jack's elbow, aching to touch her. "The Yithians should have sounded the alarm—"

Michel jogged off.

Ulriq frowned, staring after the strange male. What did he say wrong?

"Relax, Ulriq, it's me," Jack placed her fingers on his arm, drawing his attention more than her words did. "He storms off when I'm winning an argument."

Ulriq twitched. "You were arguing?" Needing to hurry, he gathered her hand in his and led her toward the back of the mine.

"About Taylor." Jack squeezed his fingers. "Why the frown?" Slipping an arm around his waist, she leaned in to press the side of her body to his.

"I wanted you safe." He stiffened, then willed his body to relax, to gather her into an embrace, and pin her to him. "Your brother did the honorable thing..."

"You just wish we could be alone?" Her breath feathered across his shoulder making him shiver. "How did you find us?"

When they neared the narrow mine entrance, he halted. He pressed his cheek to the crown of her head. "We analyzed the temirian, pointing to who took you. In addition, Teric left a message explaining his involvement and your location. We used a faster ship to reach Mascroba while the *Kushin* trailed. En route, we monitored the traffic and the arena vids." Ulriq recalled the battle match where he'd believed he'd lost his life force. His eyes closed as he attempted to contain the sharp pain at the memory.

"You saw Teric fight for us?"

"You should not have been in that situation in the first place," Ulriq growled, his self-directed fury too near the surface. He couldn't tamp down the anger that graveled his voice, nor lower the volume. The memory of his helplessness haunted him. Pressing his temple to hers, he fought for calm and opted for a change in subject. More for his peace of mind than for any other reason. "We need to guard this entrance."

"Why?" She frowned when he held her back to peek outside.

A blast sprayed chips of rock. He jerked away, slipping into the cool darkness just as a drone lowered itself in front of him. In white and shaped like an Etterian eye, its soulless dilating pupil and twin mini-chokaars stiffened his spine. He dove, snatching Jack out of the line of fire. When he touched her, he spun to land on his back, taking the brunt of it.

"What the—?"

"Kill-drones." He held his finger to her lips and inched them deeper into an alcove.

A grating preceded a crash, grind, whir as the drone tried to squeeze through the gap. With a whine, it darted away. He slumped.

"The Yithians know where we are." Jack rested her temple on his chest.

"Yes, and we are, for the most part, unarmed." He frowned. "Communication has been unsuccessful."

"I knew you would come for me."

He stilled, running his hand up her back. "You believed in me?"

"Yes, I knew here..." She tapped above his left nipple.

He smothered a grin, not wishing to take the time to explain that his heart was in the center of his chest. It was her words he needed to focus on. He rolled over, pinning her beneath him. With his hand under her head, he spared her from the rocky floor. Maker. He ached to kiss her.

Instead, he pushed off her to peek through the entrance again. Up high, four strikers hovered, shimmering in an ominous dark green. Jack grabbed his hips, as if to yank him inside. She leaned around him to blink at the streamline attack crafts similar to Etterian kites.

"What weaponry is on those?"

"Limited short blasts."

She scowled. "Explosive, laser, air, sonic?"

He grinned. "Air."

Drones darted across the opening, and he stepped back, forcing her to do the same. She tightened her grip on his hips. His chest swelled. He captured her fingers and tugged until her arms circled him from behind. "It cannot penetrate this rock nor can we wait here indefinitely."

"So no bath for a while." She sighed. "It's silly, I know. You came for me. I'm free. I just..." She sniffed. "Sorry, Ulriq. It's been quite an adventure."

He spun to hug her, crushing her body against him. "A cleanse will have to wait. What if you wore my tunic?"

She shook her head. "It's fine. We have more urgent things to worry about."

He leaned back to slip off his coat. Shoving it at her, he waited for her to take it before he peeled off the tunic. She watched, her eyes widening, her mouth parting for the swipe of her tongue across her bottom lip. Her heartbeat leaped. He smirked as he slid on his coat.

She did the same, offering his tunic to hold while she stripped off her vest. His gaze snagged on her breasts straining the delicate beige garment. He frowned when his tunic covered her.

She sniffed his tunic and smiled. "You smell good."

His breath caught. He curled his arm around her, yanking her against him. As he dipped his head to steal a kiss, a shriek-boom preceded a wave of light and heat, engulfing him. He spun, tucked Jack into his arms and shielded her with his body.

The shrieks of fired chokaars pierced the air. Four consecutive explosions followed.

He grinned and dared to peek outside. Six asteri peju hovered, their silver droplet shells glimmering in the bright Yithian sunlight. "Jack, we are going home."

"Ulriq?" Amusement in her voice drew his focus.

"I assumed you needed rescuing. I was incorrect." The young authoritative voice summoned Ulriq's grin.

He pulled Jack closer to him. "Prince Vytus, this is a surprise."

"I should hope so. Almost broke the *Phoenix* to reach you." The young male flashed a smirk at Jack, his gaze appraising her form.

Ulriq's hold tightened around her waist. He growled a warning at the prince.

Vytus dismissed him with a flick of a hand. "Malo is with me." He punched his O.D.I. and glanced at Ulriq again. "Danic and Sena reached Prex and brought the sample rock to him. Alodon's balls, Ulriq, Prex is truly an asset. That male realized the porting frequency must be altered to be successful." Vytus strolled across to them and placed a hand on Ulriq's shoulder. "Three to port."

"Wait," Jack yelped, but it was too late. "Damnit," she growled at Vytus, her lack of respect not alarming Ulriq as it should have. He was curious to see how the prince would handle his strong-willed Jack. "I needed to make sure my brother, Aala, and Teric are fine. But no. You willy-nilly fade me without my permission again."

"They are onboard. You were the last to port." Vytus grinned, not fazed by a human female's attitude.

Ulriq narrowed his eyes, his curiosity peaked for another reason. Jack must not be Vytus's first human female.

"Oh, sorry. You could have led with that." Pink stained Jack's cheeks.

Ulriq chuckled and using their clasped hands, tugged her to the door. "Thank you, my prince. Status on Kanzo?"

"Successful, Supreme Commander." Vytus beamed. "My father played a crucial role."

"A tale I wish to hear." Ulriq offered the prince a curt nod then addressed Nerx, awaiting his attention. "Status of the prisoners?"

Nerx gestured to the rows of prisoners eager to use the bay's replicator and rehydrator. "Prex is documenting each prisoner's history."

"Good, assign them an unused barracks, task Security to guard them. Have each prisoner delivered home. Where is Michel?"

"Once he handed over the prisoners, he bolted for his quarters." Nerx pursed his lips. "Teric?"

Jack stilled and raised her gaze to meet Ulriq's.

He cupped her cheek and rubbed his thumb across it, smudging a black streak of sand across her paler skin. "Find out the exact details that led to his...*adventure*."

Nerx arched a brow.

"All will be revealed in due course." With one last pointed look at Nerx, Ulriq rushed Jack down a passage.

"Ulriq, where are we going?" She ran behind him.

"To see your girls, of course. The quicker we do so, the quicker I can monopolize your time."

"You want to see more of me?" The shock in her voice had him growling in response.

He faced her. She slammed into his chest. Using this to his advantage, he snaked an arm around her to pin her against him.

"I want to see you all the time." His voice lowered as his gaze locked on hers under the dim lighting of the passage. "It is the Ethera, Jack."

"Oh, I didn't know what to expect." She twirled a pattern on his skin under his collarbone. "I hoped our...union would be one where affection and love comes later."

"Jack..." He closed his eyes for a second. "The Ethera starts the attraction with an addiction forming on its own."

"Addiction?" Alarm widened her eyes.

"Yes, I will become addicted to you, to everything about you."

"Wow," she gasped. "Just...wow. Will I become addicted to you?"

"I do not know. Were you an Etterian female, then yes."

"I hope I do." At her revelation, a growing tightness in his chest squeezed the air out of his lungs. "Maybe I am already. I like this..." She gestured to his chest, to being this close to him, held in his arms. "I like your cologne too. But it's elusive. No matter how much air I suck in, it's never enough to fill my lungs, to satisfy."

Pleased at her words, he grinned. "I feel the same." He tilted his head to listen to the staccato of her heart.

Surprise and delight consumed her adored face, warming her eyes.

"Come, I made a vow to your girls. By now, they must know you have arrived." He lowered her down his body, letting her feel all his edges, specifically his Fuyra-hard malehood. Her mouth parted, the pink depths tempting him to lean in and taste her. And to Alodon's hell with visiting the girls.

"Let's hurry then," she rasped.

He couldn't agree more.

CHAPTER NINETEEN

Etterian battleship, Phoenix
Speeding away from Yithia, hopefully in stealth mode
The Comms Room

CLASPED TO ULRIQ'S SIDE, they strode toward an awaiting man. Jack studied his features. In order to tell them apart, she had to pay attention to their details. He was taller than Ulriq by at least two inches. The defined edges of his face was further enhanced by a square jaw. His long, narrow nose softened his angles and wide oversized bottom lip. His round dark-blue eyes under dark slashing eyebrows added to his intimidation factor. If Jack had stumbled into him in a dark alley, she would have run.

"Supreme Commander Xan, thank you for the assistance," Ulriq greeted the taller Etterian.

"Ulriq." Xan clasped Ulriq's forearm and his shoulder. He stared into Ulriq's eyes. It almost looked romantic, like Xan was leaning in for a kiss. Jack smothered a chuckle. "It is true." His gaze darted to Jack, leveling his intense stare on her. She struggled to not twitch under his scrutiny, to not tug on the hem of Ulriq's tunic despite it engulfing her. "She is your Dar Eth?"

Heat flooded her face, and she fought the urge to hide behind Ulriq. Who was she kidding? Any excuse to snuggle against his hard body.

"Jack, this is Xan, my battle-bond." Ulriq bestowed a dazzling smile upon her.

For a moment she stood there, blinking at him like an idiot. Her ears tingled, and she thrust out her hand at Xan. The poor male stared at it. So, she tugged on his hand, which he allowed her to do, grasped his massive mitt in hers, and shook it. She dropped it after two shakes, but he reached for her hand again. It was dwarfed in his. He lifted his other hand and stroked the skin over her knuckles.

"Soft," he said, his expression relaxing.

"You do realize you are touching my Dar Eth, Xan?" Ulriq teased.

Startled, Xan dropped her hand, and his face darkened in a blush.

Jack took pity on him. "We're all *soft*, Supreme Commander."

"Why are you so strangely colored?" He gestured to her curls. "Lady Ava has black hair and green eyes. Are you not of the same species?"

"Ava? How is she? You found her?" At Xan's nod, Jack squealed and faced Ulriq. She threw her arms around him, squeezing him as she choked back her tears. Her emotions bubbled up her throat, and she arched her back to laugh.

Ulriq rumbled as he ran his hand up and down her back. "It is called a hug, Xan."

This drew Jack back to reality. She grinned, reluctantly unwinding her arms. A different warmth poured over her when she lingered on his bare chest. "Where is she now? Is she here?" She twisted to face Xan while trying to hide her flushed cheeks. It was a futile exercise.

"She is with her Eth. They will be transported to the *Kushin*." Xan's gaze traveled over Jack's face.

"Eth? When did that happen?" She gaped then grinned. "Kanzo?"

Xan scowled, his intimidation factor returned. Though, why his demeanor had changed, she didn't know. "Yes, he is her Eth. Lady Jack, you did not respond to my question; are you and Lady Ava not both human?"

"Yes, they are." Ulriq captured one of Jack's grimy curls, stroking his thumb across it. "Their colors vary greatly. Travel with us to the *Kushin* and meet her sisters."

Dazed at Ulriq's revelation, Xan gestured to a waiting shuttle.

Jack suppressed another chuckle. Hot damn, the poor man had no idea.

"Where is Malo?" Ulriq asked.

"He is on a comm with Prince Enyl," Xan said.

Jack searched for Michel but found Prince Vytus instead. He'd bent his head to whisper to Aala. Their intimate interaction arched her brow. Teric hovered beside them, resignation on his features. Jack relaxed; if Teric wasn't concerned, then she wouldn't be either.

"Why can't we teleport across?" she asked as Ulriq ushered her into the shuttle. She sat in the seat he indicated and let him strap her in, loving his caresses as his fingers rubbed across her hips, tightening the straps.

"Our shielding prevents it. If we were in safe space and not so close to Yithia, we would have lowered the shields for the time it would take to port."

"But Ava was taken from a shuttle, Ulriq."

He grimaced. "Kuta shielding has been upgraded since then. Unless a device like the one that ported you, a temirian, is used. Those are costly and rare." His brow furrowed, and he turned to Teric who'd stepped onto the shuttle. "Teric, the temirian? How could you afford such a device?"

"Another warrior provided it," Teric answered while watching Vytus buckle Aala into a seat.

Ulriq's eyes widened, then lowered into a glare. "More males are in your situation?" His stoic tone wasn't a good thing. A quiet, fuming fury rolled off him. Jack admired the narrowing of his eyes, the intense focus in his gaze, the stiffening of his battle-honed body, and sighed.

"Yes, and perhaps on every battleship?" Teric met Ulriq's gaze. "We underestimated the Yithians, Supreme Commander."

Ulriq slipped into a seat beside Jack, and activated his O.D.I. "I have tasked Nerx to document the details. Perhaps an operative should be included."

"What are you doing, Ulriq?" Jack pressed her shoulder to his to watch him tap on his holographic buttons.

"I am sending instructions to Prex to analyze all males on board the *Kushin*. Kemt from the *Phoenix* might as well do the same. I am also including Malo and Xan on the instruction."

"Are you at war with the Yithians?" She waited for him to finish sending his messages, then offered him her hand, palm facing upward.

Her heartbeat skipped when he didn't hesitate. He laced her fingers through his and brought their clasped hands to his lips for a kiss.

"No, we have a peace treaty with Yithia. This is unusual activity, but they are a dishonorable species."

Honor mattered. She got that. But it was also subjective. The Yithians had to have family they cared about. That had to be a universal value, right? "By your standards?"

He studied her face. "I can only measure against my own, Jack."

"Fair enough. I just can't fathom why they're targeting me or Ava."

"The buzz implies they do this for their arena. Perhaps humans are yet another species they wish to exploit."

Jack frowned. "Not good."

"I agree."

"I prefer this shuttle ride to the last one." She lowered her gaze to trail the column of his throat.

His angry expression melted into a heated one. "So do I." He grinned, revealing a dimple.

Mesmerized, she stared at it, longing to dip the tip of her tongue into the tiny indent.

"Do not look at me like that, Jack," he said, his voice hoarse.

Her blush confirmed where her thoughts had been. She looked anywhere but at Ulriq. Aala smiled at Vytus seated next to her.

"I can't believe he's royalty." Jack snuck a peek at Ulriq.

"He is but still young and untested."

She studied Vytus's physique, lanky and typical of a young man still to realize his full height. His face was softer somehow, his cheeks rounder. As the pilot maneuvered the shuttle smoothly out of the bay and into the vast expanse of space, she faced Ulriq.

She did like looking at him. "What happens now, my Eth?"

His hand squeezed hers convulsively. Well, that got a reaction. "We see your girls."

She gave him a pointed look.

He gave her one back before his expression altered to an eager one. "Then we will do whatever you want to do."

"I decide?" While allowing her gaze to travel to his lips, she licked hers in anticipation.

"Yes, wherever you go, I go." His bold words squeezed her heart.

He was her Eth. The full meaning of such a person descended upon her, and she raised her gaze to meet his. She studied his expression. An indescribable feeling, hot and electrifying, rushed through her. Utter conviction: that's what he portrayed. He believed they were meant for each other. And from this belief, he committed his life to hers, no fanfare and no drama.

CHAPTER TWENTY

Etterian battleship, Kushin
Speeding away from Mascroba, Yithia in stealth mode
The girls' shared quarters

ULRIQ STEPPED BACK AND leaned against the bulkhead, watching these females reunite with as much passion as they addressed everything else in their lives.

"Jack." Vicky threw herself at Jack and wrapped her arms around her. She had tears in her eyes calling forth a few from Jack, as well. There was crying, laughing, and incoherent words as Jack updated her on everything that had happened.

"What is that language they are speaking?" Xan stepped into the officer's quarters.

"Earth English," Ulriq said. "It has been added to the language protocols."

Xan activated his O.D.I. to select the language while his gaze strayed across the various shapes, sizes, and colors of the females in the room. Their emotional levels were high, manifesting on their animated faces, their mannerisms, and in the tone of their voices.

"Are they always this emotive?" Xan asked Ulriq.

Vicky, the tiniest female, approached them. Her proportions highlighted Ulriq's immense size.

"Thank you, Ulriq. You kept your word." Vicky swiped her tear-stained cheeks with one hand while her other rested on his forearm, squeezing it.

"Why is she touching you?" Xan asked in Etterian.

"They touch. It can be non-sexual." Ulriq switched to English to address her. "Lady Vicky, this is Supreme Commander Xan of the battleship *Phoenix*."

"Hello, Supreme Commander," she greeted him with a polite smile, offering her hand.

Ulriq grinned as Xan accepted Vicky's hand in his and held onto it. A sigh escaped his battle-bond's lips. Her hand was dwarfed in Xan's and would be as soft as Jack's. Vicky was wonderfully made judging by the size of her breasts and the flare of her hips. Warm, beautiful brown eyes locked onto Xan.

"Did you take part in Jack's rescue?" Her voice was melodic.

Xan stared at her upturned face, and Ulriq rumbled a laugh, nudging Xan with his elbow. "No, milady, I took part in Lady Ava's rescue."

"Ava's safe?" She gasped, and her brown eyes shimmered again. Xan glanced between Ulriq and her in alarm. "Is she here? Did you bring her?"

"She is en route with Warrior Kanzo," Xan said.

Vicky tugged on her hand, still engulfed in Xan's, and he dropped it. His cheeks darkened.

"Aaro kept you abreast of our progress. Do you have unanswered questions?" Ulriq opted to save Xan from his own awkwardness.

"He did a wonderful job." A bright smile splashed across her face.

"Do you still wish to return to Earth, milady?" At Ulriq's question, Jack gasped, drawing his attention. Her face paled, and her heartbeat leaped in alarm. Her hopeful gaze locked onto Vicky's face.

"Yes, please."

His Dar Eth's lips dipped; it pulled on his heart. He didn't like seeing her disappointed and wished he could carry her sorrow.

"Very well." He activated his O.D.I. and instructed Pilot Ksal to set a course for Earth. "It is done as soon as Kanzo's shuttle docks." He stepped away from the wall. "Please excuse us, miladies."

"Ulriq?" Jack's alarm warmed his chest as if she didn't want him to leave her. She rushed across to take his hand and keep him near. He liked the thought of it.

"I will collect you in a while, Jack. Stay with your girls." He crushed her to him and pressed a kiss to her temple.

"This evening meal is with me," he said in a commanding tone, and she grinned. With twitching fingers, he held her away from him and sidled toward the door. When it opened, Xan led the way and Ulriq forced himself to follow.

Before the door shut, Vicky whispered, "Holy crap, Jack, that was damn sexy."

The silence of the passage consumed Ulriq as he stared at the sealed door. The air felt colder somehow, now that he couldn't bask in the vibrant presence of his Dar Eth.

With a nudge from Xan, Ulriq dragged himself away.

Chapter Twenty-One

"I know. Be still my beating heart." Jack grinned. "Where's Taylor?"

"You ask? Like Mich didn't rush straight here to fetch her?" Vicky grinned. "It's about time the idiot realized how special she is." She finished with a dance. "But what I want to know is...when did that happen?" She gestured to the closed door, indicating Ulriq.

"Like I said, it started at the barbecue. You should have seen him stride into my cell. I have never been so happy to see anyone."

"Even Mich?" Vicky gaped.

"Yes, even Mich."

"I assume you're wearing Ulriq's shirt?" Vicky arched a brow. "Damn, an Etterian male in just pants..." She fanned her face as she blushed. "I'll save that for my spank bank."

"You better not." Jack rested her fists on her hips, wanting to pummel the idea out of Vicky's mind. Then Jack remembered what he looked like shirtless and sighed. "It's the sexiest thing I have ever seen," she chuckled. "I damn near had my way with him when he offered me his shirt."

"Would you like to shower and maybe eat something?" Vicky gestured to the 'kitchen.'

"Eat something, yes, change out of his shirt, no, not yet." Jack lifted the fabric to her nose to inhale deeply, capturing some of his sun-drenched cologne despite the stench of her unwashed body. Oh, he smelled so good.

"Addict," Vicky teased.

"I hope so." Jack bounded up to throw her arms around Vicky.

Her nose twitched. She broke free of the hug and skipped to the rehydrator. "So, did you find out why you were abducted?" She flicked her fingers over the black shiny surface.

Jack put distance between them. A bath would be wonderful, and perhaps, if she hurried, she could slip into Ulriq's shirt again. "Teric had to rescue his daughter, Aala."

Vicky froze, her finger hovering an inch above the glass, then her eyes darkened.

Jack smiled to show she had no hard feelings. Though, some of her Yithian encounters she could have done without. "Relax, we're friends now. He had to take me, don't you see? They'd stolen his daughter. I would have done the same if those bastards had my child."

"How old is she?" Vicky brought over a cup of chicken noodle soup.

Jack accepted it and paused to inhale the rich replicated aroma. It was almost as good as the real thing, and after all the bitter protein bars she'd eaten, it was downright decadent. "I'd say around eleven or twelve." She spooned soup into her mouth, moaning at the explosion of flavor across her tongue.

"Oh, my. She's just a child." Vicky slid into a comfy.

"You'll love her. She's the sweetest thing. And her mother didn't notify anyone that her daughter was missing. Well, I assume that's what happened." Jack forewent the spoon, slid it onto the table, and drank from the bowl.

"What?" Vicky slammed a fist into her open palm.

Jack gritted her teeth. "Just give me five minutes with the woman, and I'll treat her to a few Nancy moves."

"But Teric dotes on her. He's loving and patient. Hell, he even gave up his honor for her."

"How'd he do that?" Vicky gripped the edge of the chair between her thighs and swung her feet.

"Do you know how they measure their honor?" Jack placed the half-empty bowl on the table and leaned back to rub her achingly full belly. She'd fasted once, and the subsequent feast afterward had been torture. Pacing herself was wise.

Vicky shook her head.

"The length of their hair is a testimony to their battle accolades and service to Etteria. If they behave dishonorably, their hair is shortened." Jack frowned. "Teric knew taking me would cost him his honor, but he did it anyway. Then those Yithian bastards sliced it off and tossed him his braid as if it was worthless. I have never seen such a powerful man brought so low." She blinked tears away as she recalled his dejected shoulders and the way he'd reverently stroked his braid.

"Why didn't he fight them?" A tear trickled down Vicky's cheek, and she brushed it aside, her gaze riveted on Jack.

"He was badly injured, one punch to his side, and he went down. And they put an electric collar around Aala's neck. Any misbehavior from him or me, Aala would pay." Jack gripped her neck with her hands to mimic the collar.

Vicky stared at her stranglehold and paled. When the door chimed, she squeaked, jumping in the comfy. She granted access with a hoarse voice. The door opened to a familiar Etterian male.

Her voice croaked, so she cleared it before continuing, "Aaro, please come in."

"Greetings, miladies." The Etterian stepped in, a broad smile dimpling a cheek. The male was jovial, in contrast to most of the males Jack had met. She studied him a minute longer. He was younger than Ulriq, and of course, not as handsome.

"Would you like anything?" Vicky gestured to the rehydrator.

"I have had sufficient chocolate, thank you," Aaro teased.

Jack laughed. "There's no such thing."

"Teric has requested to visit with you as soon as you prefer." Aaro bowed before grinning again. "Aala is missing you."

"And I her." Jack threw her arm around Vicky and pulled her in for another hug. "Thank you for keeping my girls company."

"The pleasure was mine. I pray my Dar Eth is as passionate." His gaze lingered on Vicky's face.

"Could they come here? I'd prefer not to change…" Jack gestured with two fingers at Ulriq's shirt.

"Of course." Aaro punched his O.D.I. before sprawling in an available comfy. He was so relaxed around Vicky, implying he'd spent time with her. "I shall order more comfys. You never seem to have enough."

"I'll be home soon." Vicky shrugged, pursing her lips.

Aaro's eyebrows rose. "You are still leaving?"

"Of course. Just because I'm fond of you, Aaro, doesn't mean my mind has changed."

"You are fond of me?" His eyebrows met his hairline.

"You're like a brother to me." Vicky smiled and patted his knee.

"You honor me, Vicky. To have a sister is a blessing." Aaro's broad smile summoned a dimple. "Should you need anything, you have but to comm me."

The door chimed. It opened to reveal another Etterian—a freshly groomed Danic. If so many males would be visiting, perhaps she should change? She'd thought only Teric and Aala would be coming, but with the entire battleship dropping by, she was underdressed for playing hostess.

"Danic," Vicky called as she flew across to throw herself into his arms. The male caught her with a grin on his face. "Thank you for bringing Jack back."

The hug was brief, but he didn't release her immediately with his fingers lingering on her elbows. Jack arched a brow. When had this happened? Probably when she was making googly eyes at Ulriq over his uneaten potato salad.

"It was a successful mission," he said.

"May I offer you something from the rehydrator?" Vicky flashed him a smile.

"Try the hot chocolate," Aaro said helpfully.

Danic nodded in thanks at the suggestion before glancing around. He activated his O.D.I. and punched the holographic letters. "Thank you." He accepted the offered cup from Vicky and raised it to his nose to inhale deeply.

The rich, dark, and delicious aroma of chocolate teased Jack's nose. It was too soon to eat anything so decadent, so she drained her soup and slid the bowl onto the table.

Danic took a tentative sip and moaned. "This is delicious," he whispered before taking a gulp like a toddler with their first birthday cake.

The door chimed again, and Jack's eyebrows shot up. Holy crap. More visitors? At Vicky's call, the door opened, and she sat up in delight. Her arms widened, inviting a laughing Aala to rush forward. She clasped the girl to her chest, squeezing her against her while pressing a kiss to her temple.

"She missed you." Teric entered the room, his hair braided and resting mid-back.

"Father did as well," Aala said in a muffled voice.

"You did, Teric?" Jack met his chagrined gaze.

"Of course."

Jack chuckled then her smile dwindled. Teric ignored everyone in the room, specifically Vicky. And if she could read his expression, guilt plagued him. Sighing, she rubbed a hand up and down Aala's back. She'd need to talk to him, make him realize she understood and didn't blame him. Well, not anymore.

"May I offer you something from the rehydrator?" Jack glanced at Vicky, wiggling her eyebrows, silently asking her to play host.

"Here, taste this." Danic shoved the cup into Teric's startled hands.

He sniffed then sipped it. His surprised expression and deep rumble had everyone laughing. "Aala, *ensa*, come." He knelt and offered the cup to his daughter.

She clambered off Jack's lap to cross to him. Peering into the cup, she sniffed but didn't take it from him. "It smells amazing," she whispered before taking a sip as he tilted the cup. She cried out in delight and wrapped her hands around the cup, stealing it from him. "What is this?"

"Hot chocolate, Lady Aala," Aaro said.

The door opened, unannounced, with a grinning Vytus striding in as if he had a right to.

"Vytus. Only you could enter a room without permission," Jack teased him. "Vicky, this is Prince Vytus."

Vytus's eyebrow shot up at her introduction before giving her a formal bow. "I apologize for the intrusion; there are four males outside delivering comfys." He stepped aside to let the males pass. They lowered the chairs to the floor, the magnetic bases clicking where they placed them. "Thank you." He nodded at them, and once they'd exited, he faced the room. "I thought I scented hot chocolate."

"Vytus." Aala handed her father the cup before throwing herself into the prince's arms. He lifted her to hold against his chest, as if she weighed nothing.

"*Minus susa.*" Vytus smiled. Jack would have said in a sweet manner, but there was something incredibly tender about his expression. "Did you like it?"

"Yes, it is delicious, but how did you know I had some?" Everyone watched their interaction, some with smiles on their faces, some with unease.

Vytus chuckled at Aala, rubbed his thumb over her mouth to show her the dark brown droplets before sucking on his thumb.

"Oh," she mumbled. "What a waste."

He laughed and lowered her to her feet. Alarmed, Jack flicked a glance at Teric whose lips had formed a taut line. His look conveyed they would discuss this later. She need only be patient.

Vytus assumed a new comfy before facing Vicky. "Are we returning you to Earth, Lady Vicky? You have decided?"

Vicky blinked at the prince, startled at his casual manner. Jack smothered a smile, interpreting Vicky's surprise for what it was…shock that her name had been on many warriors' lips.

She wrapped her arms around her torso as she slid into a comfy. "Yes, it's done. Ulriq ordered the *Kushin* to set course after Ava arrives."

"I am sad to see you go, milady." Vytus offered his best smile. It drew forth an answering one from Vicky who wasn't accustomed to this much charm. In West Haven, only Antoine could be this amiable. "Danic has told me so much about you, Ava, and Taylor. I myself will be delivered to Aluna on our return trip from your homeworld."

"Aluna?" Vicky echoed.

"It is our northern base on Gikaet where I will start my rite of passage."

The males grumbled in acknowledgment.

"Remi is an excellent taskmaster," Danic said. "It is good you have been assigned to him."

"You will be building the new base. Your work will remain long after you have completed your rite," Aaro said.

"Vytus will be gone for four years. He must earn his honor." Aala sipped the hot chocolate from her position on her father's lap.

"And you, Aala, what will you do now?" Jack asked.

"Study, all females must do so in preparation for the Gifting."

"The what?" Vicky's brown eyes held only warmth for the girl.

"When a female comes of age, males from far and wide come to see her. The Gifting occurs once a year; a procession of females in the hopes of a pairing." Teric glanced at Jack before focusing on Aala's upturned face, his love for her evident.

Jack sighed, pleased to see such devotion on his face. It gave her hope that one day, Ulriq might be as open with his emotions. He desired her, thought her his salvation, but she didn't know if he loved her. It was probably too soon to tell. Besides, the little she knew about relationships could fit in a bullet casing.

"And if there isn't a pairing for Aala?" Jack asked.

"Then she may choose to study further or to pursue motherhood."

"As in sleep with random males in the hopes of falling pregnant?" Jack gasped, her gaze flying to Vicky, who gaped, snapped her mouth shut, and clenched her jaw. "She pimps her body out for the good of Etteria?" Jack's voice rose, along with the fire in her belly.

And Teric was so blasé about this. Blasé. The males concentrated on their O.D.I.s as they attempted to explain what she'd said. She fought the urge to lunge across and smack them all.

"It is her choice, Jack." Teric wasn't pleased either. His disgruntled expression eased Jack's anger somewhat.

"Not on my damn watch, that's for sure," Jack said, determination settling deep within her.

"Etteria needs my womb, Jack. I live to serve as is my right."

Jack blinked. Too often she forgot Etterians weren't human and shouldn't be judged accordingly. "All right." She forced a smile. "May I suggest Earth form part of your studies?"

"It is wise," Teric answered on Aala's behalf. "It would mean spending time with you if you are up for it?"

"Of course," Jack said, desperate for something to do. She had to assume Ulriq wouldn't stop being a supreme commander, and she wouldn't ask him to. Which meant hours of the day spent alone. "Vicky?"

"I would love to, Jack, while I'm on board."

Jack flashed her a grateful smile. Teric raised his gaze to look no higher than Vicky's knees. This as a good sign, a step toward Teric forgiving himself for the whole stealing-Jack debacle. Soon, he would meet everyone's gazes without self-recrimination.

"Your other subjects must not be neglected. After all, you are Etterian first." Wearing the perfect father-has-spoken expression, Teric looked at Aala.

Jack laughed. Mich had often used the same on her.

"Perhaps you can share your Etterian studies with us?" Vicky unraveled her arms to rub her palms along her thighs. "Like an exchange program?"

"It is decided." Teric smiled, flashing both dimples at Vicky's knees.

All four males glanced at their wrists.

"What is it?" Jack almost pushed out of the chair.

Teric released a bark of laughter as he read the message. "Your Eth does not like you spending so much time with other males."

"What?" Heat stained Jack's cheeks. Was Ulriq jealous? Her chest swelled. The idea of it tantalized and delighted her.

"He has increased our workload." Aaro bounded to his feet, chuckling.

"Thank you for this, Jack." Danic flashed a fake pout.

"I can talk to him?" She was a little stunned. How had he even known they were here in her quarters? She darted her gaze around the room, searching for surveillance equipment. Not that she'd know what their technology looked like. The Yithians had hidden theirs as well.

"No need to. We were indeed inactive." Aaro hugged Vicky who had risen to show them out. "Until evening meal, *ensa*." He exited with Danic close on his heels.

"Father, may I stay with Jack?" Aala clasped Jack's hand as if the thought of leaving was detestable to her.

"It is for Jack to decide." Teric waited.

"We don't mind." Vicky tugged on Aala's braid with a teasing smile.

"Of course, she can stay. We'll bring her to dinner." Jack drew Aala into her arms for another hug.

"Very well, *ensa*." Teric flashed a grateful smile and rose to leave.

For the first time, he glanced at Vicky and froze. He paled, and his eyes widened.

Jack frowned. "Teric?"

His gaze remain fixed on Vicky. With a guttural groan, he slid to his knee unhindered.

"Father." Aala wriggled in Jack's arms, wanting to rush to her father's side.

"I am fine, *ensa*," Teric said, his voice gravel.

But he wasn't fine. Jack recognized the anguished features, the pain trembling his body, his white knuckles. She peeked at Vicky, at the new concern on her face. Shit. She wasn't going to like this turn of events. Jack crushed Aala against her and looked pointedly at Vicky, gesturing to her to help Teric. She stumbled across to him, her hands hovering over his shoulders, his chest, hesitating to touch him. He grabbed her, lacing his fingers through hers, and tugged her closer. At her touch, his breathing labored. Jack feared he'd have a heart attack if he didn't calm himself.

"Teric?" Vicky squeaked.

He groaned again, his body shuddering. His skin glistened under the strain, shimmering the bronze into a beautiful metallic in the lighting.

"Be calm, Vicky," he growled, opening his eyes to reveal ice-blue orbs.

Jack smothered her smile in Aala's hair.

"Do you need a medic?" Vicky pressed her trembling hand against his chest.

"It is lessening." He snaked his arm around her and drew her against him.

She went willingly. Placating the patient. Jack grinned. Oh, she'd love to be the fly on the wall when Vicky found out what the hell just happened.

"Father, are you well?" Aala clung to Jack.

Teric's eyes closed briefly before he drew in a deep breath. "I am fine, Aala. If Lady Vicky would escort me to medical?"

Vicky slipped under his arm, offering him her body as anchorage. Teric shuddered again, and the two inched out of the quarters. The door sealed behind them.

Aala twisted to face Jack. "Was that the—?"

"Ethera," Jack said.

Aala's eyes widened as a slow smile curled her lips. "Vicky's my father's Dar Eth?"

"Looks like that, sweetheart," Jack said. "How do you feel about this?"

"This is wonderful. I hope she is as kind and soft as you are, Jack. She will be a better mother than my own. Although, I do believe I am too old for mothers."

"And if I was your mother, you'd be too old for me?" Jack teased her, running her fingers along Aala's braid, recalling when she'd finger-combed the girl's hair daily.

"Vicky's like you?" There was a hint of nervousness in Aala's voice.

"Better. You'll see." Jack snuck in another hug. It was only normal to be anxious about having a new mother. Hope and fear, that's what she'd felt when she and Mich had landed at the orphanage.

"No one's better than you, Jack."

Jack shook her head. "Thanks for that, but the moment you realize Vicky is amazing, I want you to tell me."

"Agreed." Aala bounced on her toes. "Ulriq has been kind too, Jack. He gave Father and me an officer's quarters."

"He did?" Jack's heart warmed, bright with hope that he might not punish Teric further. "Let's start with your studies, Aala. How about some of our foods?" She strode the rehydrator and held out her hand to the girl.

"Does Earth have more foods like chocolate?" Aala skipped over, her wide eyes sparkling.

"You decide." Jack chuckled before showing her the various choices available.

Chapter Twenty-Two

Etterian battleship, Kushin
Speeding toward Earth

"Alodon's balls, Ulriq. They are soft but too tiny," Xan said as they entered the comm room.

"Would it matter if such a female was your Dar Eth?" Ulriq arched a brow.

Xan blinked at Ulriq. "No, it would not."

"Pilot Ksal, comm the king," Ulriq said.

"He is on standby, Supreme Commander," Pilot Ksal said, to which both supreme commanders glared at him.

"You kept the king waiting?" Xan gasped.

"No, Supreme Commander. I kept Adviser Cales waiting." Pilot Ksal grinned unrepentantly before activating the display vid.

"My king," Ulriq greeted King Xeus. He dipped his head at Prince Enyl and Adviser Cales as well. "Thank you for accepting my comm request." Ulriq flashed a look at Ksal.

"Greetings Xan, Ulriq, we are pleased to see you are well. Are the Dar Eths secure, Ulriq? Are they unharmed?"

"They are, King Xeus, secure and well." The warmth in Ulriq's chest had blossomed since Jack's return to him. The Ethera's constant torture had been almost too unbearable. Now, it bombarded his senses with electric sparks and kept him harder than Fuyra rock.

"We are pleased to hear this," Prince Enyl said.

"Thank you for your support. Vytus and Malo assisted with Lady Jack while Prince Citus aided Kanzo and Xan with Lady Ava. The prince is en route to Etteria. I am certain he will regale you with his adventure."

"And what of Teric?"

Ulriq drew in a slow breath. "We have rescued him, his daughter, and the arena prisoners."

"Excellent. Teric will be dealt with according to our lore." King Xeus grimaced.

"I respectfully request he be given amnesty." Ulriq hoped his recent success would grant him a boon. All three males blinked at him, taking a moment to compile their thoughts. Xan had relaxed his posture enough to slice a glance at Ulriq.

"I do not understand." Xeus frowned. "It is your right to demand justice under such conditions."

"The Yithians took four feet of his honor, my king." Their growls reached across the comm stations, conveying their fury at Yithia's audacity. "He has received his punishment, and more. Under the circumstances, every male would have acted similarly." Ulriq ran a frustrated hand over his face before continuing, "He protected my Dar Eth, kept her and his daughter safe to the best of his ability. He acted honorably." Ulriq met the king's gaze. "Also, my Dar Eth champions him and has formed a close bond with his daughter. To harm him impacts his daughter and...Jack." He didn't need to add that to harm her would impact him. All who were present understood his Dar Eth came first, in all things.

"Very well, Ulriq. Your defense is in line with Malo's findings. Teric's performance has been above reproach. As per your discoveries, Malo will be investigating how deep Yithia has penetrated our ranks and what their agendas are. That our males are not able to ask for assistance is unacceptable. Nevertheless..." Xeus paused, flicked his gaze to the side, and nodded.

Ulriq waited patiently for his king to continue.

"Aala's mother, Nela, did not alert security on the non-arrival of her daughter. The female still does not know the whereabouts of her daughter. It is for this reason I have revoked any claim she may have on Aala." Xeus sighed.

Ulriq's lips curled in distaste, that an Etterian female hadn't cherished her offspring.

"As far as Etteria is concerned, Nela is without *damu*, the annals have been amended accordingly. Should the female bear forth another *damu*, Etteria will once more involve itself in her life. Please inform Teric he is not answerable for this, and all accusations have been officially withdrawn." King Xeus flashed a tight smile. "Inform him he has sole custody of his daughter."

Ulriq dipped his head, a weight lifting off his shoulders. Xeus was a wise leader and served Etteria with honor. "He will be most pleased to hear this, King Xeus."

"Is Vytus still with you?" Enyl asked.

"He is, my prince, and has requested we deliver him to Aluna post-Earth." Ulriq's brow twitched at having to harm his Jack by pleasing another female.

Cales paused, hovering a finger above his O.D.I. "You are returning to Earth?"

"A human female has chosen not to travel to Etteria. She has agreed to remain silent regarding Etteria's involvement in all this." This would sadden Jack, and no matter how he assessed the situation, no solution arose.

"Very well, Ulriq. Please ask your Dar Eth and Kanzo's whether they would willingly submit to compatibility tests. Liaise directly with Cales. All of Etteria is with you." Xeus ended the comm.

Ulriq relaxed his shoulders and shook the stiffness from his arms.

"Was Prince Enyl's eyes...?" Xan blinked, his focus a little dazed.

"Yes, his Dar Eth is a human female," Ulriq rolled his shoulders.

"This is unprecedented, Ulriq." Xan laughed. "Three Dar Eths in what? A few months?"

Xan was right. They were miracles. Ulriq couldn't forget that whenever he set his gaze on Jack. "They are all from a mid-grade planet called Earth."

"That went well, Supreme Commander," Pilot Ksal said.

Ulriq grunted. "Better than I had hoped considering you kept the adviser waiting. Location of Medic Teric?"

"He is on the viewing deck with the human Victoria."

"How do you know she is with him?"

"The human females have had O.D.I.s installed," Ksal said. "Warrior Aaro has instructed them on how to use it, as well. Lady Ava's is without an O.D.I. for medical reasons."

"Anything else?" What Ulriq wanted to demand was time to be alone with Jack. If there were no obligations awaiting him, he could...what? He gritted his teeth. She was never alone, not with her girls and his infernal males visiting her.

Ksal typed on his console. "Operations Commander Malo wishes to inform you he too is en route to Earth. He has received separate instructions from Prince Enyl."

"Very well, resume your duties, Ksal." Ulriq spun on Xan, who tapped on his O.D.I.

"The *Phoenix* has been tasked to guard Earth." Xan's expression warmed. "I could deliver Lady Vicky if you require."

Ulriq shook his head. "They would not appreciate the separation."

Xan frowned. "That is illogical, Ulriq. To waste resources in such a manner—"

Ulriq held Xan's gaze. "I vowed to return her, and I shall do so."

"Very well, since it is a matter of honor. You need only have said so, my battle-bond. Now you will have two escorts." Xan thumped him on the back.

"What I do need you to investigate was the presence of Yithian shuttles on Earth." Ulriq pinched the bridge of his nose. He hadn't thought of this since he'd been wounded. The Ethera had blurred his focus. He smiled. Or redirected it?

"What?" Xan scowled. "When did this—?"

"We traveled planetside. Yithians attacked us and did extensive damage to Michel's housing structure."

"And were there any nearby ships?"

"Yes. Have your data officer speak to mine."

Xan gripped Ulriq's arm and marched out of the comm room to return to his ship.

Ulriq's long strides swiftly covered the distance to the viewing deck. He strode through the door to where Vicky glared at Teric. As he neared, Teric glanced at him, his ice-blue eyes startling. Various scenarios played through Ulriq's mind, at the fore was the notification to Earth of Etteria's existence for Vicky would return home regardless of becoming a Dar Eth. "Teric, I have spoken to the king."

Teric grabbed Vicky's hand and hugged her against him, not allowing her the opportunity to escape. She scowled but didn't fight him.

Sensing he needed to hurry, Ulriq blurted the news. "No punishment will be meted out. And Aala is your daughter alone."

Teric's eyes grew wide. "Truth?" he rasped.

"What is it, Teric?" Vicky shuffled closer to him, her concern evident.

"The king has revoked Nela's rights as Aala's mother," he explained before flashing a joyful smile at her. He crushed her to him, laughing as he buried his face in her hair.

"I think I like your king," she said to his chest.

"Are we still bound for Earth?" Ulriq glanced between them.

"Yes," Teric responded on her behalf, and his reply snapped her focus to him. "Victoria wishes to return home, so to her homeworld we will go."

"You are remaining with her." Ulriq would inform the king but didn't anticipate any issues. An Eth must follow his Dar Eth. He left them alone, sending a quick communication to King Xeus regarding Teric's Ethera. Xeus would receive the news with joy and perhaps send an ambassador to liaise with Earth now that an Etterian male would be living there. It also meant Earth would be classified as a safe-to-visit planet. He expected to spend time there with Jack at some point in the near future.

Despite his best efforts, Ulriq found himself outside Jack's door requesting entrance. It opened immediately, and he grunted at the extra comfys placed in the room.

"I'm glad you're here, Ulriq," Taylor greeted him. "Please tell Jack to shower."

Ulriq's gaze flew to his blushing Dar Eth. She was curled into a comfy, exposing her legs, and her sun-kissed hair draped over one shoulder.

"No," he growled, elated to see her still wearing his tunic.

She smiled, pushed out of the comfy, and threw herself into his waiting arms. He crushed her to him and inhaled deeply, drawing in as much of her scent as possible.

"I missed you," she whispered for his ears only.

He rumbled his approval.

"How is my father, Supreme Commander? Have you seen him?" Aala asked, her small, concerned voice snagged his attention.

"He is well, *minus susa*." Ulriq leaned back to glance at the *damu*. "In fact, he has decided to live on Earth."

"Truth?" she gasped, bouncing on her toes.

"Yes, with Lady Vicky."

"He can have my house." Jack rested her cheek against Ulriq's chest. He gathered her near, relishing her curves warming him.

He tightened his arms around her as the Ethera leaped to life, and joy filled the recesses of his soul. She had a generous spirit. By offering her home, she didn't regret leaving Earth for Etteria, and cut all ties to her old life, hopefully, to embrace her new one with him.

"Lady Aala, you should speak to him and Lady Vicky, she may have other plans." Ulriq rubbed his chin across his Dar Eth's hair. "She is fighting it, Jack."

"Fighting what?" Taylor slid into the comfy with a coffee.

"The attraction between them." Jack chuckled. "Pointless, I know."

Aala caught up her braid and toyed with it. "Will I get to stay on Earth?"

Ulriq released Jack to kneel in front of her. "That is between you and your father. You should ask him about your mother. The king has made his decision." He brushed Aala's cheek, before gently pinching her chin. "It is good news, *damu*. Teric and Lady Vicky are on the viewing deck."

The *damu* squealed and raced through the door that barely had enough time to open.

Ulriq rose to stare after her.

"Good news?" Jack rested her fingers on his chest over his thumping heart.

He captured her hand with his; trapping it as he clasped her hip and urged her closer. "He will not be punished, and the king has awarded him sole access to his daughter. Nela is no longer acknowledged as her mother."

Jack's smile was glorious, like the magnus sun breaking across Etteria's oceans. "You defended him, didn't you?" Her mouth parted on a gasp.

His body reacted, pooling heat in his loins. He didn't answer. Tendrils of lust wrapped around his chest and squeezed. "Lady Taylor, please instruct Jack on the use of her O.D.I." He forced himself to release her.

"Why? Where are you going?" Jack tightened her fingers wherever they touched him, conveying her need to keep him near.

"Away from temptation," he groaned, running a trembling hand through her un-bound locks. "Comm me when you are ready for mealtime."

"You comm me. I'm the one doing nothing." The fire in her blue eyes called forth something primal within him.

"Alodon's balls. Do not look at me like that," he growled, his voice grating on his ears.

As he gazed at her upturned face, he hoped his expression conveyed how much he wanted her, to stay near her but how he needed to leave to maintain some measure of dignity. With one last kiss to her temple, he stormed out. It had been foolish to visit her, but he hadn't been able to resist.

Chapter Twenty-Three

Etterian battleship, Kushin
Speeding toward Earth

"The bastard," Vicky called as she burst into the room. She drew to a halt at seeing Jack still in a shirt and in the same comfy. "Shower, now." She pulled Jack out of her seat and dragged her into the cleansing room. "Think about what you should be wearing to drive Ulriq wild."

Visions of black lingerie, lace, and satin flashed through Jack's mind, and she chuckled.

Vicky's nose crinkled when she sniffed Jack. "After all, he's only seen you in leather and this shirt."

Jack's hairline tingled. No, he had seen her in less than that. Remembering standing before him in her bra should have embarrassed her. Something wild inside her had unraveled. Her nipples had hardened, and she had liked the intensity in his eyes, the reverence in his gaze.

"True." Her laughter faded as she peeled off his tunic, pausing to bury her nose in it.

There was just something about his scent. Her heart fluttered, and deep within her core, flash grenades went off making her weep between her thighs. She ached for him, though knowing what the intensity meant and how he would ease the throbbing didn't lessen the anticipation. Sighing, she let the tunic fall from her fingers. She stared at the pooled garment before stepping into the cubicle. The water activated immediately.

"The water washes your hair, skin, and teeth...all without soap." Vicky settled on the closed toilet seat and sighed, loud enough to be heard above the spray. "Tell me the truth, Jack. How do you feel about this Ethera nonsense?"

"A little stunned, a lot aroused." Jack snuck in the last bit to embarrass Vicky. She peeked in time to catch her friend's blush.

Vicky rubbed her palms down her thighs. Her hair splayed out, her cheeks were pink, and her eyes wide—classic signs of shock. "And you're happy to stay with these Etterians?"

"My emotions don't play a role, Vicky. I *need* to be with Ulriq. I can't explain the deep level of fear at the thought of a life without him."

A slow smile cracked Vicky's rigid face. "Oh, Jack, I'm happy for you. You've been waiting so long."

"I'm still waiting, apparently." Jack spun under the water to face her. "He has yet to kiss me, Vicky."

"How many hours have you two had together, Jack? Two, three hours?"

Jack chuckled at her insecurities. "I'd swear it was longer."

"Besides, since when do we wait for a man to kiss us first?"

Heat exploded in Jack's core at the idea of smashing her lips across Ulriq's. "Maybe with a human man, Vicky, but Ulriq's huge. I would need to stand on a chair to reach his lips."

"Trust you to have thought this through." Vicky laughed. "Very well, wait for him to make the first move." She shrugged, and her smile lingered. What mattered more to Jack was Vicky's relaxed posture. "It won't be long now, that I can promise you."

"And Teric?" Jack stepped out of the cubicle, standing in the middle of the room until Vicky rushed past her and pressed a blue button. They stood there and waited the required time for Jack to dry.

"His eyes change color, and now I must stay with him forever?" Vicky stomped her foot while holding out a robe. "I mean, just think about it? In what universe do these men live?"

"He's so hot, he melts your socks, doesn't he?" Jack teased, laughing at Vicky's instant blush.

She huffed. "Regardless, he's so arrogant..."

Jack stilled when the robe conformed to her body. She bit her lip to smother her gasp. Like the caress of a ghost, the fabric skimmed across her curves. "And sexy."

"Stubborn."

"And caring." Jack smirked.

"Opinionated."

Jack ticked off the points on her fingers, as Vicky had done for her. "And gentle."

"Jack, you're not helping," Vicky said, panic straining her voice. She dropped onto the toilet seat with less grace this time.

"I *am* helping. Vicky, he's gorgeous and is willing to uproot his and Aala's life to be near you."

Vicky slumped. "Well, when you put it like that..."

"And the way he'll treat you will be like one of your romance novels."

"He does already." Vicky shivered and ran her hands up and down her arms.

"And wait till he tastes one of your croissants; that male will fall madly in love with you."

"Now, you're being silly." She smiled.

"I'm not. Mich declared his love for you every time. It irritated the hell out of Taylor." Jack sighed when Vicky dismissed her attempts to ease her concerns. "So, tell me what's bothering you? I mean, Teric's attracted to you, he's sexy, and a wonderful father. He's committed to you, enough to live on Earth when he can choose anywhere in the universe."

Vicky raised her wide brown eyes. "I just don't know how long-term this is? I can't have my heart broken, not again."

"It's forever." Jack stepped out of the cleansing room.

"Forever's good, right?" At Taylor's soft voice, Jack grinned.

"I'm glad Mich finally released you," Vicky teased.

"Can you walk?" Jack hugged Taylor in greeting. The shower and the wrap did make her feel like a new person. Though, she mourned the loss of Ulriq's scent.

"Mich is standing right here." He rolled his eyes from his position next to the rehydrator.

"When did you sneak in?" Vicky asked.

"Can *you* walk?" Jack flashed him a grin.

"Ha-ha, very funny." Her brother had the decency to blush. "Where's Ava?"

"I don't know. She's coming from the *Phoenix*." Vicky shrugged and dropped into a comfy. "It's been one heck of a day."

"Vicky is Teric's Dar Eth," Jack told Mich and Taylor.

"What's a Dar Eth?" Mich's brow furrowed. "Ulriq called you his Dar Eth. All the males act like this is an important thing."

"The Etterians believe God designed a female perfect for each male. When they meet, their eyes change color in a painful transition they call the Ethera," Vicky said by rote.

Jack laughed, hearing Teric's voice behind the words.

Mich gaped. "Holy shit. Ulriq, Kanzo, and now Teric?"

"Kanzo?" Vicky's eyes widened.

"You should have seen him. He read Yithian transcript after transcript, trying to find news of Ava. I doubt he slept." Mich wrapped an arm around Taylor, holding her against him. "He was determined to find her. We were ported down to rescue Jack, but Kanzo had to meet with Supreme Commander Xan. I don't know what happened after we split."

"But she's safe and healthy, right?" Not that Jack distrusted Ulriq. But why the delay?

"She's with Kanzo. That's all I know."

A sensation tingled up Jack's arm, startling her. "My first message." She gaped and jumped up, as if sitting meant she couldn't read it. Her forefinger twitched when she activated her O.D.I. The message was from Ulriq. He'd finished his shift and was on his way. "Shit. I'm not dressed."

Vicky huffed and ushered her over to the replicator. "Then choose your clothes. Jeans and a T-shirt?"

Jack chewed on her bottom lip. "Is that sexy?"

"Do I need to be here for this?" Mich complained in general, giving Taylor a quick kiss before rushing out.

"A dress?" Taylor suggested, raising her brow in query, then hurried to join them at the replicator.

"Jeans, tight, low hipped," Jack squeaked.

Conflicting emotions tumbled in her stomach, and the lucky draw was panic. Nausea churned, her heart rate scattered, and her leg bounced as she waited for Vicky to place the order, entering her dimensions so it would fit properly. Jack hadn't given replicator-instructions her full attention. And mastering the rehydrator had been out of necessity.

When the pair of jeans appeared on the glass surface, she grabbed it, shrugged off her robe, and tugged them on. They clung snugly to her ass and hung low on her hips—a perfect fit.

"Now a shirt?" With Vicky's guidance, Jack chose something loose yet flowing in a flower-printed cream fabric. The shirt crisscrossed around her waist and tied with a knot. She fastened it while Taylor's brushed her curls with a hairbrush Vicky had ordered.

"Shoes?" Vicky punched something into the replicator before tossing gold sandals at Jack, who snatched them out of the air.

She dropped into the closest comfy and slipped them on. "How do I look?"

"Kissable," Vicky teased as the door chimed.

The rush of excitement was unlike anything she had experienced. Those grenades were on full flashbang mode, and she couldn't suck air in deep enough. Taylor opened the door for Ulriq. He paused halfway through the door, his gaze fixed on Jack.

"Alodon's balls, Jack," he growled, his gaze traveling up and down her figure.

He was still in his black armor, but she doubted he owned anything else. Not that his armor didn't do him justice. The way it clung to his legs dazzled her. She loved his thighs and desperately wanted to see them naked.

"Come, Ulriq, I'm hungry." She crossed the room to lace her fingers through his.

Snaking an arm around her, he tugged her closer and lifted her off the floor. He pinned her against his chest to brush his lips across the shell of her ear.

"So am I," he rasped, leaving Jack with no doubt he hadn't meant for food.

She shivered. Her skin tingled as if he'd permanently imprinted the shape of his lips onto her. He lowered her slowly down his body, and she moaned, wanting to wrap her legs around his hips and pin an open-mouthed kiss to the strong column of his neck. Pressing against her stomach was his hard and ready arousal.

"Miladies," he greeted a gaping Vicky and beaming Taylor before he escorted Jack out the room. "You go first, Jack."

"But I don't know where—"

"I'll direct you." He nudged her.

Hesitating, she strode ahead. He ruffled something and the realization of what it could be summoned a bright giddy laugh. He had to be adjusting himself. And he needed to. She'd say he had an impressive package, without having something to compare it to. When they strolled into the common, Aala ran toward them to throw herself into Jack's waiting arms.

"Father said we are staying on Earth." Aala wiggled, a smile ready, and her eyes sparkling like the azure seas.

"I'm happy for you, Aala, and you can have my house. Go tell your father. If he wants it, that is." She lowered Aala to the floor, who skipped over to Teric seated at a bench.

"You spoil her with your affection, Jack." Ulriq curled his thumb into the back of her jeans.

She liked that he touched her so casually. Liked the feel of his skin on hers. But when his fingers slid into her back pocket and squeezed her backside, his touch turned from casual to intimate. She spun into his arms and pressed her palms to his chest, raising her gaze to meet his.

"When we have a son, I'll love him so much. Even if you send him off to become an Etterian warrior, I'll hug and kiss him until he begs me not to. Don't ask me to act against my nature, Ulriq."

"Our son?" His voice was thick with emotion.

"Of course. You do want children, don't you?"

His face hardened, while his gaze lowered to her lips. "Yes. But you are talking about *damu* when I have yet to kiss you."

"Oh, kissing *will* happen, when you get around to it."

He jerked back. "When I get around to it?"

"Well, you're much taller and bigger than me. I can't tackle you to the ground to get to your lips."

He rumbled a laugh and crushed her in his embrace. His hard edges against her curves and the warmth seeping through his uniform made her shiver. "You have kissing on your world?"

"Oh, yes." She licked her lips, settling her gaze on his, and wishing he would close the distance.

"I am happy to hear this, Jack. I have been longing to kiss you since Earth." His raspy voice sent goosebumps skittering across her skin.

"I remember." Her cheeks burned as she recalled his words to her.

"I will spread those beautiful thighs of yours when I find a quiet place." By his determined expression, he planned to deliver on his promise.

She damn well hoped so, or she'd be screaming false advertising. "Aren't your quarters quiet?" What she wanted to ask was why hadn't they gone there yet? She knew he desired her, yet he didn't want to be alone with her.

His fingertip rose to trace her jaw. The heat of his skin scorched her, and she gasped.

"Why don't you two get a room?" Mich teased as he entered the common hand-in-hand with Taylor.

"Mich, if you keep this up, I will shave your eyebrows...again," Jack threatened but ruined her serious tone by grinning.

Shaving his eyebrows had been fun and the subsequent months with the concerned do-gooders hovering over a sickly-looking Mich. She'd taken pleasure in playing along, and when she couldn't contain her mirth any long, had pointed out his missing eyebrows.

"And I'll help you." Taylor smacked Mich on the arm.

Chapter Twenty-Four

TERIC'S ANNOUNCEMENT PAUSED JACK'S downward motion. She gasped, reversing her actions when she was about to sit on a bench. She flicked a glance at the beaming girls, joy bubbling up her throat. She whooped, spinning to throw her arms around Ulriq for a quick hug.

"Come, Jack. Let's hurry." Taylor took off, dragging Michel behind her.

Vicky bounced on her toes, excitement flowing off her in waves. She slipped her hand into Teric's then reached to grab Aala's as well; her enthusiasm spreading to them through touch. Aala grinned, her eyes wide. An awkward shuffle occurred at the door when Vicky had to release their hands to hurry single file along the passages. Teric trailed, leaving Jack and Ulriq to follow.

Teric's fingers shook where they hovered at the small of Vicky's back. And when Ulriq's hand rested at the base of Jack's spine, she imagined his trembled as well. She was so enjoying watching her two friends succumb to the Ethera. It was inevitable, just like she knew they'd find their happily-ever-after.

When Ava stepped off the shuttle, Vicky ran toward her, tears streaming down her cheeks unheeded. She wrapped her arms around her, not complaining when it looked like Ava squeezed her to within an inch of her life. Jack nudged Vicky out of the way to hug Ava, with Taylor joining in. Mich wrapped his arms around them all.

"What the hell happened, Angel? One moment you were there then...poof." Jack leaned back to look at her sister, taking in the weight loss. But there was something else; this wasn't the Ava she knew. There was a confidence in her gaze, a strength in her stance, but also a hint of sadness.

"Yes, and Kanzo went next-level crazy when you vanished," Taylor chuckled.

Ava did the strangest thing. She turned to Kanzo—who hovered behind her—and lisped in Yithian. Jack's head jerked back.

"Please tell them, Kanzo," Ava said to him. "Tell them I can't understand them."

"What the hell, babe?" Jack lisped in Yithian, tugging Ava to the side. "What do you mean you can't understand English?"

Kanzo explained to Taylor and Vicky how to activate the Yithian Language Protocol on their O.D.I.s.

Ava shrugged. "Sorry, Jacks. The damn shark damaged me when he inserted the interpreter."

Jack hugged her again, tight enough to cut off her breathing. "They do look like sharks, right?" She forced a smile even as tears stung her eyes. "Thought that was just me."

"I sound like a lisping cat." Vicky bumped Jack out of the way with her hip. "Welcome back, Ava-honey," she whispered, giving her sister another quick hug.

"So, what happened?" Taylor asked from within Mich's embrace.

"Oh, nothing out of the ordinary." Ava smiled. Kanzo's grumble piqued Jack's interest. So, there was more to tell; she'd get it out of Ava eventually. "Until Kanzo rescued me, of course." Ava winked and blew him a kiss, replacing his smile with a lustful expression. "And you, Jacks?"

"A long, long story," Jack shrugged. "It's why my O.D.I. was set to Yithian."

"Lady Ava, Warrior Kanzo, I am pleased you have returned safely," another tall Etterian greeted Ava.

Jack took the moment to study his face with its defined edges, a square jawline, and a wide forehead. His nose was long and narrow, almost too pretty for his masculine face, with a wide oversized upper lip and dark-blue hooded eyes under arched eyebrows as black as Ulriq's. He looked familiar though she knew damn well she had never met him before.

"Thank you so much for your assistance, my prince." Ava dipped her head.

"My prince? After what I have seen, Lady Ava." He flashed a teasing smile.

More and more Etterian males were showing humor. Why did Ulriq and Nerx not do the same? Jack glanced at Ulriq and winked at him, unable to stop herself from doing so. He'd snuck in when they'd been in a cuddle puddle. Ulriq's gaze was already on Jack when she faced him. His answering smile was immediate.

"You may address me as Citus." Those words drew Jack's attention back to 'Citus.'

Ava grinned, but the pink on her cheeks said there was some juicy stuff to her adventure.

"Are you leaving soon, my prince?" Kanzo asked in an abrupt manner.

Said prince didn't take offense but laughed. "Yes, I will be leaving shortly, Warrior Kanzo. I have seen Vytus, my son, and am now determined to rush home to rub this in Xeus's face."

Ah. Jack nodded. That's who he reminded her of. This was Vytus's father? The man looked way too young to have a grown son.

"I doubt you will be able to, my prince. Prince Enyl has found his Dar Eth." Ulriq strode toward them. He looped his arm around Jack's waist without hesitation and tugged her against him.

"Alodon's balls," the prince boomed.

"His one to your two?" Ava pointed out.

"Three," Vicky said.

"What?" Ava gasped, and the joy bursting across her face was one of pure delight.

Jack couldn't remember when last she'd seen Ava so happy, not since Billy proposed. Vicky gestured to Teric watching her from the raised platform. She unknowingly gave him the sweetest smile. Next to Teric, Aala bounced on her heels and peppered him with questions. Jack wished she could eavesdrop on their conversation.

"Something happened." Jack twisted in Ulriq's arms to whisper to him.

"Explain." He tightened his arms around her waist, pressing her to his hard length.

"Ava's changed; she's calmer, stronger, more confident." Jack stroked him from elbows to shoulders, along his collarbones and down again, while she sought the words to explain what she sensed. "You don't know what she's been through on Earth, Ulriq. It's as if she has put that all behind her. As if she's finally free." Jack leaned back to meet his gaze and smiled. His eyes were closed, and his blissful expression made her realize he liked how she touched him.

"Continue," he commanded.

She smiled. Did he mean the explanation or the stroking? She shrugged and did both. "Kanzo's in love with her too." That had Ulriq's eyes opening and the shock on his face worried her. "What's wrong with that?"

"Love is an intense emotion; it is not often experienced by Etterians... Are you certain?"

Jack blinked, not at him doubting her, but at the realization he may never love her. She didn't like the idea at all. But as he'd said, love wasn't often experienced. Who was to say he would recognize it even if it hit him in his face. He didn't see it in Kanzo's eyes, in his soft expression, in his lingering gaze and hands.

"I'm certain." She resumed stroking his shoulders and arms. "I'm surprised I didn't see the signs before."

"Signs?" Ulriq echoed, and she fought the urge to laugh. He was so easy to bait.

"Yes, when she was taken, he acted like a male in mourning."

"That was the Ethera," Ulriq said.

She smothered a chuckle by nuzzling his chest with her nose. Was Ethera their word for love? They blamed Kanzo's actions and reactions on the Ethera. That wouldn't work on Earth. *I'm sorry, officer, I had to steal it, the Ethera made me do it.* Nope, definitely wouldn't work.

"If you say so." Jack ran her hands up his arms again, but this time all the way up his neck to play with his earlobes before trailing her hands down. If he was a cat, he would have purred.

"I do, and I need to comm my king." He twitched, rocking on his heels. His hesitancy showed his desire to remain where he was.

"Go. I'll be with Ava." Jack let her fingers feather over his armor-encased chest.

His breath hitched, and he embedded his fingers in her curls, tilting her head to gaze into her eyes. She hoped he would kiss her now.

"Stay on the battleship," he teased, and his crinkling eyes turned serious. "Please, Jack."

She nodded since she couldn't speak past the lump in her throat.

He strolled off, leaving her staring at the black fabric of his military pants clinging to his gorgeous backside. Damn.

Chapter Twenty-Five

"So, what happened?" Jack lisped the moment they ushered Ava into their quarters. Nerx had informed them they could share or each receive their own, and the girls had opted to share. "You look thinner; did the sharks not feed you?"

"A white paste which was inedible, so I lived off water." Ava shrugged.

Jack shuddered as her tongue summoned the texture of the paste. Due to her revulsion, she missed the beginning of Ava's tale. Tuning in from when she mentioned the verbal letters she had written.

"Wait, are you saying you're over Billy?" Vicky asked.

Ava nodded, sharing a serene smile.

"And forgave Kanzo?" Jack asked, although the answer to that was a little too obvious with the way they gazed at each other.

"Forgave?" Ava's brow furrowed. "Why would I need to—?"

"You looked super angry on the shuttle. I assumed he'd done something..." Jack shrugged.

Ava laughed. "I thought he didn't like touching me with the way he tossed me over his shoulder. He did so to keep his fighting arm free. I was such an idiot. When I met Prince Citus, I had hope I'd been rescued, and in abundance. Then when Kanzo entered the room..." She sighed as her gaze turned distant.

Taylor threw out her hands. "Whoa, jumping ahead here."

Ava blinked and blushed at their knowing looks. So, she told them about her Yithian guard, Vlax, and how he had instructed her to charm the Yithian king. Her meeting of said king and her subsequent release to the Maloidian Ambassador and her sale to Citus. Then finally to Kanzo taking her away.

"And with you, Jack?" Ava twisted in the comfy to face her.

"Not much to say, kidnapped by an Etterian male named Teric, ported over to the Yithians, found his daughter and united her with Teric. We fought in the arena and killed two alien panthers then Ulriq rescued me...us."

"And imagine, in such a short space of time, Jack's all aflame with longing for Ulriq," Vicky teased. "It took ages to get her out of his tunic and into her own clothes."

"He smells *so* good," Jack moaned, dragging out the 'so' for emphasis.

"They do." Ava curled her feet under her. "Sun-drenched sheets, oranges, lemons, freshly cut grass, and with no cologne."

"None?" Vicky leaned in, clasping her hands in front of her.

"Yes, it offends their senses. Now what? What happens after they find their Dar Eths? It kind of sounds long term." Ava settled her gaze on Jack.

"It's forever, babe."

"Forever?" She blinked as a slow smile dimpled her cheek.

The door chimed.

Taylor peered at the panel then grinned. "It's Kanzo," she sang and activated the door.

The Etterian male filled the doorframe with his impressive, well, frame. Just seeing him splashed Ava's cheeks pink. Jack wondered if she did the same every time she saw Ulriq.

"Kanzo." Ava smiled in welcome.

Jack glanced between the two of them; Ulriq could suck it. She was right. They were in love.

"What is it?" Ava pushed out of the comfy to cross to him.

He gripped her elbow, pulling her close. "Please, Ava, you need to—"

"Sit." Danic gestured to the comfy, nudging Kanzo forward before entering the quarters himself.

Jack shook her head at Danic's high-handedness.

Glaring at him, Kanzo continued, "...hear this." He gathered Ava into his arms, holding her as if he cherished her. "The interpreter is..."

A tingle began at the back of Jack's neck and trickled down her spine. She rose to her feet, trying to hear what Kanzo was saying to Ava. Something wasn't right. Ava's face twisted with fear, reminiscent of when her fiancé had died. She whispered to Kanzo, but the way she hugged his body was the way she'd clung to Fred after Billy's death.

"What's going on?" Vicky rose from her comfy.

Taylor hovered beside the door, her face deathly pale. She was close enough to hear more.

"Medic Der needs to see me." Ava offered a stiff shrug, but none of them believed it was something casual. Kanzo and Ava continued to lisp at one another, the Yithian words not discernible from their whispers.

"I will inform them, you two go to Der," Danic growled out, opened the door and gestured to it.

"If you tell them, Danic, I'll be furious with you," Ava threatened, waving a finger in his face.

Danic smirked, not taking an irate human woman seriously. "I also told Kanzo about Billy, add that to my transgressions."

Ava frowned. "I don't understand. Billy isn't a secret I need to keep." She faced Kanzo and pressed a hand to his chest. "I didn't tell you, my Eth, because I don't think about him anymore. He's no longer in here." She touched her chest over her heart.

Kanzo cupped her elbow. "We will speak of this, *thamani*, I vow. For now, I need Der to ensure your wellbeing."

"I know, to be by your side for a long time. I remember." Her smile was tremulous. "I'm happy to have known you, Kanzo."

Ava left the quarters but must have waited in the passage within Kanzo's line of sight for he stared straight through the door, like a deer in solarlights.

"You are not leaving me, Ava. This is a simple procedure." And the door closed behind him, leaving Jack stunned, still staring at the door.

"You better start sharing some info, Danic, or I'm going to go next-level crazy on your ass." Jack poked him in the chest, tempted to smack him on the back of the head instead. The only problem was, he was too damn tall.

"It is a simple procedure, Der must remove the interpreter to..."

"It's still inside her? Will she speak English again?" Jack gritted her teeth. "Speak, damnit."

"There is a signal originating from the interpreter..."

"An explosive?" Jack's mouth dropped open, now understanding the few whispered words her O.D.I. managed to translate.

"No, our concern is that it is vulnerable to a kill command." Danic scowled at her.

He folded his arms across his chest, and his jaw hardened. Jack didn't give a shit that she was trying his patience. They'd just gotten Ava back, and she wouldn't stand by and lose her.

"The interpreter inserted was not equipped for a human brain and damaged her ear in the process. The Yithian language overwrote her natural language and caused her brain to swell. Until the swelling reduces, she cannot have an O.D.I. installed as we are uncertain as to what impact it may have on her. Discovering the signal means the device needs to be removed now. Der cannot say whether English will return or Yithian will be permanent."

"They are removing it now?" Jack lunged for the door.

"She did not want you to know, Lady Jack." Danic leaped in front of her, blocking her exit and forcing her to listen. "She did not want you to be concerned. Kanzo is with her, and he will escort her to you when the procedure is complete. This I vow."

"How long is this supposed to take?" Jack folded her arms across her chest and used her instructor's icy glare on him. The one that cowered the students in their boots. Danic seemed unfazed, damn him.

"Fifteen to twenty minutes." He tapped on his O.D.I. and gestured to the display vid mounted on the wall. "We can observe from here."

An image of medical appeared; Ava was on the med-bed with Kanzo holding her hand. In the background, there was another display vid showing the procedure as it played out. Danic glanced at Jack before splitting the display vid into two. The procedure dominated the right panel.

"There's no blood." Taylor gaped.

"Nano-meds are inserted via her ear. They will dismantle the interpreter piece by piece." Danic gestured to the left panel as he increased the magnification, showing tiny pieces placed on her cheek.

"This...is incredible." Jack grinned at Danic then at the vids, afraid she'd miss something. "Thank you for showing us." He shrugged. "I'm fully aware you were tempted to throw me over your shoulder and lock me in a room somewhere." She chuckled at his startled expression.

"Ulriq would have my hair for that, but under the circumstances, if you had disrupted the procedure and unknowingly endangered yourself by proximity…"

"True, so thank you again for this." Jack threw an arm around Vicky and Taylor and continued to watch the procedure.

Minutes later, Jack's breath rushed out in a whoosh when Ava's eyelids fluttered open. She crushed Vicky and Taylor in a hug, tossing Danic a smile in apology for her behavior. All was once again well in her world.

Chapter Twenty-Six

ULRIQ WAS UNABLE TO sit still and paced the comm room while drawing curious glances from his males. His inability to control himself added fury to the mix and had him pacing more, slamming down his data tab, or barking out orders. The Ethera drove him to seek out Jack, to scent her, touch her, but when he did, it only made things worse. He was aroused all the time, and his lack of focus affected his communication with his males.

Not that he could get a moment alone with her. Her quarters was always occupied, but if he had her near a bed, as in his quarters... He shuddered. The temptation was unbearable. The common was out, the comm room also. That left the viewing deck. Just today, he had tasked Pilot Ksal to block access to all personnel except him.

As he guided her there, he kept his twitching fingers pressed against her lower back, relishing her heat through the thin fabric of her dress. And he liked her in this garment, as well. The fabric was soft and flowed over her curves, all the way to the floor. A slit to the side of the dress blessed him with glimpses of her calves and sandaled feet. If she dressed to entice him, she was successful. His hard arousal was a permanent feature. His heart thumped in his chest, in anticipation. Soon, he promised himself.

As he entered the deck, the door sealed behind them, trapping them inside. He spun and lifted her, crushing her to his chest with an arm wrapped around her back.

"Ulriq?" She frowned.

He'd moved too quickly, but he wouldn't apologize, not now that he had her alone and in his arms...at last.

"Stay still, Jack," he said, his control almost shredded.

She looked a little dazed as he lowered his head to feather his lips across hers. Her sigh merged with his. Marveling at the warmth of her mouth, he did nothing else but hold her, brushing his lips across hers, back and forth. Her soft skin and pink lips, her sweet breath, and fruity scent pummeled his senses. Her heartbeat pounded as erratically as his.

Beyond his control, his hips swayed from side-to-side, letting her feel his achingly hard arousal. The pain didn't lessen with her proximity.

As his malehood notched into the juncture of her thighs, a sharp dart of fire shot through him. Her intoxicating scent grew stronger, encouraged by their heated bodies. His nostrils flared. He closed his eyes as he unashamedly inhaled, then released his breath on a moan.

"You try my strength, *ensa*," he said, his gravel voice no longer his to control.

"I'm sorry," she whispered.

"Do not be." He zeroed his gaze on hers. "Open your mouth for me."

She gasped, and her scent darkened. He couldn't take the time to admire her reaction to his words. His need was too great.

With a deep growl, he slashed his mouth over hers, his tongue delving in, unrepentant in its demand. He groaned at the taste and silkiness of her, his appreciation vibrating through her. She trembled in his arms as he ravaged the contours of her mouth.

"Jacqueline," he whispered, allowing their breaths to mingle as if their souls could unite.

"Ulriq." She panted as she fought for air. "May I kiss you back?"

"Yes," he rasped, shivering in response to her request.

Cupping his face, she held him still as she rubbed her lips across his, before licking his bottom lip. She sucked it into her mouth, briefly, then slipped her tongue between his lips, tracing them from the inside. Moaning, she plundered him, teasing his tongue, inviting him to duel with hers. He rumbled his approval, crushing her to him, drinking deeply from her.

They drew apart, gasping for air.

"As a first kiss, that was wonderful." She ran her nails over his scalp, sparking fire across his skin.

"If you touch me so, you *will* receive more than a kiss," he vowed.

"Promise?" she teased, a sensual smile curling her kiss-swollen lips.

He laughed and loosened his grip to roam his hands over her body. His hand itched, and so he slid it straight down to cup her backside. As the softness filled his palm, he froze.

"Jack?" he grumbled. "Please tell me you are wearing undergarments?" Rubbing her fabric-covered backside, he searched. He was desperate to find an undergarment seam, anything to denote she was covered, protected, shielded from his eager lust. His greatest fear was harming her if he lost control.

"I am." She blushed.

He groaned, pinning his forehead against hers to draw in ragged breaths.

"It's just small." She tightened her arms around him.

Shuddering, he reached down the front of her garment to slip his hand through the slit, his searching fingers finding bare skin. He slid his hand up her calf, over a firm knee, along a muscled yet soft thigh to grasp her bare backside. Unable to resist filling his hand, skin on skin, he squeezed it, careful not to bruise her.

"Jack, you are killing me," he rasped as he cupped her other cheek. The entire garment rose, exposing her thighs, allowing her to spread them to wrap around his waist. He crashed his mouth over hers with urgency, granting her no mercy. When she shivered, the sensation of her excitement sent waves of heat to nestle in his balls. She buried her fingers in his hair, crushing her body against him, tormenting him further as she overwhelmed his senses.

He lowered her as quickly as he'd picked her up, though his trembling hands did linger to ensure she maintained her balance. His body twitched with the effort to control himself.

"Can you find your way back?" His voice was hoarse, but he didn't care.

For his sanity, perhaps even hers, he needed to...claim her? The Ethera demanded. But he couldn't. She was human, smaller in stature, softer, not as hardy as Etterian females. More than this, with the Ethera working on the mated pair, affection and attachment was a given. Rushing their union, hurting Jack wouldn't add his long-term goal, that of affection. Which meant he needed to move at a slower pace. He winced at the thought. Going slow was killing him.

She nodded in a daze, her eyes wide.

"Good." He stole a quick kiss and strode away, his hands clenched at his sides.

Chapter Twenty-Seven

Etterian battleship, Kushin
Speeding toward Earth
The girls' shared quarters

JACK WAS STARTLED AWAKE, uncertain what disturbed her. Ava and Vicky slept soundly next to her. Neither slept restlessly. Jack threw a bare leg out to stretch it on top of the blanket. She stroked from collarbone to breast to taut nipple through her sleep shirt. Her body was in a constant state of need since Ulriq rescued her. Sighing, she wished he would relieve the ache between her thighs.

As if conjured from hope, the shape of a kneeling Ulriq formed beside her bed. Her squeak of fright might have been heard had he not pressed his hand over her mouth. The room's lights had been set to ten percent luminosity, so she could make out his gorgeous, *naked* chest.

"Ulriq? Are you naked?" she gasped.

"Be still, Jack."

He released her and dipped his hands under the blankets, burrowing between her and the mattress. Careful not to agitate the bed with Ava and Vicky asleep, he scooped Jack into his arms. She clung to his shoulders as he clasped her to his chest. The velvet texture of his skin imploded those damn stun grenades within her stomach. To inhale his scent, she buried her nose in the curve of his neck. She was so tempted to press a kiss to his skin, even slip out her tongue to taste him, but she managed to rein herself in.

As he carried her out of her quarters, she didn't say anything. Nor did she speak as he strode along various passages to his quarters. Once inside, he lowered her feet to the floor when the door sealed behind them. He kept his arm around her, ensuring she remained close to him.

"What's wrong?" she asked now that she was free to talk.

His facial expression had said not-a-word, and she had respected him enough to save her questions. She rested her hand on his cheek in concern, running her thumb across the dark circles under an eye.

"I cannot sleep," he muttered, frustration thickening his voice.

"Okay, what do you need from me?"

"I need you in my bed." He hesitated, then winced. "I need to hold you."

"Of course, Ulriq, whatever you need," she assured—like she would a new trainee—and gestured to his room.

He growled, startling her. She jerked to a halt and faced him.

"What I truly need is to spread your thighs and bury myself deep in your softness, what I need is to taste every inch of you." He ran a trembling hand over his face, his gaze not leaving hers, even for the moment his hand passed over his eyes. "I am trying to go slowly with you..."

An overwhelming warmth flooded her chest, burning the backs of her eyes with unshed tears. That he cared enough not to rush her was unexpected, considerate, and unnecessary. She crossed to him and raised her hands to his face, cupping him, her touch tender.

"I'm going to tell you something, but you must promise not to react until I'm done speaking." She met his gaze and waited until he nodded. "This evening, you *will* rest. Tomorrow, you can spread my thighs as many times as you wish." His breath hitched, with his eyes widening in surprise. "But, for the first time, you'll need to go slowly, Ulriq. I'm... I have...never been with a man." He released a long-drawn-out moan, but did and said nothing. When he waited, she offered him a quick smile. "You can talk now."

Then he grabbed her, scooped her into his arms, and carried her to his bed, lowering her to it with infinite gentleness.

"Alodon's balls, my Jack. I do not know which to address first. That you would let me have you pleases me immensely, *thamani*. But that you are untouched, a female as beautiful as you, it shatters my control." The tremor in his voice validated his words.

He thought her beautiful? Blinking back the tears, she smiled. She didn't know what to say to that. "I'm...happy you find me beautiful, Ulriq." Wincing at her girlish reply, she hurried to cover her shyness. "I find you as handsome." She shifted to make space for him on the bed.

When he sprawled on his back, she curved her body into his, resting her head on his shoulder. He looped his arm around her to cup her hip, his touch possessive. With a deep sigh, she placed her hand, palm down, on his bare chest. She snuggled into the heat of him and allowed his erratic heartbeat to lull her.

But his stroking fingers caressing her hip didn't still. Every time she dozed off, she awoke to his fingers still squeezing and stroking her hip.

"Can you not sleep?" she whispered, in case he had fallen asleep.

"No," he said.

"Why not?"

"You are here with me in my bed. It is understandable that I cannot rest."

She lay there thinking, analyzing. If they made love now, they would rush it, and she had specified he needed to sleep first. Would it make a difference if they did make love now? Did they have to wait? And her body did ache with need for him. She shivered when she imagined Ulriq making love to her. The erotic image plagued her dreams.

"Would you like to make love now, Ulriq?"

He groaned and flexed his arm around her, drawing her closer. "I would like nothing more, but you are correct, my Jack. I need to rest." He patted her hip. "You sleep. I will follow shortly."

She sighed, and with a shake of her head, sat up. "Lights twenty percent," she said and looked at him. He settled a hooded and intense gaze upon her, spiking her heart rate and sending shivers of anticipation from her scalp to her toes. "Do you trust me, Ulriq?"

"Of course." His response was without hesitation.

"Then remove your pants."

"What?" he said, his voice hoarse.

She arched a brow, and he rose to yank his pants off, tossing them on the floor. He returned to the bed. Her gaze settled on his erection. He was hard…and big, but similar to humans. Except the head was rounder and dark ridges ran along the length of him. She gaped in delight, eager to explore.

The hot velvet texture of his skin warmed her fingers when she touched his chin. She traced a path down his ribbed stomach, over the valleys and peaks to circle the base of his erection. He gasped and stilled, waiting. She curled a hand around the silky, heated, granite girth of him, her fingertips barely closing. Beneath her touch were more ridges running along bottom of his erection.

When she stroked them he hissed but held himself still, his hands locked into fists. "Jack," he warned, his voice unrecognizable.

She ignored him and ran her hand up and down the length of him, allowing her fingers to brush over his head to the moisture dewing. He arched, his teeth dimpling his bottom lip to silence his responses, but a groan escaped, and his chest rumbled. He trembled under her touch. She slipped her other hand down to caress his balls, and he shuddered again, fresh dew forming on his tip.

"Jack," he gritted out, his voice harsh with emotion.

"Do you like that?" She pumped him again, careful to use his own lubrication as she worked his hard length between feathered touches across the head. Then she ran her tongue from base to tip, marveling at the hot, saltiness of him.

"*Thamani*, that feels—" His mouth dropped open, and with a roar, he orgasmed, shooting his release across his taut stomach.

She grinned, as his powerful body trembled while he regained his breath. Her body flushed with an answering desire, that she could bring pleasure to such a commanding man.

"How did you know to do that?" he panted, his ice-blue gaze adoring her.

She blushed under his admiration. "Vicky has these romance novels she's particularly fond of. I'll read you sections if you like."

He used his discarded pants to wipe himself. His focus didn't shift from her, and his chest rose and fell, snagging her admiration. "Your turn," he whispered as he grabbed her ankle, tugging her leg straight.

Chapter Twenty-Eight

Etterian battleship, Kushin
Speeding toward Planet Earth
Ulriq's quarters

"I DON'T NEED A turn," Jack assured, even though her thighs drenched at Ulriq's implication.

He paused to inhale her scent, allowing himself the requisite time to savor it.

"Yes, you do." He grabbed her other ankle to tug the leg straight too.

With her ankles in his hands, she sprawled backward. She looked at him from the position on her elbows. Her long, bare legs glowed under the lighting, and her tunic pooled at the juncture of her thighs. Her curls cascaded behind her with her blue eyes smiling at him. It was a vision he would treasure. When he slid his hands along her calves, applying pressure to part her thighs, she twitched.

He inhaled again, unable to fill his lungs to his satisfaction. "You are aroused." With a gentle gathering of her sleep tunic, he exposed her feminine folds to his hungry gaze. Her pale curls glistened with her need, like dewdrops on hahyt petals.

"Beautiful...Jack, you are beautiful," he whispered, unable to strip the deep reverence from his voice. Her sexual organs were like Etterian females, but he prayed he didn't harm her.

He brushed his fingers across her curls before slipping between her folds. She was slick, silky, smooth, and so addictive to stroke. Her response was immediate, her hips twisting as he tormented her. Her eyes darkened, narrowed, with the intensity in them hardening him again. He rubbed her nub. She cried out, and tremors racked her body.

"Do you like that?" he teased, repeating her question.

She answered with a throaty moan and lashed out to grip the bedding. He slid a finger into her channel and froze. Despite his joy at finding her so hot, soft, and wet, his finger encountered what he hoped was just a barrier.

"What is this, Jack?" he asked, concerned that this was as deep as she went or that he might hurt her. He twirled the tip of his finger across the barrier.

"It's my hymen. Proof that I'm a virgin." She lifted a hand to cup his cheek. "Tomorrow, you will pierce it to be my first lover."

"First and only," he growled. She nodded, her teeth dimpling her lip as he rubbed his thumb over her nub. "Will it hurt?"

She stilled and met his gaze. "Yes, and I'll bleed, but it's minor, Ulriq. I won't feel it seconds after you fuck me."

His eyelids fluttered and he grinned. "Truth?"

She smiled at him. "I promise."

"Good," he said before dipping his head to suck her nub into his mouth. Her taste exploded across his senses. He shuddered and flattened his tongue, unable to get enough of her.

"Ulriq, please...I need..." She gasped and whimpered, peppering her responses with his name.

Licking his lips as he savored her arousal, he leaned back to marvel at her lack of control. She didn't know what was happening to her. But she showed no fear, his Jack. She trusted him to guide and care for her.

"What do you need, *thamani*?" he rumbled as he nestled into her curls, burying his face in what he would forever think of as heaven. With his hands on her hips, he held her gyrating hips to the bed.

"Don't stop," she demanded.

Chuckling, he ran his tongue over her seam to her nub and down again. He was merciless as he lapped at her, tasted, and suckled until she froze.

"Ulriq," she screamed.

The way her body trembled, then stiffened, her hips twitching beneath him meant her fulfillment was close. Sadness warred with the overwhelming burn of victory. He would have loved to spend more time between her thighs. But he didn't slow his onslaught. She keened, and shattered, her body convulsing as pleasure tore through her. The moans and purrs she made had him shuddering in reaction.

He drank her release, loving having his mouth and nose buried so intimately in her folds. Kissing his way up her quivering stomach, he suckled on her nipple through her tunic before meeting her lips, delving into the recesses of her mouth and claiming her. "Did you enjoy your first fulfillment?"

"Oh, yes." She caressed his shoulders as if she couldn't resist touching him. He liked that thought. "You have a talented tongue."

He pressed his temple to hers as he fought to regulate his breathing. "You please me, Jack," he said, his voice hoarse with many emotions thickening it.

The strongest made him want to shout out her name, call her his *thamani* from the top of the royal palace at Issneen. Falling onto his side, he tucked her into the curve of his body. He wrapped his arms around her to hold her tight against him, wishing he could rip off her tunic, and press her bare skin against his.

"Can you sleep now, Ulriq?" she teased with a sleepy chuckle.

"Yes, my Jack," he promised, and with her in his arms, the scent of her on his fingers, and the taste of her on his tongue, sleep claimed him swiftly.

Chapter Twenty-Nine

Etterian battleship, Kushin
Speeding toward Earth
Ulriq's Quarters

ULRIQ DRIFTED AWAKE, MORE rested than he could remember ever feeling. He lay there as still as could be, trying to ascertain why peace had settled upon him. A soft backside snuggled into him, snagging his focus. His Jack lay in his bed, having allowed her abduction. She'd let him touch and hold her until sleep claimed him. He drew her securely against him as he inhaled her scent deep into his lungs. Maker, how he adored her.

"Morning, Ulriq," she said in a voice husky from sleep. She squeezed his forearms wrapped around her waist and tucked under her breasts.

"Morning, *thamani.*" He planted kisses on her shoulder, up her neck to her earlobe.

"I like waking up like this." She rolled over, pressing her chest against his, and a kiss to his chin.

"As do I." He captured her lips with his, drawing her breath into his lungs. "I am rested." His enthusiasm brought forth an answering chuckle from her. "I get to claim you this day."

"Yes, you do." Her touch feathered along his jaw, pausing to tease his bottom lip. He flicked his tongue out to taste her finger, pleased she touched him at will. "Want to share a shower with me?"

Heat burst in his chest, a supernova, bright and devastating. Something constricted him. He wanted to share this aspect of her life and hadn't realized how much such an opportunity would mean to him.

"Yes." He cleared his clogged throat and tried again. "I would be honored."

She laughed as she slid off the bed and stripped off her sleep tunic. For the second time since meeting her, she stood before him naked.

He groaned at the sight of her, drinking her in like a starved male. Her long legs, silky and toned. Those breasts, bouncing with taut nipples. The curve of her hips...the light curls at the apex of her thighs.

"Jack..." He trembled, curling his fingers into tight fists.

"Come, Ulriq." She sashayed away from him, her hands rising to unravel her braided hair.

Eager to be near her, he bounded after her. As she stepped under the water, he wrapped his arms around her back as she placed her hands against his chest. Contentment settled upon him, and with it, the realization of what it meant to have a Dar Eth.

Unable to resist, he feathered kisses from her temple, across her cheeks and lips, happy to do nothing else for now. He held her in his arms, cherishing her. Not wanting to mar the paleness of her skin with a too-eager grip, he kept his touch gentle.

Time was inconsequential, standing under the water, kissing, and touching each other in adoration. He didn't care and ignored his O.D.I.'s buzzes. For now, he was her Eth, and that was all that mattered.

When her stomach growled, he deactivated the water and pressed the blue button for the dryer. Time stretched ahead, a promise, a reward, with the few more minutes he could spend kissing her and did just that. He deepened the kiss though, in desperation to retain the taste of her. This wasn't logical for he would eat and drench his mouth with momaberry sauce. But there were no annals that said the Ethera was logical. When the dryer deactivated, he forced himself to release her. He trailed his fingers across her hips, regretting the end to this remarkable experience.

"What would you like for breakfast?"

"Besides you?" She flashed him a lustful smile that had him groaning, his fingers flexing where he gripped the wrap. "Bacon and cheese sandwich with a vanilla latte."

He slipped the wrap around her, activating it, admiring her as it molded to her form.

"Sounds appetizing." He slipped his wrap on, allowing it to conform to his shape before he reached for her hand, lacing his fingers through hers.

"I'll share mine if you share yours," she suggested as they strode to his rehydrator.

"Agreed." He grinned.

She ordered hers then settled on a comfy, balancing her plate on her knees.

"You first," she said when he sat next to her.

She offered him a brown triangle. When he sniffed it, she laughed. He took a big bite and chewed, a slow smile forming. The texture was crunchy and smooth, the flavor salty and rich. She offered her latte. He sniffed again before filling his mouth with the hot sweet liquid that held a hint of bitter smokiness.

"Unusual yet delicious." He offered her a forkful of kreso dipped in momaberry sauce.

She opened her mouth and slid the morsel off the fork with the tip of her tongue. His gaze heated, and his fingers clenched the fork, almost buckling it. She didn't notice, with her eyes closing on a moan. The meat would be soft, savory, the dark sauce thick and tart. He offered his giyua juice.

"Delicious," she said before biting into her brown triangle. They finished their meals in silence even as their gazes lingered.

After breakfast, she jumped on the bed and curled her legs under her to watch him change into his armor. There was pleasure in her appreciative attention as he covered each part of his nudity.

"I will not last this day if you look at me like that, Jack."

"I can't help it." She shrugged and ran her hand down his back when he sat on the bed to tug on his footwear. When he strolled to his door, he was reluctant to leave. He drew her close to him for a deep kiss, one filled with longing. Holding her away from him with trembling hands, he spun on his heel and left her alone in his quarters. He took two steps down the darkened passage and bolted back to her. Panic with an irrational fear and deep-seated need tore through him.

"Ulriq?" she squeaked in alarm.

He said nothing, just pinned her to the bulkhead, breathing her in deeply. "Stay with me," he whispered into her mouth, urgency peppering his plundering tongue. "As my Dar Eth, please...stay with me," he begged her between soul-destroying kisses, allowing his hands to cup her unbound breasts. He rubbed his thumbs across her taut nipples, their hardness tenting her wrap. "Forever, Jack. I need you forever."

She stared at him for a long moment, her thoughts and expressions flitting across her face, too fast for him to register. He recognized joy, hope, fear but none of the others.

"Tell me your thoughts."

She pinched her lips then sighed. "My...heart is beating so fast, Ulriq...I knew the Ethera was forever, and I want that. I just never expected it this quickly, or that you might feel the same way. Teric explained the Ethera to me but none of this emotional turmoil." She pressed a kiss to Ulriq's lips to silence his need to convince her, wordlessly conveying to let her finish. "I want to grasp this...gift, with both hands. Maybe I'm being naïve, maybe I'm jumping in recklessly, but what I know about you makes me appreciate the wonderful male you are. You're incredibly handsome, Ulriq, but it isn't just that. I like your thoughtfulness, your kindness, your honor. I love that you feel the need to please me. You make me happy, and if saying yes to forever means a repeat of last night and this morning, then yes...I'd like forever with you, Ulriq."

He growled his appreciation and crushed her to him for yet another mind-blowing kiss that snatched his wits and his ability to breathe.

"Call your king and tell him you're sick...," she teased as he stepped back, her fingers trailing down his armored chest, "...that you need a day off."

"Temptress." Unable to contain the joy within him, his smile broadened into a grin. Her arousal's scent rose to greet him, and his nostrils flared with the force of his inhalation. "Your scent is enticing, delicious. You make my mouth water."

"I make your mouth water?" She fake-gasped. "Your smile's to blame for my current scent."

"You react like this to my smile? Then I will be sure to use it more often."

"You do that, and you won't be able to walk tomorrow," she teased.

"That is not a threat, Jack, it is a vow." He kissed her again, unable to resist. Why did she taste so good? "What will you do today?"

"Visit with Aala, Vicky, and Ava. Hopefully Mich will let Taylor come up for air." Her eyes twinkled, and she leaned her head back to chuckle, one filled with desire and mischief. "At your shift-end, I'll be here, naked." She let her wrap fall open, exposing her nudity to his gaze. "Like this."

He growled, and with a sharp flick, closed her wrap.

She laughed, the sound husky and alluring, before opening the door and giving him a gentle shove out. "Have a lovely day, my Eth."

He groaned as he stared at the steel door, wishing he would command it to open. Turning away from the temptation, he adjusted his arousal in his breeches. A smile curled his lips as he recalled Jack's expression. His Jack, laughing, teasing, filled his chest with a joy that saturated the corners of his heart, smothering the darkness that had once reigned there. Alodon's balls, how was he going to survive the day without her?

Chapter Thirty

Etterian battleship, Kushin
Speeding toward Earth

ULRIQ GLANCED AT HIS O.D.I. again, the time a few minutes past when he'd last checked it. Even though he no longer barked orders at his males, he might as well not be present for the attention he gave his tasks. Nerx stormed in, snatched the data tab from Ulriq's numb fingers before striding out again. Point made. Not that it changed Ulriq's current situation. He wanted to be with Jack, not stuck in the comm room approving requisitions.

A supreme commander meant honor, duty... he sighed, drawing Ksal's gaze. Ulriq squared his shoulders, hoping to not embarrass himself further. It was just a few hours, then he would see her...

"Pilot Ksal?"

Ulriq's head shot up as those uttered words came across the comm's audio. It was a feminine voice he would recognize anywhere.

"Hello? Anyone? Damn, is this thing broken too?"

A grin spread across his face. His males in the comm room faced him, this time for another reason than his deep sighs.

"Morning, milady," Ksal said.

"Did you not answer me on purpose?" She huffed.

"How can I assist you, milady?"

She hesitated. "Um, for one, could you let me out of Ulriq's quarters?"

Ulriq frowned, hearing her embarrassment at his thoughtlessness.

"Full access has been granted, milady." Ksal's shoulders shook. "I apologize for my oversight."

Ulriq nodded at Ksal, grateful for the assist, but he had forgotten. Perhaps on a subconscious level, he hadn't wanted to grant her access lest she left him. He liked that she was in his quarters, awaiting his return. Warmth flooded his chest at this morning's memory. And she had agreed to stay with him...forever.

"So, there are no special words to command the door to open?"

Ksal rolled his lips, his eyes sparkling with unexpressed humor. "Special words, milady?"

"You know, like open sesame?" A smile filled her voice.

Ulriq ached to charge out the comm room, bolt to her, and bury himself in any part of her she would allow him access to.

"No, milady. Walk toward it, and it will open. It senses your movement."

She groaned at Ksal's words, the sound indicating her disbelief. "Like I didn't try that, you damn alien," she muttered.

Ksal jerked back at her words, but then he bit his fist to smother his laughter.

"Thank you, Ksal," Jack said in a louder voice. "Now, how do I communicate with Teric?"

Ulriq frowned, not liking the idea of a male alone with his Dar Eth in his quarters. That the male was Teric, her kidnapper, worsened his unhappiness. He gritted his teeth, fighting the illogical urge to imprison the male.

"Did you comm him via your O.D.I.?" Ksal's brow furrowed while his eyes shimmered.

"Shit, I forgot I had that. Thank you again, Ksal. Please don't tell Ulriq I was being an idiot."

"Of course, milady." Ksal's laughter didn't reflect in his voice.

"Monitor my quarters, Ksal, for the duration of this day," Ulriq said. "Monitor Teric's location at all times."

"He will steal her again?" Ksal raised an eyebrow while wiping his eyes.

Ulriq grumbled at having the impossibility pointed out to him. "I would prefer not to find out."

"Supreme Commander, Teric has requested access to your quarters." Ksal's words startled Ulriq, bringing forth a strong reaction that bordered on violence.

Was Jack even clothed? Alodon's balls, why hadn't he seen to her needs this morning? He was proving to be a thoughtless Eth. Bolting to Ksal, he leaned over the multi-lit console, his gaze locked on the audio button. Ksal gestured to a mini display vid, and Ulriq flicked his focus there. With yet another grateful nod to Ksal, he read his replicator history, indicating she'd clothed herself. Half of the tension drained from his body.

"Enter." At the sound of Jack's voice, Ulriq scowled. He hadn't even heard the door chime. "Come in, Teric. Where's Aala?"

"She is with the girls and my Dar Eth." Teric's voice was thick with emotion Ulriq recognized: gratitude, awe, disbelief, yearning, to name a few.

"Good, now we can chat. Would you like something from the rehydrator? A hot chocolate?"

Ulriq growled. What in Alodon's hell was a hot chocolate?

"Please." Teric's familiarity with a human beverage irked Ulriq, and his fingers twitched. He curled them into a fist and fought the urge to thump the console.

"So, tell me, how do you *feel* about finding your Dar Eth?" Jack's voice was fainter as she walked to the rehydrator.

"It was unexpected," Teric answered noncommittally.

"But you're happy about it?" Jack's voice grew louder.

"Of course." Teric's inflection remained constant.

"Honestly, Teric, talking to you is like drawing blood from a stone. I'll not tell Vicky anything you say to me. I thought you knew that already."

"Alodon's balls, Jack. What are you expecting me to say? My only reason for living was my daughter. And how could I, a dishonored male, be gifted with a Dar Eth? Now, I have two females to protect."

Sadness darkened Jack's voice. "You aren't happy?"

"Of course, I am joyful." His rough tone defied his words.

"All right." She hesitated. "But Vicky's being difficult?"

"Human females are nothing compared to our females. Vicky is sweet, considerate, gentle, appreciative. All the things a Dar Eth should be."

Jack huffed. "Then why are you so grumpy?"

Teric groaned. "Look at me, Jack. My hands are shaking, and my heart refuses to stay in a steady rhythm. I cannot breathe with her near me. I cannot think when she touches me, yet I need to scent her...all the time."

Jack gasped. "Do all Etterian males feel like this? Does the Ethera affect you all the same?"

Ulriq smiled. It was good she understood what he endured for her.

"I do not know, Jack. The annals only mention sharp pain, weak knees, uncontrollable lust. I *feel* far more than this. I need to see her smile. I need to have her touch me, and when she does, I am grateful. But what threatens my control is the constant craving to scent her."

"Then why not keep something of hers in your pocket? Every time it gets too unbearable, then take a sniff." Silence met Jack's suggestion, but Ulriq nodded. It was good advice. "Since we're on this subject, what is the Ethera exactly?"

"A few centuries ago, the Great War of Darriz cost Etteria many males due to a single emotional outburst between ambassadors. Sides were chosen. King Prius attempted to force peace, but in the end, formed the third faction in the war. Agendas shifted from revenge, justice, to the quest for power. As the victor, King Prius had to restore our broken world."

When Teric paused, Jack said, "Sounds like human history."

"True for most worlds. King Prius turned to an advanced civilization, the Durns. Genetic modifications granted us control over our emotions and the ability to mate the ideal partner. The Durn designed and implemented the training regime we still utilize. Each *damu* is taught how to control their emotions, their energies honed into worthwhile pursuits. As time passes, our vigilant existence becomes dull routine, the joy we once found fades, leaving the nothingness. The void circles our souls. I sense it now. Mine is dormant thanks to Vicky. But those who do not find their Dar Eths, they will sacrifice their lives in the pursuit of battle, to feel something other than emptiness." Teric released a steady breath. "When I saw Vicky, I...the pain was excruciating, Jack. All at once, emotions long suppressed flooded me. I once again know deep affection, comradery, gratitude, lust, and my eye color is that of my birth."

"And..." Jack cleared her throat. "If a Dar Eth dies?"

"The void returns. The male cannot be saved. He is doomed for no other female exists for him."

"Thanks for explaining, Teric. I suggest you share this with Vicky. Now tell me, what was that thing between Aala and Vytus?"

Teri's voice hardened. "I suspect they are a pairing."

Jack gasped. "How's that possible? She's so young."

"The Ethera will trigger when she is of age. For now, they are friends. I am grateful the Ethera did not happen. I would have had a Dar Eth and a new son on the same day."

"What...what do you mean?" Jack whispered.

"The Ethera forms a lifetime commitment and is recognized by Etterian law the moment it happens."

"I'm married?" she squeaked. Silence met her question, but since Ulriq himself awaited his O.D.I.'s guidance, Teric had to do the same.

"Yes," Teric said.

"No wedding or dress?" At Jack's whimper, Ulriq stretched across the console and flicked a button. The display vid filled with the image of his quarters. Jack slumped in a comfy, curling into herself with her hands clasped between her thighs.

Ulriq growled, not liking his Dar Eth's distress.

"Etteria has no such ceremony, Jack." Seated in the comfy across from her, Teric leaned forward, resting his elbows on his knees. "Are yours necessary?"

"Oh, yes, Teric. Especially the dress. All our friends and family gather to witness the joyous union between man and woman. It's celebrated, and all women dream of their day."

Ulriq's mouth fell open; he was startled at the level of emotion in Jack's voice. He was also angry they hadn't known of this human tradition and the importance thereof. Ksal called forth images on his smaller display vid, showing various human females in gowns of white. They looked happy, excited. Ulriq grunted.

"Jack, we didn't know," Teric said. "Would Vicky want the same?"

Jack offered a strained smile. "Of course. The wedding ceremony makes us feel special, desired, cherished."

"Thank you, Jack." Teric released his breath on a whoosh. "I will ensure Vicky receives such a ceremony."

"You will make a good Eth, Teric." Jack reached across to pat his knee.

Her confidence in him angered Ulriq, staining his vision red. He tightened his fingers on the back of Ksal's chair, denting the metal. As if she'd implied Ulriq was wanting.

"You are not upset I am her Eth?"

Jack chuckled, and her posture relaxed. "I once wanted to kill you, but I don't feel like that anymore."

"I am honored to know you. Your forgiveness humbles me."

"So formal, Teric." She laughed, her curls catching the lighting and shimmering. "Now, I'm sure Aala mentioned you can have my house?"

"Yes, she did." Teric frowned. "It is an unusual gift."

"Nonsense. My life is with Ulriq now. Where he goes, I go." Her confident words, spoken in her husky voice, soothed Ulriq, specifically easing the feeling that he'd failed her. "I'll sign over the ownership. I had solar panels installed, so you should have power indefinitely. You may need to pay for water, though, but Vicky will guide you through all the travails of being a property owner."

"Are you going planetside with us?"

"I hope so. I haven't spoken to Ulriq about it yet. There are a few things I need. A few mementos of my parents. I'd also like to see Fred, my father, of sorts." A comfortable silence fell for a few minutes before Jack spoke again. "Tell me, Teric, is it possible to contact Earth? I'd like to let Fred know I'm still alive."

Teric pointed to the display vid mounted on the wall. "Address the display vid. It will search for your Fred and attempt a communication link via the various technologies your planet may have available."

"It's that easy?" She bounded up, exposing her long legs in her tight blue pants to Ulriq's eager gaze. With her nose an inch from the black vid, she said, "Ava Hamilton?"

"Jack? What the hell? You disappeared in the middle of the night. I hope he was worth it." Ava's image flickered on the vid.

"So far, yes." Joy seeped into every cell of Ulriq's body. So, he wasn't such a disaster of an Eth. It was that or his Jack was a forgiving female. He liked to think it was both.

"Good. I want details later when Teric isn't eavesdropping."

"I am doing no such thing," Teric said, thus confirming he was indeed listening.

Ulriq dipped his focus at Ksal. The male's smile mimicked Ulriq's.

"Hello, big guy." Vicky's face held fondness.

"Greetings, *minus susa*." Teric's voice had taken on a gruffer quality.

Aala threw herself into the conversation, peeking up from between Vicky and Ava. "Father, look at my hair. Vicky did it, is it not beautiful?" Two thick braids ran from her temple down her back with strands tucking in from the sides.

"Everything is beautiful on you, *ensa*," Teric teased his daughter.

"Shall we meet in the common for lunch?" Jack asked. "I have a craving for a burger."

"Add fries, and I'm there. With a strawberry milkshake?" Vicky's cheeks flushed. "Aala, wait until you try one of those."

"Teric and I will see you there shortly." Jack ended the communication. "You don't mind joining us for lunch, Teric? We didn't just overrule your plans for your day?"

"I am pleased to join you, Jack."

Ulriq stared long after the display vid reverted to the stars ahead.

"They have left your quarters, Supreme Commander," Pilot Ksal said, receiving an arched brow from Ulriq for this needless information.

Ksal widened his eyes, attempting to convey Ulriq should join them. Nerx gripped Ulriq's shoulder, having been listening in from the position of the comm room's door.

"I am hungry myself. The...uh, burger, sounded interesting." At Nerx's comment, Ulriq glared at him.

"You complained about my distraction, and now you wish to worsen it? Once I see Jack, the remaining hours of my shift will be unbearable."

"Where is the evidence proving such? Seeing her might ease the Ethera. In truth, I *am* hungry. Ksal, you have the comm." With a firm grip on his arm, Nerx escorted Ulriq to the common, not that he dragged his feet. Excitement jolted through him in anticipation.

The moment he entered the room, his gaze unerringly found her. She was so beautiful he feared his breathing would never return to normal. Dressed in dark-blue leggings that hugged her thighs, and a white tunic that molded to the shape of her breasts, she looked delectable. She'd braided her hair, and it curled into the enticing curve of her neck. Her hands in her pockets pulled her pants down in the front, exposing an inch more of smooth skin. If he had a choice, he would rather make a meal out of her.

"Ulriq," Jack called from across the room, rushing over to slide her arm around his waist.

Her open display of affection startled any witnessing warrior but pleased him. As if she was laying claim to him. He rumbled his approval. Nerx indicated from across the room, that he'd secured a table. Ulriq tugged Jack against him, his fingers twitching where they touched bare skin.

"Where is Mich, Jack?" Nerx asked as they approached.

She shrugged, but a hahyt-pink stained her cheeks. Ulriq brushed a finger along her skin, relishing the heat of her embarrassment.

"With Taylor, I assume. And Ava will join us later." Jack twisted to scan the common, searching for her. Ulriq's gaze followed. Ava argued with Kanzo, her arms flying wide or folding across her body. By the frown on Jack's brow, their unhappiness displeased her.

"What will you be eating?" Nerx threw an irritated glance at Ulriq who had yet to speak.

"A burger, with fries, and a strawberry milkshake." Jack raised her gaze to meet Ulriq's. Excitement poured from their blue depths, enchanting him. "Do you want to try, Ulriq?"

She paused, her mouth parted as she studied his face. The rich scent of her arousal rose to greet him. Did she know how aroused he was? Was it his eyes, his touch that revealed his current state? His nostrils flared, unable to resist the scent of her allure. She licked her bottom lip as she focused on his mouth. He narrowed his hearing, listening to her erratic heartbeat. A joyful chuckle rumbled through him.

"I will try, Jack. Ulriq will as well." Then Nerx grumbled for Ulriq's ears only, "You are behaving like a fool. Etterian females do not drive males this senseless."

"For us as well, please, Jack." Teric rested his laughing gaze on Nerx. "Wait till you have your own Dar Eth, Sub-Commander."

"Wonderful, I'll go get it then." Jack bounced up, her fingers trailing along Ulriq's shoulders as she hurried past him.

"Alodon's balls, Ulriq. You have more control than this," Nerx rasped.

Ulriq flashed a grin at his battle-bond, briefly removing his gaze from appreciating Jack's blue-encased backside. "Your Dar Eth will do the same to you, Nerx," he vowed with a chuckle, then let his attention rest on Jack at the rehydrator.

"It is a humbling experience, Sub-Commander. And it will test your control. Not even Gikaet compares." Teric sighed. "Although, what Base Commander Remi could do to prepare us, I cannot say."

Jack carried the plates to the table, serving everyone, before rushing back for her own. Once she'd done that, she weaved through the gathering males to the rehydrator to order the pink beverages. After she'd placed a tall glass in front of each of them, she slid onto the bench beside him and explained what she'd ordered.

He was mesmerized by the way she nibbled on her fries, by her lips wrapping around a straw, the way her fingers gripped the burger. Every moan of pleasure she made tore through him, filling his body with unbearable need. He stifled his responses to the best of his current ability. He mimicked her actions since the proper consuming of such a meal was unknown to him.

"This was remarkable, Jack." Nerx pushed his empty plate to the side. "I especially liked this..." He held up the empty milkshake glass.

"You have a sweet tooth?" Jack asked.

"My teeth are not sweet," he glared.

Her husky laugh unraveled and tangled tendrils of lust around Ulriq's malehood. "No, silly, it means you like sweet things."

Nerx glowered. "Speak to your Dar Eth, Ulriq. She cannot assume it is wise to call males silly." His grumbles only made her laugh more, not that she knew what he'd said.

"If calling you silly makes her laugh so, I will insist she does so daily," Ulriq muttered, his gaze riveted by the joy on Jack's face. He loved how her laughter came from her belly, throaty...sensual.

"What did you think, Aala? Teric?" A wide smile split Jack's cheeks and crinkled her beautiful eyes.

"The fries were a strange texture, the burger too big, but the milkshake is my favorite." Aala rose to order another.

"I preferred the burger." Teric grinned, tugging on one of his daughter's new braids as she passed him.

"What is a hot chocolate?" Ulriq asked.

"Why would you...?" Jack stilled. Anger and pain flitted across her face, cutting deeply into his heart. "Were you listening in on my conversation with Teric?"

"I do not trust Teric." Ulriq rubbed his chest to ease the tightness there.

"Why not?" She faced him. Hahyt pink stained her cheeks anew. By the rise and fall of her chest and the furious beating of her heart, this pink wasn't one of embarrassment.

Aid came from the least likely person. "He has a right to not trust me, Jack. I would feel the same." Teric ran his thumb along the glass and sucked the pink off it.

"Don't you dare defend him. Damnit, Ulriq, we've been together a day, and you can't even trust me that long." Her lips pursed. The darkness in her gaze alarmed him.

He reached for her, needing to keep her near. "It is not you I distrust, my Jack. I cannot...lose you. I am not strong enough to endure your parting."

"Ulriq is protective of you, Jack. What's not to like?" Ava slid onto a seat next to Nerx. Kanzo joined her.

"How would you feel if Kanzo listened in on your conversations?" Jack snapped.

Ava laughed at her dismissively. "I have nothing to hide." She jumped up to order something from the rehydrator.

Jack sighed and twisted her body, breaking contact. She didn't pull away, though, but leaned in and cupped his jaw. "Trust me, big guy. I'm not going anywhere. I promised you forever, remember."

He pressed a kiss to her palm. "You have forgiven Teric, this I admire. I have not, cannot. The pain is still raw..."

She stared at him, tracing his face with her blue gaze while her thumb plucked at his bottom lip. "Point made." Rising to her knees on the bench, she cupped his cheek and feathered a kiss across his lips. He drowned in her eyes as she did so. "You can have as much time as you need, and if you never forgive Teric, I won't judge you for it."

"Here we go, three hot chocolates with extra mini marshmallows." Ava slid a mug over to Ulriq and Nerx. "I don't know where you'll put it. You'd think burgers would fill you." She slid a bowl of mini marshmallows over to Aala. The girl dove right in with a greedy grin, but she had to share with her father who helped himself.

Nerx, Ulriq, and Kanzo tentatively pulled their mugs closer, but it was Nerx who took the first sip. His eyes widened, and he sipped again. A slow smile conquered his harsh features. Ulriq hadn't seen his battle-bond this joyful since the Ethera struck.

"Alodon." He moaned. "This is incredible." He gulped, uncaring that something dark with stringy white pieces clung to his lips. Bolstered by Nerx's reaction, Ulriq took a sip and rumbled. He smiled at Jack, the sweet, smoky, intense flavor drenched his mouth. His mouth twitched with the same detritus that Nerx sported. She stared at it before brushing her lips across Ulriq's ear.

"I want to lick that off you," she whispered and flashed him a heated gaze.

As he licked his lips, Jack hissed, her scent darkening as her breasts quivered.

"You do know we have advanced hearing?" Nerx smirked with his nose still buried in his mug.

Fresh hahyt-pink stained Jack's cheeks. Her gaze snagged Ulriq's before lingering on his lips. "And an excellent sense of smell." She looked at Nerx with an arched brow and a delicious curl to her upper lip.

Ulriq chuckled, enjoying their banter.

Nerx scowled, his nostrils flaring as he inhaled. He flinched and stood up abruptly. "Alodon's hell, females." He glared at Ulriq, blaming him for the delicious scent of human females. "Do they always scent this good? Do all of them?" Nerx turned his glare on Ava, as well. Not waiting for a response, he stormed over to the rehydrator, ordered another hot chocolate, and left the common.

"That was unkind, Jack," Teric mumbled a second before his thundering laughter broke free and shook his shoulders.

"His holier-than-thou attitude gets annoying." Jack slipped her hand into Ulriq's. "Should I apologize, my Eth?"

Ulriq stared at her upturned face, his gaze caressing her features. "No," he said, his voice rough as he struggled not to kidnap her. "He is correct though; your scent is evocative."

"You never complained before." Jack threw the accusation at Teric.

"You scented good, Jack. Arousal intensifies it and since you were not stimulated in my presence... Now, I do not scent you at all." Teric's face darkened with intense emotion, one Ulriq recognized as yearning. "I only scent my Dar Eth."

"Where is Vicky?" Jack scanned the common, searching for her friend.

"She wanted to comm a human male...Antoine, she called him."

Jack nodded at Teric before leaning into the curve of Ulriq's arm. He sighed and pressed a kiss into her hair.

"So, let me get this straight, excellent hearing and sense of smell?" Ava shoved a fry into her mouth. "And well-hung?" Jack's gasp and subsequent blush had Ulriq smiling. Her reaction brought an answering laugh from Ava. "There's my innocent Jack."

"Are you speaking about my...?" Ulriq asked in disbelief as her strange words were at last explained by his O.D.I.

Jack patted Ulriq's hand, unknowing that her touch turned into a caress. "I hope to limp tomorrow, are you planning on doing the same?" she asked.

Ava's face flushed. He didn't know what had just happened, but it looked like Jack was victorious.

"Ava can give sexual innuendo but can't take it without blushing," Jack whispered to Ulriq who arched his brow at her words. Sexual innuendo?

"Limping?" Ulriq frowned. He would never harm her.

Jack laughed, giving his hand a squeeze.

"I'll show you later," she rasped and snatched a sweet kiss.

He groaned in response.

Chapter Thirty-One

Etterian battleship, Kushin
Speeding Toward Earth

Ksal was sipping his hot chocolate when Ulriq returned to the comm room. The rich aroma filled the room. He raised an eyebrow in query. Nerx shrugged at him before glancing at his data tablet.

"I did not expect you to return this afternoon, Supreme Commander." Ksal rested his mug on the console.

"I am on shift," Ulriq said, though he did wish it wasn't so.

He'd escorted Jack to their quarters and plastered her to the bulkhead, eager to kiss her, to traverse the recesses of her hot mouth. His hands had unerringly found her lovely breasts, the taut nipples begging for his attention. In fact, recalling her moans made him rock hard, again. He shifted, uncomfortable in his too-tight armored breeches.

"I would recommend you take time to be with your Dar Eth." Nerx handed over the data tab.

It held endless requisitions and other dull documentation requiring Ulriq's attention. With a sense of obligation, Ulriq had attended to this repetitive side of his ranking. But today, he lacked the tolerance.

He slid the data tab back to Nerx with a look. "You mentioned Malo is en route to Earth?" A change of topic might bolster Ulriq's dwindling control.

"I commed him yesterday. He was not pleased with the assignment." Nerx chuckled.

Ulriq studied him, finding his pleasant demeanor unnerving. "Our males would be most eager to assist should he need us."

Nerx ran a finger down the data tab. "I assured him of our availability."

"Good." Ulriq studied the various display vids and flickering lights that decorated the console. "Any Yithian movement to report?"

Ksal shook his head. "There have been a few transport junkets. I have scanned them for abnormal life readings." Boredom was unavoidable, but it meant no danger loomed on the horizon, and the human females in their care were secure.

Time passed, and the incessant tapping finally reached through to Ulriq's unfocused mind.

"What seems to be the problem, Ksal?" His voice bordered on harsh.

Ksal's drumming fingers stopped, and he appeared surprised at his actions. "I apologize, Supreme Commander. I was unaware—"

"It is the hot chocolate," Nerx said, with a twitch at the corner of his lips as if he was tempted to smile. "It has an overabundance of fuel with little nutritional value."

"It is delicious, though." Ksal grinned but curled his fingers into fists to still them.

"The human food is as passionate as they are." Nerx slumped and allowed a full smile to form. "Bold flavors for a bold species."

"A species with no self-control." Ksal rubbed his palms together, his braid swinging opposite directions to his jerking shoulders.

"That, Pilot Ksal, is appreciated in their females, but when their males lack control, it is unwise." Ulriq did value Jack's uninhibited nature, even when it stirred something primal within him.

Nerx tapped the side of the data tab, a deep frown furrowing his temple. "They are exceedingly affectionate. They like this hug. I do not think it is appropriate to force one's presence upon another."

"You do not like it?" Ksal's eyebrows rose then lowered on a faraway gaze.

"It is unbearable when a male has no Dar Eth," Nerx mumbled. "The human females lack consideration."

"But their scents *are* good," Pilot Ksal groaned.

The silence of the comm room reached through to Ulriq. The males on-duty attended to their conversation. Their excellent hearing didn't mean they could ignore protocol. Yet he sympathized with them, having recently faced the void himself.

"I assume you are curious?" He directed this question to his males present. "It is true. Warriors Teric and Kanzo and I are experiencing the Ethera." Having it so factually confirmed murmured surprise and excitement through his males. "Prince Enyl is also experiencing his Ethera. All the Dar Eths are human females. I trust King Xeus to ensure more females are welcomed into our world. Be patient, specifically for those enduring the encroaching void."

"And now you should leave..." Nerx glanced at Ulriq's trembling hands.

Ulriq grunted and clenched them into fists, tight enough to whiten his knuckles. Still, he hesitated. To not attend to his duty was unacceptable.

Nerx rose, and with a nod to Pilot Ksal, he too scrambled out of his chair. "If you do not heed me on this, Supreme Commander, I will ensure Der enforces your off-time."

"I reserve the right to torment you when you experience your Ethera, Nerx," Ulriq grumbled.

"An experience I am beginning to dread," Nerx muttered.

Ulriq laughed at his frowning battle-bond. And his humor dissipated the final effects of the hot chocolate.

"Truly?" Ksal stared at Nerx in disbelief.

Nerx threw out his arm in a wide sweep. "Look at him, Ksal. He is trembling, cannot focus on the task at hand, and growls at all."

"I do not," Ulriq roared, proving Nerx correct. He grinned at the male in acquiescence, realizing the volatility of his emotions. "Very well, Nerx. You have the comm."

ULRIQ ENTERED HIS QUARTERS, pausing to search for Jack, having expected her to be waiting in a comfy. She'd spread out a meal on the counter at which he grunted, appreciating the gesture. His brow furrowed as he listened with his preternatural hearing and turned toward the cleansing room. Her huffs and the swishing of fabric reached him.

"Jack?"

"Here," she said, though her voice was husky. She stepped through the door, just wearing the wrap as she'd promised.

"You prepared a meal?" He strode across to her, unable to stop himself from being near her. "The only thing I want to eat is you."

"It's pizza, silly; it's best eaten cold." She pressed the magnetic clasp and her wrap gaped.

With a shrug of her shoulder, the garment slipped off her to pool on the floor. Beautifully naked, her soft curves called to him. He growled and lunged. She dodged his arms and smacked him on his backside as she darted around him.

Tutting, she swept a hand from her breast to her hip. "I'm so not impressed, Ulriq. You can't catch little old me?"

She squealed as he charged her, snatching her off the floor to swing over his shoulder in a smooth motion. While carrying her to the room, he stroked her bare, soft backside, letting his fingers slide up her inner thighs, along her seam, and dip into her silken folds.

"You are so ready for me," he groaned. He found her nub to massage and tease, while he stroked her bare cheek, along her thigh, and up again, with his other hand. Her husky moans and shivering body had him dribbling inside his armored breeches. The scent of her arousal made his mouth water.

"I'm going to orgasm if you keep doing that," she whispered.

Then he felt it, her hands cupping his armor-encased backside. His balls spasmed, and he hastened his strides toward the bed. He gently flipped her over until he held her to his chest. With his arms crushing her to him, he crashed his mouth across hers, eager for her taste. There was no tenderness, just an unadulterated need.

He ravaged her, not letting her breathe. With each demand he made, she met him, kiss for kiss, touch for touch, the level of desperation climbing. He spread her on the bed, keeping his lips on hers as he climbed over her. Without effort, he supported his weight on his elbows as he buried his fingers in her white-gold curls and stared in the crystalline blue depths of her eyes.

"Jack." He moaned his need, his lips tugging on hers, spreading wet heat along her jaw to her earlobe.

She panted her response. Lying on his side, he freed his fingertips to brush across her lips, marveling at their softness, at the sweet spiciness of her mouth. Running his thumb across her chin, he trailed a path down the curve of her throat to stroke over her collarbone. With the flat of his palm, he brushed across a taut nipple.

"You have exquisite breasts, Jack," he said in a rough voice. He cupped her breast, relishing the softness filling his hand. Her nipple hardened, and he halted to tease it. She trembled, releasing a husky moan.

Her fingers dug into his upper arm as his mouth latched onto her pebbled nipple. He sucked on it with forceful, rhythmic motions. Hot need and a deep, sweet ache ricocheted through him with every tug of his mouth.

"Touch me, please, Ulriq," she begged.

He chuckled. "Do you not have self-control, Jack?"

A sensual smile crawled across her kiss-swollen lips. "What? Why would I need control when you have yours?" Her fingers feathered across his shoulders. "Are you going to get naked anytime soon?"

"You want to see me unclothed?" He teased her in return.

"Damnit, Ulriq, I want to feel your chest on my nipples. I want to have your arms wrapped around me as you fuck me. I want to scream your name as I orgasm."

His eyelashes fluttered as his O.D.I. instructed him. When he gazed upon her, reflected in her eyes, his irises had faded to the palest of blues. His cheeks trembled while a pulse thumped below his jaw.

"Jack," he moaned, ripping his chest armor off and yanking her into his arms. Her sigh of pleasure as his chest brushed her nipples made him crush his mouth over hers. She was so uninhibited, his Jack.

Leaning back but not breaking contact with her mouth, he trailed his fingers down her stomach to the curls at the apex of her thighs. He dipped into her heated folds, slick with need. A groan rumbled from his belly. He loved that she desired him so. Flicking his fingers, he teased her until she trembled. Her heart thundered as she plundered his mouth, forcefully, drawing forth a moan from him. He forgot for a second where his fingers were.

She made primal noises in the back of her throat as he continued his onslaught, her hands buried in his hair, clasping him to her as she dragged her mouth from his to latch onto his earlobe. His malehood spasmed in response.

"Supreme Commander," Pilot Ksal's voice came through Ulriq's O.D.I.

He groaned in agony, fighting for control. A potent, furious fire ripped through him at the intrusion, at another male's voice reverberating through his room with his Dar Eth so vulnerable and alive with need.

"Report," he growled as his fingers dipped into her channel, then up and over her nub again. She arched, twisted, writhed on the bed, her teeth dimpling her bottom lip as she struggled to not make a sound. Maker. He shuddered.

"Four Yithian battleships have appeared out of fusion pulse, one klik away."

Ulriq closed his eyes, drawing in deep breaths through his mouth as he fought for control.

"Nerx can handle this." He did not recognize his own voice.

"Get here now, Ulriq," Nerx boomed down the comm.

"I will be there shortly." After Ulriq made his Jack scream his name. Not making an effort to dress, he slid his thumb over her nub while his fingers teased her channel.

"Ulriq, you can't...you need to go."

He blinked, amazed that she would insist he leave her this aroused and unfulfilled.

"Then be quick, my *ensa*." He sucked her nipple into his mouth, not ceasing his torment with his fingers, sliding and stroking her. She whimpered, then stilled, her eyes growing wide.

"Ulriq." She screamed her release, her body convulsed, and her hips thrust upward in offering, demanding he fill her.

Closing his eyes, he brushed kisses up her quivering body to her lips, claiming her mouth again. He wanted and needed to be in her with a desperation bordering on painful.

"Thank you." She graced him with a smile that shot bolts of heat along the hardened length of his malehood. "I'll stay right here, just like this." When she feathered her fingers across his lips, he shivered, relishing the skitter of fire and ice along his senses. "So, hurry back."

"You are so sensual, Jack." He claimed her mouth again then hastily released her. She lay there exposed, replete, and smiling seductively at him. With a grumble, he yanked his armor on and stomped out of his quarters.

Chapter Thirty-Two

ULRIQ WAS READY TO blast those bastards, just because they dared to interrupt his first union with his Dar Eth. He was livid and vibrated with burgeoning anger. Nerx was in the comm room, awaiting his arrival. For which Ulriq was grateful; he needed his assistance since Ulriq's judgment was leaning toward annihilation. He nodded at him and Ksal as he faced the large display vid.

"What do you want, Yithian?" Ulriq growled when they were within comm range, any semblance of diplomacy gone.

"You took something from us, Etterian. We demand you return it."

"I took something...," he boomed, his fingers curled into fists, fighting for his elusive control. He was tempted to command Ksal to fire the Chokaar.

"Please specify what was taken, Yithian?" Nerx shot Ulriq a dark look.

"I wish to take this private," the Yithian said.

"Hyper-secure the call, Pilot Ksal." When the blue light appeared in the right bottom corner of the display, Nerx addressed the vid. "We are secure, Yithian."

"Excellent. I am Commander Pyo, and we wish to entreat the Etterians for assistance to overthrow our monarchy."

As if Pyo had punched him, Ulriq twitched. Alodon's balls. He drew in a long, silent breath, willing his malehood to quit throbbing.

"For many reasons, we are dissatisfied with our king and his narrow-minded offspring. Yithia has become a nation focused on instant gratification with no thoughts or plans for the future," Pyo lisped through his clenched lips.

"Why not contact our king directly?" Ulriq asked, hesitant to believe the authenticity of Pyo's request.

"Direct contact with your king would raise suspicions, speaking to an Etterian battleship while on patrol...not so suspicious," he lisped. "Also, understanding our situation, we are unimpressed with royalty, and therefore, cannot trust your king not to notify Urio of our plans."

"And why would you need Etteria? You have sufficient Yithian soldiers." Ulriq frowned. This was too unexpected, too surreal. Nor would he reveal he trusted Pyo less than he trusted a blaster in Alodon's clumsy fingers. The poor male had shot off his balls and was now infamous.

"Many will not step away from tradition for fear of failure. Should we have the backing of the Etterian warriors, we might yet save Yithia."

"Very well, Pyo. I will take your entreaty to my king. I guarantee a response within the hour," Ulriq vowed, bowing formally.

"We will remain within comm range for one hour." Pyo held up one of three fingers then ended the transmission.

Ulriq turned to Nerx. "What say you?"

Nerx folded his arms across his chest and spread his legs, at ease. "Unexpected yet plausible."

Ulriq settled his gaze on Ksal. "Pilot Ksal, comm the king." He watched the black display vid expectantly.

"It is a secure line, Supreme Commander," Ksal said seconds before Xeus appeared on the vid.

"My king," Ulriq said in greeting. "I apologize for the comm. It is urgent. We have a Yithian Commander seeking assistance to overthrow Urio."

Xeus blinked at him, a little stunned.

Ulriq clasped his trembling hands behind his back and forced himself to stand still, to endure the Ethera's demands in silence. "How do you wish to proceed, my king?"

"A trap?" Xeus straightened, yet eager energy flowed off him, as if he would appreciate some battle action.

"It's possible, my king, but why reach out to us for assistance? What could they hope to gain if it is a trap?" Ulriq sliced a glance at Nerx, who tapped his bottom lip with his forefinger, his eyes shadowed in thought.

"Suggest we meet halfway between your location and Etteria." Xeus rolled his shoulders.

Nerx shook his head. "He may not agree, my king. He is cautious and does not wish to alarm his superiors."

"Supreme Commander?" Pilot Ksal mumbled.

The three males focused on the pilot.

"You have a suggestion, Pilot Ksal?" Ulriq offered a nod of encouragement.

"Why not open the comm to include Pyo? I can manipulate it in such a way that it will appear as if the source is this battleship."

"Do it, Pilot," King Xeus commanded. Ksal's fingers flew over the console and the vid split into two displays. "Greetings Yithian Commander. How may Etteria assist?"

Pyo's cheeks darkened, and a tremulous smile gaped across his jagged teeth. "King Xeus, thank you for taking the time."

Xeus's eyes narrowed. "I repeat, Yithian, how may Etteria assist? I assume you need warriors?"

"Not at the moment. I need to know Etteria would support the new ruler, whoever is chosen."

Ulriq gritted his teeth at Pyo's vague answer. Had he just wasted his king's time?

"What is his name, Yithian?" Xeus inched closer until his face dominated the vid.

Pyo twitched and shuffled. "We have not—"

"Unacceptable. One cannot follow a faceless ruler." Xeus's tone brooked no argument as he stared Pyo down.

"Kbal," Pyo lisped, his gray skin darkening in anger.

"I wish to speak to Kbal. We have various ships traveling this route. Ensure Kbal encounters one of them. Comm me again. For now, you have our initial support." Xeus nodded at Ulriq before ending the communication.

"Your king...is impressive, Supreme Commander. I will convey his wishes. Thank you for the assist." Pyo ended the communication from his side.

Chapter Thirty-Three

"I PLACE YOU IN command, Nerx. I *need* to bond with my Dar Eth." Ulriq faced his Sub-Commander. "Unless King Xeus ports onboard or the entire Yithian fleet circles the *Kushin*. If I am disturbed for any other reason, that warrior will know the sharp edge of my dagger." His voice vibrated with thick emotion. Yet more evidence he'd lost what hold he'd had on his control.

"Understood, Supreme Commander." Nerx clasped his hands behind his back.

"Excellent work, Ksal. I will ensure my report mentions your performance." And with that said, Ulriq strode out of the comm room. He punched his O.D.I. and informed all under his command that Sub-Commander Nerx had his authority.

Excitement bubbled through him as he jogged to his quarters. He burst through the door, taking the time to lock it, removing security access, as well. He wouldn't tolerate any further interruptions.

When he strode into his bedroom, Jack lay where he'd left her, but she'd fallen asleep. She'd rolled onto her side, her curls cascading around her, partially covering her nudity. His vision narrowed, bright colors exploding as strong emotions roiled inside him. She was so beautiful.

He stripped off his garments, tossing them on the floor as he slipped onto the bed. He spread his body over hers, feathering kisses over her bare shoulder, along her neck, across her cheek to her lips. Hovering there, he inhaled her breath, tasting her life essence. He brushed his lips over hers while his aching fingers stroked across her body. They sought to learn the curves, her valleys, her sensitive spots. He sought to memorize every inch of her.

"Ulriq?" she rasped as her eyelids fluttered open. She rolled onto her back within the space he allowed her, her hands fluttering up to rest on his shoulders.

"You waited for me," he said, joyful she had.

"I'm sorry I fell asleep," she pouted.

He grumbled at the deep pink of her bottom lip. He dipped to suck it into his mouth, nibbling on its softness. She moaned her approval, hooking her left leg around his hip, pulling him closer.

"But waking up to this? Perfect," she mumbled, running her hands down his bare chest.

"I am pleased you approve. I plan to make this a habit," he said into her parted mouth as he caressed her waist.

Molding his fingers around her breast, her nipple puckered under his attentive touch. He admired her body's response, then dipped to run his mouth across the taut bud, back and forth until her fingers tightened in his hair. Sucking the nipple deep into his mouth summoned her husky cry.

He stopped tormenting her to meet her gaze. "Do you like that?" he teased before drawing it into his mouth again, rolling his tongue across it, and gently tugging on it with his teeth. She writhed in response, panting and whimpering, with her heart pounding in his ears.

"Ulriq, please," she begged.

"What is it, *thamani*?" He smiled while he toyed with her wet and pebbled nipple.

He slipped his hand over her stomach to brush her curls, marveling at the softness. As a gate to her essence, it was a weak one, more alluring than defensive. A strangled noise escaped her as her hips rose to meet his searching fingers, encouraging him to venture deeper.

"Just do me already," she begged as she arched her back.

"I want to savor this, Jack, to savor you," he said gruffly.

"Why?" She lifted her head to look at him, her pale-blue eyes hooded with need. "You have me forever, Ulriq. You can savor me every damn day." Her hand rose to clasp his cheek, running a thumb across his parted and swollen lips. "No more teasing me, please."

He responded to the need in her eyes, to her trembling hands. "I scent your arousal, Jack. I need to touch you, may I?" he asked, with his fingertips dipping between her curls but not yet touching her moistness.

"My body is yours, Ulriq, as yours is mine." Her voice cracked when he slid his fingers between her folds, unerringly finding her nub.

He circled it mercilessly, slipping into her channel, before finding the nub again. She trembled under his onslaught; gasping and mewling while her hands clawed the bedding.

"Ulriq. Damnit, take me now or so help me...." She broke off on a keening moan. "I ache for you."

He shuddered in reaction to her scent, her demand. Pushing off the bed, he placed a knee between her parted thighs, then the other, moving over her to position his arousal at her channel. The tip of it dipped in her slick essence. She raised her leg and wrapped them both tighter around his hips, bringing him closer.

Clawing at his arms, she thrashed, pleading and enticing him with her body. He fought for sanity, her scent and responses driving him wild. Pressing into her tightness was breathtaking. She surrounded his malehood with wet softness. He trembled with longing, using the last vestiges of his control, to not thrust into her, to take it slow. Hurting her with his eagerness wasn't an option.

"Jack, please, be still..." he pleaded, but she didn't listen.

Her heels dug into his bare backside, driving him deeper. He groaned his pleasure as he slid farther in and encountered her barrier.

His gaze rose to meet her lust-filled eyes. In one smooth movement, he thrust in, breaching and claiming her as his. Pain darkened her face, her brow, and he waited, breathless, concerned. Then her sensual and enticing mouth parted in wonder. The possessiveness claiming his soul, his heart, rivaled burying himself inside her, surrounded by her silky, tight heat.

"Jack, the feel of you is indescribable." His voice broke with the force of his emotions cleaving through him.

"You fill me, Ulriq. You feel incredible, intimate." Her fingernails scraped his scalp as her hips began to swirl and grind.

His malehood felt every move she made; ripple after shudder flowed along his length, the sensations exquisite. As gently as he could, he withdrew, until his tip brushed her folds before he slammed into her. She keened and arched almost off the bed. Her thighs tightened around him, urging him on, harder and faster. Ulriq shuddered as tingles skittered down his spine to settle in his balls. His gaze focused on her, her eyes, her parted pink lips, her flushed cheeks, her husky whimpers.

Nothing else existed, only this female, his Dar Eth. He withdrew again and rammed in, his balls slapping against her skin. She moaned, arching into him, unintentionally rubbing her taut nipples across his chest. He growled in reaction as tingling and intense heat slid from his balls to his arousal. Pulling out and plunging into her, the head of his arousal throbbed, threatening to bring forth his release. But he held back, she wasn't ready. He wasn't ready to end this experience either.

She stilled with her mouth open, her eyes rolled back, and her breathing labored. Then her nails dug into his back, her channel tightened around him almost to a painful degree, spasms rippled along the length of him, and she cried out. She milked him, tugging him deeper into her, melding them as one. Shards of pure joy and heat surged to his malehood, calling forth a release that inflamed his body, from his scalp to his toes. He roared her name. His backside tightened to shoot his seed into her.

His arms trembled when he held himself off her, losing himself in the warm blue of her eyes. He had never experienced anything so intense. Tiny pulses of pleasure rippled through him, and he grunted, collapsing alongside her. Grasping her with a reverent gentleness, he pulled her into his arms for another kiss, careful not to slip out of her. He wanted to remain inside her for as long as she'd allow.

"I am glad you are mine, Jack. You are perfect to me." He brushed the curls from her flushed face. "Are you in pain? I scent blood."

"No, and I like having you deep inside me." She dragged her nails down his chest to toy with his belly button.

Her eyes narrowed into a hooded expression as she leaned forward to press a kiss over his pebbled nipple. He rumbled his approval, embedding his fingers in her hips in response.

"How long before we can do it again?" She sucked his nipple into her mouth, nipping it before dragging the flat of her tongue across it.

A guttural growl scored his throat, and a fresh wave of need wrapped its tendrils around his malehood, twitching it. "Females can do it once per day." He stroked his hand to the base of her spine, with his fingers splaying out.

"Etterian females?" She released his nipple with an exaggerated 'pop' of her mouth.

She toyed with his other nipple, swirling her fingers and brushing over it until the urge to bury himself in her again was almost unbearable. But he needed to focus on her words. What was she saying?

He shook his head, trying to clear the seductive haze of desire. "Are humans not the same?"

"No, our males can do it once per day, maybe every two days. We can do it many times within a day."

"And you find fulfillment each time?" Ulriq growled, just at the mention of having her again made his malehood throb in anticipation.

She chuckled, wiggling her hips. "Yes."

He groaned and pinned her to the bed, sliding his erect malehood out to slam it into her. She writhed, keening her pleasure.

"Wait, Ulriq," she called out, and he froze, immediate concern on his mind. "Move back, pull out." He did so instantly. She rolled onto her hands and knees, spread her thighs, and arched her back. Her femininity was like the blossoming petals of a hahyt flower. "Now enter me," she commanded.

"Truly?" Concern still dampened his ardor...a little.

"Trust me, Ulriq. I heard this position is spectacular."

He grumbled, but he positioned the head of his arousal at the entrance of her channel and smoothly slid into her. Her pleasure was immediate with her hands flying out to grip the bedding.

"Ulriq," she panted. "I'm dying...don't stop."

He chuckled as he withdrew to slam into her. With his right hand, he gripped her hip, while his other hand, he slid down her spine from nape to backside. She shivered in response. Mewling with each thrust, she arched back, creating a friction so exquisite, so breathtaking. The skitters of need and joy were too intense. She screamed her release, clenching around him to milk him again. A delicious warmth engulfed his length, and a fresh wave of sparks rushed from his balls to his tip. He roared, biting her shoulder as bright lights burst across his vision, and his body trembled under the barrage of pleasure.

"Jack," he whispered, cuddling her against him, not willing to be separated from her for a moment.

"We need to do that again." She smiled between the kisses she pressed to his chest just above his heart.

"Agreed." He tightened his hold and held his lips to her temple, closing his eyes against the gift she was.

Her fingers fluttered over his chest, and she glanced down, hiding her beautiful eyes from him.

He frowned, not knowing what that serious expression meant. "What is wrong, Jack?" Tilting her chin up with his forefinger, he peered into her eyes.

"I'm so happy to be here with you, Ulriq." Her answer startled him. The heat that burst in his chest overwhelmed him, his thoughts, what remained of the void. He didn't understand what it was, except intensely joyful. Her words were important, they mattered.

"I too am content." His voice deepened with emotion.

"Can we eat now?" she asked with a small smile.

He grinned before rolling off the bed, taking her with him. All he could say about the meal was that it was delicious. His gaze lingered on her face, on her fingers gripping a slice. The curve of her hips and the bounce of her breasts, his entertainment. There was an immense pleasure to be had eating pizza naked. The need to say something gripped him, but he knew not what. How could he tell her how she made him feel when he didn't recognize these emotions burning within him? All he could say was he was honored to be hers.

'You please me' didn't convey how much she *did* please him.

'I am content with you' didn't show how much he enjoyed being with her, listening to her melodic voice, or having her grace him with a bright smile.

He'd task Pilot Ksal and Data Officer Prex to investigate. Perhaps the Earthian annals might offer guidance.

Chapter Thirty-Four

JACK AWOKE IN THE middle of the bed, naked. She lay there blinking, trying to remember. She shifted her legs and groaned at the tenderness between her thighs. A smile burst forth, and she chuckled, rolling onto her back and stretching. She arched and ran her hands over her breasts, relishing their well-loved and tender state. Ulriq had woken her up many times to show her the meaning of cherished.

"You make me hard when you do that." His voice reverberated through the room.

She squeaked and blushed at having been caught fondling her breasts. He blessed her with a smile from where he leaned his bulky frame against the wall. She took a moment to admire his loose yoga pants hanging low on his hips and draped over his muscled thighs. The low lighting caressed the ripped ridges of his torso, and his skin glowed like molten toffee. Damn.

He strolled over to the bed, dropping onto the edge to look at her. He stroked up one knee to her thigh to rest on her hip. "Would you like to comm Fred this morning?"

"Yes, please." She sat up in a smooth motion to brush Ulriq's lips with hers. Loving his arms wrapping around her to crush her to his hot bare chest, she feasted on his mouth. "Now it's a good morning," she said into his mouth.

He scooped her off the bed, easing her feet to the floor while cupping her backside with his long-fingered hands. A whimper escaped as he kneaded her there, summoning delicious tendrils of desire.

"If you keep looking at me like that, Jack, we will not leave this room today," he threatened.

The idea sparked a deep excitement within her. Oh, yes, please. "Promise?" She brushed her fingers over his taut nipples.

"Come, temptress, I requested your meal." He laced his fingers through hers and tugged her to the replicator. "I will not make it through our breakfast if you stay so gloriously bare, Jack."

She sighed and requested a nightshirt, pulling it on as soon as it formed on the glass surface.

He gestured to her to assume a comfy, then handed her a plate with a bacon and cheese sandwich. Her vanilla latte he placed on the table before her. She smiled, pleased he'd remembered. While she chewed on the bite of her sandwich, she studied her husband. This was too unbelievable. She wanted to pinch herself. Maybe she was dreaming? Maybe she had just watched an illegal vid on Galactic Bachelor and one of the contestants had infiltrated her subconscious? It could even be the pain meds talking after being shot.

Ulriq gripped her knee while he ate his kreso. His touch was hot, and her nerve endings burst to life, running up her thigh to pool in her core. This was no dream. He was real and hers. She admired his outstretched arm, rippling with muscle. Shifting in her comfy, she tried to ease the ache overriding her soreness.

He stilled, raised his face to the ceiling, and sniffed. When he settled his gaze on her, the ice-blue of his eyes swirled, darkened, lightened and he blessed her with a sensual smile.

Holy cow. She shivered, staring at her forgotten sandwich. Time for a subject change.

"Ulriq, I wanted to ask you for something to keep me busy. Etterians don't need my particular skill set as we've already discussed." She paused, and he nodded, his mouth full of kreso and momaberry sauce. "Would I be able to train as an Etterian male? Combat training, I mean." When his eyebrows shot to his hairline and he choked on his kreso, she laughed. "Or learn about your weapons? Shadow a medic or a mechanic? Or learn about spaceships? Train as a pilot?"

"Why not try it all?" he asked. "Except for the Etterian combat training. You cannot hold our greatswords, *thamani*."

"I can do all of it?" She gasped as excitement burst through her. Wait till she told Mich. She bit into her cold sandwich, smiling at Ulriq. Her gaze returned to his face no matter how many times she snatched it away. Her favorite path was from the shape of his eyebrows and high cheekbones, dipping to his chin, and along his jaw. She knew damn well how much she sighed at him between mouthfuls, how she became flustered when she glanced at his bare chest. He had to be aware of her fascination with his preternatural senses. The sensual smile showing his dimple confirmed this. Her heart skipped a beat. He was so handsome, and so hers. How did she get so lucky? Joy warmed her chest, overwhelming her with an intense emotion that wasn't sexual. She would almost say it was...love?

He sucked momaberry sauce off his thumb and sparked another wave of desire in her belly. "What would you start with?"

"I don't know. Maybe I should research first." She shrugged as she slid her empty plate onto the table and leaned back with the latte in hand.

"Research?" His frown was formidable.

"I shouldn't research first?" She stiffened, concerned she might have offended him or crossed some sort of alien boundary.

He winced and closed his eyes for a second. "I do not like you talking to other males. My anxious emotion is illogical. This does not stop me from feeling it."

She beamed. He didn't know he was jealous, that he didn't want to share her. He didn't distrust his males. He was simply selfish. But she wasn't going to explain jealousy to him when most human men denied it existed.

"If the roles were reversed, I wouldn't want you talking to other women...females, either. You could approach your males on my behalf?"

"This is acceptable." He was pleased with her solution and rewarded her with a sinfully decadent smile. That same had done amazing things to her. "I appreciate your understanding, Jack. Perhaps Michel would participate in your research?"

"He might. Thank you, Ulriq." Unable to handle the distance between them, she rose to kiss him.

Wrapping an arm around her to keep her close, he rumbled his approval.

Chapter Thirty-Five

Etterian battleship, Kushin
Speeding toward Earth
Ulriq's quarters

"Fred Munroe." Jack spoke into the display vid. She didn't have to wait long when a startled Fred appeared. He was a sight for sore eyes. Warmth and familiarity soaked through her.

"Damnit, Jack. How did you activate my video function? I have never used it."

She sighed at the thick emotion in his voice. He had been the one consistency in her somewhat unstable life.

"How are you, Jackie, my girl?"

Tears misted her eyes, and she sniffed, dashing them away. "Better now that I hear your voice, Fred."

Sprawled in a comfy in his yoga pants, Ulriq raised his gaze from his data tab. He arched his brow, concern in the depths of his eyes. She flashed him a smile, trying to convey crying was normal for a human woman.

"How are the girls doing? Mich?"

Jack scowled at the red-haired Fred, his pale cheeks darkening his green eyes. "Why aren't you shocked to see me alive?" She rested her fists on her hips in a universal 'I'm pissed with you' stance.

"Mich let me know you were fine. Gave me a nasty scare there. And it's been busy this side trying to ensure everything continues as per usual. Antoine hasn't burned down Vicky's bakery, that's the one good thing. Both you and Ava lost your jobs, no hard feelings, though, once I explained what happened."

"What did happen? Or rather, what did Mich say happened?"

"Some sort of gas leak, and now you're quarantined by the Disease Center while they run tests." Fred laughed, smacking the bar counter. "He must think I'm an idiot. I can see your room, Jackie. It's next-level shit. No way do we have that technology."

She spun to study the quarters through Fred's eyes. The bulkheads were seamless, the metal plating and panels smooth, and of course, the kitchen with nothing in it but the two shiny surfaces.

She laughed, and Ulriq grunted off display. "We're on our way to drop off Vicky. But the girls, Mich, and I are leaving indefinitely."

Fred frowned, clenched his jaw, then met her gaze. "Shit, Jackie, what the hell happened?"

"I'll explain everything when we see you," she said.

"You better." He gave her a tight smile. "When do you arrive?"

She glanced at Ulriq, and he whispered, "One week."

Sprawled in the comfy, she got lost trailing her gaze over his form, his bare chest, and almost forgot she had called Fred. "One week," she blurted.

"What? Where are you that the journey will take that long?"

"She's with me." Ulriq pushed out of the comfy and stepped into the display range. Fred's eyes widened.

Ulriq kissed her temple then returned to his comfy to read his data tab.

"Bloody hell, Jackie, you have some explaining to do." Fred ran a freckled hand over his face and through his short hair. "Are you sure about this, Jackie, sweetheart? He's looking at you worse than Steve did," he whispered.

"They have excellent hearing, Fred."

And as she said that, Ulriq grumbled, "Who is Steve?"

"I'll explain later." She darted her gaze to the side to meet Ulriq's before facing Fred again. "We thought it might be better if everyone believed we died in the explosion. But now that we're coming back, I guess that won't be feasible anymore."

"Obviously." Fred's sarcasm brought forth an answering chuckle from Ulriq.

His soft laughter warmed her and fired a wave of pure energy through her, bouncing her on her toes.

"Maybe you should come with us?" She struggled to hide the hope in her voice. She glanced at Ulriq. "Is that possible, my Eth?"

He stilled, raised his gaze to her, and an intense emotion poured from his eyes. "Yes, for you."

"See." Jack faced Fred, throwing him a pointed look.

"Leave the bar?" Instead of looking aghast, Fred twisted his lips at the possibility.

"Bring your finest stock, hire a manager, and fly the stars with me."

"I can come home anytime?" He straightened his shoulders and raised his arms as he did a little shimmy.

"We have various ships traveling between Earth and Etteria." Ulriq stepped into the display vid again and clasped her to the heated velvet of his chest. "If Jack wants you, then we want you."

Heat burned her cheeks to her ears, but she looped her arm around his waist. She shot a 'see what I mean' look at Fred.

"I don't have a say, it seems." Fred chuckled. "Very well, I'll be ready."

"Wonderful, Fred. I'll let the girls know. Hurry up and pack. We're coming." Jack ended the communication. So happy she was giddy with it, she twisted in Ulriq's embrace. "First, let me show you my appreciation." She buried her face in his chest to inhale his scent.

"Appreciation is not necessary." He crushed her to him, tilting her chin up to meet his gaze.

"But you won't say no," she said between kisses on his collarbone, chin, and lips

"I will not." He grinned.

She dipped her tongue into his deep dimple, then slithered down his body to her knees. Tapping the magnetic fastener, she slid his pants down his legs. His impressive erection sprang free. She moaned her delight, and her mouth watered while she curled her fingers around the shaft. Flicking her tongue across his moist trip drew a groan from him.

"Jack." He feathered his trembling hands through her curls.

"Want me to stop?" With a wicked grin, she stroked him from balls to tip.

He purred, his head falling back to rest on the bulkhead. "You are showing your appreciation," he growled.

Moments later, she wrapped her mouth around him, sucking him in, swirling her tongue across the sensitive ridges. He tasted hot and spicy. Hungry for more, she sucked the hard length of him. She tried to be gentle, too scared to hurt him. With only Vicky's books to guide her, Jack was a fool to try this. Releasing him to slide her tongue along the length then up to suck on the tip, she gently dragged her teeth across his length. He grabbed her, kicked off his pants, and bolted for their bedroom.

He sprawled her onto the bed. "I do not think I will ever have my fill of you." He slid between her parted thighs and positioned his tip at her entrance. When he slipped between her folds, he blessed her with his sensual smile, the sight of which hummed pleasure through her. "Never, my Jack."

He popped his finger into his mouth and mumbled in appreciation. Heat flushed her body, spiking tingles and uncoiling need. She hadn't known how much she would enjoy licking him. Gripping her hips, he dipped to meet her gaze, and in one thrust, buried himself to the hilt, his growl drowning her gasp.

Chapter Thirty-Six

Etterian battleship, Kushin
Speeding toward Earth
Ava's and Vicky's quarters

"WHAT'S WRONG WITH YOU?" Jack asked a fidgeting Vicky. "You're nervous."

"I should be, Jack. I'm about to start a new life without you and the girls."

"In three days, it will be you, Teric, and Aala." At Jack's reminder, Vicky's face flushed, and delight gleamed in her eyes. "You Ava? What has you so jumpy?"

"Same reason, a life without Vicky." Ava shrugged, but Jack wasn't buying it.

They were acting strangely. She hadn't had an opportunity to chat with Ava after her and Kanzo's fight in the common. Especially since it turned out Jack had caused the argument. She'd shared with Ava that she too was a married woman. Kanzo hadn't informed her, either. Perhaps they'd taken for granted that humans knew about the Ethera and the law around it?

Unlike Jack's sex-less past, Ava had a fiancé. He'd died in a car accident, losing control of his vehicle in a thunderstorm to plough into a tree. It had happened weeks before their wedding. Jack sighed and wondered what was going on in Ava's head now. Since the kidnapping, she had returned a changed woman. She'd said she was free of Billy, of past pains. Only now did Jack believe her.

"I received a message from Fred. He wants an afternoon with us girls, one last time." Vicky chewed on her thumbnail which she did when she was anxious.

"That sounds intriguing. I wonder what the old man has up his sleeve," Jack grinned.

"Me too.' Ava bounced on her seat.

Jack frowned, her concern deepening. The two of them wouldn't even meet her gaze. Her instincts leaped and danced, having been dormant since the arena. "All right, now you're just freaking me out."

"Nonsense." Vicky threw a warning look at Ava, one Jack interpreted as 'behave.' "I thought we could take our males for a picnic, Earth-style. What do you think, Jack?"

"Close to dusk so we can catch our last blue-sky sunset on Earth." Ava drew in a steadying breath. It did nothing to cool her perspiring face, but Jack decided not to point that out to her.

"Why?" Jack jerked back. Not once had she considered that Etteria wouldn't look like Earth. "What color is Etteria's sky?"

Taylor strolled into the room and assumed a comfy as if she hadn't been otherwise occupied.

"You mean you haven't asked Ulriq?" Vicky teased, giving Taylor a wink in greeting.

"She hasn't come up for air," Ava said.

"I know how that feels." Taylor chuckled.

"I'll comm Antoine and have him organize a few picnic hampers for us." Vicky huffed as if she was herding cats into a bag.

Jack laughed, sympathizing with her. She'd done that before. Not cats per se. Usually her students into the local morgue for a cadaver demonstration. "Please do. I can't believe I'll say this, but I haven't missed his chocolate croissants." She shrugged, having found something more addictive than chocolate. "Just don't tell him that."

"Did you and Ulriq stop to eat, Jack?" Vicky ran an assessing gaze over Jack's jeans and shirt.

"Nope, besides, who cares about food?" Jack tucked her twitching fingers under her ass.

"Amen, sister." Taylor rose to high-five her, forcing Jack to reveal how self-conscious she was feeling.

"So, Taylor, is Mich going to make an honest woman out of you?" Ava blurted out.

Jack grinned. Loving the pink that burst across Taylor's cheeks. Ava's ability to address sensitive topics was something Jack had always admired since she lacked the courage herself.

"Do I need to have a talk with him?" Jack puffed out her chest like she'd seen men do, then playfully thumped it in a macho fashion.

"No, please…just no." Taylor ran a frustrated hand through her hair, disheveling it. "Ulriq cornered Mich the other day."

"He did?" Pleasure shot through Jack as her heart leaped into her throat. He was so honorable, so thoughtful.

"I heard him say something about a wedding and marriage." Taylor frowned.

Jack gasped. "I didn't even know he knew those words." Wait, something tugged at the edges of her memory. What had she and Teric discussed when Ulriq eavesdropped? The answer was elusive.

"Your man's awesome, Jack, acting the perfect brother-in-law." Vicky grinned.

"He is, and I appreciate his efforts. But forcing Mich to propose doesn't mean the same thing…" Taylor's voice dwindled.

"As if he did it on his own?" Ava finished with a nod.

Jack stretched and groaned; her body ached all over. "I wish we had a bathtub on this battleship," she mumbled then blushed at the three knowing looks she received.

"Comm Der and ask him to add anesthetic to your cleanse," Taylor suggested and pinkened as the three knowing looks settled on her.

Jack wished she'd thought to do so sooner. She messaged Der. "And on that note, I'm going back to Ulriq's quarters. I could do with a nap." She stood and beamed at her friends. "Oh, almost forgot to tell you. Fred's coming with us into charted space."

Vicky stilled. "He is?" She cleared her throat but couldn't hide the new shimmer in her eyes. "I'll truly be alone."

"There's still time to change your mind." Taylor rose to order a coffee.

Vicky shook her head. "I'll cope."

"I'm so happy he's coming with." Ava's energy bounced off her, calling forth another frown from Jack. "I give up." She threw her hands into the air and stormed out of the room.

Jack stared at the closed door. "What's with her?"

"You have to ask, Jack? With how Kanzo has her as giddy as a schoolgirl? I doubt Billy ever made her feel this way." Vicky patted under an eye, catching an escaped tear.

Jack winced. She hadn't given Vicky a thought when she'd asked Fred to join her. How long had she been this selfish? "I'll go easy on her, Vicky, I swear."

"They can't keep their hands off each other, but he's quite adamant they can't use his quarters. And since they can't be alone here…"

"She'll sort him out. You know how Ava is, Vicky," Taylor said. "She'll take it, and take it, then she'll snap. She'll strip him such a new one, he won't be able to find the old one."

Jack blinked at Taylor for a second, then laughter bubbled out of her.

"Or she'll take matters into her own hands," Vicky added.

"Or that," Jack agreed and was still chuckling five minutes later when she left the quarters. A shower, a nap, then she would be ready for this evening, for hours in Ulriq's arms.

"I HEARD ABOUT YOUR talk with Mich." Jack twirled shapes over and around Ulriq's nipple.

She sprawled across him with her legs entwined with his. He'd just made love to her, thoroughly, and she was lethargic, blissful, and content. He rubbed his hand up and down her bare back, twisting strands of her hair around his fingers. His caress stilled at her words.

"Thank you for talking to him for me, Ulriq. I hope he does marry Taylor; nothing would make me happier."

Ulriq relaxed, and she frowned, but then he slid a hand over her ass to cup her cheek, distracting her. She released a moan when he dipped his fingers into her folds.

"I needed to talk to him, Jack. Humans do not have the Ethera."

She spread her thighs to grant him easier access. "That you thought to do it is what I am thankful for. I didn't. I let my friend down."

"I am certain she does not agree." Ulriq feathered kisses along her temple. "Are you excited for tomorrow?"

"Yes, I need to see Fred, get some things..." A gasp parted her mouth in reaction to his naughty fingers.

"Who is Steve?" His gruff question startled her.

"Steve's someone who wanted to know me like this?" She gestured to their entangled bodies. Ulriq growled, making her laugh. "Relax, babe. You rock my world. He never did."

"Babe?" Ulriq's voice rose.

"It's a human term of endearment. I could call you sugar, honey…"

"Ulriq. You can call me Ulriq," he said, to which she smothered a smile. "I rock your world?"

His eyebrow arched.

"Yes." She flicked the tip of her tongue across his taut nipple. His rumble vibrated through her, setting off an answering hum in her core. "I tremble in your arms." She lifted her gaze to meet his ice-blue eyes. Sometimes around him, shyness tangled her tongue—an unusual experience for her. No man had ever rattled her composure.

"As do I, in yours," he said with conviction.

She smiled at the sweetness of his words. "Do you mind that Fred wants to spend time with me?" She nibbled on her lip, dreading his response.

"No."

"What will you be doing?" She tried to focus on him, but his searching hands had found sensitive valleys, and it was making concentrating hard.

"We will help Teric settle in."

"You're a good male." She cupped his face and brushed a tender kiss across his parted lips. "I'm honored to know you, Ulriq."

He growled and flipped her onto her back. With one smooth movement, he thrust into her.

She moaned, looping her legs around his hips in an attempt to trap those delicious sensations his pounding cock generated.

"I am honored you are mine, *thamani*. More than you will ever know." He kissed her then, plundering her, claiming her, and she groaned under his forceful onslaught.

She didn't speak again, not until the morning.

Chapter Thirty-Seven

Earth

Fred's Bar, Cromdon Park

JACK OPENED THE DOOR of the bar and strolled in as if she was on Earth to stay. It had gone noon, and the rush had yet to happen. Only a few repeat customers were present.

"Jackie?" Fred called from behind the bar. Within seconds, he circled the counter and yanked her into his arms. "My girl, I'm glad to see you."

"Hi, Fred," she mumbled into his shirt, wrapping her arms tight around him. Had he lost weight? She frowned, hoping their disappearance hadn't added too much stress on his heart.

"Come, sit, tell me everything." He patted the bar stool.

She climbed onto it, appearing obedient, but she'd learned years ago to choose her battles wisely. Keeping her voice low, she regaled him, starting at the barbecue. Her reflection in the mirror behind the bar revealed how she felt every time she mentioned Ulriq's name. The warmth emanating from her body and the omnipresent smile showed she was happy. "So, that's the story, Fred."

"Jack?"

At the whine in that particular voice, she groaned. She buried her face in the glass of cognac Fred slid before her.

"I thought you'd died." Slamming the door behind him, Steve approached her.

She mumbled under her breath about his persistence but didn't lift her face from her glass.

"Sorry, Jackie, he found out about your visit," Fred whispered.

Steve stopped beside her, lifting his arm to drape across her shoulders.

"Do not touch what is mine." Ulriq's lethal warning whipped her head up. Pleasure at seeing him exploded those flash grenades in the pit of her stomach, slicing through her with a blinding joy.

Steve gaped at Ulriq, before shuffling back.

She wasn't sure if it was to make eye contact or if the sheer size of Ulriq intimidated. "Steve, I'd like you to meet my husband, Ulriq." She bit the bullet, so to speak. Knowing how Steve struggled with hints, she wasn't going to be subtle about her status change.

"Your what?" His curls bobbed as he twisted to gawk at her.

"Ulriq, this is Steve." She gestured to her ex-colleague.

Ulriq ran a cold, calculating gaze over Steve before pulling her into the curve of his arm. "Greetings, my *ensa*. Michel delivered me to this door. He has other tasks to attend to and will collect us later."

She shivered as Ulriq's breath fanned across her ear. "Ulriq, this is Fred, my father."

Fred's eyes misted at her introduction, and he held his hand out to Ulriq in welcome. "A pleasure to meet you." They shook hands. "Do I call you Supreme Commander or Ulriq?"

"Ulriq is fine," Ulriq smiled while Steve mouthed 'Supreme Commander.'

Jack gestured to a booth at the back. "Get us a table, while I order you something. What would you like?"

"You choose, my Jack." Ulriq sauntered off.

Fred had to clear his throat twice to drag her attention away from Ulriq's black armor-encased ass.

"One coke, one beer, please, Fred." She smiled at him, unrepentant that she'd stared and was probably drooling too.

"How?" Steve blustered, his face glowed red in anger.

"Your husband, Jack? When? How? Why so fast?" Fred asked at the same time, drowning out Steve.

She laughed, unable to contain her joy. "He proposed the moment we met. I just didn't realize it when he fell to a knee before me. It was love at first sight for me."

"That still happens? So, you love him?" Fred wore a silly grin.

"There is no such thing as love at first sight," Steve muttered.

Jack grinned, holding no regret, no animosity toward him. With love bubbling with warmth through her, she couldn't hold a grudge.

"I love him with every cell of my body," she answered Fred.

A roar at the back of the bar startled everyone; well, it should, with a two hundred and fifty-pound male charging toward her.

Ulriq's long strides had him reaching her in seconds. "You love me?" he rasped.

She met his gaze and smiled, despite the warmth across her face. This wasn't how she wanted to confess her love. "Yes, my Eth."

He crushed her to him, lifted her off the floor, and slanted his mouth over hers a second later. His tongue delved in, drawing a throaty moan from her, but he stopped too soon. He leaned back to look at her. She'd never seen such a huge smile, dimpling both cheeks. She adored his smile. It did amazing things to her insides. Those silly stun grenades were out in full force.

"Alodon's balls, Jack. I love you too. Why did you not tell me?" He softened his voice as he feathered his fingers along her jaw.

"I didn't think I needed to, Ulriq. I show you every second of every day."

"You do." Even as he agreed with her, his eyes widened as he realized the truth in her words.

"As you show me, my Eth,"

"I feel it here." He pressed his hand over the middle of his chest. His heart was there? Well, that was good to know. "Especially when you smile at me, like now."

"I'll stop smiling then. I want to spend some time with Fred." She smiled despite her words. "Besides, you've had me twice today."

"It is never enough." He nodded at a gaping Steve and a pleased Fred. "But my Jack is correct, this time is reserved for you, Fred. Come, join us, tell me why my Jack cherishes you."

Fred beamed under such praise.

"Goodbye, Steve." She patted his hand and followed Ulriq, sliding into the booth beside him. The intimacy of her grasping his upper thigh, clarified to all who saw it, exactly how she felt about the big hulking male. As was her intention.

"WHAT DO YOU MEAN we're going to try on wedding dresses? Did Mich propose?" Jack climbed into Fred's car. Her girls filled the remaining seats. Aala looped her arm around Jack's, a bright smile on her dark face.

"I insisted since I won't get to walk you down the aisle." Fred twisted to speak to Jack and reached back to tap Aala on the nose. After Jack buckled in, he faced forward and started the drive to West Haven's only bridal shop. "Please, Jackie, do this for me. I want to see each of you as you might have looked on your wedding day."

Her eyes misted, and she offered a watery smile at Ava, Vicky, and Taylor. Their excitement and sadness mimicked her own.

"Okay, Fred, for you." She offered him a tremulous smile, sniffing through the tears. It wasn't what she'd anticipated he'd wanted to do, but who was she to deny him?

"Wedding day?" Aala's eyelids fluttered. She gasped then released Jack to clap her hands. "The garments are so beautiful."

"We'll get you a dress too, sweetheart." Vicky patted her cheeks. "Antoine will meet us at the park with the picnic hampers."

"Mich and the guys will meet us there as well," Taylor said. "Where is Ulriq? I thought he was with you?"

"We dropped him off at my house on the way here." Jack blushed at the memory of his goodbye kiss. Her toes were still curled in her slippers.

"Wouldn't it be funny if we arrived in our wedding dresses?" Ava chuckled.

Her excitement was a little too much for Jack who sighed. "No, it wouldn't."

"Jack." Fred admonished her. "Ava, ignore grumpy Jack, of course you can wear your wedding dress to the park." He winked at her via the review mirror.

"Aala and I will wear ours too." Vicky leaned back to clasp Ava's hand.

"Let's find dresses first before we decide if we're wearing them out or not." Jack wrapped her arm around Ava's shoulders in apology, crushing Aala between them.

"We're here," Taylor squealed, jumping out before Fred had fully stopped the car.

"Tell me now, did Mich propose?" Jack asked the group as she watched Taylor rush into the bridal store. When no one answered her, she met their gazes, arching a brow.

"No, he didn't." Vicky slid out, helping Aala across the seat.

With a frown, Jack followed. She paused to admire the dress in the window.

"I think you should try that one first," Ava squeezed Jack's forearm before tugging her through the ornate doors.

"Did you say four weddings?" the poor sales assistant whispered, her gaze fixed on Aala browsing the bridesmaids dresses alongside Taylor eyeing a blue creation.

She ushered a few more assistants over and soon Jack was trying on the pale pink dress from the window's display. It had a sweetheart neckline with spaghetti straps. The gown fitted her curves until her hips then flared into a full skirt with shifting tulle hinting at her legs beneath. The bareback exposed just the right amount of skin. Sequins and pearls adorned the satin bodice. She blinked at her smiling reflection.

"Shit, Jack, I think you found your dress..." Taylor gaped. She stood there with a few dresses thrown over her arm, ready to try on.

"You look amazing, Jackie." Fred sat on the couch, holding an untouched glass of champagne.

"I don't think I'll ever have a wedding day, Fred." She brushed a tear aside as he rose to hug her. "I love Ulriq and don't need the whole bride thing. The Ethera is far more precious to me."

"He adores you too." Ava glided over to them.

Jack's breath hitched. Ava had never looked more beautiful. She wore a high-collared scooped front and lace open-back wedding dress in a mermaid style. The soft fabric clung to her curves sensually. It was crisp white contrasting mesmerizingly with her black hair and mocha skin. She'd also twisted her hair up with curls cascading everywhere.

"Ava, is this the one?" Jack asked. Ava nodded through a batch of tears. "How many did you try on?"

"Only two." She stopped next to Jack and in front of the large walled mirror. Sidling behind Jack, she gathered her curls and held them on top of her head. They both admired the image and laughed. "Okay, maybe leave it down."

Jack shrugged. "Ulriq likes it down, anyway." A smile lingered after her laughter faded, but excitement began to burn in the depths of her belly.

"Now, let's check in on Taylor, Vicky, and Aala." Ava chuckled as she rushed off.

Jack grinned, heading to Fred instead. She sat carefully on the faux-leather chairs, not willing to damage the dress. The growing excitement burst through her, clutching her heart, at the thought of Ulriq seeing her in it. Maybe she should wear it to the park? It wasn't as if he knew what such a dress was worn for, anyway.

"Fred, how are you doing?"

Before he could answer, Taylor came out in a baby blue gown with a sweetheart neckline. The fabric spiraled around her figure.

"Taylor." Jack gasped, rising to her feet in a graceful motion, before sashaying over to the mirror, where Taylor had stopped to admire the full-length reflection.

"That gown is perfect for you, Taylor." Fred handed the untouched champagne to a passing assistant. Another strolled by and gave him a fresh glass. He blinked at it, shrugged, and took a sip.

"Fred's right, Taylor. Mich would have a heart attack at the sight of you in this." Jack circled her, fluffing the tulle frills. "But what do you think?"

"I love it. I mean, it's the same color blue as my hair, Jack. What are the odds?"

Jack chuckled—Taylor's enthusiasm contagious.

She pursed her lips as she spun to look at the back of the gown. "I think it's a bridesmaid's dress, but who cares, right?"

"You look stunning in it." Jack hugged her from behind, meeting her gaze in the mirror. "So, it's just Vicky and Aala now?"

"Aala's found a pink dress. She's twirling herself dizzy. But Vicky's struggling to decide," Taylor said.

Ava rushed out, still in her chosen gown. Beaming, she fell into place beside them with mischief in her eyes. Aala trailed her, skipping along to pause in front of the mirror before tossing a smile over her shoulder to join the lineup.

"You look beautiful, Aala," Jack whispered when she kissed the girl's temple.

"You too, Jack." She grabbed her skirts and fluffed them. Her smile was so broad, Jack half-expected her cheeks to crack under the strain.

"This is the one, watch..." Ava gestured to the archway where Vicky hesitated.

Her gown was off-white, with a bateau bodice in sheer fabric, lace detailing, and a cinched-in waist. From there, yards of fabric flared out in an A-line. It looked simple in design until she strode toward them. The yards of fabric parted to reveal her leg, all the way to her upper thigh.

"Holy shit, Vicky." Taylor gawked.

"Stunning." Jack laughed. "Teric's going to—"

"I know, right?" Vicky smirked.

"Do any of you need alterations?" Fred asked, his eyes sparkling.

"Even if we did, there isn't time." Taylor shrugged.

"Mine could be a little tighter." Vicky spun to show them the many pins holding the dress on.

"We can make the alterations within the hour," the assistant said and led her away.

"Mine's perfect," Aala beamed.

Vicky hugged her. "It's perfect on you."

"Ava?" Taylor ran an assessing gaze over Ava's accentuated curves.

Ava played with Taylor's hair, combing it with her fingers. "Mine is too tight, but with this style, I can get away with it."

"Jack?"

Jack admired the feminine woman in the mirror. It wasn't an image of herself she had ever envisioned. The bare shoulders, sweetheart neckline, and flowing fabric made her look enchanting, young, happy, although, that might have been Ulriq's declaration still affecting her. She caught a tear before it could slip free.

Meeting Taylor's gaze in the reflection, Jack sighed. "Mine's perfect." She ran her hands over the beadwork, then fluffed the skirt. The fabric was amazing, sensual, and suited her well. If only Ulriq could see her in it.

"Excellent, now shoes." Fred gestured to the wall of shoes behind him.

Two and a half hours later, four fully dressed brides and a bridesmaid waltzed out of the shop.

"Oh, look. There's a wedding happening in the park." Ava bounced on the seat as they pulled into a parking bay.

"Truly?" Aala plastered her face to the window.

"We best avoid it. If I was the bride, I'd hate if four strange women spoiled my day for me." Vicky chuckled.

"Not if those brides were my sisters." Taylor climbed out of the car. Teetering in high heels was a new experience for her, so she stepped with careful precision. It was a sight Jack would cherish. Sometimes Taylor would raise her knees too high and look like a prancing peacock. Not that Jack would ever tell her that.

"Wouldn't that be awesome? If we got married at the same time?" Vicky stepped gingerly forward, exposing more leg than she'd ever before.

Aala skipped ahead, following the path into the forest.

"Too late for that, Vicky. We're already married." Jack trailed her and sashayed down a paved pathway. Gone was her stomping stride, and in its place, she glided while swaying her hips.

"Are we there yet?" Taylor called out five minutes later. "As pretty as these shoes are, they're killer on the toes."

"The pain of beauty, babe," Ava teased from behind Jack.

"I have to admit; it looks pretty strange from back here." Fred chuckled. "I'm the Pied Piper ushering brides away from their grooms."

"Well, next time, you can wear the shoes," Taylor whined.

"Hell, no, sweetheart." He barked out a laugh. "They don't make them in my size."

Vicky stepped off the path to adjust her shoe and gestured to all to pass. Jack winced as she walked another few steps, her shoes pinching her too. She gathered the gown's fabric and adjusted the straps, trying to figure out what hurt. Masculine black shoes appeared in her line of vision. Her gaze traveled up black tailored pants and a cumber band, then a black bow tie, to a grinning Mich...in a tuxedo. He had an exquisite pale pink lily in his lapel. She stroked a petal of her favorite flower.

"You proposed?" She grinned. "Does she know?" she whispered to her brother.

"She has no idea." Mich beamed then offered Jack the crook of his arm.

She stared at it with a frown, then peeked behind her. Her girls were far back, admiring each other's shoes. "You should hide—"

"Fred's keeping Taylor busy. I asked for a few minutes alone with you first."

"Oh." Jack looped her arm through his, placing her fingers on his forearm. "Okay, brother, what is it? Why didn't you tell me?"

She strolled where he led, assuming he wanted privacy. He continued along a side path that twisted in many directions before opening into another clearing.

"How private do we need to be?" She panted after trying to walk in the gladiator-style shoes she'd chosen. Silk ribbons wrapped around her ankles and calves. She had loved them on sight.

"Here's fine, then." Mich grinned at her. "She's all yours, Ulriq."

Jack's head shot up since her focus had been on the path and not her surroundings. With a gasp, her eyes widened at the sight of Ulriq in a tuxedo. It hugged him, enhancing his shoulders, his narrow waist, and incredible thighs. He too had a lily in his lapel. His loving and intense eyes made her knees tremble.

Mich pressed a kiss to her temple and stepped aside. Her gaze flew to her brother, who had assumed the position beside a grinning Taylor.

"What's going on?" Jack squeaked despite beginning to realize.

"It's your wedding, Jack." Mich gestured to Ulriq who waited for her.

She gaped at her Eth. Pastor Harris studied the crowd, his eyes wide, his digi-pad clasped before him in a white-knuckled grip. Even Aaro, Danic, Kanzo, and Teric wore tuxedos. She smiled; her breath catching at the depth of her emotion overwhelming her. A tear slid down her cheek, but she ignored it. Instead, she sashayed toward Ulriq, her focus on him and him alone. His heated gaze traveled the length of her. Joy exploded like a thousand flash grenades. She was grateful for Fred and her sisters in insisting they do this. Grateful for Mich for leading her down the 'aisle' and for Ulriq in organizing this in secret. As she neared him, he held out his hand, and she slipped hers into his, lacing their fingers. With a gentle tug from him, she stood in front of him.

"Ulriq? You did this for me?"

He smiled, calling up a dimple. "I apologize for robbing you of this day, Jack."

"The Ethera is more precious than a wedding day, my Eth." She swallowed past the lump in her throat and the hot tightness in her chest. "Thank you for this." She met his gaze and lifted her hand to caress his cheek and jaw.

He released a deep sigh then glanced at the pastor to begin.

Her adoring gaze fixed on Ulriq's, and she never broke focus as the pastor said words. Words she never heard in the daze she was in.

"I love you," she mouthed to him, squeezing his hand.

He squeezed back just before he said, "I do."

"Do you take Ulriq et Abariq to be your lawful wedded husband—"

"I do, with all my heart." She didn't let the pastor finish.

The poor man smiled as if this was a common occurrence for him. "I now pronounce you husband and wife; you may kiss the bride."

And Ulriq did; he drew her tightly into his arms and crushed his mouth to hers. The emotions he was feeling he revealed in his claiming kiss.

"Alodon's balls, Jack, you look beautiful," he growled. "I never knew a garment could make you more so."

"May I kiss the bride?" Fred laughed, tugging a reluctant Jack away from Ulriq's firm embrace. Fred kissed her on her temple and smiled at her. "You do look beautifully happy, Jackie."

"Congratulations, Jack." Mich bounded over and hugged her, shook Ulriq's hand, and slapped him on the shoulder as well.

"And Taylor?" Jack whispered.

Mich grimaced. "Wants to marry on some exotic planet. Says she'll know when she sees it."

Ah. Jack chuckled. "Now that sounds like Taylor."

"I'm sorry, Jack. I almost ruined it with my excitement." Ava sniffed, but when she tried to hug her, Kanzo held her back. Pain twisted his features, and his trousers emphasized a growing bulge.

"You are so forgiven, all of you." Jack laughed, unable to contain her joy. "I had no idea, not a clue." She studied her friends and family.

Vicky and Teric stood to the side. Teric stared at Vicky, his focus intense, unconsciously adjusting his black tailored trousers around his groin.

He dipped his head to say, "Keep the dress for our wedding."

Her cheeks bloomed and she cast a wide-eyed gaze at him.

Jack winked at Aala, flashing her a smile, and released Ulriq to hug the girl.

Taylor hovered behind Mich, who held onto her hand like a drowning man.

Kanzo ran his gaze down Ava's back, but there was something else in his eyes, something too evocative to identify. For a moment, he shared his focus with Pastor Harris who hovered, a smile twitching his lips.

He held the pad out for Jack to sign the marriage certificate. "Never expected you to marry anyone outside West Haven, Jack." He snuck a glance at Ulriq. "For an alien, he's impressive."

A contented sigh rushed out of her. "Yes, he is."

Aaro and Danic congratulated Ulriq with their regular arm-clasping, and they seemed pleased for their supreme commander.

As she scanned her family, she tried her damndest not to cry, but patted under her eyes to catch the tears.

After Ulriq signed the pad, Pastor Harris bid everyone goodbye and scurried down the path.

Ulriq hugged her from behind. He wrapped his arms around her waist and buried his nose into the curve of her neck. "You are everything to me, Jack." He pressed a kiss to her skin.

She shivered at the contact. "When we get home, I'll show you my appreciation." She draped her arms over his, rubbing her ass across his groin.

As expected, he inhaled sharply. "Appreciation is not necessary." He spun her within his arms to crush her to him, brushing his lips across hers.

She laughed. "But you won't say no."

"I will not." He grinned.

Glossary

Etterians worship one God, one Maker, since the universes have only His finger-print on all of it, a single golden thread through all of creation.

Tokens: intergalactic form of currency

Kliks: predetermined length of distance.

Hatimaye – To bring an end (Hutt-ee-my-ee)

Etterian

Alodon (A-low-donn): who accidentally shot his balls off with his own blaster.

Teacher: lima (lee-ma)

Great teacher: lima kuu: (lee-ma koo)

Directions: semit (semm-it)

Lemon: giyua (gee-you-a)

Young one: damu (daa-moo)

Heart: ensa (enn-sa)

Heart of my heart: ensa ra ensa (enn-sa raa enn-sa)

Beloved: thamani (ta-mar-nee)

Little joy: minus susa (mee-nas soo-sa)

Little cat: minus cesu (mee-nas sess-oo)

Large: magnus (mag-nis)

Orgasm: fulfillment/deite asteri (see stars) / released (day-ta ass-tare-ree)

Starfighter: asteri peju (ass-tare-ree pear-joo)

Collection of glass vials: virak (vee-ruck)

Scum of the galaxies: xemi (ze-mee)

Hair up: malia pa (Mar-lee-a par)

Hair down: malia pado (Mar-lee-a par-dow)

Lysaran

Visitor: kashi (Kaa-shee)

God: Kaiha (Kigh-haa)

King: Kuna (Koo-na)

Orange fleshy fruit: Lemte (Lem-ta)

White flowers: Myameru (My-a-me-roo)

Precious: Delica (Dell-ee-ka)

Sweetheart: Sali (Saa-lee)

Arum Lily-type flower: D'nastu (D-nass-too)

Love Blossom: aroa loulu (A-row-a low-loo)

Maloidian

Title of respect: lommia (Lomm-ee-a)

Stubborn, lethal tree: tewaa (Tee-wah)

Tokauri/Kulai

Blade – Sulac (soo-lack)

Bone – Ukog (you-cog) - bone from some dumb animal, probably an ukog.

Braided – Gisul (gee-sool)

Father – Danno (dan-no)

Heart – Kassu (cass-soo)

Maker – Mugbu (Mug-boo)

Mother – Manno (man-no)

Sapphires – Buha (boo-ha)

Shit – Saho (sa-ho)

Star - stuon (stoo-on)

Stupid – Ungog (oon-gog)

Vessel/ship - sakay (sa-kay)

Pronunciations

Names

Aaro - Ah-row

Adda – Ay-dah

Aldur - Al-durr

Alllero - A-le-row

Balllio – Bah-leee-oh

Bos - Boss

Bry-dar - Brigh-darr

Brynr - Brin-ner

Cales - Cale-es

Cento - Sen-tow

Citus - Sigh-tuss

Coldar - Coal-daar

Cria - Kree-ah

Eriz - Sigh-low

Danic - Dan-eek

Deeezo – Dee-zoh

Der - Durr

Diso - Dee-sow

Diyo - Die-oh

Eira - Eye-raa

Enyl - E-neel

Eriz - E-rizz

Garix - Ga-ricks

Gayn - Gain

Iddan - Ee-dann

Idon - Eye-donn

Illan - Ee-lann

Jarg – Jar-g

Jokta - Jock-tar

Kanzo - Can-zow

Keelu – Key-loo

Keryr – Kerr-eer

Ksal - Ka-sell

Lazu – Lah-zoo

Lurz - Lurr-z

Malo - Mail-oh

Matir - Mat-teer

Myan - My-ann

Myn-ras - Min-russ

Naio – Nay-oh

Nerx - Nurcks

Nuos - New-oss

Oyaz - Oh-yaz

Prex - Precks

Ronin - Row-nin

Saan - Sarn

Sena - See-na

Sy'mar - Sigh-marr

Syna - Sigh-na

Tamra – Tum-rah

Taro - Tah-row

Tenu - Ten-oo

Trav - Trahv

Tinh - Tin

Vytus - Vie-tuss

Vodin - Vo-din

Ulriq - Yule-rick

Vorn - Vawn

Vyar - Vie-arr

Xan - Zan

Xeus – Zeus

Zaro - Zah-row

Ziot - Zye-ott

Places

Argaxx – Are-jax

Crustiiu – Criss-tee-oo

Dyuqa - Dee-you-ka

Etteria – E-tare-rea

Galaza – Gah-Lar-Zah

Gikaet – Gee-ka-ett

Iphara = Ee-far-ra

Kulai – koo-ligh

Lysara – Liss-saa-ra

Mascroba – Mus-crow-ba

Resia Cay – Ress-Ee-ahh Kay

Sarvis – Sarr-viss

Sosu – Sow-soo

Tokauri – Too-cow-ree

Yithia – Yith-ee-a

Battleships

Chikara – Chee-kar-a - Force

Gladio – Glad-ee-oh - Sword

Kushin – Cush-shin - To Pierce

Surata – Soo-ra-tah – Beginning

Usaha – Oo-saa-hah - Endeavor

Shuttles

Celeeri – See-lee-ree - swift

    Denessi – Denn-ess-ee - sodge

    Eshima – Ee-shee-ma - respect

    Kevol – Kev-oll - agony

    Kuta – Koo-tah - modular shuttle.

    Liri-ny – Lee-ree-nye – freedom

    Misaia – Miss-aye-a - memory

    Sasay – Sass-ay - whispers

    Yakin – Yuck-kin - belief

Creatures

Asnu – Ass-Noo – buffalo/donkey

    Eiltur – Ale-turr

    Gracc – Grrr-ack

    Ilag – Ee-Lug– leggy slugs that feast on sol.

    Kreso – Kreh-soo

    Omeika – Oh-may-ka

    Pagsu – Pug-Soo - cocksuckers

    Reshy – Resh-Ee - huge, like the size of a kuta shuttle, with massive jaws and rows of sharp teeth.

    Sogair – Sow-gare

    Wilanegy – Will-anna-jee

About the Author

Sevannah Storm is a fiction writer who immerses herself in fantastical worlds both magical and science fiction. She has a flair for the creative having studied art and interior architecture and spends her time drawing, oil painting, and writing. An avid reader from an early age, Sevannah finds her inspiration from various sources: games, novels, music, and the land of make-believe. The unique versus the practical has brought on numerous debates. In her spare time, she does Krav Maga, CrossFit, and rereads novels that snatch her breath away. Having embraced the social media world, you can find her on most platforms.

Her home is a land south of Wakanda, where animals roam free. Born in Zimbabwe, she grew up in South Africa. The crisp blue skies with cotton-candy sunsets expand her heart and soul, encapsulating a sense of freedom.

Words she lives by: "Know your pothole and dodge it. Don't work in a pencil factory if you're a vampire."

Sevannah loves to hear from her readers. You can find and connect with her at the links below.

Website/Newsletter:

https://www.sevannahstorm.com/

Facebook:

https://www.facebook.com/sevannah.storm

Instagram:

https://www.instagram.com/sevannah.storm/

Twitter:

https://twitter.com/sevannah_storm

Thank you for taking the time to read Fate Forged. If you enjoyed the story, please tell your friends and leave a review. Reviews support authors and ensure they continue to bring readers books to love and enjoy.

https://sevannahstorm.com

SOUL FORGED

The Gifting Series #1

Know-it-all Oriana agreed to travel with aliens who need women. But she didn't agree to abduction, life/death battles, and escaping with a bossy, arrogant man. She was sabotaged, attacked, and kidnapped, but she is far from beaten. Forced to participate in an alien battle arena with no promise of freedom, she has to forget the loss of her family and focus on surviving.

Enyl has given up hope. His people are dying due to a genetic modification gone awry. Darkness is consuming his warriors, and his world, as he knows it, will end. His father, the king, has rolled out a plan to save them all. But Enyl doubts a solution will be found in time.

And when a compatible female is found...and lost, he must rescue her, a human female capable of surviving despite all odds. However, freeing Oriana serves to anger the aliens holding her captive. Ensuring she is cared for—as per Etterian protocol—he is stunned by the strong connection between the two of them. Such a bond was only experienced between Etterian mates.

Is she his salvation or is that wishful thinking on his part?

Read it here:

https://books2read.com/u/mlAWr9

SUN FORGED

WAR FORGED

Being kidnapped by aliens does not sit well with Quinlan. Not only would her seven guardians give her hell if she doesn't attempt some sort of escape, but she refuses to be at anybody's mercy. With her practiced military skills, the help of an underground lounge singer and a personal assistant, she takes over the alien slave ship. Not knowing how to fly the damn thing, she sends a distress signal. ...The rescue comes swiftly in the form of a bronzed man with exquisite ice-blue eyes. Leaving her to ask the true question: has she just given up her newfound freedom for a gorgeous man who seems determined to have her for eternity?

As Elite Supreme Commander of the Etterian Forces, Xan answers a distress call in Earth English. That is all he did. The female who captured the slave ship shows remarkable skill, making her a warrior in her own right. Said skills should be respected and honored. Except she is his Dar Eth, calling forth the Ethera—the soulmate bond. How can he protect his female when she can do so herself? What can she possibly need from him? What can he offer a female, not Etterian but human? Not that he can think clearly in her presence when she scents so good and makes him want to kiss all of her.

Maker help him.

Read it here:

https://books2read.com/u/bz1QGD

STAR FORGED

Macy is feeling a little left out, as usual. Who would have thought moving from one planet to another wouldn't change that loneliness? She is never alone these days since Etterians guard human women with an urgency she understands. But the lack of companionship is like a dark aching abyss inside her chest. On some days, it threatens to implode, and Macy Mitchell would cease to exist. Looming is her impending meeting with King Xeus of Etteria. How is she supposed to keep her shit together when presented to royalty? Not after she ran from the last king she met.

For Xeus, the void expands daily. Duty, honor, concern for his dying people, and endless loneliness fill his life. Having decided to search for pairings among other worlds, he is pleased his son found his soulmate among human women. It doesn't mean that Xeus's loneliness and longing haven't ended until he stumbles upon a crying female. Meaning only to soothe, he is spellbound when her presence brings him peace. Unable to resist, he forms an attachment to a female he can never have

Read it here:

https://books2read.com/u/3nXgp5

SHADOW FORGED

The Gifting Series #6

Forty-year-old Caroline is too old to start dating and too bored with her vibrator, but what other choices does she have. On the day she burns her shirt and breaks a fingernail, she meets Etterian warriors. As part of her job at E.S.A. (Earth Space Association,) she must 'entertain' the hot-as-apple-pie Chief Engineer she suspects isn't who he claims to be.

Operations Commander Malo, Head of Espionage, must act as an engineer and ambassador, hoping to invite human females to visit Etteria and save his dying race. From Princess Oriana, he has strict instructions to distrust humans. What he finds he cannot trust are his emotions and his body whenever in the presence of the human ambassador, Caroline. She does not believe in soulmates or in a forever with him. Convincing her to choose him is the greatest task ever set before him, one he cannot afford to fail.

Until she is stolen from him. He calls in favors, utilizes all his resources to find her. And *when* he does, he is never letting her off his battleship...or his bed.

Read it here:

https://books2read.com/u/bPNd8j

EARTH FORGED

Guilt hounds Izzy, who caused her sister's injury and subsequent blindness. But no matter how she cares for Simone or what she sacrifices, it doesn't ease the ache in her chest. With Simone and naive Caro, her best friend, Izzy's role as protector is fully realized. The cost? Hiding behind quirkiness, pseudo-joy, and giving up her hopes and dreams. What she needs is a knight in any armor. After all, beggars can't be fussy. She has no idea that armor, in her case, means black military and that a knight could come in any color, specifically bronze.

Oyaz wants to find his life force, his soulmate, and he'd like her to be human. Earth's females are soft, amusing, passionate, and their scents rival a garden of hahyt blossoms. His task is to guard their planet that promises so many salvations for his males. It's a duty he's pleased to perform, one he would die for. When Operations Commander Malo orders Oyaz to retrieve a human female, he's eager to oblige. That it would lead to his salvation is something he couldn't anticipate. What he hadn't planned for is an ambush that costs him more than his memory, the loss of his soulmate.

Now what? Nothing in their training prepared him for this.

And yet, despite not remembering kneeling for Izzy, he longs to claim her with every inch of his soul.

Read it here:

https://books2read.com/u/31V82D

LUST FORGED

The Gifting Series #8

Ex-socialite Leona wants nothing more than to enhance the mechanics within sex-cybs, not to mention improve their performances with their 'lovers.' It's a job where she's safe in an all-woman factory on Callisto, and far from her matchmaking mama. When the chief engineer is incapacitated, Leona's required to gift—her term would be pimp—sex-cyborgs to prospective clients. On an Etterian battleship, surrounded by gorgeous males, she tries not to think of sex when it's her work, especially with the Sub-Commander Aaro whose neon-blue eyes are the stuff of her erotic dreams.

As a diplomatic favor, Aaro must abandon his task to guard Earth, and perhaps find his Dar Eth or soulmate, all to protect cargo en route to many worlds, including the dangerous and unpredictable Yithia. Princess Oriana is most concerned for the two human female engineers determined to ensure the deliveries are successful. A simple enough mission until one human enters Aaro's cargo bay, dropping him to his knees.

But revealing to independent Leona that she's now trapped in a marriage isn't something Aaro can bring himself to do. He violates all he stands for, every ounce of honor by not telling her the truth. All in the hopes that she will choose to love him.

Read it here:

https://books2read.com/u/3LdA1w